Carolina Cousins Series

1

S0-ASJ-152

A Perilous Proposal

Books by Michael Phillips

Is Jesus Coming Back As Soon As We Think?
Destiny Junction • *Kings Crossroads*
Make Me Like Jesus • *God, A Good Father*
Jesus, An Obedient Son
Best Friends for Life (with Judy Phillips)
George MacDonald, Scotland's Beloved Storyteller
A Rift in Time • *Hidden in Time*
Legend of the Celtic Stone
Your Life in Christ (George MacDonald)

AMERICAN DREAMS

Dream of Freedom • *Dream of Life*

CAROLINA COUSINS

A Perilous Proposal

THE SECRET OF THE ROSE

The Eleventh Hour • *A Rose Remembered*
Escape to Freedom • *Dawn of Liberty*

THE SECRETS OF HEATHERSLEIGH HALL

Wild Grows the Heather in Devon
Wayward Winds
Heathersleigh Homecoming
A New Dawn Over Devon

SHENANDOAH SISTERS

Angels Watching Over Me
A Day to Pick Your Own Cotton
The Color of Your Skin Ain't the Color of Your Heart
Together Is All We Need

CAROLINA COUSINS

A Perilous Proposal

NOVEL

MICHAEL PHILLIPS

DISCARD
MASSANUTTEN REGIONAL LIBRARY
Harrisonburg, VA 22801

BETHANY HOUSE PUBLISHERS

Minneapolis, Minnesota

F
Phi

A Perilous Proposal
Copyright © 2005
Michael Phillips

Cover design by John Hamilton/UDG DesignWorks
Cover photography by Steve Gardner

All rights reserved. No part of this publication may be reproduced, stored in a retrieval system, or transmitted in any form or by any means—electronic, mechanical, photocopying, recording, or otherwise—without the prior written permission of the publisher and copyright owners.

Scripture quotations are from the King James Version of the Bible.

Published by Bethany House Publishers
11400 Hampshire Avenue South
Bloomington, Minnesota 55438

Bethany House Publishers is a division of
Baker Publishing Group, Grand Rapids, Michigan.

Printed in the United States of America

ISBN 0-7642-0041-0 (Paperback)
ISBN 0-7642-0062-3 (Hardcover)
ISBN 0-7642-0085-2 (Large Print)

Library of Congress Cataloging-in-Publication Data

Phillips, Michael R., 1946-
    A perilous proposal / by Michael Phillips.
        p.   cm. —(Carolina cousins ; bk. 1)
        Summary: "In a new series related to his bestselling Shenandoah sisters,
Michael Phillips returns to the post-Civil War South in a story of forgiveness,
danger and love"—Provided by publisher.
        ISBN 0-7642-0062-3 (hardcover : alk. paper) —ISBN 0-7642-0041-0 (pbk. :
alk. paper) —ISBN 0-7642-0085-2 (large print pbk.) 1. Reconstruction (U.S.
history, 1865–1877)—Fiction. 2. Women plantation owners—Fiction.
3. Female friendship—Fiction. 4. Plantation life—Fiction. 5. Race
relations—Fiction. 6. North Carolina—Fiction. 7. Young women—Fiction.
8. Racism—Fiction. I. Title II. Series: Phillips, Michael R. 1946- . Carolina
cousins ; bk. 1.
        PS3566.H492P425   2005
        813'.54—dc22   2005005235

To the friends of my youth from many years ago at Lincoln University in southeastern Pennsylvania.

From you I learned, to the limited extent such a thing is possible in this fallen world, to love and understand in some small measure a race other than my own. For the hearts of such men as Frank Brewington and Rufus Nance and many others of you who took me in as one of you, I will always be more grateful than words can say. Being part of your lives, for however briefly, enriched me, broadened me, and changed me in more ways than I am sure I even realize myself.

I have not forgotten you . . . and never will.

CONTENTS

PROLOGUE

❧ ✳ ❧

Maybe we shouldn't have been surprised by what happened. But we were. We had been living in danger for so long, I reckon we forgot how dangerous it really was—especially for blacks like us. Considering all that had happened before, and how folks 'round there felt about a black boy touching a white girl—even if it was only to protect her—we should have known what was coming. We probably should have hidden him away, or sent him north or . . . something. But we didn't.

It is still so painful to recall that it brings tears to my eyes—having the man I loved ripped away from me. How I wished, in that awful fire-flickering moment when I could still see his face, that I hadn't put him off, that I had agreed to his proposal when I'd had the chance . . . in spite of the danger. But it was too late now.

I could not help wondering if I would ever see his face again, or if I would even live through the night myself.

❧ ✳ ❧

Night Riders in White

1

THE SKY WAS SO BLACK NO ONE COULD HAVE SEEN their own hand in front of their face. Everyone in the big house was asleep, and had been for hours. There wasn't a moon.

Only silence.

But the stillness would soon be broken. For murder approached through the night.

The distant thunder of horses' hooves gradually intruded into the senses of the dogs where they lay. Even asleep, their ears turned instinctively toward the sound. Instantly they jumped to their feet. A few barks echoed into the night. They weren't enough to wake anyone inside . . . not yet.

But the riders were coming fast. Within a minute or two the dogs were howling at whatever was moving toward them. Uneven flames played against the black horizon . . . and the pounding of hooves grew ominous. The dogs saw the strange lights and barked the louder. Five or six sleepers stirred in their beds.

Two minutes later a posse of riders galloped recklessly into the yard. Dust rose in all directions. The dogs flew about in a yowling frenzy at the horses' feet. Chickens in their sheds cackled in an uproar of confusion, and a few cows in the barn began to low restlessly. Lanterns appeared in a couple of the windows. They were hardly needed. The torches of flame held from every rider's hand jumped high in the blackness and cast eerie shadows on the walls of house and barn and lit up the open space between.

"Hey you inside!" called the deep voice of the lead horseman. "You got a nigger in there—we're here for him!"

The band of white-hooded riders around him sat waiting. Their prancing mounts fidgeted with jittery energy after the long ride.

Daring a few glances outside, the women in the house trembled with terror.

After a long minute, at last the door of the house opened. A white man holding a lantern stepped onto the porch. He did not carry a gun. He hoped somehow to deal with this peaceably. Though he was not a man easily cowed, the sight that met his eye was enough to send a chill up his spine. He had spent most of his life talking rather than shooting his way out of trouble. Whether he would be able to do so on this present occasion looked doubtful. In front of him sat twelve riders draped in white sheets and with masked faces.

"We're here for the nigger . . . you know why!" said the rider.

"You know who we've got here," replied the white man. "They're none of your concern."

"That young buck made himself our concern yesterday. This is what comes of being too friendly with that little girl of yours. Now he's going to pay! Hand him over or these torches'll be through your windows and that house of yours'll be nothing but cinders come morning."

"He doesn't live here. We've just got a couple of house darkies."

"Word has it he's been out—"

"Hey, Dwight—" interrupted another voice.

"Shut up, you fool," spat the spokesman, turning in his

saddle. "—I told you . . . no names."

"But I got him . . . he was hiding in the barn!"

All eyes turned toward the voice. A tall young man wearing one of the white capes was dragging a young black man, still rubbing sleep out of his eyes, through the barn door into the torchlit night.

"That's him!" cried another of the riders.

Half the saddles emptied. Within seconds a small crowd was viciously kicking and beating the black man into the dirt. A few moans were his only reply.

"That's enough—plenty of time for all that later," yelled the man called Dwight. "We don't want to kill him here. Just get the rope around him and put him up on that horse."

"All right, you boys have had your fun," said the white man, walking toward them from the house. He still hoped to end the incident without bloodshed. "He's done nothing to any of you."

"He forgot what color his skin is—that's enough!" yelled another of the riders. "You seem to have forgotten it too."

"Ain't no good can come to a nigger-lover around here, mister," chided another. "That's something you maybe oughta remember. You and your kind ain't welcome in these parts."

Behind them, the door of the house opened again. Out stepped a white woman, by appearance close to twenty. Terrified at the sight that met her gaze, she drew in a steadying breath. Then she stepped off the porch and came forward with more apparent courage than she felt inside. She knew, in one way, that she was herself the cause of this incident. She hoped she could keep it from becoming still more dangerous.

"He meant nothing by what he did," she said, walking forward and speaking to the lead rider. "It was my fault, not his. I shouldn't have interfered."

"Then he should have known better, miss—and you should have yourself. Now that it's done, he's got to pay."

Out of the corner of her eye she saw the black man being shoved onto the back of one of the horses with his hands tied behind his back. One of the other men began forcing a noose around his neck.

"Get it tight!" yelled another with an evil laugh.

"But you can't do this!" she cried in a pleading voice. She ran toward them. "He's done nothing wrong!"

Rude hands restrained her and yanked her back. A surge of fury filled the white man where he stood a few yards away. He took several steps forward. But there was nothing he could do against so many. The young woman ran to his side in desperation.

"Let's go, Dwight," yelled one of the men, "—we got him!"

The last of the riders remounted. The rest began to swing their horses around.

Out of the house now flew another woman, this one black. She ran straight for the captive. Before the riders could stop her she threw herself against the horse where he was bound and clung to one of his legs. He looked down and tried to reassure her with a smile. The light from the surrounding torches danced in her eyes, wet with tears of terror that she would never see him again.

The eyes of the two former slaves met but for a moment. Though the noose had already begun to choke his neck, the young man tried to speak.

"I love . . . we'll—" he began.

A rude slap across the mouth from the nearest of the horsemen silenced him. At the same instant, a booted foot from another shoved the girl away.

"Get away from him, nigger girl!" he yelled as she stumbled back and fell to the ground. "Otherwise we'll string you up beside him! We got plenty of rope for the two of you."

A few shouts and slashes from whips and reins, and the mob galloped away. On the ground, the girl picked herself up and ran a few steps toward them.

"No!" she wailed. The forlorn cry was lost in the night. Her horrified protests soon gave way to sobs. She hardly felt the arms of the man and her friend as they approached and tried to comfort her. Slowly they led her back to the house.

"But why . . . why?" was all she could whimper in her grief. Neither of the other two had an answer. There was no "why" to hatred.

⌒ ❄ ⌒

For the first time in my brief life as a free colored girl, I almost wished we were slaves again. Had Mr. Lincoln never set us free, a whipping and a beating might take place on a night like this. But at least the man I loved would be left with his life.

But times had changed. I knew that. Living in the South after the War Between the States was different than before. I had been glad of that . . . before now. But now coloreds like me no longer had value as slaves. Before 1862, our very slavery, though our curse, had also been our protection. Whites may have looked down on us, and whipped us, even despised us. But not too many hated us. In the white man's eyes, we weren't worth hating. I hadn't liked it. None of us had. But it's how things were.

But the war changed everything.

Once we were free, hatred came to the South. A new kind of hatred. An evil hatred. Slaves had always been beaten. But blacks were now being hung. And now the young man I had come to love was about to become one of them!

I wept as I watched the torches disappear into the night. Dread filled my heart. I knew I would probably never see him again. What good was the freedom we had been given if we couldn't live long enough to enjoy it?

No, I did not want to go back. Not even now. Freedom was better than anything. But hatred created invisible bonds of its own just as bad as slavery. I had changed so much, we all had, in such a short period of time. But was it worth it?

The nation called the United States of America was supposed to be one of liberty and opportunity for all, or so I had heard. It did not seem so to me at that moment.

As a result of our newfound freedom, many black people might possibly rise up and prosper in this land that had long been our home.

But on this night it seemed clear that many would also die. . . .

☙ ❀ ❧

SLAVE BOY
2

LIFE WAS SIMPLER BACK WHEN NEGROES WERE slaves.

White masters controlled life. Every bit of it. There was nothing to do, nothing to think, nothing to plan, nothing to hope for . . . nothing to do anything about except do what you were told.

But was freedom from such drudgery worth life itself?

That was the question on the mind of the young black man now riding through the darkness with a noose of death around his neck. He was terrified—that was for sure. But even more than his own fate, his sickened heart was filled with the wail of love that had sounded behind him as he had been taken away. It was a dreadful sound. He would never forget it.

As he jostled along in the saddle, his past life flitted through his memory. He recalled where he had come from. It had been a long search that had brought him here three years before. Now it seemed the quest hadn't been such a good idea after all.

He had found family. He had discovered love. But what would either matter if his life ended tonight with his body dangling from the end of a white man's rope?

All he could think was that he should never have left Alabama, where he was born.

Back then as long as he obeyed his white master and kept his eyes to the ground, all went on day by day in relative peace.

That hadn't prevented the whippings. But at least the simplicity of life had kept him alive.

Alive . . . but angry.

He had hoped the smoldering demon of anger had left him for good. But the white man hated soft-spoken free Negroes no less than brash and belligerent slaves. What made him think life would ever be different?

What did any of it matter now?

A quiet anger had been his silent companion almost longer than he could remember. Perhaps it was destined to be a curse that accompanied the newfound freedom of his race.

The day he first felt it rise up within him was also the day his own whippings had begun. Years later, by the age of fourteen when the Emancipation Proclamation had come, he had countless scars on his back. The marks of the whip were plain enough evidence that keeping his mouth shut hadn't been easy.

And all the while a silent rage seethed inside him to accompany the scars. It was not an anger directed merely at his white master or his men, but also against the man who had given him life. Scars on his back were not in themselves a burden. No scar could keep a man from becoming anything he wanted to be. But anger like his was a different thing. It could keep a man in an unseen bondage from which no one else could free him. Or a woman too, though women weren't quite so prone to it as men. Not even Abraham Lincoln could free the young man called Jake from the anger in his own heart. He would have to fight his own personal war to win that freedom.

The battle would not be an easy one.

Jake's youngest years playing with the other slave children and the master's son hadn't been so bad. There had been enough to eat. Though the work for grown-up slaves was hard, life had pattern and predictability. He came from a people who took happiness where they could find it. Laughter and song were never far away, ready to brighten any day when the master's whip was silent.

But Master Clarkson was a shrewd one. He knew how to control his slaves with more than just the whip. He instilled fear early in life. He didn't want his black youngsters growing up too comfortable.

Jake never forgot the day the master came out and gathered all the slave children, then looked at them sternly. Jake was probably four or five, but there were some as young as three in the little group.

"Just look here," said the master, nodding toward the dog beside him. He was holding it by a leash as it strained and growled to get at the children. "This here's what's called a nigger dog," he said. "I got it to ketch niggers when they run away."

He looked around, making sure his eyes probed straight into every child's face. He wanted them to understand that he was talking to each one of them.

"He's a mighty strong dog," said Clarkson. "He can run faster'n any man alive. Look at them teeth—they'd just snap a nigger's leg right off. This dog likes the taste of nigger blood, he does. He's just waiting every day, hoping I'll say the word and send him after some nigger trying to run away. Might be your daddy, might be your mama . . . it might even be *you*, 'cause this dog don't care if it's a grown-up or what. He likes nigger blood wherever it comes from."

Again he stopped and stared every little boy and girl in the eyes. Most of them, just like young Jake's, were by this time wide as round white saucers in the middle of their black faces. If Master Clarkson wanted them to be afraid, he had already succeeded. But he wasn't done yet.

"Just look how strong his jaws are," he went on. "When a nigger don't behave, all I got to do is just say the word and this here dog'll grab hold of him and pull him to the ground and then he'll just snap a nigger's head right off as easy as I'd whack off a chicken's head with an ax. He likes the taste of nigger young'uns best."[1]

By the time the master was finished, Jake and all the other children were scared to death. The master's speech had exactly the effect he wanted. Fear of disobedience was the earliest and most important lesson he wanted to teach every slave. And white masters like Massa Clarkson had a thousand ways to teach it.

The very thought of escape always brought to the minds of boys and girls like Jake reminders of the fangs of "Massa's houn' dog." None of them had ever seen a dog take off a man's leg, much less a head. But most had seen enough to know that a dog's teeth could draw blood and leave a vicious scar on the calf. Half the men on the Clarkson plantation could pull up a ragged trouser leg to show proof of it.

For generations before that time, since their ancestors had first been brought as captives from their African homeland, not too many slaves ever thought about trying to escape. A thousand men like Master Clarkson, with five thousand overseers and ten thousand whips and more ornery "nigger dogs" than you could count, had seen to that.

But young Jake was growing up in the turbulent 1850s. Times were changing. Even in the Deep South of Alabama.

Sounds of freedom were in the air.

Those sounds of freedom took many forms. The white masters learned to recognize them and tried to stamp them out whenever they saw signs of them. But that wasn't so easy.

---

[1] This "nigger dog" description was recounted in the book *Black Bondage: The Life of Slaves in the South*, by Walter Goodman. Published by Farrar Straus & Giroux, 1969.

Once a people who have been oppressed get a notion of what freedom is like, they want it more and more. That's how it was for the black slaves in America's South. They started thinking about Moses and the children of Israel in their slavery in Egypt. They realized that they might someday have a Moses to deliver them too, or lots of Moseses working together. And they started talking and singing about their own promised land, and the day when they'd be free just like the Israelites.

Though the white masters and their white families all went to their white churches all prim and proper every Sunday, when their Negro slaves started talking and singing about Israel and Moses and the Promised Land, they started to get nervous. They didn't like their slaves getting *too* familiar with the white man's religion because that could lead to only one thing—talk of freedom. That's what salvation was, after all—freedom from sin . . . and maybe other kinds of freedom too.

So it was outlawed throughout the South for Negroes to preach to other Negroes. Black churches had white preachers who preached to them about obedience and submission and the sin of rebellion. The most quoted verses of Scripture in those black churches were Ephesians 6:5—*Servants, be obedient to them that are your masters*—and Colossians 3:22—*Servants, obey in all things your masters.*

For two centuries white masters had kept their black slaves mostly uneducated and illiterate. When a black man or woman taught himself or herself to read the Bible and to speak with sense and intelligence, there was nothing so threatening to the white man's world.

Most dangerous of all to their white masters were those uncommon blacks of strong religious conviction. They knew they could never subdue the spirits of such men and women. And that made them dangerous. Hardworking and obedient, taking whippings without complaint, their strength came from within. Such men were the most respected of all in the Negro community. As stirrings of freedom mounted, whites hated spiritual leaders more than every other kind of black. A fiery slave-prophet called Nat Turner had proved that in 1831. Ever since, whites had feared the appearance of his like again.

Among black slaves there was rebellion and there was religion. Put the two together, and by the mid-1850s there were runaways everywhere. The white schoolteachers had their three Rs. But white masters had another "three Rs" they hated when they saw them among their slaves—*rebellion, religion,* and *runaways.* They were determined to get rid of them.

They weren't afraid *of* their slaves, like slaves were of their masters. But they were afraid of what might happen if enough blacks felt the stirrings of those first two Rs down in their hearts. And all the while, out in the fields more and more of the low melancholy music of freedom spirituals could be heard.

BOY, PAPA, AND MASTER
3

J AKE'S PAPA WAS ONE OF THOSE KINDS OF SPIRITUAL men that the white masters hated.

He wasn't what folks might call a "religious" man, he was a *spiritual* man. His faith was his own. He wasn't interested in leading a slave rebellion. He knew well enough about Nat Turner and other black preachers who intermingled religion and rebellion.

But that wasn't his kind of spirituality. He knew the two passages from the Bible just like everyone else. But the difference was, he took them to heart. He believed that he really *was* supposed to obey his master. And not just the first part of the verses either—he believed he was supposed to obey the rest of them too, which said that slaves were to obey their masters cheerfully as if they were serving the Lord instead of a man.

If you'd have asked him, he'd have said that all he wanted to do was do what Jesus Christ's Father told him to do. He'd have said he could do that just as well being a slave as if he was free. He'd have preferred to be free. Who wouldn't? But he wasn't the kind of man who would fight for it. He was content to let God see to his needs, and his freedom too. He wanted to spend his energy just trying to obey the words of his Master.

And by that he meant his spiritual master, not the white man who legally owned him. Even Jake could see that his father was a pretty unusual kind of man and most folks liked him for it.

But Master Clarkson, whose plantation he worked on, came to hate soft-spoken Hank almost more than any of the rabble-rousers among his slaves. He was sure the quiet Negro would never lead a rebellion. For all he knew, if there was a rebellion he wouldn't even go along with it. He might even try to stop it. But he also knew that Hank would never call any earthly man "master."

That simple fact gnawed away at the soul of Garfield Clarkson. Though every other black on his plantation dutifully referred to him as "Massa Clarkson," every time he heard Jake's father's quiet "*Mister* Clarkson," the proud white man silently seethed with resentment. He hated it that he could not break the proud fool's spirit. In time he came to hate Hank all the more that he was hardworking, diligent, and obedient. He hated him because he knew that his obedience was only secondarily to him as his white owner. He could never tell what the ridiculous fellow might say. One minute he might be quoting some Scripture or another—as if any black man could presume to preach to his betters—and the next be working harder than any three of Clarkson's other slaves.

It incensed Clarkson all the more whenever Hank took his side in any dispute. In time he even came to despise the way he encouraged his fellow slaves to obey respectfully and without complaint. As if he needed such a man's help! He had his whip and his dogs. They would do fine without any of the slave's idiotic preaching. Men like Clarkson, contrary as it seems, didn't like people he thought were too good. Maybe because he was mean himself, he was suspicious of anyone who wasn't.

If he could get rid of Hank, he would, thought Clarkson. But he was too valuable a man to lose. Clarkson knew that he would never get anything close to him to repay his value to the smooth functioning of his plantation. Though he hated him, he couldn't deny, lanky though Hank was, that he was strong as an ox and had a calming influence on the other slaves. And his uncanny ability with horses was like nothing Clarkson had ever seen—from the devil, no doubt.

But in spite of Hank's value, his master was on the look-out for some way to punish the proud fellow. He had to teach him his place. Threats of his "nigger dog" may have worked on children, but not on a man like Hank.

Jake was too young to grasp what any of this meant. He liked nothing better than to sit on his father's lap and feel his long strong arms around him, or to feel his father's kiss and his big rough hand holding his little one. To listen to his father's laughter when he told stories was just about the best thing there was. When he was with his father, it seemed that nothing in the whole world could be wrong. But Jake also knew that sometimes his father was the cause of trouble and angry outbursts from Master Clarkson, though he didn't know why. Why would anyone get angry at his papa?

Then one day his father did something Jake couldn't understand.

Jake had always been friends with the master's son John. They played together while Jake's mama watched over both little boys. But as they grew older, John slowly began to change. He talked more and more like the white men, while Jake's speech became like his papa's. By the time they were seven, little John started bossing Jake around.

One day he told Jake to pick up a pile of firewood and move it about ten feet away.

"Now why you tellin' me ter do dat, Johnny?" said Jake. "Dat's a silly thing ter do."

"Don't call me that, Jake," retorted the white boy. "From now on, I want you to call me Master John."

"Why dat?" laughed Jake.

"Because I said so."

"You ain't my massa."

"I'm white. That makes me your boss."

"No it don't."

"It does too."

"It don't!"

"And I tell you it does. Whites are masters and coloreds have to do what they say."

"But dat wood dere don't need ter be moved," insisted Jake.

"If I tell you to move it, then you have to move it. You're a slave."

Still thinking Johnny was playing a game on him, Jake started laughing again.

Angrily "Master John" picked up a long, thin stick from the woodpile and whacked it across Jake's back.

"What you do dat for!" yelled Jake. The game was suddenly over. He grabbed another stick to fight back.

Before long they were hitting and fighting and yelling and rolling over each other on the ground. In the midst of the skirmish Jake's papa came by. Immediately he put a stop to it. Expecting to be vindicated, Jake stood up, hot from the battle, with a smile of satisfaction on his face. But he was in for a surprise.

Jake's papa sent Johnny Clarkson on his way back home. Then he turned seriously to Jake.

"Don't you neber fight back, son," he said. "Fightin' back ain't no way ter foller da master."

"But Johnny was bossin' at me, Papa," replied Jake.

"Dat don't matter, son," said his father. "When sumbody

from da big house duz sumfin ter you, or tells you ter do sum-fin, you gots ter min' what dey say."

"But it wuz jes' Johnny."

"He be Mister Clarkson's son, an' so you gots ter min' whateber Master John tell you ter do."

"But he tol' me ter move dat pile er wood."

"Den you bes' move it," said his father.

"But it don't need ter be moved."

"Dat don' matter, son. We gots ter obey what we's tol' ter do. Lots er what we's tol' don' seem ter make sense. We gots ter obey neber da less. We's slaves, an' da Bible tells us ter obey."

Feeling betrayed by his own father, Jake set about moving the wood. Out of the corner of his eye he saw Johnny watching from behind a tree with a smirk on his face. Jake didn't know whom to be most angry at—Johnny or his own papa.

Instead of trusting his father to know what was best, Jake let himself sulk about it. Then he let it fester in his thoughts and heart. And that tiny seed of anger began to grow inside young Jake's heart.

It wasn't too long afterward, when he was still stewing about what his papa had done, that Jake came home one day from swimming in the creek with Johnny and some of the other children. He came around the corner of the shack and heard something he had never heard before in his life. His mother was speaking heatedly to his father.

"Why can't chu be like da other men an' jes' keep yo mouf shut?" she said. "Why you gots ter be such a talker? Don' chu know Massa don' want none er yer religious noshuns? An' he don' want none er yer help wiffen da other men neither, not nohow."

"I gots ter say what da Lawd gib me ter say," said her husband calmly.

"Eben effen it gits you whipped?"

"Maybe sumtimes dat's da way it gots ter be."

"Dat soun's right foolish ter me. Why can't chu jes' let ever'body else be? You's gwine git us *all* whupped one er dese days."

Hank did not reply immediately.

Jake crept away and heard no more. He didn't like seeing his mama upset. He could not have explained why, but the incident deepened his irritation toward his father.

Separations
4

G ARFIELD CLARKSON WAS A CRUEL MAN.
At last he devised a plan to get back at Jake's father
for his uppity ways. The very thought of it brought an evil
smile to his lips.

Jake was eight when his father disappeared. He came in
from playing one day and found his mother crying in the
shack they called home.

"Why's you cryin', Mama?" he said.

"Yer daddy's gone" was her only reply. In her desire to
mask her own pain, she unknowingly added more to her
son's. She felt bad that she'd argued with him about the very
thing that got him sent away.

"Why . . . where'd he go?" asked Jake. He was too young
to realize the full truth.

"Ah don' know, Jake . . . ah don' know," she answered in
a mournful tone. "He's jes' gone, dat's all . . . he's jes' gone.
Dey said Massa Clarkson dun sol' him!"

Jake's father did not come back that evening. Nor ever
again.

The next time Jake saw the overseer in the field with the
slave men, he walked up to him.

"What do you want, boy?" said the man gruffly.

"Please, suh . . . where's my daddy?" asked Jake.

"How should I know?" laughed the white man.

"But he's gone?"

"That he is, boy—and he ain't never coming back."

"But why's he gone, suh?"

The man seemed to think a few seconds, then stooped down and stared into Jake's face. Slowly the hint of a grin came to his lips. "Didn't they tell you, boy?" he asked.

"No, suh."

"He left 'cause he couldn't stand the sight of you no more," said Master Clarkson's foreman. "Yes, sir—he said to the master, 'Marsa,' he said, 'dat boy ob mine's jes' too ugly an' I can' stan' sight er him no mo. So I'z leavin', I am. Effen you don' sell me, den I'll run away, I will. Dat's how despert I be ter git away from dat boy.' That's what he said, and it must be the truth because Mister Clarkson sold him the very next day, and I know he wouldn't have sold him if he hadn't had a mighty good reason."

Jake swallowed, blinking hard to keep from crying in front of the white man. The more he tried to swallow, the bigger got the lump in his throat.

Feeling his eyes starting to sting, he turned and walked away. Behind him he heard the sound of laughter. It followed him all the way until he was out of sight of the workers. He crept behind the trunk of a big oak, then sat down on the ground and cried and cried. Finally he cried himself to sleep.

When he woke up the overseer's laughter still rang in Jake's ears. Though the thought that his father would want to leave because of him was too painful to bear, he now remembered his mother's tears from two days before. He thought of his mama's pain. Again anger toward his father filled his heart. How could he do a thing like this to his mother!

A week later Jake walked into the house and saw his mother packing up what few things they had to call their own.

"What you doin', Mama?" he asked.

MASSANUTTEN REGIONAL LIBRARY
Harrisonburg, VA 22801

"We's leavin' here, Jake," she said.

"Is it 'cause er Papa?"

"No, it ain't got nuffin' ter do wiff him. Now git yer clothes. We's bein' sold. Massa's takin' us ter da slave auction dis afternoon."

The words filled Jake with dread. But when the time came, it wasn't as bad as he had expected. A few white men looked him over with mean expressions and stuck their fingers in his mouth and poked him in the stomach. They did the same to his mama, and a few men said things about her looks. In the end they were both sold to the same man, and Jake knew enough to know that all slave families weren't so lucky.

By late that same day they were on their way to their new home. His mama didn't say much. She just held him in the wagon. He knew she was relieved they were still together.

WORDS OF ANGER
5

J AKE WAS EIGHT, AND AT THE NEW PLANTATION HE was expected to work like a man.

His mother never seemed the same after that. She didn't talk as much, or sing around the house. As Jake grew, he gradually forgot his father, even forgot his face and what his voice sounded like. He came to realize that in a slave's life, family was a luxury not everyone got to enjoy.

In time Jake forgot the lips that had laughed and kissed and told him old slave stories and had soothed his hurts and fears. He forgot the expression and color of the eyes that had once looked upon him with tenderness and affection. But though he forgot the good, he allowed the resentment in his heart toward the man he'd once called *Papa* to smolder and grow. The faceless memory of his father became for him the cause and blame of everything that made life unpleasant. He blamed his father for every grievance he suffered at the hands of others. It made no sense. The resentments of children toward parents are often illogical. But irrational resentments eat away at the soul just as destructively as rational ones.

Thus the anger in Jake's heart festered and deepened its hold on his dawning character.

As the decade of the 1850s came to an end, talk of freedom was everywhere. Some folks were even talking about war. Jake had never heard the name Abraham Lincoln and knew nothing about elections or politics. But he could tell that things were changing.

Jake was changing too. By 1860 he was twelve and growing into a strong, strapping Negro teenager. He had a man's voice and was putting in long days with the other black men. But like most boys his age he wasn't particularly eager to work any harder than he had to. It was something he would live to regret.

The fall of 1860 progressed, and the election that would change the country and its history drew closer. Master Winegaard was working everyone on the plantation hard in preparation for winter, but also in preparation for what might happen if the Republican upstart from Illinois was elected. He had a cousin from the North who had written him about a rumor saying that the fellow called Lincoln might free the South's slaves if he was elected. Whites throughout the South were scared to death of what might happen to their way of life. There was even talk about the Southern states forming a new country where slavery would be allowed whether Mr. Lincoln liked it or not. Some folks said the division between North and South could lead to war.

All Jake and his mama knew was that Master Winegaard was working them harder than he ever had before. They were tired. The master didn't usually take on extra hands because he had enough slaves to do the work of the plantation. But he was even hiring temporary whites now too. There were several new faces around the place, including a couple of drifters Jake's mama didn't like the look of.

One hot day early in October, the master walked toward Jake where he was working with a dozen or so of the slaves.

It was about eleven o'clock in the morning. They had been up at dawn and had been ploughing the hard ground of one of the fields ever since. There wasn't a breath of wind. Flies were buzzing about. The men were all bare chested and sweating freely. Jake was so tired he could have fallen asleep right there on his feet, though the day wasn't half done yet.

"Jake," said Master Winegaard, "here's a satchel of fence staples. Take it out to where Tavish is working on that fence—you know, the twenty-acre parcel across the creek."

"I don't know effen I know who Tavish is, suh," said Jake.

"I just hired him last week. Big white fellow—twenty-eight or thirty, black hair . . . he's alone out there anyway. Just take the path beyond the slave village to the bridge across the creek. You'll hear him working. Now get going—I want him to finish that stretch of fence today."

Winegaard handed him the leather pouch and Jake walked off in the direction of the slave cabins. On the way, he realized how tired he was. A cold glass of water would taste mighty good. Something to eat along with it would be even better!

He walked into his little house ten minutes later, threw the satchel on the floor, picked up a tin cup, and went back outside to the water pump. His mother returned from the vegetable garden as he was splashing cold water over his head after taking several long, satisfying drinks. He fell in step with her back toward the house.

"Wha'chu doin' here at dis time er day, Jake?" she asked.

"Massa Winegaard sent me on a errand ter sumbody workin' 'cross da creek."

"You don't look like you's on yer way ter nobody."

"I jes' stopped by ter git a cup er water an' take a little rest an' git sumfin ter eat," said Jake. He followed her inside and plopped down on his blanket on the far side of the room.

"Wha'chu layin' down for?" said his mother. "Git up, Jake."

"I's plumb tuckered out, Mama. I been out diggin' in dat hard dirt all day."

"An' I been workin' in da garden mos' er da day. What's so unushul 'bout dat? Now what you supposed ter be doin'?"

"Sum white man on da other side er da bridge needs dat dere satchel. But I figger he can wait a spell fo it."

"Effen Massa gib you sumfin ter do, den you best git it dun or you's feel his whip on yo back."

"A few minutes won't make no dif'rence," said Jake. "'Sides dat, Massa's busy over t' da other side er da big house. He'll neber know."

"He'll neber know! What kind er talk dat be?"

"Nuthin', Mama—I jes' meant he won't fin' out dat I stopped by here. He can't whip me fo what he don't know."

"Jake Patterson, you oughter be 'shamed er yo'self. Da good Lawd'll know, eben effen Massa don't. Tryin' ter hide what you's doin' be jes' like lyin'. Ain't no good can come er dat, nohow."

"It ain't lyin', Mama," retorted Jake a little testily. "I jes' want ter rest a bit. Dere ain't nuthin' so bad 'bout dat. Why you takin' da massa's side?"

"I ain't takin' nobody's side. I's jes' tellin' you what's right, dat's all. Yer papa wudn't neber do such a thing. He wuz a man er his word, an' effen he said he gwine do sumfin, he'd do it wiffout no sneakin' roun' pretendin' ter be one place, den goin' off sumwheres else."

"Well, Papa's gone!" Jake shot back. "He left us an' dat's dat. I's sick er hearin' 'bout him."

"Wha'chu sayin'! He got sol'. He didn't leab us."

"Dat ain't da way I heard it."

"He wudn't neber do dat. Now you git up and git goin',
Jake."

"An' I tell you I ain't ready jes' yet. Why you always
throwin' Papa up at me like he wuz sum blame saint er sumfin!"

"Jake, you watch yer mouf! How dare you talk like dat
'bout yer papa!"

"It's true—you make him soun' like he was sumfin special."

"Dat he wuz as shure as you's standin' dere! Yer papa was
a good man. He always did what Massa tol' him. Effen he
said he wud do sumfin he did it. Wudn't hurt you none ter
be a little mo like him neither."

"Like him! He's da las' man I'd want ter be like! What he
eber do fo me?"

"Wha'chu sayin'! What's got inter yer head? He gib
you life, dat what, an' he loved you like no papa I eber
seen."

"Loved me!" Jake said sarcastically. "I don't 'member no
love from him. He'd whip my back soon as da massa effen I
did sumfin he didn't like."

"He neber whipped yer back! Where you git a noshun like
dat!"

"He spanked me sumthin' fierce!"

"Only w'en you didn't do what you wuz tol'. Dat ain't no
whippin'!"

"When I got in er fight wif Johnny Clarkson, he sided wiff
Johnny, not me, an' den made me do what Johnny said. He
wuz always lookin' ter see what I done wrong an' gittin' after
me fo it."

"Jes' cuz he wanted you ter be da bes' boy you cud," said
his mama. "Dat's da job God gib papas ter do, an' good papas
try ter do it. It's jes' lazy papas dat let dere young'uns do
whatever dey wants."

"Well, maybe I didn't want ter be what he wanted me ter be."

"An' maybe dat weren't fer you ter say. Dat's a papa's job, an' a mama's too. An' I tried ter do it, jes' like yer daddy did. But you jes' sulk round an' gib me ornery looks like I's sum kind er dog instead er yer mama. Sumtimes I wonder what you's thinkin', Jake, da way you act roun' me. Mos' kids got respec' fer dere mamas, but you jes' ax me ter do dis an' do dat an' den gib me nasty looks like you can't stan' da sight er me."

But by now Jake was too worked up about his father for his mother's words to sink in.

"You's always sayin' how good Papa wuz," he went on irritably. "You say he cared 'bout us, but he didn't. He didn't care enuff ter stay. You say he wuz sold, but I'm thinkin' you's sayin' it jes' ter keep me from knowin' da truf, an' dat's dat he turned his back an' lef' us. I know dat happened cuz one er da massa's men tol' me. Papa lef' us. An' I hate him. I hate da thought ob him!"

Jake began to storm out of the house. Stunned at what she had heard, and having no idea how strong was the silent anger that had built inside him, Jake's mother stared after him with her mouth hanging open. His words had angered her too. But she was filled with the righteous indignation of a loving wife, not the selfish anger of a teenager. She found her voice a few seconds later.

"Jake, don't you turn yer back on me!" she yelled after him. "You come back here!"

Jake stopped and glanced back.

"You take back dose awful words," she said. "You take 'em back, you hear me. Den you pick up dat dere satchel an' take it where Massa tol' you like yer papa wud er dun."

"I won't take back what I said!" Jake retorted. "I meant it. Dere ain't no love in my heart fo da man, whateber you say."

"Why, Jeremi—" she began.

"Don't you call me dat name!" Jake shot back angrily. "Dat's what he always called me when he wuz getting' after me fo sumthin', an' I don't want ter eber hear it agin!"

His mother's heart sank. Her son's words were so painful that she felt like a knife had plunged into her heart. Tears rose in her eyes.

"Jake, Jake," she said in a sad, almost pleading, voice, "w'en you gwine stop blamin' yer daddy fo everythin' you don' like in life? Dere comes a time w'en folks gotter grow up an' take a look inside theirselves 'stead er heapin' dere own problems on sumbody else. Looks ter me like dat time's 'bout come fer you. You got a heart full er resentment dat's nobody's fault but yer own. Yer daddy wuz a fine man dat honored da Lawd Jesus in everythin' he said an' dun. He tried ter honor da Lawd tards you too, an' you's got da wrong grip on it. You's lookin' at what he wuz an' what he dun tards you all backwards. Looks ter me like da devil's got hold ob yer heart 'stead er da Lawd himsel'."

"My heart's my own biz'ness!" spat Jake rudely. "I don't need you preachin' at me neither, not 'bout Papa or Jesus or nobody else. I reckon I can take care of mysel' wiffout either ob dem!"

He turned again and stomped angrily away.

His mother watched his back till he was out of sight, then began to cry in earnest. It broke her heart to hear him talk so. But it would break her heart even more for him to be whipped for disobeying, or, worse, to be sold as a troublemaker. Right now she couldn't afford the luxury of sinking into the grief she felt. Whatever cruel words he had spoken, she had to protect them both from the consequences of his irresponsibility.

She wiped back her tears, then picked up the satchel that still lay on the floor. If she delivered it herself, maybe the master wouldn't find out that Jake hadn't done what he'd told him. That wouldn't be lying like what she'd said to Jake, but just making sure the job got done. At least that's the way it seemed at the moment.

The argument with her son was her fault anyway. She shouldn't have pushed Jake so hard. If he did find out, that's what she would tell the master. Hopefully whatever punishment fell would come to her instead of him.

JAKE'S MAMA
6

I T WAS A CURSE FOR A BLACK WOMAN TO BE PRETTY IN those days, and Jake's mama was. Every day she lived in fear that the master would make her marry someone she didn't want to, or bed her down with one of his men. She was even afraid that one of the whites around the place would appear at her doorstep one day and order her onto the pad that was her bed. But Master Winegaard wasn't cruel like Master Clarkson. Though he worked his slaves hard, he didn't allow things like that to happen if he could help it.

But he couldn't be everywhere at once. A couple of the new men had been looking at her in ways that made her uncomfortable. With poor whites like them, you could never tell what might happen.

Jake's mama didn't know where Jake had stormed off to, but as she crossed the bridge over the stream she knew well enough from the pounding echo of a hammer where he'd been supposed to take the satchel. She walked toward the sound.

As she emerged into the clearing from where the sound was coming, she stopped abruptly. There stood a man she recognized as one of the new hands who had been around the plantation about a week. Beside him on the ground, along with his jacket, she saw what looked to be a bottle of whiskey.

He saw the movement of her approach and turned.

"Massa sent you down a supply er staples," she said. "I's set 'em right here."

She put the leather satchel she had been carrying on the ground, then quickly turned and began to walk away.

"Hey, wait just a minute, missy," the man called after her. "Where you off to in such an all-fired hurry?"

Not wanting to anger him, she stopped, but stood facing the opposite direction.

"I'm talking to you, missy," said the man. "You turn around when a white man's talking to you."

Slowly she turned. His eyes roamed up and down her body.

"Anyone come down here with you?" he asked.

"No, suh."

"You alone?"

"Yes, suh," she replied, her heart beginning to pound.

Slowly an evil grin spread across his face.

"Ain't no one nearby," he said, tossing down his hammer and walking toward her. "Why don't you and I go over there and lay down in that nice soft grass and have us some fun. You'd like that, wouldn't you, missy?"

"No, suh . . . I don't think so, suh," she said. She took a few steps backward.

"You refusing me, missy?"

"No, suh. It's jes' dat I gots ter git back so dey—"

"You're lyin', missy," he interrupted as he began to unbutton his shirt. His voice contained more than a hint of anger. "There ain't no one expecting you for nothing, is there? Ten minutes for a little fun . . . ain't nobody gonna know but you and me. Now you come here, missy, and get that dress off," he said, throwing his shirt on the ground.

In panic she turned and ran. But it was the wrong thing to do. More than half drunk and running clumsily, he was still able to overtake her. She felt the strong grip of his hand on her shoulder as he grabbed her and yanked her back, pulling her dress down. She stumbled with a little cry and fell to the ground.

"Now you didn't need to go running off like that, missy," he said. "You didn't need to make Tavish mad." He stooped to one knee and began to lie down on top of her.

With a sudden strength that took him completely by surprise, she shoved him away. He fell on his back as she jumped to her feet. She pulled her dress up to her waist and bolted toward the bridge. Incensed with rage, he struggled up, yelling terrible curses after her, and tried to run. He stumbled, found his feet, and hurried after her. She made it farther this time, but again she was no match for his younger legs. When he caught her this time, his fury unleashed itself and he beat violently at her face and shoulders.

Terrified for her life, she screamed as loud as she could and called desperately for help. Her cries enraged him all the more. He whacked with a clenched fist at her mouth to silence her, then continued beating at her head as if he had been fighting a man. A terrible blow to the side of her jaw stunned her with a sharp bolt of pain to the back of her skull. Wobbling dizzily, she staggered and fell limp to the ground. Her head thudded dully to the hard-packed dirt of the path.

Even as he had left the shack, his mother staring at his back and his own heated words ringing in his ears, Jake knew how wrong he had been. Whatever he might feel about his father, he had never before raised his voice to his mother. His heart stung him for what he had said. The argument had also brought to the surface the overseer's cruel and painful words from years before. True or not, they were the kind of words a boy never forgets. They had hurt him so deeply that he could never escape them. How much of his present anger was an attempt to fight back against the pain of such rejection, who could say.

"*He couldn't stand the sight of you no more . . . Dat boy ob mine's jes' too ugly . . . I can't stan' sight er him no mo.*"

Over and over the overseer's words repeated themselves. *Jes' too ugly . . . can't stan' sight er him . . . too ugly . . . too ugly.*

All Jake wanted to do was erase the terrible words from his mind. But that was the one thing he could never do.

He had to settle down. His temper had got the better of him a time or two with Master Winegaard's overseer. He had tasted the man's whip as a result. But now that his temper had erupted against his own mother, Jake suddenly saw that the demon inside him had grown larger than he had realized. But he kept walking away.

He was too proud to admit it immediately. But it didn't take long before he knew what he had to do.

Jake walked sheepishly back into the house about five minutes later, cooled off and embarrassed. Already he was rehearsing in his mind the apology to his mother he knew he had to make. The house was still and quiet. He glanced around. His eyes fell on the floor where he had dumped the leather satchel.

It was gone.

Immediately he suspected the truth. The same instant a wave of panic surged through him. He had seen the same leering looks on Tavish's face that his mother had. He knew well enough the cause of them.

The next moment he was sprinting out of the house and running toward the creek.

Jake heard the screams he knew were his mother's well before he reached the bridge. When they went silent he increased his pace. He pounded across the footbridge, then slowed. He listened intently for any sound, then made for the field where he thought Tavish had been working.

Halfway between the bridge and the clearing, he saw Tavish ahead. He had just unbuttoned his trousers, knelt down, and begun to rip at Jake's mother's dress. Jake flew the remaining distance and leaped at the man, hitting him in full flight and knocking him flat on his back. Even half drunk, Tavish had been able to overpower Jake's mother. But he was no match for the son. His alcohol-soaked brain had no more begun trying to make sense of what had happened, and his eyes attempted to focus on the sky and treetops above him, than the fists and booted feet of what seemed like a dozen men began pummeling him with a frenzy that soon lost all sense of reason.

Two or three minutes later, Jake was dragging the limp form off the path into the nearby underbrush. Behind him he heard his mother moaning in pain.

Jake hurried back, glanced about, then ran ahead to the clearing, picked up the man's shirt and jacket, ran back, and threw them into the brush out of sight. Now first he saw the color on his hands. But the horror of what he had done had not yet fully dawned on him. He ran to the creek to wash. As he did, it was the creek that gave him the idea of how to get rid of Tavish for good.

A few minutes later he hurried back to his mother, who was struggling to come to herself.

"Mama, Mama," he said, stooping down beside her. "Oh, Mama, I's sorry . . . I's sorry for all da things I said."

"Jake . . . Jake," she moaned feebly, "dat be you?"

"Yes, Mama. It's me. I's here now."

"Where dat terrible man?"

"He's gone, Mama. I run him off. He's gone now."

"He hit me, Jake . . . he hit me bad."

"He's gone, Mama . . . he won't hurt you no mo."

"My head . . . it's painin' me sumfin dreadful."

"I'll git you home, Mama," said Jake, gently slipping his hands beneath her shoulders and knees and lifting her as he stood.

Ten minutes later his mother was resting on her own bed

pad while Jake wiped her face and forehead and arms with a damp cloth. Already welts and bruises were beginning to show color around her eyes and across her cheeks. But the blows to her jaw and back of her head were more serious than the rest. Young Jake was not physician enough to recognize that she was feverish, nor to know the danger of allowing her to drift off to sleep so soon after hurting her head.

Once she was asleep, the reality of his own plight began to press itself upon him.

What should he do?

He had to get help for his mother. That was the first thing. But if it was discovered that he had attacked a white man, even fair-minded Master Winegaard would mete out the white man's justice swiftly and harshly. Whatever form that justice took, it would not be favorable for young Jake Patterson. And he knew it.

First he would find the rest of the women where they were working in the garden. He would get old Mammy Jenks to sit with his mother. Then he would go back to the master with whatever story he could devise to account for the length of his absence.

FAREWELL
7

THERE WAS NO MISTAKING THAT MASTER WINE-gaard was growing perturbed by Jake's delay. But before a tongue-lashing could erupt, Jake ran up saying his mother had had a bad fall, had hit her head, and that he had helped see her to bed and had sat with her for a while. The obvious panic on Jake's face confirmed that he was not making the story up.

Winegaard nodded with concern and asked if she was being looked after. Jake said Mammy Jenks was with her. Had the accident happened before or after he had seen Tavish? Jake answered that he had delivered the satchel and then helped his mother to her bed.

The vague reply did not seem to bother the master. He took in the information, then returned to his own affairs while Jake rejoined the rest of the slaves in the field.

When Tavish did not return to the big house for supper that evening, Winegaard sent one of his men after him. They returned saying they could find no trace of him. The only evidence he had been there at all was a hammer, a whiskey bottle, and the satchel of staples on the ground that Jake had delivered. When Tavish still made no appearance the following day, Winegaard chalked it up to drink, the irresponsibility of a slacker, or the itchy feet of a drifter. He said to himself that he had received the best of the bargain anyway, since he had not yet paid anything for the half-week's work.

The missing man was not quite so easily dismissed from Jake's mind.

He hardly slept for a week, haunted by nightmares of what he had done and what might be the consequences. More than once, dozing in the quiet, lonely hours of blackness, he awoke suddenly in a cold sweat, fingers clutching at the imaginary rope he had felt tightening about his neck.

But there was no escape for him. His mother needed him. Still she lay, day after day and night after night, coming in and out of consciousness. She took water occasionally but ate nothing. By appearances she was getting no better. All Mammy Jenks could do was shake her head and mumble unintelligibly. Her countenance did not look hopeful. Everyone knew Mammy Jenks possessed a sixth sense about these things.

After several days, Master Winegaard sent for the white doctor in town. By now the swelling of the face, as well as the bruises and welts around both eyes, was well pronounced. The doctor questioned everyone as to their cause. No one knew a thing. Jake professed truthfully that he had not seen the accident but had found his mother lying on the ground moaning in pain and complaining about her head. His story, short on detail as it might be, was the only account to be had; there was nothing to conclude but that the injuries to Jake's mother involved mysteries they might never get to the bottom of.

Then came a day when she became still more feverish. Mammy Jenks appealed to Master Winegaard. Again he sent for the doctor. He said there was nothing to do but keep the fever under control with cold compresses. He added that she had probably suffered a concussion and that eventually the fever would pass if they could keep her cool.

Mammy Jenks watched him go, shaking her head. "What dat fool white man knows 'bout doctorin'," she mumbled under her breath, "is jes' 'bout what ah knows 'bout dat ol' Greek language dey say da Good Book come from."

When Jake returned from the fields that evening, Mammy Jenks gave him instructions about keeping his mama's skin moist and cool. She showed him the soup she had made for his supper, and told him to spoon some of it into his mother's mouth if he could. Then she returned to her shack to see to her own people.

Jake spent the night at his mama's bedside. He tried to be stoic, for he was poised at that moment between childhood and manhood, where he thought that to show his emotions indicated weakness. He had seen on Mammy Jenks' face that his mother had taken a turn for the worse. The budding man inside his young body wanted to be strong. But the boy that was still more part of him than he let on was dying with anguish for what his own foolishness had allowed to happen.

In the middle of the night, as he dozed in the chair at her side, his mama came suddenly awake. She found his hand, then clutched it with unusual strength. Jake came to himself. He felt his mother's hand holding tight to his, clammy and wet. An involuntary shudder went through him.

The fever seemed to have completely left her. Now she felt cold. Too cold. She pulled him toward her face.

"You fin' him, Jake," she said. Her voice was stronger than it had been in days. Strong and determined.

"Who, Mama . . . find who?" he said sleepily.

"Yer papa, Jake. You fin' yer father. I want him ter know dat I loved him, dat he wuz da bes' man da Lawd cud er gib me. You tell him, Jake. You tell him I neber stopped lovin' him, dat I wuz neber wiff anudder man in all my life but him. You tell him, Jake."

"I'll try, Mama."

"Sumday you'll be free," she continued. "I knows it, sumday we all be free. An' w'en dat day comes, you fin' him, you hear—you fin' yer daddy an' you tell him he wuz da bes' man I eber knowed. I don't care what you say 'bout him, you's wrong, Jake, an' don't you say nuthin' like dat ter me . . . not now."

"I won't, Mama. I's real sorry fo what I said dat day. I love you, Mama. I's real sorry."

"Dat's good er you ter say, Jake," she said softly, a feeble smile coming to her face. "I's be better now, jes' hearin' dat. I cudn't bear ter say good-bye wiffout it right atween us again."

"Good-bye . . . what you mean, Mama?" said Jake, fear clutching his heart.

"Jake, my boy," replied his mother weakly, barely whispering now, "it's time you gots ter be a man. I's goin' where you can't go wiff me. Ain't no one can go wiff me but da Lawd, an' I's almost see Him comin' fer me . . . it's all white dere in da distance. I know it's Him. I can jes' kinder make out da white er His robe . . . an' He's walkin' tards me wiff His hand out ter take mine. Dere's a smile on His face . . . He smilin' jes' ter see me! An' He's by hissel' too, so I knows yer daddy's still here on dis side er dat ol' ribber called Jordan. He's still here cuz da good Lawd, He wants you an' yer papa ter fin' one anudder's arms agin. I knows it . . . so you fin' him, Jake."

"How will I fin' him, Mama?" said Jake, his deep man-voice trembling like a boy's.

"Dere wuz talk from one er Massa Clarkson's house slaves dat he wuz sol' up norf where Massa Clarkson had a brudder, sumwheres in Carolina. So you fin' Carolina, Jake."

"What's Carolina, Mama?"

"Don' know, Jake. Sumwheres up norf . . . you fin' it."

She fumbled weakly in her bedclothes. A moment later her hand emerged clutching a tiny object. She took Jake's hand, then opened her own. In it she held a small carved wooden horse.

"Take dis, Jake," she said in a voice that had grown so weak he had to lean down with his ear next to her mouth to make out her words. "Yer papa gib it ter me. Take it ter him . . . it be my way er tellin' him I neber fergot how good he wuz ter me."

Jake nodded as he took the tiny horse his father had carved many years before.

"You fin' Carolina, Jake," his mother added, "whateber it be, whereber it be. I know dat sumday you'll see dat freedom me an' yer papa prayed ter see. So w'en you's free, you fin' him. You hear me . . . you fin' him."

The talk had taxed her. She fell back on the blanket and closed her eyes. Jake sat, holding the carving in one hand and her limp hand in his other. Her breathing was labored and weak. He sniffed and dabbed at his eyes, then replaced her hand under the blanket.

Jake longed to cry. His heart was breaking for fear of what was surely at hand. But even in the middle of the night with no human eyes upon him, the floodgates of emotion within him were accompanied by too many memories of his father yet to open themselves.

By morning his mother was gone.

Jake knew it the moment he woke again two hours after drifting off to sleep where he sat. His eyes fell upon her face. Her eyes were closed but her mouth was open a crack. A pallor of grey had begun to invade the brown of her skin.

"Mama . . ." he whispered, though he knew she could not reply. A trickle of moisture filled his eyes. He brushed at it, then leaned down and kissed her mouth. Her lips were cold.

Jake pulled quickly away, then rose and went for Mammy Jenks.

They buried her the day after in the small plot on a distant corner of the Winegaard plantation where slaves were laid to rest. Most of their fellow slaves, as well as Master and Mistress Winegaard and the white preacher from town, stood beside the grave. Jake stood stoic with the others, saying nothing. Still his tears remained inside. Their season had not yet come. The pain he felt in his young heart was too mingled with other things to do anything but fill him with conflict and confusion.

The secret of what he had done haunted him. Every day he grew more fearful that Master Winegaard or one of his men would discover the truth, or that the missing man would turn up to betray him. Nothing now held him to this place. Two nights later, in the quiet hours between midnight and the first sound of the cock, Jake stole quietly from the small cabin he alone now occupied.

With only the few clothes he could carry, he crept through the woods to the creek, which alone knew of his terrible deed. He then began to run across fields barely lit with a quarter moon.

He ran and ran until his lungs were ready to burst. He rested, then ran again.

All night he ran, until the day's first light began to grow in the east. He searched for a secluded place to lie down and sleep. How many miles from the Winegaard plantation he had gone, and in what direction, he had no idea.

He only knew two things for certain. For the first time in his life he was on his own. And he was a runaway.

If he was found, it would not go well for him. He had never forgotten Master Clarkson's overseer's words about his father. He had never forgotten the master's words about nigger dogs. And he knew that nigger dogs thirsting for the taste of nigger blood were everywhere.

As soon as he woke he searched about for water to drink. From what he knew about the sun in the sky, Jake Patterson then began to make his way in the only direction that promised safety for a black man on the run.

North.

Terrifying Encounter
8

N OT ONLY WERE THERE NIGGER DOGS EVERYWHERE, there were runaway slaves everywhere too. Slavery was tearing the country apart at the seams. One of the results was a flood of escapees from plantations large and small. More and more blacks were setting out for freedom in the North.

No bond among men and women is quite so instantly felt as the camaraderie of shared affliction. In the South of those *dis*-United States of America, the lines of antagonism between slave owners and blacks were more and more strident. Therefore, any fellow of dark skin was an immediate comrade, no matter what might be his circumstances.

It did not take Jake long to find that he had friends everywhere among the innumerable brothers and sisters of his race. All he had to say was, "A white man killed my mama and I'm a runaway," and he was instantly taken in, fed, clothed, and provided a place to sleep for as long as he chose to remain.

After his first few weeks on the run, Jake never went hungry. He moved from plantation to plantation, field to field, from slave hut to slave hut. He passed from family to relative to acquaintance. He was given directions, instructions, names, and passwords. Anyone and everyone with black skin was only too eager to help him. Blacks, whether slave or free, may not have had much. But what they had they would happily share with any pilgrim in need.

Gradually came word that the man called Lincoln had been elected president, and that the states of the South were joining together to form a new country.

None of that meant much to the slaves until April of 1861, when even more shocking news began to spread—war had broken out between the old country and the new, the North and the South.

All this time Jake had had no definite plan. He only knew that the Carolinas were somewhere vaguely north and east of him. His northward sojourn had taken him to northern Alabama and near the border about the time the war broke out. Having to hide out more now because of the war, and traveling with other blacks making their way north, his steps now followed a northerly route into Tennessee. There he first saw signs of the war for himself.

He was just looking for a place to sleep one night, traveling alone, when the small company of grey-clad soldiers came into sight in the distance. His first thought was panic. He didn't know much about the war, only that it was being fought over slaves and slavery. But soldiers meant government, and the government didn't look kindly on runaway slaves. There was no telling what might happen if they saw him.

But Jake had no time to decide what to do. While he still stood watching, suddenly a small band of riders galloped through the woods behind him.

He glanced back. Their uniforms were grey just like the troops in the distance. Every face among them was white.

He sprinted for the cover of some nearby undergrowth. But it was too late to hide. They had seen him.

"Hey, boys!" cried the lead rider. "Look what we found— a nigger kid! Hey, boy . . . come back here!"

The soldier lashed his mount and bolted after him.

Terrified, Jake kept running. But he was no match for a man on horseback, much less six of them. Within seconds they had him surrounded.

"Where you think you're going, nigger boy?" said another of the soldiers. He inched his horse close to Jake and gave him a shove with his boot.

Jake stumbled back and fell against the flank of another of the horses.

"From the look of it," said another, "he's a runaway. Where you goin', boy?"

"Nowhere, suh," replied Jake.

"Then what you doing out here alone? You're lyin', boy!"

"Maybe he's a spy for the Union," suggested one of the soldiers.

"Nah, he's too young and ugly for that. He's a runaway if you ask me."

"Then we gotta do something about that, don't we, boys?"

"Yeah," laughed another. "Looks like we got to teach this nigger boy a lesson!"

"I ain't no runaway or no spy—" Jake began. Another kick in the ribs silenced him.

"Hey, boy! You ain't got no call to talk unless your betters ask you a question. So you just shut your mouth!"

At last Jake's anger got the better of his fear.

"President Lincoln's gonna free us all one er dese days, an' den I'll say whateber I feels like sayin'!"

It was a foolish outburst. Jake still hadn't learned to control his anger.

"You hear that, boys! He says ol' Abe's gonna free him." Cruel laughter followed, along with a few more shoves and jabs and kicks against his head and shoulders.

"Ain't you never heard of the Confederate States of America, nigger boy?" said one of the riders. "That's where you are now. Abe Lincoln don't got no power here. Ain't that right, boys? You ain't in Abe Lincoln's country no more—you're in the South, where Jeff Davis is president. Niggers ain't free here and you're still a slave. That's why we got to teach you your place. You been speaking with disrespect to your betters. We got to learn you some manners."

One of the men took a rope from behind his saddle. He made a loop and tossed it over Jake's head and coiled it around his shoulders and chest, then yanked tight. Jake struggled, but his efforts only tightened the cords all the worse. Two or three of the riders jumped off their horses and grabbed his hands. Soon they were tied behind his back. The men took the other end of the rope and tied it somewhere, though Jake couldn't see, then they scrambled back up onto their horses. Hardly knowing what they were doing, suddenly Jake heard a few shouts.

The horses galloped away. For a second or two he stood bewildered, then suddenly felt himself pulled viciously off his feet and along the ground. Up and down the rider dragged him behind his horse over the hard dirt. With his hands tied, Jake was powerless to protect his head. He twisted and bumped and tumbled behind the horse like a sack of potatoes. The rope cinched so tight around his chest that he could hardly breathe.

Laughter, shouts, and taunts mingled with the pounding of galloping hooves. He felt almost as if the horses themselves were trampling on his head.

Back and forth the soldier dragged him. His clothes ripped and tore. His bare skin was soon scraped and bleeding and caked with dirt. His head was pummeled to near unconsciousness.

The thought came into Jake's battered mind that he was about to die. Fleeting memories of his mother, and even dimly behind them of his father, flitted through his brain.

Just as Jake's awareness began to fade completely, an explosion of gunfire sounded. Another followed. Jake's dull thought was that other riders were shooting as he tumbled over the ground. Their next shots would surely be through his head. His brain spun confused and out of control.

Shouts . . . more gunshots, louder this time. Why hadn't his head been blown apart? Still he felt no bullet smashing into his chest or skull. How could they miss? Why was he still alive?

The horse had stopped. He lay flat on his stomach. Everything became still and quiet.

Though barely conscious, he struggled to listen. Horses were galloping away in the distance. Faintly he heard footsteps approaching. Then they stopped. Someone was standing next to him. He was dead now for sure. Standing straight above him, no one could possibly miss.

Warm, dreamy exhaustion filled him. His head swam in swirling light.

Then slowly everything went black.

MICAH DUFF
9

W HEN JAKE PATTERSON SLOWLY BEGAN TO COME TO himself, his first sensation was of a faint crackling sound. His brain was blurry and confused. Blackness surrounded him. He was cold.

Suddenly he knew what it was—it was the sound of a fire, the crackling of flames.

Was he dead? Had he woken up in hell!

The next thoughts that came were reminders of his dreadful secret, and what he had done and the terrible things he had said to his mother. No wonder he was here. He belonged to the devil now. It was nothing more than he deserved.

Slowly another sensation gradually filtered through into his senses . . . more crackling and sizzling. But with it came . . . what was it?

Jake sniffed at the chilly air.

It was the smell of bacon frying.

He struggled to turn toward it. Suddenly within him a thousand places screamed in pain. Every muscle, every bone, every inch of his body was scraped, cut, bruised . . . or worse.

A groan sounded. It seemed far away, yet Jake realized it had come from his own mouth.

He managed to open his eyes a crack. He could hardly

move, but he could see. A few yards from him burned a small fire. A black pan sat on top of its coals from which apparently came the sound and smell of frying bacon. Now he noticed, along with it, the smell of coffee coming from a pot next to the pan.

Wherever he was, he thought, it couldn't be hell. The fire was too small. And the old devil surely didn't treat his guests with such luxuries!

Now he saw a few trees. The grey light of daybreak began to awaken his consciousness further . . . now more sounds . . . shuffling feet . . . indistinct voices . . . the occasional snort of horses from nearby.

He detected movement. He opened his eyes wider. There were men around, stirring in the morning mist . . . milling about . . . getting dressed . . . tending to their horses. They all wore the same color . . . the color of uniforms . . . he was surrounded by soldiers!

Another groan escaped Jake's lips, this one of fear. He was alert now. He knew he was in danger! He had to get up . . . get away . . . get to the woods before they noticed he was awake! He had to get out of here!

But his groans had attracted someone's attention. Jake struggled to turn his head. Beside the fire someone in a uniform stooped to one knee and stirred at the pan. He was dressed head to foot in dark blue.

The soldier turned toward him. The light of the fire flickered and reflected from the man's face. Jake's eyes shot open at the sight of it.

"So . . . you've come to at last," said the man, revealing a smile of friendly greeting. He stood and walked toward where Jake lay. "I was beginning to think I'd lost you for good."

All Jake could do was stare up in astonishment. The face looking down at him was *black*!

"Who . . . who are you?" Jake tried to say. He could

scarcely speak. The words came out like the croak of a dying frog.

The man chuckled.

"You just lie still, son," he said. "Don't try to talk. Don't try to do nothing."

"But I gotta git outer here," Jake said in a groaning whisper.

Again the man laughed. "You're not going anywhere anytime soon, brother," he said. "You got yourself mighty banged up. You got welts and bruises all over you, two or three broken ribs and maybe a broken arm besides. I don't know if you could walk right now if you tried. So you lay still. You'll be fine right here."

"But where am I . . . who are you . . . what happened to those—"

Jake's voice cracked. His mouth was too dry and his lips too cut and swollen to continue. The man saw him trying to lick at his lips, turned away for a minute, then returned and bent to one knee beside him. He slid a hand under Jake's shoulders and lifted him slightly, then with his other hand put a cup of cold water to Jake's mouth. With great effort Jake managed to sip at it, though it was painful to swallow, until he had downed about a third of it. The man eased him back down.

"The name's Micah Duff, son," said the soldier. "Private Duff. You're with a company of Illinois volunteers heading for Chattanooga."

"But . . . dose others . . . dose soldiers that . . ." Jake began.

"That was a small detail of rebs. They'd have killed you sure if I hadn't come along. But they're gone now. You don't have to worry about them no more. I was out ahead of our company. That's what I do—I'm a scout. And I tend the horses. I was scouting when I ran into them. Lucky for you I did too. In case you hadn't noticed, they were wearing the grey of the Confederate rebels. We're wearing the blue of the U.S. infantry. So are you.''

For the first time Jake looked at himself. His legs were covered by a blanket, and he saw that he too was wearing a blue army coat.

"It was all I had to wrap you in to keep you warm," said the man named Duff. In Jake's eyes, wearing the uniform of a soldier and having saved him from what would probably have been death, the fellow called Micah Duff looked fully a man. In Jake's estimation, Duff might have been anywhere from twenty to thirty. In fact, he was but eighteen. He was only a few years older than Jake and hardly more than a boy himself.

Jake lay back and closed his eyes and tried to take in this latest change in his life. He had no idea how long he'd been unconscious. But he knew he was weak. And as he came more fully awake he realized the truth of what the young man had said—that he was seriously hurt and wasn't going anywhere on his own anytime soon. He hurt everywhere!

He did his best to keep sipping at the water in the cup. Gradually he finished it and asked for a refill. After a little while, with Duff's help, he managed to sit up. Now his ribs and left arm really screamed out at him!

Duff handed him a cup of coffee. "Here," he said, "this ought to help clear some of the fog out of your brain. It might not be too good, but it's strong, which is all the men of this company expect. I'm not the cook, but a lot of them still come to my fire for their first cup of coffee in the morning. They say the cook's coffee's too weak."

Jake took it with a grateful nod, and began sipping at the edges of the steaming cup. It was strong, all right!

"Now let's see about that bacon!" said Duff. "You hungry?''

"I ain't had no chance ter be hungry, suh," replied Jake.

"I'm barely waked up enuff . . . I's still tryin' ter figger out all what's goin' on."

Duff laughed. "Well, you'll be hungry soon enough, I reckon. By the way . . . what's your name, brother?"

"Jake Patterson, suh."

"Well, I'm pleased to meet you, Jake," said Duff, forking out several slabs of the sizzling pork onto two tin plates. He handed one to Jake. "But one thing we gotta get straight," he went on, "—I ain't no *sir*. I'm just a black man like you."

"I ain't no man, Mr. Duff," said Jake. "I's just a kid on da run tryin' ter keep out er sight an' make it to da norf."

"How old are you, Jake?"

"I don't know . . . twelve, I reckon, maybe thirteen by now. I kinder lose track er time hidin' out like I been doin'."

"Hey, Duff, looks like your invalid's gonna make it after all," a voice interrupted them. Jake turned to see a white man looking him over as he approached.

"Yes, sir," said Duff. "I'm trying to get some coffee into him."

"If anything will bring the life back into him, it's your coffee! How you doing, son?" he said, glancing down at Jake.

"Uh . . . okay, suh."

"Gimme a cup of that coffee of yours, Duff," he said, handing the private an empty cup.

Duff filled it. The man took a sip, grimaced, then walked away.

"Well, Jake," said Duff when he was gone, "I'm eighteen, so that makes me a little older than you, but not old enough for you to call me no *sir*. So you see, I'm just a few years ahead of you, though being a soldier makes a man of you quicker than other things."

"Why are you a soldier, Mr. Duff? Ain't you a slave?"

"A slave! I've never been a slave, Jake. I'm from Illinois and I'm as free as any white man alive. Why . . . were you a slave?"

"I's still a slave, Mr. Duff," said Jake.

"Talking to you, I'm not sure I like the *mister* any more than I do the *sir*. Nobody's called me a mister in my life. All the men around here just call me Duff, or Private Duff. So why don't you do that too, Jake, if you don't want to call me by my name."

"I'll try, Mr. Duff."

"What I want to know, then, is what all this is about with you being a slave. You can't still be a slave . . . not while you're here with us. Why do you say you're still a slave?"

Jake glanced around and lowered his voice. "I's a runaway, Mr. Duff," he said. "Dat's why I's tryin' ter git to da norf. I's in a heap er trouble. Dat's why I's on da run."

"Why you say you're in trouble? What happened?"

Briefly Jake told him about his mother and about attacking the white drifter. But he didn't tell him the worst of his secrets.

"What will dey do ter me, Duff?" Jake asked when he was through. "Da white soldiers . . . what dey do when dey fin' out I'm a runaway?"

"They won't do anything. That's what I've been trying to tell you—you're with friends now. You might as well get used to it, 'cause you're going to be with us for a spell, at least until you get recovered enough to walk."

"But what will I do? I ain't no soldier like you."

"You let me worry about that," said Duff. "You can help me with the horses. Nobody's going to bother you. Once you're up and about, I'll make sure you earn your grub. You know anything about horses?"

"A little. My papa wuz real good wiff horses. Dat's what he did."

"He was a slave too?"

Jake nodded. "Till he lef' us," he said. "I ain't seen him since I wuz a little kid."

Duff took in the statement thoughtfully but did not reply.

He could tell from the cloud that came over Jake's face, there was more to the story. He was curious, but he would let whatever he might need to know come out when the time was right. Micah Duff may have been young, but he was wise enough to know that there is a time to press and a time not to.

NEW SURROUNDINGS
10

PRIVATE DUFF WAS RIGHT. IT TOOK JAKE A LONG time to recover from his injuries. The company couldn't stop and take time for him to mend just because they'd picked up a runaway black. They had to keep going. And those next few days were mighty painful for Jake.

Private Duff did his best to make a comfortable place for him to lie in one of the wagons, with as many blankets as they could spare. But the bouncing and bumping hurt so much that there were times Jake didn't think he could stand it. There is nothing quite so painful as broken ribs. Every bump the wagon wheels went over sent jabs from a hot iron straight into his chest. But Jake didn't have much choice, unless he wanted to ride on a horse. That would have hurt even more.

Getting used to his new surroundings, getting used to the routine, and getting used to the kindness both the white and the black soldiers showed him helped the days gradually pass. Ribs are also mighty slow to heal, but gradually he was able to put up with the pain a little better.

There were only three blacks in the company. It took a lot of getting used to being around so many white men who didn't treat him like a slave. Watching Micah Duff and the other two colored men behave around the white soldiers was like nothing Jake had ever seen before. They acted like he'd never seen any black person act around whites.

Though Private Duff was busy doing all the things that soldiers do, he had time to take care of Jake too. Whenever the company stopped, and especially every evening when they made camp, he tended most of the horses—though some of the officers took care of their own. But he still did everything he could to make Jake comfortable. He brought him food and water and checked his bandages every once in a while. Jake began to think that Duff was part doctor as well as everything else he did!

After a week or so, Jake began to get around pretty good. He could use his right arm to eat and get his shirt on and off and do most of the things he needed to do. But Private Duff still tended him as faithfully as ever. A lot of the white soldiers took an interest in Jake too. They came around when they were camped to ask about him and see if there was anything they could to do help. Before long, the whole company had adopted Jake as if he was one of their own men.

Though he was always busy, in his own way Micah Duff was a quiet young man. There were times as Jake woke up in the morning, before he said anything or tried to get up, when he just watched his new friend—whether Duff was feeding and watering the horses in the distance, or tending the fire or brewing his well-known early morning pot of coffee, Jake found himself wondering what Private Duff was thinking about. There was a look in his eyes that made Jake curious, a look that made it seem as if more was going on inside his brain than he let on. At least that's how it seemed to Jake. Of course, there was more going on in Jake than he let on too.

Cheerful and friendly though he was, Micah Duff knew the value of quiet. He knew how to let silence speak, how to let the quiet say what it had to say. He didn't try to fill the air up with words every minute. At first, after he got to feeling better, Jake squirmed a bit at the silence. But gradually he grew more comfortable with it. That helped him pay more attention to things around him. Watching Micah Duff not only taught him how to enjoy the quiet, it also taught him how to look and observe and notice things he wouldn't have seen before.

Private Duff didn't come right out and tell Jake what he was thinking. He didn't say, "Now, Jake, you need to learn to listen to what the silence has to show you." He let him sit with him at the fire and stare into it, neither of them saying a word for maybe twenty minutes until Jake was at peace with the silence. He let Jake figure out for himself that sitting quietly with your own thoughts was a good thing.

As time went on, he taught Jake a lot with words too. But the words always followed the quiet watching and observing and listening. First came the silence, then came the words. For a long time the two of them would sit staring into the red and yellow and orange flames licking at the chunks of wood, which popped and sizzled occasionally.

Fire's got an attraction and lure to it. You can't help staring into it. Mesmerizing is what you'd call it. Staring into a fire helps quiet you down. One day after waking up early, everything was already quiet around them.

After a long time, Private Duff finally spoke. His voice was soft.

"Light's a pretty amazing thing, isn't it, Jake?" he said.

"Uh . . . I reckon so," said Jake.

"Just think what it would be like without light," Duff went on. "We wouldn't know what anything looked like. Imagine what night must have been like before there was fire. Must have been pretty fearsome, not knowing if the sun was going to come up again."

"Why would dey hab thought dat?" asked Jake.

"I don't know that they did," replied Duff. "But back in those days a long time ago, the world was a fearsome place to the first men and women who didn't know how things were.

I imagine them being afraid when the cold and darkness came, and maybe being afraid the sun was gone forever. Darkness is a fearsome thing, don't you think, Jake?"

"I reckon so."

Again it was quiet. They stared into the fire a long time. After a while Duff stood up and took a few steps away from the fire. Jake hadn't noticed from staring into the flames, but the light of dawn had begun to show at the eastern horizon. Duff stood staring at it for the longest time, with Jake staring at him. The men around the rest of the camp were beginning to stir.

Finally Duff turned back toward the fire and poured them each a cup of coffee. By then a few more of the men were wandering in their direction, drawn by the aroma of the pot. Within another thirty minutes the camp was abuzz with activity.

Two mornings later, Jake awoke as usual. But when he got up he found the fire already burning low, like it had been fed an hour or two earlier. Private Duff was nowhere to be seen.

Jake got up, added a few more chunks to the fire, looked about, then went to fill the coffeepot with water and put it on the fire.

When Private Duff finally galloped into camp two hours later, he looked as if he'd been riding all night. After giving Jake the reins to his horse and asking him to feed and water him, he went straight to the captain's tent.

"There's a big movement of rebs heading this way, Captain," he said. "Ten or fifteen times bigger than us at least— maybe more."

"You think they know we're here, Duff?" asked the captain.

"I don't know, sir. I saw no evidence of it. But they're already on the march this morning. If they spot us, there's no way we could fight them off."

The captain rose and paced about his tent. "What do you

suggest, Duff—hole up somewhere?"

"We've got no choice, sir. Not unless you wanted to make a run for it."

"No, that would be suicide," said the captain, shaking his head. "Once on our tail, they'd never let up. You spot any-place nearby we could keep thirty men and horses out of sight?"

"There's a small farm two or three miles ahead, sir. Couple of big barns. Otherwise, it's just the woods."

"Hmm . . . I see. Any idea how many people at this place?"

"I only saw a man and his wife and a girl. Might be a hired hand or two, but I couldn't tell."

"No slaves?"

"No, sir. No slave crops—just cattle, horses . . . a few sheep."

"All right, then . . . good work, Duff. We'd better get camp broken."

Duff left Captain Taylor's tent. He found Jake tending the horses.

"Hey, Jake," he said, "taking over for me, I see!"

"I didn't know when you'd be back, so I figgered dese horses oughter hab dere breakfast."

"Good for you. From what some of the men tell me, your coffee is as bad as mine! Sounds like I'll be out of a job before long."

Two hours later the company paused within sight of the farm buildings Private Duff had told the captain about.

"Okay," said the captain, "we're going to have to com-mandeer the place, and they're not going to take too kindly to it. Barkley, Jones, Shenahan, Carter—you come with me. We'll have to do it at gunpoint, but I don't suppose it can be helped. The rest of you wait here."

The captain and his four officers rode on toward the house, dismounted in front, and walked up the porch to the door. Five minutes later, from where they watched, they saw Captain Taylor reemerge from the house and ride back to where the rest of his men were waiting.

"All right," he said, "we'll put up in that biggest of the barns there if it'll hold us. Duff, you go see what you think. We'll have to corral our horses and keep them separate from theirs, and get all the rest of our stuff out of sight. The man's an ornery cuss—we had to tie him up. But I don't think his wife and daughter will cause any trouble."

"Anyone else around, sir?" asked one of the men.

"Nope—just the three of them. The woman said they had two hands, but they both joined up when the war broke out."

Several hours later they were settled in makeshift quarters in the barn and two other outbuildings. They split the horses into groups in two of the corrals, though the captain was worried that there were so many of them that if the Confederates came, they would get suspicious. Then he had an idea.

"Billings," he said to one of the white soldiers. The man walked over. "You used to be from the South, didn't you?"

"Yes, sir."

"You can talk like a Southerner?"

"That I can, Captain, sir," laughed Billings, speaking in his thickest Mississippi drawl.

"All right, then, you take Jake here—get some of the other men to help you—and take half the horses out to that fenced pasture we passed coming in. Make sure they're secure, then you and Jake keep an eye on them. The two of you can watch over our horses and won't need to stay out of sight if the rebels come. Jake's got a black twang as thick as yours. Just pretend you're the fellow's hired hand and that Jake's the man's slave. Can you do that, Jake?" he asked, turning to where Jake stood.

"Dat I can, Captain," Jake replied. "I been a slave all my life. I don' reckon I'll hab ter do much pretendin'! What effen dey ax 'bout my patched-up shoulder?"

"Tell them Billings got drunk and beat the tar out of you," laughed the Captain. "Nobody'll suspect either of you of being with the Union Army."

"What about my uniform, Captain?" asked Billings. "They just might suspect *that!*"

"Right . . . I'll get some work clothes from the fellow in the house. He's about your size."

SCUFFLE
11

CAPTAIN TAYLOR'S PRECAUTIONS WERE WELL founded, all right.

The battalion of Confederate troops marched through the area two days later. It was a good thing the soldiers Jake was with were hiding out, because they were outnumbered twenty to one. Private Duff had been out scouting and watching the movements of the big grey army. Finally he galloped into the farmyard and ran to tell the captain that they were close and coming toward them.

They had to untie the farmer so that things would look normal. He was still fighting mad to be a prisoner of what he called the "damn Yankees" right in his own home. But he couldn't give them away because Captain Taylor took the fifteen-year-old girl with him to hide in the loft of the barn. He told the farmer that if he did anything to betray them, he wouldn't be able to protect the girl from his men. Whether Captain Taylor would really have let anything happen to her, who knows? All that mattered was that the farmer believed it. He was steaming inside and would probably have killed them all if he could have. He was a loyal Southerner and hated everyone from the North.

Then everybody hid, in the barns and the lofts and the

cellars, hoping the man and his wife were worried enough about their daughter not to give their presence away. Luckily only the general commanding the battalion and a few of his officers rode in, and nothing aroused their suspicions to make them think they needed to search the place. They asked the farmer if he'd seen any Union troops around and when he shook his head asked if they could camp their men in his fields for a day. They came and went a few times, but not so much that Private Duff and all the others weren't able to keep out of sight.

But out where they had corralled their horses, it was different for Jake and Sergeant Billings. They saw a lot of the Confederates and had to be on their guard not to say anything that might give them away. The first day, when they were looking for a place to make their camp, a troop of Confederates rode up and stopped.

"That's a lot of fine-looking horses," said the man in charge as he reined in and looked over the small enclosed pasture.

"Yes, sir. We's right proud of them," said Billings in his Southern twang.

"Lot of horses for a place this small."

"My boss, he likes horses. You killed any Yankees yet, sir?"

"Not yet, but that's what we're on our way to do. We'll kill every one that sets foot down here where they don't belong."

The soldier glanced toward Jake where he stood silently watching.

"What you lookin' at, boy?" he said.

"Nuffin', suh. I's jes' standin' here."

"Well, I don't like your looks. You're an ugly cuss.—He give you any trouble?" he said, turning again to Sergeant Billings.

"Just the usual with their kind," answered Billings. "You

know how dim-witted they are."

"And you know what to do if he does?"

"Yes, sir. He knows the taste of a horse whip, all right."

"Good man! Well, if he gives you any backtalk as long as we're here, you come see me. I'm overseer for a big plantation down in Louisiana. I know how to handle his kind."

"Yes, sir."

The man turned his horse around and he and his men rode off. It was silent a minute.

"You mean what you said 'bout me bein' dim-witted, suh?" said Jake after a bit.

"Aw, heck no—I was just saying what that Johnny Reb wanted to hear," said Billings. "If he'd have thought I was too soft, he might have made us some trouble."

But there wasn't any trouble. After two days, the battalion of Confederate soldiers moved on and Captain Taylor's company came out of hiding. They planned to wait another day or two before moving on.

On the day they were leaving, in early afternoon, Jake and Sergeant Billings saw someone walking toward them from the direction of the farmhouse. The house was about half a mile away and was an eight or ten minute walk. When the walker got closer, they saw that it was the farmer's fifteen-year-old daughter. Though Jake had heard some of the men talking about her, he hadn't seen her before. Now that he did, he thought she must be about the most beautiful girl he had ever seen of any color, white or black. She was short and had long hair that was kind of halfway between blond and auburn red and came down over her shoulders. As she walked up to them and glanced over at Jake, the look that came over her face was almost one of hatred. She didn't look so pretty then! No one can look pretty or handsome when hatred is in their eyes.

Jake realized he'd been staring at her without thinking about it. Quickly he looked away.

"Hi," she said, and her voice was as pretty as her face. "Are you Sergeant Billings?"

"That I am, pretty lady," said Billings.

"My mama sent me out to tell you that she's made up a stew and biscuits if you'd like to come into the house and join your men."

"Well, that's right neighborly of her. You see anything of my captain?"

"He was inside talking to her. He said it'd be all right, and to tell you that the Confederates have left and that you could come and have something to eat and that you'd bring the horses in afterward."

Billings walked slowly toward her. "What about your daddy?" he said. "He there too?"

"Yes, and he's madder than a wet hen," said the girl, laughing lightly as if she thought it funny. "He's storming and cursing like I've never heard him before. He about hit the roof when Mama started fixing up a stew on the cook stove and asked me to stir up a batch of biscuits. He asked her what she was doing and she said that those poor young men in the barn hadn't had a hot meal in two days and that she was going to fix them something to eat. That's when he got really mad and then finally your captain had to come in and calm him down and Daddy didn't like that at all."

"What did he do?"

"He stormed and fussed and your captain said that if he didn't stop it he'd have to tie him up again and gag his mouth."

"That's Captain Taylor, all right!" Billings laughed. "So how long till that stew and those biscuits are ready?"

"I don't know—half an hour, maybe," answered the girl.

"Then you and I ain't in any hurry, are we?" He took the girl's hand and began leading her away. "You watch the horses, Jake," he said.

"Where's you goin', Sergeant?" said Jake.

"Never you mind, Jake. You just keep your eyes on those horses."

Jake watched as the sergeant led the girl toward a clump of trees bordering the pasture.

"The house is over that way, Sergeant," she said.

"But like I said, you and I ain't in no hurry. I figure we'll take the long way around and get to know each other a little better. You'd like that, wouldn't you?"

"I don't think so, Sergeant," said the girl, now pulling her hand away. "I think we should go straight home."

"What's your hurry? There ain't no harm in us having a little fun."

Genuinely frightened now, the girl turned and began running back the way she had come. But Billings' blood was by now running hot and he wasn't about to give up so easily.

"Hey, what's that for, missy!" he yelled, running after her. "I'm trying to be friendly and you go running away. What kind of Southern hospitality is that?"

Jake's blood was rising too. He was filled with anger at what he saw. He hadn't done what he should have a year ago and it had cost his mother her life. He wasn't going to make that mistake again.

The girl cried for help. But Sergeant Billings caught up with her quickly. He took hold of her hand again and half dragged, half carried her toward the woods.

Suddenly Jake crashed into him like a huge black locomotive.

"What the—" he cried, trying desperately to right himself as he fell to the ground.

"Git outta here, girl," said Jake, struggling to keep his own feet beneath him. "You jes' git back ter yo mama . . . git goin'!"

The girl glanced back and forth between the white man and big Negro boy, then turned and dashed for the house. Billings climbed back to his feet.

"What in tarnation you doing, Jake!" he yelled.

"I seen dat look in yo eye, suh," replied Jake, breathing hard from the exertion of the run. "I din't think you wuz gwine do right by dat girl."

"And what business is it of yours?"

"Likely none, suh. But I had ter proteck da girl."

"*Protect* her!" fumed Billings. "You, a slave kid . . . *you* protect a white girl from *me*!"

Before Jake could defend himself, the sergeant charged him and delivered two quick blows of his fist to Jake's jaw and nose. But Jake was too big to be knocked down so easily. The blows stunned him awake. Heedless of his bandages and sling, he turned on Sergeant Billings with a pent-up wrath that it might have been wiser to keep under control. Though eight years older, Billings found Jake more than he could handle. A few swift jabs from Jake's good arm to his own face brought blood from his nose and a nasty cut above his right eye. For a minute or two it looked as if Jake might thrash him good. But from where he had fallen, Billings lifted one foot. As Jake stooped down to hit him again, he kicked at his chest with all his might.

Jake howled and stumbled back. The sergeant's boot had hit dead center against Jake's broken ribs and injured left arm. Jake's eyes filled in an agony of pain, and his whole left side was suddenly useless. Billings jumped to his feet and ran toward him.

"You blamed fool nigger!" he cried, pounding at Jake's face. "You should have minded your own business! Now I gotta teach you what your kind never seems to learn—not to interfere with your betters!"

No longer trying to fight back but merely to protect himself with his one good arm, Jake was no match for Billings' two good fists. A moment later he was on his back.

"Please, suh, Sergeant . . . please stop!" Jake cried. "My ribs is busted . . . I's sorry, Sergeant!"

But Billings was in no mood to let up now. He knocked Jake to the ground, then continued the fight with his boots. Two minutes later, sweating, dirty, and breathing heavily, he stood back, realized he'd gone too far, and went to retrieve his hat.

He began to walk back toward the house, leaving Jake unconscious and bleeding, two more broken ribs to go with the others. His arm, which had just begun to heal, was broken again in the same spot. Suddenly Captain Taylor galloped toward him. Taylor glanced about the scene as he reined in. He saw Jake lying on the ground, and blood all over Billings' face.

"What's this the girl says about Jake trying to rape her?" he asked.

"It's over now," replied Billings. "He's over there," he said with a nod of his head. "He won't be bothering anyone for a while. That true what she said about stew and biscuits?"

"Yeah . . . yeah, it's true," said the captain a little hesitantly, still looking about as if trying to figure out what had happened. "All right," he said, reaching down one hand, "hop up behind me. Looks like you took a few licks yourself. We'll go have some of that stew, then come back and get the horses and decide what's to be done with the kid."

Left Behind
12

Word of Jake's attack against Samantha Dawson, and that Sergeant Billings had beaten him within an inch of his life, was all over the Dawson farm before Jake had even begun to come to himself in the field where he lay with several of the company's horses licking at his face.

Micah Duff heard about it within minutes of returning from the scouting ride that had reported the last position of the Confederate regiment. Immediately he had his suspicions. He said nothing, however. He looked about for Jake. Not finding him, he remounted his horse and rode out to the field where the rest of their horses had been grazing for two days. It wasn't hard to find Jake on the ground. Four or five horses were sniffing and snorting about him. Duff dismounted and ran toward them.

It wasn't hard to see that the reports he'd heard were true. Jake was hurt, and bad. His old injuries, with new ones added to them, would take longer than ever to heal. Duff also knew that he couldn't move Jake out of the field alone. Even as he galloped back to the farmhouse for help and a wagon, he was resolving in his mind what to do. As he had expected, the captain was already making plans to move on at daybreak the following morning.

He got Jake loaded into the back of a small work cart and took him back to the farm. There he made him as comfortable as possible on a bed of straw in the barn, then went to find Captain Taylor.

"Captain, sir," he said, "there ain't no way the Patterson kid can travel—not in the condition he's in."

"What's that to me?" said Taylor a little irritably. "You nursemaided him and we fed him for two weeks. He'll be okay, and we've got our orders."

"He won't be okay, sir, not here. That Mr. Dawson will kill him the minute we're out of sight."

"Jake should have thought of that before he went fooling around with the girl."

"You really think he tried to rape her, Captain Taylor?"

"That's what the girl says."

"Have you questioned Billings?"

"I saw no need to."

"Maybe you ought to."

"What are you driving at, Duff?"

"Nothing, sir. I just ain't sure Jake's that kind of young man."

"They're all that way."

"What do you mean, Captain?"

"Meaning no disrespect to you, Duff, you know well enough what I mean. Your kind is different. Kids like Patterson—they're all the same. You've got to watch them."

"Is that how you think of me, Captain?" said the private.

"I don't know, Duff. I've never seen you around women."

Duff did not reply. He turned and went to the barn to tend to his invalid. As he cleaned Jake's wounds and got a fresh sling around his arm and shoulders, he asked Jake a few questions. It was obvious Jake himself had no idea of the reports circulating about him. An hour later Duff again sought the captain.

"Captain," he said, "I'm going to stay here with Jake for

a few days, at least until he can travel again.''

"What are you talking about, Private?" asked Taylor, none too happily. "I need you."

"I know, sir. I'll rejoin you as soon as I can. But Jake needs me too, probably more than you do. His life may depend on it. I'm not going to desert him now."

"The farmer won't be pleased."

"He's exactly who I'm worried about," said Duff. "Leaving him here . . . there's just no telling what he might do. Whatever happened, Billings hurt Jake bad, and he can no more travel than tame a wild horse right now. He'll either slow us down or we'll have to leave him somewhere else. That's why he's got to stay here, and why I'm staying with him."

"Suit yourself, Duff," said Taylor. "I could order you to come, and have you shot for desertion if you refuse."

"That you could, Captain," replied Duff. "But like I said about Jake, I don't think you're *that* kind of man."

The captain eyed him seriously a moment. "You know what'll happen if any more Confederates happen along and find the two of you?"

Duff nodded. "The farmer will tell them about us, and the soldiers will kill us—probably hang us."

"You want to take that chance?"

"I've got to, sir."

"You want me to tell Dawson what you aim to do?" asked Taylor.

"No, I'll go talk to him," replied Duff. "If he's going to be furious, he may as well hear that he's going to have two Negroes holing up on his farm straight from my own mouth. Then he can take his wrath out on me."

Duff walked toward the farmhouse and up the steps of the porch. He knocked on the door. The farmer's wife answered it.

"Who is it, Bess?" called a voice from inside.

"It's . . . uh, one of the soldiers," said the woman, glancing behind her.

The farmer came toward them from across the room. When he saw who it was, his face filled with rage.

"Get back, boy!" he shouted, hurrying toward the open door as his wife took a step back. "Don't you even think about stepping inside my house."

"I had no such intention, Mr. Dawson," said Duff.

"What do you want, then?" asked the farmer, his eyes squinting imperceptibly as he looked over the Negro standing before him. The man sounded more like a white man than a slave.

"I wanted to tell you, sir," said Private Duff, "that two of us will be staying on a few days after the rest of our men move on. We will keep out of your way and—"

"Why do *you* need to stay on?" interrupted the farmer.

"The young man who was hurt out in the fields a little while ago—"

"You're talking about the nigger kid who attacked my daughter?"

"Yes, sir. He's injured pretty bad and won't be able to travel again for a spell."

"He tried to rape her . . . and you want me to put him up!"

"I'm not at all certain he did so, Mr. Dawson. In any event, he is—"

"I'll see him rot in hell for what he did before I see him nursed to health under my roof!"

"We'll stay in the barn, sir."

"You'll be nowhere on my property!"

"We have no choice, sir. You won't even know we're here."

"And you won't be! We'll see how the two of you fare without twenty Yankee cowards keeping you from what you deserve."

A voice spoke from behind them.

"What harm can it do, John?" said the man's wife. "A few more days won't make any difference."

"You stay out of this, Bess!" snapped her husband.

Out of the corner of his eye, Duff saw the girl who was at the center of the storm watching them. Like her father's, her eyes were full of hatred toward him for no other reason than the color of his skin. Her expression confirmed in his mind the truth of what had probably happened.

With no more words between them, Private Duff turned and left the house. As soon as they were alone and Jake was feeling a little better, he asked him again what had happened with Billings. Again Jake told him. Duff explained what was being said among the men. For the first time he was almost glad Jake was confined to his back and in too much pain to get up. Had he been capable of it, Billings might soon have found himself in far worse shape. As it was, Jake could do nothing but rant and fume.

"But it ain't true, Micah!" he said.

"I didn't think it was, Jake."

"You gotter tell 'em."

"It wouldn't do any good, Jake. Once people's minds are made up about a lie, it doesn't matter what you say—you can't make them stop believing it. Most folks'll be convinced of a lie easier than they'll believe the truth. I believe you, Jake. You're probably going to have to be satisfied with that."

"But it ain't right, Micah . . . it jes' ain't right!"

"Lots of things ain't right, Jake. It's something you've got to learn to live with if your skin is black. You and I aren't going to set the world right. The sooner we come to terms with the fact that lots of things aren't right, the sooner we'll be at peace with ourselves."

Jake let out a long sigh. But he was still angry.

Duff left him. He also knew it would do no good to tell Captain Taylor. He had seen the look in his eyes too. Though he was as tolerant and respectful of blacks as any white man Micah Duff had ever known, he was still not likely to be quite fair-minded enough to take the word of a black boy none of them knew over one of the white soldiers under his command. There were limits to what you could expect, even from good white men like Captain Taylor. Micah Duff had learned long ago that there were times it was best just not to make too much of a fuss.

Before the sun had climbed an hour off the horizon the following morning, Captain Taylor and his small Union company continued their march to the southeast. Behind them they left two black men in the barn of a white Southerner who would gladly have seen them hanging from its rafters if he could figure out a way to accomplish it. If he'd had any neighbors nearby, he most likely would have gathered a lynch mob to hang them both before the day was out. His daughter would happily have helped, though his wife would never have stood for it.

But alone, he was not quite brave enough to try it. John Dawson may have been a bigot, but he knew well enough that he was no match for Micah Duff.

RECOVERY AND REFLECTION
13

T HEIR FIRST DAY ALONE PASSED WITHOUT INCIDENT.
Neither Micah nor Jake saw so much as a glimpse of
John, Bess, or Samantha Dawson.

Micah had kept three horses behind and enough supplies
to last them as long as it took to get Jake back on a horse and
for the two of them to rejoin the company before it reached
Chattanooga. There Captain Taylor's small detachment was
to join a larger Union regiment making its way down from
the North.

There was nothing to do and Jake could hardly move.
Micah did not want to leave him alone for even five minutes.
He was reasonably sure his movements were being watched
from the house. The man Dawson was no murderer. But prejudice strikes deep and makes otherwise good people do evil
things, which, if they were sitting in a church, they would not
even attribute to a demon. So Private Duff would take no
chances. Hate was too powerful a force, and Jake in too vul-
nerable a condition, to regard their situation lightly.

Not only was he a prudent man, Micah Duff was not the
sort who could stand to be idle. By late afternoon on that first
day, he was already growing bored. He stood and slowly wandered about the barn. It was so quiet that the afternoon sun,

sending slanted shafts of light into the darkened place that was their temporary home, added to the silence. He noticed where their men had been and had moved things about to make themselves comfortable. He began setting everything back to its original condition. Slowly other things came to his attention. A frayed harness hanging from a peg, a broken wheel of a buggy, several stalls whose boards were split or loose . . . all these he noticed as he wandered about the barn.

When Jake groaned and came awake some time later, he saw Micah across the dirt floor nailing up a new board he had just cut for one of the stalls.

"Dat you, Duff," he said hoarsely, "—wha'chu doin' dere?"

"Hey, Jake," said Micah, turning and walking toward him in the dim light. "I'm just trying to make myself useful. I figured I might as well fix up a few things in exchange for these folks' hospitality in letting us stay here. How you feeling?"

"Bad, Duff. I's hurt everywhere."

"I don't doubt it. That's why you've got to lay still and let me take care of you."

"Why you do all dis, Duff . . . *why* you helpin' me like dis?"

"You'd do the same for me, wouldn't you, Jake?"

"I don't know . . . I reckon. But dat still don't tell me why."

Duff laughed lightly, set down the hammer in his hand, and sat down on a bail of straw beside Jake's makeshift bed. He sat for several minutes, but gave Jake no idea what he was thinking. When he finally did speak, what he said wasn't at all what Jake had expected.

"I'm helping you, Jake," he said, "because I've had a hard life."

Jake stared up at him where he lay.

"Wha'chu talkin' 'bout?"

"Just what I said."

"What dat got ter do wiff it?"

"Everything."

"Dat don't make no sense," said Jake. "Why dat make you want ter help me?"

"I suppose to most folks it might not make sense," said Duff. "But that's my answer to your question."

"What made yo life so hard, Micah?" asked Jake. "You don't look like nobody dat's had ter suffer dat much."

Micah smiled. "There's all kinds of pain, Jake," he said. "Not all pain comes from a whip across your back. There's lots of different kinds of suffering, lots of different ways that life can be hard. Not all of them are easy to see."

"You said you wuzn't no slave. I don't reckon dere's a much harder life den dat."

"No, I wasn't a slave. And I'm thankful for that. But there's pains that hurt inside—hurts no one else sees. They can hurt in their own way too, maybe even worse sometimes. Everybody's got hurts, Jake. Some you see, some you can't. But in their own way, everybody's life is hard."

"I neber thought 'bout dat. You reckon life be hard . . . even fo white folks?"

Micah nodded. "Yep, even for white folks, Jake . . . life is hard even for white folks."

Jake took in his words as if he'd never considered such an idea before.

"But I still don't see," he said after a minute, "how dat'd make you want ter help sumbody like me dat jes' comes along dat you don't eben know," he said after a bit.

"All right, I'll see if I can explain it," said Duff. "It's like this, Jake . . . when life gets hard—whether you're white or black doesn't make any difference—folks have got a choice what to do about it. I didn't always know about choices. But when I was eleven, that's when I realized what a big thing choices were. After that I started watching people real close. You know what I saw, Jake?"

"No . . . what?"

"I saw that it wasn't the pain or the suffering or the whippings or the hardships that made the difference in folks' lives. I saw that it was something else."

"What wuz dat?"

"It was what they did about it, Jake. That's what makes folks different—not that some people have a hard life and some have an easy one, or that one man's white and another's black, that one man's poor and one man's rich, or that one man's a slave and another's free. In one way, I saw that none of that makes much difference."

"Wha'chu mean? Seems ter me dat'd make *all* da difference."

"Maybe not, Jake. Maybe it doesn't make as much difference as you think. What I saw was that folks decide what they're going to do when the hard things come. And *that's* what makes the difference—what they decide to do. When the whippings come, what are you going to do? And life can send invisible whippings that I reckon hurt in their own way just as much as those a slave gets. Some folks get angry and they blame everybody else they can think of. Others don't."

"I reckon dat's so, all right."

"There's a lot of angry people in the world, Jake—lots and lots of angry people. Some are angry down inside where nobody sees. Others you can tell just from looking at them. I've seen a lot of folks with anger inside them, Jake. It's not pleasant to see. Anger's not a pretty thing. It makes people miserable inside. Then there's other folks that get sad and discouraged at all the hardships that come in their lives. Maybe they don't get angry, but they go around being sad and miserable and letting people know it. They want people to feel sorry for them, and that's not too pretty to see either."

"So what did you do w'en you wuz eleben?"

"Well, it didn't come to me all at once, that's only when it began. But eventually I decided I wasn't going to get sad or angry and let either of those things eat me up inside. I didn't want people feeling sorry for me and I didn't want to be angry inside. I said to myself, *Look here, Duff,* I said, *you think your life is hard, well, lots of other folks' lives are hard too. Some of them are even harder than yours! So you quit feeling so sorry for yourself like you've got it so bad. You're alive, aren't you? You're healthy and strong, aren't you? You don't have it nearly so bad as you think. No matter what you've been through, life can be a pretty good thing if you'll let it.* And then I made my choice, Jake."

"What wuz dat?"

"I decided that I didn't want to let my own hurts make me into a selfish person. I wanted to be a better person, not a sad or angry or discouraged person. So that's when I decided that I was going to spend my life trying to do good things for other folks, especially folks with pains and the marks of invisible whippings down inside them. I began looking at folks I met just a little different. I said to myself, *Maybe that man or that woman or that little boy or girl . . . maybe they've got hurts inside. Maybe there's something that's paining them in a way I can't see. And maybe I can help a bit.* That's when I decided that I'd keep my eye out for folks that might need a helping hand or a kind word, and that maybe I could help make their lives just a little bit easier and happier."

He paused briefly. "So that's why, Jake. You got the marks of real whips on your back. You've had some hurts and pains in your life. So I figure that maybe God sent me along to help make your life just a little better. I made my choice about what kind of person I wanted to be. Maybe I can help you make yours."

Jake asked nothing further. He had enough to think about for one day. After another minute or two, Micah rose and returned to his repairs on the horse stalls.

Not wanting to risk a fire in the barn, or make their presence more visible outside than was necessary, water, jerky, and cold biscuits were all they ate and drank that day. But the following morning Micah ventured to build a small fire out of sight behind the barn, and the fresh coffee and bacon from it considerably picked up their spirits. Jake's injuries, however, made even a simple task like trying to sit up to eat or drink excruciatingly painful.

Helping him get to the woods to do his necessaries about midmorning, Micah glanced toward the house. From an upper window he saw Mrs. Dawson watching them.

Later that day he heard the barn door open. There stood the farmer's wife. In the thin light Micah saw a sheepish and somewhat anxious look on her face.

"I . . . I just baked some bread," she said, glancing behind her. "I thought you might like a loaf."

"That is very kind of you, Mrs. Dawson," said Micah, walking toward her with a smile. "It smells delicious. Thank you very much."

She nodded, struggled to smile as he took it from her, then hurried away. Micah was sure her husband knew nothing of her errand of kindness. From the frightened look on her face, it was clear that he would not be pleased if he found out about it.

THE ORDER OF THINGS
14

THE NEXT COUPLE OF DAYS PASSED ALMOST LIKE A dream for Jake Patterson. He slept and woke, ate what he could, dozed, woke again, drank, hobbled with Micah's help outside a time or two to do his necessaries, then eased back down onto his bed of straw again to wake and doze again. Sometimes he lay awake thinking. Surprisingly, he found that being alone with Micah Duff presented him with much to think about. And slowly the minutes and hours and eventually days passed like a blur. Since his legs were generally all right except for a few bruises, the trips to the woods became easier and easier and he walked around a little more each day. But moving and shifting his position, even just a few inches, remained painful, not only from his ribs but from the blows that had been delivered to his stomach and back and chest, and even his head, by Sergeant Billings.

Sometimes Jake talked to Micah, sometimes he just lay watching him putter about the barn fixing things and tidying it up. In later years, Jake Patterson always looked back on these few days as the season of his life when he began to come awake. The deeper part of him . . . the real him, the thoughtful him, the spiritual part of him—what folks might call his soul. Jake didn't realize it yet. Most people don't realize when they begin to come awake. It's only later, when they look back, that they can see that things were happening to poke at the sleepiness of their soul to make it wake up. That's how it was for Jake. He was still young and at an age when most people's souls are still mostly asleep. All through life, situations and circumstances poke at people's souls, trying to make them uncomfortable enough to realize that they're asleep. Some people wake up when they grow into adulthood. Other people never wake up no matter how long they live.

"What do you think, Duff?" Jake asked one time. "You think I'll eber be a free man like you?"

"That depends on what you mean, Jake."

"I mean, duz you think I'll eber be free instead ob a slave?"

"There's all kinds of freedom and all kinds of slavery."

"Dere you go agin sayin' da most out ob da way things so's I don't know what you's talkin' 'bout!"

Micah laughed. "You know more than you think you know, Jake," he said. "You just gotta figure out what you know."

"So what you talkin' 'bout wiff dat different kinds er freedom talk?"

"There's freedom inside and outside," replied Duff. "There's lots of men like me who are free on the outside but aren't free inside. They aren't free from themselves. There are also lots of slaves like you who are really free on the inside because they've discovered what life means. That's the only kind of freedom that really matters in the end."

"Dere you go talkin' riddles agin, Duff!"

It's not easy to describe what one person does for another. It's not always in outward ways, in things that are actually said. It's the small experiences that add up to a different way of looking at things. That's what Micah Duff did for Jake— he helped him look at things different, and to see and understand things that most folks never look at.

Like when he was chopping some wood one day to add to the Dawsons' woodpile, Micah stopped and picked up two chunks of the pine, looked at them back and forth, then turned to Jake.

"What do these two pieces of wood remind you of, Jake?" he said, holding them toward him in his hands.

"Dey jes' look like two pieces ob wood ter me."

"They're more than that, Jake. When God made the two trees that these two pieces came from, He put meaning inside those trees. Did you know that God put meaning into everything He made?"

"Guess I neber thought 'bout it afore."

"Well, think about it, Jake. You gotta think about it. We're supposed to think about it. Whenever we look around us, we're supposed to find out the meaning God put into the things we see. That's the only way to figure out what life means. We've got to figure out the meaning God put into the things around us."

"So what dose two bits er wood in yo hands—what dey mean, Duff? Dey don't look like dey mean nuthin'. Dey jes' wood, dat's all."

"Just wood—I reckon you're right, Jake. But wood with God's meaning inside it.—Look, here's a piece with straight grain running from top to bottom, straight and even and true. But look at this other piece. It's full of knots. Its grain is all twisted and gnarled and going all kinds of directions. When I look at these two pieces of wood, Jake, I see two people. I see a person who's straight and true and good. I see a person who, when he tells you something, you know it's right because his word is as straight and true as he is inside. He's a person whose grain is straight. But when I look at this other chunk of wood, I see a person who is all twisted up, whose inside is full of knots. He's a pretty confused person who doesn't know which direction he wants to grow and doesn't know what kind of person he wants to be. That's why his grain is growing in so many directions, because he's all mixed up inside. You ever know a gnarled-up person, Jake, who looked like this piece of wood?"

"I don't know, Duff."

"I have. I don't doubt this man whose farm we're staying at is pretty gnarled up inside. He's full of a lot of things going a lot of different directions in him, making knots in his character. So is his daughter, if she lied about what you did. What kind of person tells lies, Jake? A person who's twisted up inside, and whose grain doesn't run straight and true."

Duff turned around, set the two chunks on the chopping block, then brought the ax down first on one, then the other, until they were split into smaller pieces, then tossed them into the woodbox and continued on. For a while the sound of the ax and the splitting wood was the only sound to be heard. Then Jake spoke up again from where he lay.

"How'd you git ter be such a deep thinker, Duff?" he said. "Sumtimes you remin' me of a preacher. You eber been a preacher, Duff?"

Micah laughed like Jake had never heard him.

"I'm no preacher, that's for sure!"

"You sounds like one ter me."

"I suppose I am a thinker," Duff went on. "But everybody's got a brain. It's just that some folks put theirs to use. That's another thing I decided after I was eleven, that I wanted to use the brain God gave me. Everybody thinks, Jake. Some people don't point their brains in directions that do them any good. They just think about things that are gone the next day, like smoke from that fire out there cooking our supper. Their thoughts just go up and are gone."

"Yeah, I reckon I can see dat, all right."

"I decided that I ought to spend my time thinking about things that mattered. That's when I began to think about myself and whether the grain in my life was straight and true, or all knotted up."

"Dat soun's like mighty big things fo sum eleben-year-old boy ter be thinkin' 'bout. I shore neber did. I neber eben wud er thought 'bout none ob dis now effen it weren't fo you. What made you think 'bout such things, Duff?"

"I didn't think about them all when I was eleven. That's just when it started. That's when I met an old man who took care of me for a spell. He taught me how to think."

"What kind er man? A colored man?"

"No, a white man. A mysterious fellow with a big beard who kept to himself. But he happened along when I was in a bad fix. He helped me maybe a little bit like I'm helping you, Jake, though in a different way. He helped me begin thinking and understanding life and God and the order of things and fitting in with that order."

"I ain't shore what you mean by dat, Duff," said Jake. "What exactly?"

"Da order ob things . . . what you mean by dat?"

"I just mean life and God and how things work and how you and I fit into them," replied Duff. "I'll explain it to you like the old man explained it to me. He said that there were two kinds of people in the world—those who were content and at peace with themselves, and those who weren't. The first kind were usually happy and were the kind of people you liked to be with. But the second kind were selfish and mixed up inside."

"Like dose two chunks er wood."

"Just like that. Then he asked me which kind of person I wanted to be. I wasn't much more than a kid, but he always made me think about those kinds of things. Then he told me to start looking at animals. He said that the difference between animals and men was that animals don't have a choice about what they do. They just do what animals do. But with men it's different. We've got a choice whether to fall into harmony with the order of things in the world. When we do, the grain in our lives runs straight and true. When we don't, we get all knotted and twisted up inside."

"But what dat mean, dat fallin' in wiff da order ob things you's talkin' 'bout?"

"To find out what that natural order of things is, you have to know what life and the world means. That's when God comes into it. God must have made everything for a reason. It's like I was saying before, we've got to figure out what God means with things around us. We've also got to figure out what God means *inside* us. Why did He make us, Jake? Why did God make *you*?"

"I don't know . . . I figgered I just happened when I wuz born."

"Nothing just happens, Jake. Everything means something because God made it. You *mean* something. Figuring out what life means is the same as figuring out what *you* mean. What's your life supposed to be about? That's what falling in with the order of things means—living in the way God means you to live. You ever heard about being created in the image of God, Jake?"

"I reckon so . . . but dat's jes' fo white folk—everybody knows dat, don't dey?"

"It's for everybody, Jake, but not too many folks think much about what it really means."

"What duz it mean, den?"

"That we're supposed to be like God ourselves. That's what it means to fall in with the natural order of the world. That's why we're alive. That's our purpose. Even though we're just ordinary people who can't do it very well, we're supposed to try to act like God wants us to. We're supposed to be kind and nice and unselfish because that's the way God is. When we fall in with how God means us to be, that's when our grain grows straight and true. Life can't be a good and happy thing if we don't go along with that purpose. It's like the sap in a tree trying to go against the way it's supposed to grow. When you go against the way you're supposed to grow, you can't help but grow crooked. There's twisted-up crooked people just like there's twisted-up and crooked trees. Then there are people whose insides are straight just like trees. That's what it means to fall in with the way things are supposed to be—growing the straight way we were meant to grow.''

"But we don't got no sap inside us tellin' us how ter grow straight like trees duz.''

"We *do*, Jake. We've got the best kind of sap inside us of all.''

"What dat?''

"God's life is inside us tellin' us a thousand ways every day how straight people are supposed to grow. That's the human sap growing in us—God's life and God's voice telling us how to grow into straight, true people.''

"I neber heard God tellin' me nuthin' like dat.''

"His voice is so quiet, most folks never learn to hear it, Jake. But it's there just like the sap in a tree. That's what I mean about finding out what things around us mean. When we learn how trees grow, that helps us know how people are supposed to grow too.''

Jake sighed and shook his head. "I don't know, Duff," he said. "Dat's gwine take sum hard thinkin' 'bout. An' I ain't so shore I believe what you said dat you weren't neber a preacher.''

Micah just smiled and went about his work. He knew seeds were getting planted in the soil of Jake's heart, just like the bearded white man called Hawk had planted seeds in his. Now it was his own turn, Micah thought. If he kept gently watering them with hands of kindness, he hoped the seeds in Jake's heart would sprout and grow in time.

Twisted Grain
15

An hour later Micah was outside tending the small fire where he was making a stew for their supper from what meat he had left from his own supply and a few vegetables he had retrieved from the table scraps the farmer's wife had brought out to the pigpen that morning. The pig seemed fat enough, Micah thought, and wouldn't miss them. The moment Mrs. Dawson was out of sight, he had dashed for the trough before the old sow had been able to waddle to it from the other side of her pen.

He'd been outside a good long while. When he went back into the barn, he froze. There was Samantha Dawson across the dirt floor staring down at Jake, who was sound asleep. In her two hands she held the ax she'd picked up from the woodpile, where Micah had been chopping wood earlier that day.

Micah stood stock-still. She hadn't heard him. Even unable to see her face, it was clear enough what she was thinking.

Slowly she raised the ax into the air over Jake's head.

Micah waited no longer. He leapt and wrenched the ax handle from the girl's hand. Losing her balance, she toppled to the ground with a cry of anger and surprise.

She scarcely had time to recover her shock before a huge

black hand took hold of her arm and yanked her to her feet as if she weighed no more than twenty pounds. She spun around to see two great flaring eyes boring into hers from the middle of a stern black face.

"Let me go!" she cried, struggling to free herself from his grip.

"I will not let you become a murderer," Micah said, still holding her tight.

"You let go of me! I'll kill you too if I get the chance!"

"If you want to let your hate eat you up, you foolish girl," said Micah, "I can't help you, though I pity you for it. But you're not going to kill anybody."

He let go of her and she made a dash for the ax. But Micah reached it first and stood to face her.

"Aren't you listening to what I'm saying, you stupid girl!" he said. "Maybe I can't stop you hating. But to let you destroy yourself by killing a man that did his best to protect you, that I can prevent. Now you get out of here and you think about what I said."

"You evil nigger man—I hate you!" she screamed, then ran from the barn.

The incident unnerved both invalid and his protector. In spite of Jake's condition, things had suddenly taken a serious turn. Micah began to think that maybe it was time for them to move on.

But the day was not over yet.

His daughter's shrieks and hysterical reports that the man in the barn had attacked her brought the boiling furnace of rage within the heart of the father to the surface. Above his wife's terrified objections, he ran to the gun cabinet. He stormed out of the house a minute later. He had every intention of emptying both barrels of his shotgun into the chests of the two niggers who had dared defile his home.

He charged into the darkened barn. Hastily he struggled to adapt his eyes to the dim light. Fortunately for Jake, he did not wait long enough. The explosion that brought Micah running from where he had been working blew a hole six inches across through the thin board of a wall about two feet above where Jake lay.

Jake cried out in terror. Even as echoes from the shot and Jake's yells were still reverberating in his ears, John Dawson heard the sound of running footsteps behind him. He spun around to meet them. But suddenly he felt the barrel of his gun wrested from his hands. The instant it thudded to the floor, a fist smashed into the side of its owner's head just above one ear. The blow sent him sprawling to the ground.

A string of horrible obscenities burst from Dawson's mouth. He leapt to his feet, his vision even less dependable now than it had been a moment earlier, and charged at Micah like an enraged bear. John Dawson was a powerful man with great skill with his fists. Had they been outside in the sunlight, it might well have been that both blacks would have been dead within five minutes. As it was, however, having just come inside out of the bright afternoon, he was no match for one who had been working in the barn's darkness. Micah received two or three glancing blows to shoulder, side, and back of the head. But in the end, several more sharp, well-aimed jabs from his own fists sent the farmer again to the ground, this time flat on his back. As his eyes at last began to adjust to the light, he found himself staring up into the wrong end of his own shotgun.

"Look, Mr. Dawson," said Micah heatedly, his righteous anger at last fully aroused, "maybe I won't kill you to keep Jake alive. His life is not worth more than yours. But neither is it worth less. Now I'm going to give you a chance to get up and walk out of here before you do any more mischief. I don't know what evil has gotten into you and your daughter. But if you try to hurt him again, I'll put you in bed beside him with the other barrel of this gun if I have to. Then maybe I'll have to nurse you both back to health and teach you some respect for your fellow man by making you lie beside one black man and take food and drink from the hands of another. I'd rather it didn't come to that. I don't want to hurt you, but if that's what it takes to keep you both alive, then I'll do what I have to do. I bear you no animosity, Mr. Dawson. I'm appreciative of your hospitality. But I will not let you hurt that boy."

Almost beside himself with wrath to hear a black man lecture him, Dawson struggled to his feet. "You are a dead man, you hell-bound nigger!" he said, spitting the words out with venom. "You're both dead or my name's not John Dawson! I'll kill you with my own two hands!"

He strode angrily from the barn and across the yard to the house.

Hearing the shot and fearing for what it meant, his poor wife met him at the door and followed him with a barrage of anxious questions. He shoved her away with a rude remark and for the second time in less than ten minutes made straight for the gun cabinet. By the time he had another gun loaded, however, a vicious throbbing had begun in his head. His right eye had also begun to swell shut. Along with this came the reminder that the black man in the barn still had the shotgun with one loaded barrel. And, as long as he remained in the barn, would have the advantage of the light.

For all his raging bluster, he was not yet quite ready to die. He had not heard a word Micah had said. He had no doubt that the wild man out in the barn would blow a hole in his head if given half the chance. He still had no inkling that in Micah Duff he had probably encountered the gentlest man he would ever meet.

Slowly he closed the door of the gun cabinet. He might try something after dark, Dawson said to himself. For the present he would have to content himself with fuming about the house. For the rest of the day he complained bitterly to his wife about the cruel lot of being at the mercy of such nigger trash, as if she herself were the object of his fury.

Back in the barn, Micah set the gun down and hurried to make sure Jake had not received any ricocheting shot.

"We gots ter git outta dis place, Duff!" said Jake, by now on his feet. "Dese blamed white folks is plumb crazy!"

"They're a man and daughter with some mighty twisted-up ideas, that's for sure," said Micah as he regained his breath. "Yep, it's probably time we were moving on. You think you can sit a saddle?"

"Don't know unless I try. But it's better'n bein' dead. Dat's a crazy man, Duff!"

"Well, if you have too hard a time riding, we'll stop again. But you're right. We can't risk one of these people doing something else stupid. We better wait till tonight and slip out when it's dark."

"Why dat?"

"You heard what he said. I think if given half the chance, he'd follow us and ambush us first chance he got. I'd rather he didn't know which way we were headed."

"Dat's right smart, Duff. I'm glad you thought ob dat. I don't want dat man puttin' no gun to my head when I's asleep!"

"I'll round up our things and keep the horses inside and out of sight for the rest of the day. We'll saddle them, and after they're asleep we'll head out across the field behind the barn out of sight from the house. Once we make the cover of the trees, we'll move back and forth for a while so he can't follow us and see how you are, then make camp somewhere till morning. How's that sound?"

"Anythin' ter git outta dis fool place!"

FREEDOM COUSINS
16

S OMETIME BETWEEN MIDNIGHT AND TWO IN THE morning, with the light of a three-quarter moon glowing in and out from between a night sky half full of clouds, Micah Duff and Jake Patterson slowly walked away from the Dawson farm with their three horses. After reaching the trees, with some difficulty Micah helped Jake into the saddle. Then they continued on.

They rode for perhaps two hours, then stopped to get what sleep they could before daybreak. By the time the sun was high in the sky, they had put enough distance between themselves and the Dawsons that they had no more worries about being followed. They stopped again and slept for most of the afternoon.

Jake's pain was not gone by any means. But he could sit in the saddle without it being too much worse. As long as they went slowly and he sat upright and straight, he managed fine. They did not cover many miles a day, but their progress toward Chattanooga was steady. Micah's main worry was that they would encounter more Confederate troops, or Southern civilians like the Dawsons. If they encountered danger, in Jake's condition they could hardly hope to make a run for it. Two blacks traveling alone in the South, one a runaway slave and both wearing Union blue, were anything but safe. Thus they kept to back roads and wooded areas, and traveled as much as possible at night. Whether they would ever catch up with their detachment, that part of his own anxiety Micah kept to himself.

"What's gwine happen ter me, Duff?" asked Jake as they rode slowly along. "When we git back ter yo men, I mean. After what happened, dey's not gwine be none too glad ter see da likes er me agin. Dat man Billings, he's likely told 'em a heap more lies 'bout me."

"You let me worry about Billings and the rest of them, Jake," replied Micah. "Until you feel healthy and well and want to move on, you can stay with me as long as you want. If you help me tend the horses and learn to make coffee for the men, they're not going to complain."

"But what 'bout da lies, Duff?"

"Lies can't hurt you, Jake, as long as you're true yourself."

"But dey *do* hurt, Duff."

"I know. What I meant is that they can't hurt the real you, the you that's down inside that's who you really are. So there's nothing you can do except ignore them and be true yourself."

Jake rode on in silence. Micah's words had stabbed deep into him. He *wasn't* true inside, and he knew it. He had a terrible secret and it ate away at him. Micah sensed a change in the atmosphere and let the quiet do its work without disturbing it with more words. Several long minutes passed.

"You think I's be safe wiff yo men?" asked Jake at length. "Dey won't do nuthin' ter me?"

"You'll be safe," replied Micah. "Most Northern men don't mind coloreds like us as long as we don't push them and get what they call uppity. I doubt even Billings will bother you again as long as you stay out of his way."

"But dey don't *like* us, do dey, Duff?"

Now it was Micah's turn to grow reflective. "That's a good question, Jake," he said. "I don't think I know the answer. They *tolerate* us . . . maybe that's the best we can expect. I don't know."

"Why you talk like er white man, Duff? You been ter sum kind er college er sumfin like dat?"

"No, Jake, I've likely got no more education than you."

"You kin read, can't you?"

"Yes, I can read."

"Kin you read books, Duff?"

"I can."

"You read any?"

"I have."

"What kind er books?"

"Stories about people and faraway places. I haven't read that many books, Jake—just whatever I could get my hands on."

"How kin you talk so good, den, Duff?"

"I decided I was going to learn how, and I did."

"You jes' learned yo'self?"

Micah nodded. "That's how I learned to read too."

"Why did you do it, learn yo'self to talk better?"

"Because I noticed that folks treat people different because of how they talk. I figured that if I could talk better, maybe folks would treat me like somebody they could respect. I don't know whether white folks can ever really respect a colored man the same way they do one of their own kind. But I know they treat me with more respect now. And I figure that's a good thing."

"You think I cud eber talk like you, Duff?"

"If you want to, Jake. People can do anything they want if they set their minds to it. You could learn to talk better and read books and do whatever you want. Anybody can."

Being around Micah Duff, watching him, listening to him, and now riding beside him was already changing Jake Patter-

son far more than he realized. Slowly he had invisibly begun
to absorb one of the most valuable lessons anybody can learn
in life—that a person can change and grow and improve himself and make something more of himself than he is. Micah
didn't always say it in so many words like he just had about
reading and speaking. But being around him just made Jake
feel like life was a good thing. It made him realize that there
was always something more you could find if you looked for
it and wanted to find it. Micah's heart and brain were alive
and awake with ideas and thoughts and possibilities and chal-
lenges. Slowly that awakeness of heart began to rub off on
Jake.

"You got kin, Duff?" asked Jake.

"Nope. I'm alone, Jake. How about you?"

"My mama's dead."

"How'd she die?"

"A white man killed her," said Jake moodily.

"What about your daddy?"

The very word he hadn't heard in so long brought undefined emotions of anger and resentment to the surface in
Jake's heart. Micah instantly felt a change come over his
young companion.

"My daddy lef' us when I was a kid," said Jake. "He's
supposed ter be in Carolina sumwheres. Dat's where I'm
boun', effen I eber git dere."

"What kind of man is your daddy?" asked Micah.

Jake didn't answer. Micah sensed that the cloud that had
come over Jake's countenance had darkened all the more as a
result of his question.

"Well, if you and I are alone in the world," said Micah
cheerily, "at least until you find your pa, then we'll be family
to each other, Jake. We're all from the same people anyway,
all coloreds like us. We came from the same place. That
makes us cousins, Jake, you and me and all blacks . . . cousins
in this fight for freedom we're part of."

They reached the outskirts of Chattanooga about ten days later. Coming so near such an important Southern town increased the danger to them. They had to find the Union regiment quickly or else move on and head north.

Stashing Jake and two of their horses in as out-of-the-way a place as they could find—near a stream where there was water and surrounded by thick woods—and dressed as a civilian, Micah set out to scout around the town.

He knew the general kinds of terrain suitable for the encampment of a large number of troops. Captain Taylor had said they were to meet the regiment near a junction some five miles north of the town. It took him most of the day to find them, and it was with great relief that at last he saw uniforms of the Union blue with the Stars and Stripes waving overhead. Only a portion of the Northern regiment had yet arrived. Some four or five hundred troops were encamped in a small valley. Questioning one company after another, he finally walked into the familiar camp of Captain Taylor's small Illinois detachment.

"How's the kid?" asked the captain after they had greeted one another.

"He's doing okay," replied Micah. "I've got him hidden out a few miles away. I wanted to find you first. Your permission to keep him with us a while longer?"

Taylor eyed him without expression.

"I'm convinced he's innocent in the affair with Billings, sir," said Micah.

Taylor shrugged. "You may be right, Duff," he said. "I suppose it hardly matters. It's over now. But if you're not right, he could spell trouble."

"I'll vouch for him, sir. He'll cause no trouble as long as he's with me."

"All right, then, Duff. You can bring him back to camp. But I'm going to hold you to what you just said."

"Fair enough, sir," nodded Micah. "Thank you."

THE FREEDOM WAR
17

J AKE PATTERSON REMAINED WITH MICAH DUFF AND
Captain Taylor's Illinois company for three years. No
more trouble arose with Billings.

There were no major engagements with the Confederate
Army, only a few brief skirmishes, for the rest of that year.
Throughout the winter of 1861, the war quieted down almost
completely. As winter gave way to the spring of 1862, however, with both sides now at full strength, major bloodshed
loomed on the horizon.

In September of that year, President Lincoln issued a
stern ultimatum to the rebel states of the South: Return to the
Union or all slaves would be declared free.

His words were met with ridicule and resentment
throughout the South. But he intended to back them up.

Thus, in January of 1863, the president issued his famous
decree setting every slave in the land free.

Suddenly, astonishing news began to spread like a brush-
fire through the South. "Dat ol' mancerpashun proklerma-
shun," as the blacks called it, had abolished and outlawed
slavery itself! Whether the decree could be enforced against
the newly formed Confederacy remained to be seen. But

blacks themselves took the new law from Washington as if it had come from God himself.

The dream of Jake Patterson's mama had come true. Her son now knew something she had prayed for but never experienced for herself—that precious thing called *freedom*.

Many couldn't believe it at first. Most of the older slaves didn't know what to make of it. What did it all mean? What was to become of them? What were they to do?

How could the words *freedom* and *colored* possibly go together? And yet as time went on, gradually they became accustomed to the amazing truth—if they wanted, they could turn their backs and walk away from their masters and never have to do anything they said again.

They were truly . . . free.

Within months of the news Jake wasn't the only colored on the move. The world of slavery had been turned upside down. Blacks everywhere were traveling and looking for work and trying to accustom themselves to a new way of life without "Massa" controlling every detail of their lives.

But their newfound freedom did not bring them an easy life. If Massa wasn't telling them what to do, neither was he feeding and clothing them and providing them a place to live. Those who chose to stay on with their former masters now had to be given nominal pay for their labor, since they were no longer slaves. But those who stayed found that freedom brought corresponding obligations. And those who chose not to stay found that life on their own could be a hard, and dangerous, thing.

In the midst of the war, more and more former slaves set out on the long trek north. There they hoped opportunity would be waiting for them.

But for the present, Jake Patterson's quest had been interrupted by the war. His newfound home and family was with the 23rd Illinois Company. He had not been trying to get to the North anyway, but to Carolina. Right now, the Carolinas

A Perilous Proposal

were not a safe place for a young black traveling alone.

As the war progressed, Jake continued to grow. By the time he was fifteen he had put on six more inches and another twenty pounds and was as big as Micah Duff himself.

All his life, especially since his flight from the Winegaard plantation, Jake had regarded the white man as his enemy. But among Captain Taylor's men, with Billings now gone to join another regiment, he discovered a different kind of white man, who spoke in a different tongue, and who treated blacks with respect, sometimes even kindness. These blue-clad soldiers of the North saw themselves as liberators and friends to former slaves. They wanted to help them, not hurt them. And just as surely, as the war progressed, he learned that the grey coats of the Confederacy hated blacks, whose freedom was the cause of ruining the Southern way of life. While a Northern soldier in blue would usually help a black in need, a Southern soldier in grey would be happy to kill him if given the opportunity.

The more he was around horses, as the slow dawning maturity of youth advanced him little by little toward adulthood, hints and reminders of his father came back to him. A vision might come to him of his father in the distance speaking gently into the ear of a jittery horse to calm it down. At another time came the vision of a man bent to one knee speaking tenderly into the face of a young boy. The words of such images remained a mystery. Jake's memory of the incidents was too faint to recall them with clarity. But they aroused within him a feeling of curiosity and wonder. And then came the faraway sense that it had something to do with horses.

Little did Jake realize that in a host of unseen ways his father had passed on to him a rare gift with horses. It was to understand and be understood by them. Not realizing why, more and more Jake was drawn to his father's occupation. But in spite of his love for the noble four-footed creatures, reminders of his father remained bitter in his memory.

Instead of cherishing the tender visions, he refused to see them with the innocent eyes of happy childhood. Instead he overlaid the memories with the anger of his later youth.

Instead of bringing healing, as such memories could have done, they only deepened the anger fomenting beneath the surface in his heart.

But the memory of his father and horses had one benefit. The more useful he became to Micah Duff in the care of the horses, the more respect he gained among the rest of the men.

"You got some knack with horses, Jake," said one of the soldiers as he came upon Jake walking out of the makeshift corral one day. "Where'd it come from?"

"Don't know," answered Jake. "Jes' one ob dose things, I reckon."

Jake did not add that his father had also been gifted with horses. He did not want to admit that perhaps he was more like his father than he realized. All the while his work subtly drew him in unseen ways closer to his father's memory. In time he would grow to understand much about his father by staring into the great eyes of his horse-companions, knowing that his father shared the same special bond with the unspeaking creatures that he felt.

LIGHT
18

ONE MORNING JAKE WOKE EARLY. IT WAS STILL mostly dark. The merest hint of something that would eventually be sunrise was off in the east. It was more like the *thought* of light than light itself.

Jake lay in his bedroll staring into the darkness. Gradually he became aware that someone sat not far away. As the hint of dawn slowly grew, he saw that it was Micah Duff. He was just sitting there staring toward the east.

Jake got up, walked over, and sat down beside him.

"Wha'chu doin', Duff?" he asked.

"Waiting for the sunrise," answered Micah.

"Why?"

"It's my favorite part of the day," replied Micah. "Every chance I get, I like to watch it all the way from darkness to the first of the sun's rays shooting over the horizon."

"But dat don't explain why."

For a long time Micah did not answer. He continued looking east. Jake sat beside him, watching the approaching dawn too, though not seeing everything in it Micah did. Before long the chilly grey of morning had come. After a while longer, a slight glow of orange started to show where the earth met the sky.

The glow increased, then focused its intensity more and more into the one place that, in another twenty minutes or so, would explode with fire from the heavens.

"Just think of all the things light does for us, Jake," said Micah at length.

"Like what?"

"Look how the darkness runs from it."

"How you mean?" asked Jake.

"When the sun starts coming up every morning, the darkness begins to evaporate and all the shadows run and hide. Look around us—the darkness is disappearing. We were sitting in the dark just a little while ago, Jake. But now look—the light has chased it away!"

"I reckon dat's so, all right. But it's jes' what happens when da sun comes up."

"It's more than that, Jake. Everything has meaning."

"So what dis light mean?"

"The light is just like God."

"How dat?"

"That's what God does too—chases darkness away . . . defeats the darkness in *us*, just like the sun coming up over the horizon, so that we can be more full of light."

He paused a second or two.

"You know what I think of, Jake," he added, "whenever I sit here like this and watch the sunrise?"

"What?"

"I think of the light that God's trying to get inside us, sending little shoots and arrows and rays to chase away all the shadows and clear out all the dark corners of our hearts, so that we can be full of light. I can't think of anything I want more than to be clean and clear and pure and full of light inside."

Micah paused and drew in a deep breath of satisfaction and wonder. There was a long silence before he spoke again.

"When are you going to let the light all the way inside

your heart, Jake?" he said in a soft but serious tone.

"What you talkin' 'bout?" said Jake.

"When are you going to let it shine into those dark spots that are keeping you from being clean and whole?"

"I don't know wha'chu mean."

"I think you do, Jake. You're an angry young man. I can see it in your eyes. That anger is like a darkness inside you that you haven't let the sun reach yet."

"What kind er fool talk is dat?"

"You're full of anger inside. I think you know it. You're trying to run from it, trying to hide from the light. But you can't escape it, Jake."

"You'd be angry too effen you'd been a slave, ef you'd been whupped like I hab."

"So it's anger against whites, against your owner? You're angry because you were a slave?"

Jake was silent. Micah's unexpected questions irritated him.

"It's more than that, isn't it, Jake? It's got to do with your father, hasn't it?"

"Maybe dat ain' none ob yo affair," Jake snapped back.

"You're right," said Micah. "It isn't. But *you* are. God put you and me together for me to do my best for you. I wouldn't be doing that if I didn't do my best to try to shine light on what's keeping you twisted up inside."

"You always preachin' at me like *he* wuz," Jake snapped. "I didn't ax you ter do none ob dat!"

"No you didn't, Jake. But that doesn't change the fact that it's anger that's making you grow crooked. That's why you gotta let the light in so you can look at it and let the light chase it away. Maybe you don't like me saying it. But what kind of a friend would I be if I didn't?"

Another moody silence followed.

"Why are you angry at your pa, Jake?" Micah asked.

"He run away from us, dat's why! He didn't care nuthin' 'bout me!"

Saying the words stung Jake's heart like a hot knife. With them came the memory of the overseer's cruel laughter: *"Dat boy ob mine's jes' too ugly an' I can't stan' sight er him no mo. I be despert ter git away from dat boy."* He felt tears trying to rise in his eyes. They were the tears of boyhood anguish and a father's rejection. But he forced them away.

Other memories flooded him. But Jake could not face them. The guilt and confusion were too overpowering.

"He lef' me an' my mama!" he said, angrily now. "He lef' her alone jes' like he lef' me an' called me names. He lef' her to die! Now she's dead because of him!"

Jake jumped to his feet and paced about. He was obviously agitated.

Micah took in his heated words calmly. He said nothing for a long while. When he glanced up, Jake was gone. Micah sighed and rose to his feet, made a fire, then put the water on for coffee. Before long the camp was bustling with weary soldiers getting ready for the day.

Jake was silent and moody for the rest of the morning. As they rode along beside each other, midway through the afternoon, Micah ventured to bring the subject up again.

"You know, Jake, nobody's got a perfect daddy," he said. "That's because no daddy can possibly be perfect. They weren't supposed to be. They make mistakes 'cause they're just men like the rest of us. But they gave us life. If it weren't for them, we wouldn't be here at all. No matter what they may have done, and no matter what we may think they have done, they deserve our love and honor for that alone."

"Why you know so much 'bout fathers?" said Jake irritably. "What makes you think you kin preach ter me like all dis?"

A look of pain passed over Micah's face.

"I know nothing about my own pa, Jake. I never saw him,

never knew who he was. I still don't. Not having a father at all teaches you a lot about how precious a thing a pa is. So I've probably thought about it more than you have. I can't even realize what having a pa is, and what memories of feeling a father's touch must be like, even if he wasn't a perfect pa. I can't realize it because I don't have those memories, and I never will. You've got them, Jake. But instead of being thankful for them, you're angry about them. I'd give anything to have memories of a pa like you've got, Jake. I'd give anything even to have a pa that left me. I wouldn't even mind a pa that beat me or was mean to me . . . just to have a pa at all. But I never had one, Jake. That's why I know what a precious thing a pa is."

Hard Words
19

T HE WAR WAS ALL AROUND THEM, AND JAKE PAT-
terson saw things no one ought ever to have to see. But
as long as men were determined to fight other men, and as
long as neither side was willing to back down, there would be
war. And as long as there was war, there would be bloodshed,
and there would be killing, and there would be heartache.

As the war began to turn more and more toward the North
after the battles of Gettysburg and Vicksburg in July of 1863,
the Confederates they encountered fought all the harder to
keep hold of their dying dream. As the year 1864 arrived and
warmed into spring, Jake, now sixteen, had seen more than
his share of bloodshed.

He and Micah were dressing wounds of several of the
company's horses. Micah had just returned from having to
put a mare down who had broken two legs in the battle of the
previous day. He was more somber for hours afterward as
they went about their unpleasant work.

"That was hard, Jake," he said finally with a weary sigh.
"There's nothing worse than having to shoot a horse. I loved
that animal."

Jake had nothing to say. It was quiet a long time.

"That was a mighty brave thing you did yesterday, Jake,"

said Micah after a while, "—running in when the captain went down, getting his horse's reins and then pulling them both out of there. When I saw you at first with all that gun and cannon fire, I was sure I'd see you going down splattered in your own blood. But you did it. You proved you got one kind of courage, all right."

Jake glanced up, a look of bewilderment on his face. But he didn't say anything, and neither did Micah. But Micah's statement stuck with him for days.

"Wha'chu mean da other day," said Jake several days later, "'bout me havin' one kin' ob courage?"

"Just what I said," replied Micah, "that you did a brave thing."

"But dere's sum other kin' er courage dat I ain't got?"

"I don't know whether you've got it or not, Jake."

"What is dat other kin' er courage?"

"The courage to be a man, to look inside yourself and see what you're made of. It takes a different kind of courage."

"How you mean?"

"It's easy enough to be brave when you're facing something outside yourself, even something terrifying like death, like you did that day when you pulled the captain out of the battle. You probably saved his life. But when you're facing something inside yourself—that's what takes real courage. That's when you have to find out if you're really a man."

"You had ter do dat, Duff?"

"I've had to a few times. Nothing's harder than facing your own doubts, fears . . . your past. That's where the greatest courage comes from—when what you have to battle against is yourself. It takes a man to do that."

"What 'bout da kind er bravery on da battlefield? You said dat took courage, what I done."

"It did. It showed you've got guts, Jake. There's men doing brave things all around us every day. But any fool can go out and get his head blown off, or fight and show how tough he is. Sometimes the men who talk the most about being tough are the biggest fools of all. Any fool can act brave if all he wants is to prove he's tougher than someone else. Don't get me wrong—I was proud of what you did the other day. Putting yourself in danger for someone else took real courage. All I'm saying is that by itself, that kind of courage can't make a man of you."

"So what kin make a man er me, Duff?"

"That you've got to find out for yourself, Jake. And I'm thinking it's just about time you did."

"Wha'chu mean by dat?"

"I'm just wondering if it's not about time you took a look inside yourself about that anger that's eating away there."

"Dere you go agin—you gwine start preachin' at me agin!"

"You just tell me to shut up if you want, Jake, and I won't say another word. You asked what I meant by courage, so I figured I'd try to tell you."

Jake looked away but said nothing.

"So what do you want, Jake?" said Micah. "You want me to shut up? Or are you brave enough to hear what I've got to say?"

Jake shrugged and muttered something Micah didn't hear.

"I didn't catch what you said, Jake."

"Aw, go on an' say whateber you want . . . dat's what I said."

Again they rode on for a while in silence.

"All I'm saying, Jake," said Micah after a while, "is nothing more than I've had to do myself—look inside and own up to things that were wrong there, to look at my crooked places and get them straightened around. That's the thing that I say takes a kind of courage that most men don't learn soon enough in life. Some never learn it at all. That's where the real fearsome kinds of things are—inside us. Most men go through life trying to prove that they're men in all the wrong ways. They try to prove that they can take care of themselves and that they don't need anybody else. That's what the man I was telling you about helped me see. But I decided I didn't want to be that kind of man. I decided I wanted to be a *real* man, the kind of man with courage to face what's inside, to face those places in me that no one else had ever seen."

Micah glanced at Jake, but he was just looking ahead.

"That's not an easy thing to do, Jake," Micah continued. "Growing into a man with that kind of courage is a hard thing. But it's the only way to be a whole man. Otherwise, you'll only be half a man. As many brave things as you might do, you'll still only be half a man. That's why I've been trying to get you to take an honest look at the anger that's inside you, Jake—because I want you to be a whole man."

Micah paused again. Jake was still staring at the saddle horn in front of him, showing nothing by his expression of what he thought.

"Who knows where anger comes from, Jake," Micah went on. "But lots of men have it deep down inside them. Most folks have got some kind of anger inside them toward either their ma or their pa. Kind of a mystery, it's always seemed to me, that the folks that gave them life are the ones folks get angriest at. But that anger toward your pa will kill you, Jake, if you don't someday summon the courage to face it. All of us have got to learn to forgive. It takes courage. It takes humility to forgive. But no one can be a whole man without being able to do both."

Micah stopped. He had said what he had to say. Now it was Jake's turn. Micah Duff knew that Jake's future was now in his own hands.

Away

20

T HAT NIGHT JAKE LAY AWAKE LONG AFTER EVERY-
one else was asleep. He couldn't have admitted it to
him, but Micah's words had hit him hard.

He didn't like them.

And as he lay fussing and fuming and turning them over
and back in his mind, the slow anger in his heart grew.

He was a man, he said to himself. He was sixteen. But
Micah was treating him like a boy, always preaching at him
and lecturing him about everything that was wrong with him.
All that nonsense about courage and looking inside yourself.

He didn't need it!

What business was it of Micah Duff's anyway? His
insides were his own business, nobody else's.

He'd had enough of it!

But try as he might, he couldn't stop the many words that
Micah had spoken during their three years together.

*"Anger's not a pretty thing. It makes people miserable
inside. . . ."*

The longer he lay awake the more agitated he became.
Agitated and angry.

*"When we fall in with how God means us to be, that's when
our grain grows straight and true. . . ."*

He couldn't stop the plaguing voice.

"When are you going to let the light all the way inside your heart, Jake? . . ."

Finally he couldn't stand it another minute. He got up out of his bedroll. There was enough of a moon to see by and he walked a little way off from the camp. He paced back and forth on the other side of the roped-off horse corral that he and Micah had strung up that afternoon. But still the words hounded him.

"You're full of anger. . . . You're trying to run from it, trying to hide from the light. But you can't escape it. . . ."

He was in a sweat now and pacing more rapidly, trying desperately to escape the one thing no one can ever escape— his own thoughts.

He continued to get more and more stirred up. Suddenly burst out from inside him—though in the blackness of night the words exploded silently in his own mind:

Heck wiff you, Micah Duff. . . ! I don't need none ob yo blamed preachin' no mo! I don't need you neither. I don't need nobody! I kin take care ob mysel'. I don't need you meddlin' wiff me, carryin' on all 'bout darkness an' courage an' da like. I don't need it, Duff!

When Jake came to himself, he was standing over Micah Duff's bedroll, listening to the quiet rhythmic breathing of his sleeping companion. For two or three minutes he stood, just staring down at the indistinct form in the darkness.

Then slowly he returned to where he had himself been sleeping. He stooped down and picked up the few things he could call his own. Finally he rolled up a single blanket of the Union Army he hoped they wouldn't mind if he took, and again left the camp.

This time he did not turn back.

Haunted by a Mother's Words
21

T HOUGH THERE WAS ENOUGH OF A MOON TO SEE BY, Jake knew that he had to choose his steps with care. He was pretty sure the Confederate Army they had engaged two days before had retreated toward the east. He did his best to follow what he thought was a northerly course, though he wasn't altogether sure which way that was.

He managed to avoid any encampments or farms or stray dogs. He changed his direction so many times, by the time he collapsed in sleepy exhaustion several hours later, he had no idea whether he had been walking north or south or east or west.

When he woke the sun was high in the sky. Whichever way he had been going, he was miles away and could not have hoped to find Captain Taylor's Illinois company now had he tried.

For the first time since his flight from the Winegaard plantation, Jake Patterson was again alone.

Though there had been a lot of talk lately that the war might not last much longer, he knew that traveling in the South still meant danger. Even though he might be free as a result of President Lincoln's proclamation, he knew that there was danger everywhere for a black like him.

For the first time in years, his mother's words from the past began to return to him as he went.

"You fin' yer papa, Jake . . . you fin' Carolina . . . I know dat sumday you'll see dat freedom me an' yer papa prayed ter see. So w'en you's free, you fin' him . . . you fin' him . . . you fin' Carolina, Jake."

After all that Micah Duff had said to him, he had no interest in finding his father. Yet he was alone in the world again. He had nothing else to cling to but his mother's words.

With a vague mingling of many conflicting emotions, he made his way like before. He found food and gradually encountered other blacks on the move like himself. And as he did, he began asking, "Which way ter Carolina?"

Not consciously even forming the idea in his brain that he had set upon a journey to search for his father, *Find Carolina* became the underlying impulse guiding his movements. He could not have said why. Drawn to the memory of his mother, and racked by the gnawing torment of guilt that he was responsible for her death, images of her face and the sound of her voice haunted the long nights of his sojourning loneliness. For reasons he could not himself define, he could do nothing else but obey her dying wish. The two words of his mother became the vague notion of his calling and present destiny. He had failed her in life. He could not fail her in death. He little realized in what ways his own life and future would be marked by footsteps that now set themselves to carry out her final charge from mother to son.

He had no idea where he was. But in time he learned that he had left his Union regiment near Fort Donelson in northwestern Tennessee and that Carolina lay east. And he knew enough from listening to Micah Duff talk about the sunrise to know that every morning the sun pointed him afresh in the direction he was compelled to follow. He was now walking toward the sunrise every day—though not exactly spiritually yet. As he went he did not realize how close he had returned to where he had been before. After traveling with the company throughout Missouri, Arkansas, and Mississippi, he was again near the very spot where Micah Duff had first rescued him and where he had spent his first days with Captain Taylor's small detachment.

Slowly he began to vaguely recognize some of the terrain from his earlier travels. He had also come into a region of great troop activity and movement. Every day required more and more care to keep from being seen. He did not know about General Sherman's destruction of Atlanta and march to the sea. Neither did he know that he was in the very path where Southern General Hood was now invading southern Tennessee with a huge army, hoping to cut Sherman's northwest supply lines.

The first inkling he had of his danger was waking one morning to a distant rumble. Jake sat up and listened. He could not be sure, but it sounded like horses—hundreds of horses . . . maybe thousands.

Hurriedly he jumped to his feet and grabbed up his things. It was close! The sounds came from everywhere around him.

Without thinking, he glanced about and had scarcely had time to scramble up into a nearby oak when one of the flanks of Hood's army emerged through the woods. Within minutes, Jake was staring down upon a passing sea of grey uniforms. Had they been looking for a place to camp, or had they paused for any reason, he would surely have been seen. But they were on the march. It was obvious they were tired and worn. No one was looking up into the trees for frightened Negro runaways hiding among the birds.

In terror Jake watched for an hour. At last the tramp of

dust and marching feet and horses' hooves retreated into the distance toward the north.

Still he waited. After twenty minutes of silence about him, at last he let himself down to the ground, glanced up at the sky, then continued east toward the rising sun.

Unsought Tragedy
22

Midway through the day, Jake suddenly perked up his ears to listen.

The sharp report of gunfire halted his feet. Three or four more shots followed, then silence.

He glanced to his right and left, then all around in the distance.

He knew this place! He knew this very field. It was the same field where he and Sergeant Billings had kept their horses when they had had to hide out. It was the same field where Billings had beaten him to within an inch of his life.

He had stumbled right back into the middle of the Dawson farm!

What could the shots have been about? Wherever he was bound, this was one place he did not want to be! This was a place where they tried to shoot Negroes with shotguns and split their heads open with axes!

But he also knew the layout of the place. He knew where the icehouse and smoking shed were, and where they hung the cheese and where the milk cans were stored after the day's milking. And the gnawing in his stomach right now reminded him that he had hardly eaten more than several apples for two days.

If he was careful, perhaps he could snoop around and make himself a meal without them knowing he was here.

Carefully Jake began to make his way the half mile toward the farmhouse.

Once the outbuildings of the Dawson farm came into view, Jake slowed and considered his moves with care. Everything looked the same. He saw no one around. He didn't remember there being any dogs, though there might be now.

Almost on tiptoe, he crept toward the back of the barn.

He reached the rear entrance safely. The fat sow was still in her muddy pen, snorting and snooting around and doing whatever pigs do to pass the time of day. Slowly he inched inside, squinting in the blackness as his eyes tried to adjust to the light. He heard nothing but the shuffling and breathing and occasional snort from a single horse in its stable. Inside the safety of the familiar barn, which had once served as his temporary hospital, he paused to get his bearings and think what to do next. Should he go for milk or cheese, or perhaps a slab of dried meat hanging in the smokehouse?

But he had no time to wonder about it further.

Suddenly the shriek of a woman's voice sounded from the direction of the house. Jake's blood turned to ice.

His first thought was to make a run for it. If something bad was going on around this place, the last thing he wanted was to get involved in it. The farther he was from this place the better! Whatever it was, it didn't concern him!

But a second cry, obviously of terror, and then a third, was followed by the angry sounds of men's voices, then what sounded like two women pleading for their lives. Whatever might be the danger to himself, Jake could not run away from such cries. He recognized the men's voices clearly enough as black like his. He was pretty sure he recognized the women's voices as well.

He hurried across the barn to the door opposite the house and peered out. The yells and shouts and screams were coming from the kitchen. Jake glanced about the yard, then dashed across to the house and knelt down below an open window.

"Please don't hurt us," a desperate woman was whimpering. "Take whatever you want. But please . . . just go away and leave us."

"Jes' kill 'em, Rafe," said one of the men. "We gots food like we come for."

"I'll kill 'em w'en I'm ready ter kill em," barked his companion. "You jes' shut up till me an' dis little white girl has sum fun."

"Leab her alone, Rafe. We don't need dat kind er trouble."

A shriek from Samantha Dawson was all Jake needed to give him a good idea what was going on inside. He turned and dashed back for the barn.

Hurriedly he glanced around in the dim light for a weapon. His eyes fell on the woodpile. There were two axes, one stuck in a chopping block, the other broken and lying among the chunks of wood.

He started to grab the good ax, then stopped. No—too unwieldy. He didn't want to kill anyone *that* way.

Frantically he continued to look about. A pitchfork . . . no, they would shoot him while he was trying to jab it at them.

Thirty seconds later, armed with the handle of the broken ax with no head in one hand, and a horsewhip in the other, again he approached the house from out of sight of the windows. In his work around the company's stable, he had learned to use a whip with cunning precision. Slowly he inched along beneath the sills toward the kitchen door.

One more glance inside . . . one of the men and the girl had disappeared into a room off the kitchen. He could hear Samantha yelling and struggling.

He crept up onto the porch and took a standing position behind the door.

"Hey you in dere, come out here!" he called.

"Who dat?" came a deep voice from inside.

"A black brudder, dat's who," said Jake. "Wha'chu up to in dere? You gots anythin' a hungry black man might hab ter eat?"

He heard feet walking across the floor. The door opened a few inches. The head of a tall husky Negro man poked through it and looked out. Behind the door, Jake held his breath.

Slowly the door opened wider. The man stepped out and began to look about.

The next instant a butt of solid white ash came crashing down on his head. He collapsed in a heap onto the porch. Jake set down the ax handle, grabbed up the man's pistol where it had fallen, then stepped over the unconscious form into the room.

A horrifying sight met his eyes.

Mrs. Dawson sat tied to a straight-backed chair across the room, a look of sickening horror and grief on her face. Her dress was splattered with the blood of her husband, who lay dead on the floor a few feet away. On the other side of the room lay a Negro youth, by appearances not much older than Jake, dead from a blast through his chest from Dawson's shotgun.

The scene looked like a battlefield. The sight of blood and death turned Jake's stomach. He would never get used to it. Beside Dawson lay the gun that had nearly taken his own life several years before, and it did not take him long to see what had probably happened.

At the sight of Jake, Mrs. Dawson's eyes widened in terror, thinking him to be yet a fourth of the band of desperate former slaves who had attacked them.

Then she faintly recognized him. A sudden gasp escaped her lips. Jake's hand shot to his mouth and he placed a finger on his lips.

He glanced about with question, then back at the terrified woman. A dart to the left of her eyes and nod of her head told him what he wanted to know.

Only four or five seconds had passed since Jake had entered the house. The man who had disappeared into the bedroom with the frantically struggling Samantha Dawson had heard the exchange of words followed by the commotion on the porch. He now walked out of the room, bare chested, gun in hand, to see what the ruckus was about before he finished his business with Samantha.

He had but an instant to realize that a young black man he had never seen before was standing ten feet from him. What it might mean he had no time to wonder.

The next instant a vicious snap from the whip in Jake's grip ripped the gun from his hand. He screamed in pain from a sting that had torn half an inch of flesh from the inside of his wrist.

As the gun clattered to the floor, a second *swoosh* of leather sounded. The thin thong coiled twice around his ankles, and in almost the same motion Jake yanked with all his might. The stunned man fell flat on his back before he could cry out again. The next thing he knew Jake's boot was crushing into his chest and he was staring up into the barrel of his partner's pistol six inches from his nose. The enraged face of another runaway just like himself was staring down at him.

"You miserable nigger," Jake cried, trembling with fury. "What you want ter hurt dese ladies fo!"

Before the stunned man could answer, Samantha Dawson half staggered out of the bedroom. All she saw was a black man standing in front of her. She ran forward yelling hysterically and beating Jake with her fists like a child throwing a tantrum.

"Wha'chu doin' . . . hey, you stupid girl . . . you stop dat!"

"Samantha . . . Samantha, stop it!" yelled her mother

frantically. "That man won't hurt you!"

"I's yo frien', girl!" said Jake. "An' it looks ter me like you needs one—now go untie yo mother . . . git, you fool girl!"

Too confused and distraught to argue, Samantha backed away and did as Jake had told her. She still had no idea who he was. To her all Negroes looked alike.

"Hey, brudder, what you want ter be causin' all dis trouble fo?" began the man on the ground, writhing under Jake's foot. "You an' me's—"

"You shut dat face ob yors!" yelled Jake. "You an' me ain't no brudders. Any man dat'd hurt a woman an' kill anudder man, even effen he's white—"

Suddenly he stopped. A chill gripped his heart. An involuntary shudder swept through him and silenced whatever he had been about to say.

He turned to Mrs. Dawson.

"Come ober here, lady," said Jake. "Tie dis dog's han's."

She did so, though her fingers shook so badly she could hardly control them. On the other side of the room, Samantha stood paralyzed.

As soon as the man was secure, Jake tied his feet, then went to the porch and bound the unconscious man lying there with the whip. At last he turned to Mrs. Dawson. Finally the poor woman's emotions gave way. With no one else to turn to, she collapsed on Jake's chest. Slowly he put his arms around her and tried to comfort her as she broke into convulsive sobs.

How long they stood there it was hard to say, the sixteen-year-old black youth comforting the forty-year-old widow, whose husband had just been killed by one of Jake's own kind. It was long enough for Samantha to come to herself and realize what she was witnessing. The shock of her mother's behavior was almost greater than that of seeing her own dress stained with her father's blood.

Slowly Jake led Mrs. Dawson outside, over the lump of humanity tied unconscious on the porch, and away from the house. Dumbly, Samantha watched them go, then stumbled after them in a stupor.

"I's Jake Patterson, ma'am," said Jake. "I ain't wiff dose dere men—I hope you knows dat. I neber seen dem in my life. I jes' happened by an' heard da shots an' da screamin'."

"I . . . I know . . . yes . . . I remember you, uh . . . Jake," she said, struggling for words in a hoarse voice.

"You wuz kind enuff ter share sum bread wiff me one time. What happened, ma'am?"

"They . . . they came looking for food . . . my husband . . . he tried to . . . he was . . ."

She broke down and began to cry again.

She felt the gentle touch of Jake's hand on her shoulder. Unconsciously her own hand went up and clutched it for comfort and support.

"Mother!" shrieked Samantha, at last coming out of her trance and running forward. "What are you doing? Get away from that horrid colored man!"

Not moving from where she stood, Mrs. Dawson looked toward her daughter with sad red eyes.

"Samantha," she said, "your father is dead. Isn't it time for the hatred to stop?"

"But . . . he's . . . he's a Negro! Why are you letting him touch you? Mother, it's disgusting! He had his arms around you. He's nothing but a dirty—"

A great slap across her cheek from her mother's hand silenced her.

"Samantha!" cried Mrs. Dawson. "This man just saved our lives! If that isn't enough, he's the same young man who saved you from that white soldier before. If anyone has shown himself to be your friend, it's him."

At last a hint of recognition began to dawn in Samantha Dawson's eyes. But with it came no light of warmth or gratitude. The only thing visible on her face was a recollection of former hatred just as strong as what she felt toward these men who had brought tragedy to their family today.

All blacks were the same in her eyes—low, mean, disgusting, and evil. The very color of Jake's skin prevented her from being able to discern any difference between him and the two men tied up back at the house with her own father's blood on their hands.

Without another word, she turned and walked away.

Unlikely Alliance
23

B Y DEGREES JAKE MANAGED TO GET OUT OF BESS Dawson the gist of what had happened. The three Negro men, traveling north and trying to avoid the war, had come to the house looking for food. Her husband's response had angered them. Heated words had followed, as had a visit to his gun cabinet, with the result as Jake had seen it some twenty minutes later.

But what to do with the men now? Was he to take them bound into the sheriff of the nearest town? He would probably be arrested with them. He certainly could not just kill them in cold blood. But until they were gone, the two Dawson women would not be safe. And what about him? With their own companion lying dead on the floor along with the farmer, and having already shown themselves capable of killing, there was little doubt that if given the opportunity they would kill him and probably Mrs. Dawson, have their way with Samantha, and then probably kill her too.

Something had to be done with them.

For now he would secure them away from the house until he could think. The man on the porch was just coming to himself. Jake hauled him some distance away. With additional rope from the barn, he tied him to a tree. He went back for his companion. He carried him out of the house slung over his shoulders, followed by Mrs. Dawson holding the ax handle with instructions from Jake to conk him on the head as hard as she could if he uttered a peep.

He dumped him down like a sack of potatoes near his friend. Mrs. Dawson walked slowly back toward the house. Violent threats and curses followed from both men as he tied the second to another tree. Their words deepened Jake's conviction that, if they managed to get free, his actions would mean death to all three of them.

Then Jake returned to the house. He found Mrs. Dawson sitting on the steps of her porch quietly weeping.

"We gots ter think 'bout buryin' yo husband, ma'am," he said softly.

She nodded.

"I'll see ter it, ma'am, effen you'll jes' show me where . . . dat is, effen you'd take no disrespeck from a colored person like me carryin' him an' such-like."

She shook her head. Still crying, she rose. Jake followed as she led him away from the house to a small plot about fifty yards from the house, where a hedge and small garden surrounded a small grassy area. In the middle of it three or four grave markers rose out of the ground.

She pointed down. Jake nodded.

He returned to the barn, found a shovel and pickax, and returned to the site. An hour later he walked into the kitchen. Neither of the women were in sight. From somewhere he heard the sound of weeping. He stooped down and first picked up the stiffening body of the black boy and carried it outside and deposited it out of sight from the house in the vicinity of where the men were tied. He returned for Mr. Dawson, hoisting up what remained of the same man who had once tried to kill him and carried it to the grave he had dug. Being as careful as he could under the circumstances, he lowered the body off his back and half dumped, half laid it beside the hole.

Jake straightened himself, exhaled a sigh, then thought it best to speak to the man's widow before proceeding. He had never buried anyone. He didn't know exactly what to do next.

Gingerly he walked back into the house. With tentative steps he followed the whimpering sounds to one of the bedrooms. He peeped cautiously inside.

"Mrs. Dawson, ma'am," he said, "I's right sorry ter disturb you in yo grief . . . I's sorrier den I kin be, but duz you want me ter build him a box ter go in . . . or duz you want me ter jes' put him inter da groun' da way he is?"

The honest simplicity of Jake's question, and the practicality of response required, did not exactly bring the stricken woman out of her misery. But at least it forced her to confront the next moment with a decision. And once a decision has been made, any decision, the next moment is always easier to face.

She sat up on her bed, sniffed, and wiped at her nose and eyes with the handkerchief in her hand. She looked at Jake with something resembling a forlorn smile.

"It is very kind of you to help us, Jake," she said. "I don't know what we would have done if you hadn't come when you did. We would probably all be dead."

She drew in a breath and tried to steady herself.

"I . . . think we will not need a coffin, Jake," she said after a moment. "Is the hole plenty deep?"

"Sumthin' like three er fo feet, ma'am."

"That should be fine—thank you. Just put . . . my, uh, my husband to rest as he is."

"Yes'm. Shud I cover him, ma'am?"

"Yes, Jake, that will be fine."

"Duz you want ter say a few words, ma'am, or shud I jes' go ahead?"

"Go ahead, Jake. I don't think I can stand to see his face

again . . . like . . . like he is. I will be along in a few minutes."

Jake left the house and returned to the small family plot. As he was filling the grave and covering it over with the last of the dirt, he heard steps behind him.

He set the shovel aside as Mrs. Dawson came and stood beside him. They stood in silence for several minutes. Slowly Samantha came from somewhere and stood silently beside her mother.

"God bless you, John Dawson," said his wife at length. "You were a man who never learned to give your anger to the God who made you. In the end it cost you your own life—"

At the words, Jake's head jerked toward her. But he remained silent.

"—but you were a good husband," she went on without noticing. "I never went hungry. You were gentle and kind to me, and though you would rage and fuss about so many things, you never raised your voice or your hand at me. I loved you when I first met you, and I loved you when I woke up this morning. For all your faults . . . I never stopped loving you."

She choked on her words and began sobbing again. Slowly she knelt to the ground and gently placed her face near the fresh-turned earth, then whispered again, "Oh, John . . . I love you."

Several minutes more she remained kneeling at the side of the grave, then slowly rose.

Crying herself now, Samantha went to her knees, gently reached out her hand, and placed her palm on the fresh dirt. "Good-bye, Daddy . . . I love you too."

For the rest of the afternoon, Jake tried to keep his distance. He did not want to intrude. A couple hours later, Mrs. Dawson approached him where he sat beside the barn.

"Would you like something to eat, Jake?" she said.

"Dat I would, ma'am. Dat's right kind ob you. I ain't had much ob nuthin' fo two days."

"Come inside, then," she said. "I've been trying to clean up a little. I've got some meat and cheese and milk and bread and fruit on the table."

Jake followed her to the house.

"What should we do about the two men?" she asked as they walked.

"Dere any lawmen in dese parts?" Jake asked, though he wasn't sure he wanted to put himself anywhere near a white man's jail.

"Our sheriff was killed in the war. Him and so many others. . . . No one's taken his place."

"Well, I can't kill dem, ma'am. But you ain't safe so long as de're here. Dat is . . . less you'd like ter kill 'em, ma'am. I wudn't have no objections."

"I couldn't possibly do that," said Mrs. Dawson with a shudder.

"Neither could I, ma'am."

They walked into the kitchen. Mrs. Dawson told Jake to sit down. She put a plate in front of him. Jake's teenage appetite was ferocious, and he set about the provisions in front of him without delay.

"Can't you take them someplace, Jake?" asked Mrs. Dawson.

"Where, ma'am?" he asked, his mouth half full of a chunk of bread.

"I don't know, somewhere out in the woods . . . somewhere far away."

"I don't want dem chasing me down an' killin' me, ma'am."

"No, of course not—that's not what I meant. Couldn't we put them in a cart or wagon and haul them miles away and leave them?"

"What's ter keep 'em from comin' back an' doin' more mischief?"

"Yes, you're right . . . then what *are* we going to do with them?"

In the end, the plan they hatched was not without risk but was the best they could think of short of simply murdering them.

That evening, Jake hitched up a small wagon and loaded the two men, tied as tight as he could bind them, along with their dead friend, into the back of it. Just before dark that same night, he blindfolded them just as tight, then he set out with Mrs. Dawson at his side. They left the farm, moving south. As the night progressed, with Mrs. Dawson guiding Jake with silent directions, all the while speaking many misleading clues as to their route and various landmarks along the way, they gradually made their way in a wide arc until their actual direction was due north. Having grown up in the region, Mrs. Dawson knew every inch of the territory for miles. By the time they reached one of the ridges of the Cumberland about six miles as the crow flew from her home, she was confident they would need a magician to find their way back.

She motioned Jake to circle a few times, then stop. The night had been long, and the day preceding it even longer. She was exhausted. But the long hours of darkness had given her the chance to dwell somewhat upon her own thoughts concerning the tragedy that had overtaken her.

Jake dragged the dead body out onto the ground, then pulled out the two black men, shoved them onto the ground, and removed their blindfolds.

They squinted in the moonlight. At last they began to see the dim form of Mrs. Dawson standing over them.

"I am going to leave the two of you here with your friend," she said. "If you can get yourselves free, then God help you. If you can't, dying on this mountain is no more than you deserve. I will spend the rest of my life praying to be able to forgive you for what you have done. I don't know whether

I will succeed or not, but perhaps the Lord's grace will give me strength. But be assured of this, I know how to use my husband's guns. If I ever see either of you at my home again, I will shoot you dead. God be merciful to your souls.''

She turned and climbed back up beside Jake on the wagon. He flicked the reins and they rattled off into the night, heading north, listening to vile shouts and profanities and threats behind them. When she judged that they were out of earshot, Mrs. Dawson directed Jake how to make his way again in a wide circle. At length they found the road south that led them back in the direction of her home.

RESPITE
24

I T WAS ONLY TWO OR THREE HOURS BEFORE DAYBREAK
when Jake and Mrs. Dawson again rode into the yard of
the home that had been visited by death and tragedy the day
before. Mercifully Bess Dawson was exhausted. Sleep over-
came her almost before she collapsed on her bed.

Jake unhitched the team, then sought his former bed of
straw in the barn. He did not wake until nearly noon. He
found Mrs. Dawson in the kitchen, red-eyed again but strong,
as women of all eras have had to be in times of death.

"I reckon I, uh . . . oughter be movin' along," said Jake.
"Duz you mind ef I cud hab jes' a little somethin' ter eat afore
I go?"

"Of course not, Jake," she replied with a sad smile. "I will
put you up a few things."

She paused and a strange look came over her face.

"Do you . . . do you *have* to go, Jake?" she asked after a
moment.

"Uh, I don't know, ma'am . . . I don't reckon, but . . .
wha'chu mean?"

"Only that . . . I would be," she began, seemingly embarrassed, "—that is . . . my husband was mending a stretch of

fence he was concerned about, and . . . I'm frightened of those men, and . . ."

She stopped and looked away. For a Southerner to ask for the help of a Negro was about the worst form of degradation imaginable. But being married to John Dawson for more than twenty years had done much to wear away whatever pride might once have existed in the heart of Bess Dawson. She was not above asking a near stranger for help. After what had happened, she saw Jake not as a black but as a fellow human being whom she needed, and maybe whom she could help a little too. How could they consider themselves strangers after what they had been through together?

"Actually the truth is," she struggled to go on, "I would . . . I'd be obliged if . . . if you would stay for a while, Jake. I could give you jobs to do . . . it would be a big help to me."

Jake nodded. "No, ma'am," he said, "I ain't got ter go— I ain't in no hurry ter git anywheres. I don't eben rightly know where I'm going anyway."

Mrs. Dawson sighed, in obvious relief. "Then sit down and have something to eat."

Jake remained at the Dawson farm a month.

What Samantha Dawson thought of the arrangement she never said. But Jake suspected well enough from the way she looked at him that she was anything but pleased. Her father's brutal death, however, as well as her own close brush with what would likely have ended in her own, had moderated her anger toward him. She was proud and arrogant, but not completely stupid. She knew that what her mother had said after slapping her across the face was true. Jake had saved their lives, and possibly protected her from rape and becoming the mother of a colored baby. If she would never be capable of actually thanking him, that knowledge at least allowed her to tolerate him.

Mending the broken fence turned Jake's thoughts toward

his own mother and what had happened back at the Wine-gaard plantation. And the secret . . . the terrible secret that no one knew . . . the secret that haunted him . . . tormented him with the guilt of Cain. Was he too destined forever to be a wanderer . . . running from his past, trying to escape what he could never escape—the hidden evil within his own self?

He threw down the hammer in his hands and clasped his palms to his ears, desperately trying to silence the accusing voice. But it could not be stopped. For it was the voice of his own conscience.

In turmoil he walked back toward the farmhouse several hours later, relieved to have the day of inner conflict behind him.

He found Samantha Dawson alone in the kitchen.

"Mama's gone into town," she said as Jake entered and removed his cap. "She told me to give you something to eat.—Here," she said, setting a dish down on the table in front of him.

Jake thanked her and sat down. Another place was set at the table, but she made no move to join him. Finally Jake spooned out a portion of stew and began to eat.

"You gwine eat anythin', miss?" he asked.

"I'm waiting for my mama," she replied, her back turned.

Jake ate a minute or two in silence.

"Why'd you lie about me, Miz Dawson?" he said after several slow and thoughtful mouthfuls. "Before, I mean . . . when I wuz here wiff da soldiers. Why'd you say I dun what you an' I bof know I didn't do?"

"Why do you think?" she said, slowly turning around. "Because you're colored."

"But why'd dat make you tell a lie 'bout me?"

"It wasn't really a lie."

"Wha'chu mean by dat?"

"It's the kind of thing you *might* have done."

"How kin you say dat? You neber seen me afore dat."

"You're colored. Your kind does evil things."

"I neber touched a girl wrong in my life," said Jake.

"Well, you probably would have if you'd had the chance. Colored people smell different and rape people and say coarse things and don't talk right and act like animals."

Jake stared at her in disbelief.

"Where'd you learn such nonsense as all dat? I doubt you eber eben knowed a colored person. You learn all dat from yo daddy?"

"Where I learned it's none of your business."

"Do you hate me now, Miz Dawson?" Jake asked.

"I don't know—maybe not now."

"But you still think dose things 'bout me?"

"You're colored. What else can I think?"

"Are you afraid ob me, den?"

"No," she replied with a hint of a smile.

"Ef blacks do all dat you say, den you must be terrified ob me."

"I keep a gun in my room," she said. "If you try to come in, I'll shoot you. Mama doesn't know. Daddy always said she was too soft-hearted for her own good. So when you and she weren't looking I took one of those dead men's guns and I've got it hidden if I need it."

Stunned, Jake stared back at the young woman.

"Why haven't you killed me, den? You's had plenty ob chances."

"I don't know. Maybe because you're helping Mama. And you did chase those men away, and I suppose that counts for something."

"But not enuff ter make you see dat I'm a normal person jes' like you?"

She laughed as if he were a child.

"But you're not like me. We're nothing alike. I'm white, you're colored."

"So colored folks can't neber be the same in yo eyes, no

matter what dey be like on da inside, is dat it?"

"Of course not," she laughed. "Everybody knows that. Even slaves know they can never really be like white people."

"Dere aren't no mo slaves, Miz Dawson. I's free now too."

"I heard something about that. But that can't make you be like me, not ever."

Not reassured by her words and the disclosure about the gun, Jake made himself a new bed in the loft of the barn for the remainder of his stay. He did not want to be quite so accessible in case she changed her mind about tolerating his presence for her mother's sake.

He began making plans to complete enough of the work around the place so that Mrs. Dawson could get by, and then he'd move on. Samantha's mother would gladly have hired him as a permanent hand, for he had shown himself capable and trustworthy. But knowing her daughter kept a pistol under her pillow, or in the drawer of her nightstand or wherever it was, was all the convincing Jake needed that he could have no future here.

And he had not forgotten his mother's words.

As Jake prepared to leave, Mrs. Dawson shook his hand warmly. "Thank you for everything, Jake," she said.

"I'm mighty obliged to you too, ma'am," Jake replied. "You been a good frien' ter dis wanderin' colored boy."

"Well, I imagine you'll do all right for yourself now, Jake. And I want you to take this."

She reached out and handed him a fistful of money. Jake stared at the pile of coins in his hand.

"I can't take dis!" he said. "Dere must be a fortune here!"

"I want you to have it. It's only twenty dollars."

"Laws almighty, Mrs. Dawson, dat *is* a fortune!"

"I don't want you to starve before you find what you're looking for."

"I won't starve. I knows how ter work."

"That you do, and you've been a big help to me. Now take the money."

Jake put the coins in the pocket of his trousers with awe and gratitude.

"Best of luck to you, Jake."

CAROLINA
25

As Jake Patterson continued his sojourn in response to his mother's dying charge, he was much closer to his long-undefined goal than he realized. And with Mrs. Dawson's directions, within weeks he had crossed into northern Georgia and eventually across the Savannah River into the hilly western region of South Carolina.

To his inquiries now, he was met with, "Why *dis* be Carolina, son . . . you's *in* Carolina."

Now that he was in the place he had so long sought, *Find Carolina* could no longer guide his steps. What was he to do now that he was here?

With the change, he began to think more and more of his father. What would he do if he actually *did* find him? What would he say?

Was his sole responsibility to deliver his mother's final message? Would he then turn his back on the man who had given him life? Would he just walk away . . . never to see the man again?

Is that why he had followed "Find Carolina"—only to deliver *her* message?

Such questions did not exactly form themselves in Jake's brain. But he felt a subtle change coming in ways he could not define, even in ways he was not yet aware of. He felt increasingly uneasy, on edge, almost like someone was watching him . . . like *his mother* was watching him. Had it now become a quest not merely to discharge a final duty *as* a son, but to discover what it meant to *be* a son?

Only time would answer such an important question.

Mrs. Dawson's twenty dollars lasted him a long time. He spent his newfound wealth sparingly, and continued to work at whatever jobs presented themselves, mostly in small towns along the way. As he grew stronger and learned more of the ways of how things stood between blacks and whites, and as he gained confidence, his range of skills also increased. He was strong and capable. No one could be around him long without realizing that he possessed an uncanny sense with horses. He never stopped to ask himself if he had inherited the gift from his father.

His sleeping accommodations were usually a bed of straw in either barn or stable, usually clean, mostly dry, and he expected no better. Sleeping under the stars was no hardship. He had been doing so for years.

Continually he moved on. He knew that his father had taken care of horses too, shoeing them and tending them when sick and sometimes training them for special uses. He began seeking out large ranches and livery stables, asking for work himself but also hoping to find the trail of another black man who may have come before him who was known for his skill with horses.

He worked for several months in Anderson, moved on to Greenwood, then south to Aiken, Orangeburg, north to Sumter, then west across the Wateree River. But nowhere did he hear anything. He spent the end of 1864 around Columbia, then again began to move northward, through Camden and Kershaw, eventually crossing the border into North Carolina as spring began to blossom throughout the South.

Through March and April, he moved through Robeson

and Cumberland counties, always looking, always listening. Gradually he began to realize how futile his search was. He was looking for one black man who might have changed his name, who might be dead, whom he probably wouldn't recognize if he saw him anyway.

Deep, undefined emotions still drove him on. He heard that the war had ended. He was now able to travel and work more openly.

As spring advanced, he was working in a livery stable in the town of Monroe. There he chanced to make the acquaintance of a black family traveling north who said they had heard of a freedman named Patterson.

"Where?" asked Jake.

"Don't rightly know, son. North of Charlotte sumplace."

"In da city?"

"Don't think so, young feller. Some town north er there. He was in a livery too, as I recolleck."

Jake was on the road again the next day, passed through Charlotte, where he worked for another week to earn money for food, then began walking from town to town as he moved out of the city to the north. He stayed for a week or two in every town of any size, picking up what work he could and asking the blacks he encountered if they knew a man called Patterson. As soon as he was satisfied there was nothing more to learn in one place, he moved on to another.

Increasingly reminded that he had forgotten what his father looked like played tricks on Jake's mind.

Thoughts and memories and images began to haunt him with more regularity. He did not seek them, but could not prevent them. The face of his mother was now with him always—smiling, loving, but watching . . . a gentle sadness in her eyes. She was sad because she saw the anger in the heart of her son. She was in a place now where he could hide nothing from her. She *knew*. But reaching out from the grave into his memory, she was powerless to heal his bitterness and make it go away.

With images of her came also unbidden images of his father, vague and shadowy and distant—smiles and laughter, and loving caresses from a father's hand. But when they came in his dreams, Jake pushed them away, silently rejecting the very touch of love he so desperately longed for.

Jake Patterson was a soul in torment. Yet whenever Micah Duff's words returned in his brain along with his mother's, he forced them away.

He began to dream horrible dreams of the man attacking his mother, and always they ended the same, with her cries for help. But Jake was not there to answer them. Then again came Micah's words—*"You're full of anger deep inside. You're trying to run from it, trying to hide from the light. But you can't escape it."*

Sometimes he awoke screaming out terrible curses in the night, as if to banish his inner demons of anger and guilt by sheer force of will.

But deep inside he knew he was living a lie. His own words to Micah returned to haunt him too—*"She's dead because of him!"*

But it was all a lie. He was blaming his father when he had no one to blame but himself. *He* had caused her to die. Not his father. There was no one else to blame . . . only him. But to admit it would be to relinquish the object of his anger. And that he was not yet ready to do.

The spring of 1865 gradually warmed and gave way to summer. Jake turned seventeen, and a look of dawning manhood had come to his eyes and cheeks. But it was a hard look. He rarely smiled now. And he still had to face manhood's greatest challenge—discovering who he was, and what he was going to do about it.

In North Carolina he made inquiries in every town he came to. By June he had gone through a dozen or more towns without learning a thing. Finally he came to a small town some twenty miles from Charlotte. Walking through it for the first time, he was used to the stares and looks as he asked if anyone knew where a black man might find work.

Some whites ignored him, some answered rudely or cursed at him, some spit at his feet. The more respectable merely turned up their noses and moved as far away from him as circumstances would allow. But here and there one answer might lead to another. The fellow blacks he met were always friendly.

Eventually, it seemed, something always turned up.

FATEFUL DISCOVERY
26

I T WAS ABOUT A WEEK LATER THAT JAKE GLANCED UP from where he was loading some boxes onto the back of a wagon in front of the hotel.

He had heard a delivery wagon clattering along the street but had hardly paid it any attention. As he looked toward the street he saw that its driver had reined in his team. A white man on the buckboard was staring down at him. A hot sun beat down and Jake's chest was dripping with sweat. It was the first week of July.

"Don't think I've seen you around here before, have I, son?" the man asked.

"No, suh."

"How long you been here?"

"Jes' a few days, suh."

"Just passing through looking for work?"

"Dat's right, suh."

"How long you figure to be working for the hotel here?" he asked, cocking his head toward the building behind Jake.

"Don't know, suh—likely anudder day er two."

"Would you like some steady work? I pay a fair wage to black or white."

"Dat I wud, suh. Effen you's got work, I kin do it."

"Then you come see me, son," said the man on the wagon. "I'm in the next town west of here—about four miles. Ask anyone where to find me. The name's Watson—what's your name, son?"

"Jake, suh."

"Well, I hope you'll come see me, Jake," he added, then slapped the reins and yelled his team back into motion.

Three days later, after asking directions from the hotel manager who had hired him for a few day's work, Jake was on his way to the next town in his long trek.

As he entered it, the town looked like any of thirty other towns Jake had been in during the last few years. He had grown into a man moving from place to place, and in many towns just like this one. This was the first time he was going to see a white man who had actually come to him asking if he needed a job.

"I's lookin' fo Mr. Watson," he said to the first person he saw.

Within an hour, he was hard at work loading sacks of grain into a wagon for a delivery to be made that same afternoon.

He worked several days, mostly inside a grain mill, loading and unloading. Then came a day without any deliveries.

"I don't have much for you to do today, Jake," said Mr. Watson. "I've arranged for you to work at the livery up the street. The owner's a friend of mine. Go up the street and see the black man there. He's expecting you. He'll put you to work."

Jake did so. The older man handed him a pitchfork, showed him where to dump the manure and straw from the stables, then disappeared for several hours. When he returned, a wagonload of various supplies stood in the street in front and they set about unloading it. As they worked, little was said between them, though several times Jake caught sight of the lanky Negro man gazing at him with an odd look of perplexity. Something about the man's voice sounded strangely nostalgic in Jake's ear. He couldn't quite lay his finger on the reason. But whenever the man spoke, strange sensations filled him as from a far-off dream, whose disappearing fragments he could not quite catch as wakefulness returned to his brain. And, like fleeting dreams, the harder he tried to grab on to them, the more quickly they retreated into forgetfulness.

He returned to Mr. Watson's at day's end feeling strangely uneasy. Yet at the same time a strange and quiet melody of peacefulness played distantly at the edges of his consciousness. That night he passed in Mr. Watson's storage barn as he had the last several nights. But he slept little. The melody of peace was drowned out while he was tossed about by many strident and undefined emotions flitting through his brain.

Back at work the next day for Mr. Watson, though tired from his restless night, Jake managed to lose himself in his work.

Another day passed. Then one of Mr. Watson's men was laid up by an injury to his hand. The owner summoned Jake.

"I've got to take this delivery out to one of the plantations myself, Jake," he said. "I want you to come with me to help unload it."

They made the delivery, then started on the hour-long return drive. On the way back to town, Jake spoke up. It was the first day he and the mill owner had been alone together.

"You min' ef I ax you a question, Mr. Watson?" Jake asked.

"Not at all," the man replied.

"You make deliveries all roun' 'bout here, so's you must know jes' 'bout everybody."

"I suppose I do, Jake," laughed Mr. Watson.

"You eber hear ob a black man called Hank Patterson?"

Mr. Watson stared back at him. "What kind of a question is that?" he said.

"I meant nuthin', Mr. Watson. I'd jes' like ter know, dat's all."

"Sure I know him, Jake."

"You know him!"

"Of course. You spent a whole day working with him up at the livery last week."

"Dat black man . . . dat's Hank Patterson!"

Watson nodded. "I've known him for years."

Jake was silent the rest of the way back to town. When they arrived at the mill, he jumped down from the wagon and ran up the street.

He flew into the livery stable in a flurry of emotions. There stood the black man. He glanced up and saw fire gleaming in Jake's eyes.

"Mr. Watson tells me yo name's Hank Patterson," Jake said in a demanding tone.

"Dat's so, all right. Though folks round here call me Henry."

"Why didn't you tell me?"

"You didn't ask."

"Well, I been lookin' fo you."

"You lookin' fo me—why dat?"

"'Cause my name's Jake . . . Jake Patterson."

The older man's eyes filled with tears. Slowly he approached and began to open his arms to embrace the son he thought he had lost forever.

"Don't you touch me," Jake said angrily, stepping back.

Stunned, his father stopped. His loving eyes were full of confusion. "What is it . . . *son?*" he said. "What you talkin' 'bout?"

All the pent-up anger of the years suddenly exploded to the surface like a long-smoldering volcano.

"Don't you call me yo son!" said Jake heatedly. "You lef'

us alone an' you said awful things 'bout me. You neber loved me. You cared more 'bout dat white boy Johnny Clarkson den me. You neber cared 'bout me an' den you lef' Mama an' me. You lef' her t' die, an' it's cuz ob you!''

"Yo . . . yo mama's . . . dead?'' said Jake's father in a halting voice. His eyes filled with tears.

"Yes, she's dead, an' it's cuz er you. Effen you'd been dere an' hadn't axed Massa Clarkson ter sell you an' lef' us all alone like you dun, maybe she'd still be alive!''

The poor man crumpled on a bale of straw, buried his face in his hands, and wept bitterly. But Jake was too young to be moved by such a display. He had not yet shed the tears of manhood. He did not yet know that there are no tears that pull with greater anguish at the heart than the honest tears of a quiet man's love.

Jake turned and stormed out of the livery, leaving the broken man who shared his name alone with his heartache, his tears, and his loss.

Accusation and Agony

27

TWENTY OR THIRTY MINUTES LATER, JAKE WALKED back into the cool shadows of the livery stable. Hank Patterson, the man whose name he had so long sought without thinking what he would do if he one day actually stood face to face with him, was still seated where he had so cruelly left him.

Jake's spirit had calmed, but his countenance remained dark and ominous. Clouds of cold, smoldering anger still brooded across his forehead and in his eyes.

He sat down and stared at the floor.

"I reckon you got a right ter hab yo say too," said Jake after a few long seconds. He thought himself wiser and more fair-minded than he really was by such a statement. He was not really ready to *listen*. He just wanted to be eased somewhat from the brief pangs of guilt for storming out as he had. But he was ready to lash out with more of the same should his anger boil to the surface again.

Like most boys his age, humility had not yet begun to change his certainty that his own ideas were more reliable than anyone else's. He was especially not about to listen to anything his father might say. His own resentments, based on images of incidents either misunderstood, remembered inaccurately, or that had never happened at all, were absolutely real in his brain. No amount of logic or reason, especially from his father, and certainly not his own father's tears, could dislodge them.

Gloomily Jake waited. Unconsciously in his pocket, his fingers turned the little carved horse over and over that had come with him so far. But he was not thinking about his mother right then, only himself.

"But . . . but you's got it all wrong, son," said his father at last. His voice was barely above a whisper.

"Says who . . . says *you*?" retorted Jake.

"Says one who wuz dere, son."

"An' I shud believe anythin' you say 'bout it?"

"It might be dat you shud believe one who knows what happened better'n a small boy who must hab got some parful wrong noshuns in his head sumhow."

"So . . . a boy can't see da truf 'bout his daddy?" said Jake. His anger was rising again.

"Not ef he's wrong, son. Chilluns don't ushally recollect things altogether da right way. De're too young, and sometimes too selfish ter see things da way dey really is. Da truf is, son, you's wrong 'bout all you said."

"Well, maybe it's *you* dat's wrong!" Jake shot back. "Maybe it's you dat don't remember what really happened back den."

The older man sighed. His grief to hear his grown son speak so was almost more overpowering than his tender heart could take.

"I do remember it, son," he said softly. "I wuz a growed man. You wuz jes' a boy. Dat's why I recollect it right, da way it really wuz. You's rememberin' it wrong, son. It didn't happen da way you think at all."

"Yeah . . . well, maybe I don't believe you! I think you jes' don't want ter face what a cruel man you wuz."

"You kin believe da truf, or you kin believe a lie, son. But dat don't change what da truf really is."

"An' you know what's true an' I don't?"

"Dat's right, son," said Mr. Patterson softly.

"I kin see dis wuz a mistake, thinkin' I cud talk t' you,"
said Jake angrily. "Yo mind's made up. You's not gwine listen ter nuthin' I gots ter say. You jes' won't see dat what you
done ter me wuz wrong!"

Jake jumped up and began to storm off again.

"I thought you said I had a right ter my say too," said the
voice of his father behind him.

Jake stopped. The words hit him hard. The man was
right.

"Seems ter me dat you's da one not wantin' ter listen,"
added his father. "I'm sittin' here calm-like wiffout raisin' my
voice an' jes' axin' you ter let me tell you what happened, an'
you's da one rantin' an' stormin' round angrier den a hungry
bull dog when you ain't got as much cause ter be angry wiff
me as you think. Where dat anger come from, son, I don't
know. But you's a mighty angry young man. So you kin storm
off effen you want, or you kin listen to sum truf dat you's got
all twisted up in dat brain er yourn."

He stopped. Jake sat down again and waited. It was silent
a long while.

"Dere came a day in my life," began Hank Patterson at
length, "when ef I'd hab wanted ter become a hatin' man I'd
look back on dat day as when hate cud hab entered my soul
an' neber lef' it. I ain't sayin' dere ain't been bitterness an'
sum anger on account er it. But thank God I kep' hate from
consumin' me. An' I pray I'm still learnin' ter forgive fo dat
black day dat destroyed a thing dat's precious in God's sight,
a family.

"It wuz da day w'en Mr. Clarkson come ter me in da fields
an' took me an' said he was sendin' me up ter his brudder's
plantation fo a spell ter help wiff da horse trainin'. I started
ter walk back tards da slave village an' he yelled after me,

'Where you think you's goin', Patterson?' he says. An' I said dat I wuz goin' back ter tell my wife an' ter say good-bye ter my son an' tell him dat I loved him. 'You ain't goin' nowhere, Patterson,' he says back. 'You's leabin' fo Carolina right now.' An' den one er his men took me ter da train, an' afore I knowed it I was on my way wiff him.

"An' I done my work up here in Carolina fo a few munfs, an' den Mr. Clarkson's brudder, he sent me back home. An' what shud I fin' when I git dere but dat you an' yo mama'd been sol', an' Mr. Clarkson jes' laughed when I axed him where you wuz. He wudn't tell me, an' nobody'd tell me, an' I don't think none ob da other slaves eben knew, on account er Mr. Clarkson keepin' it from dem ter punish me cuz I wudn't call him *Master*.

"My heart wuz like ter break in two. I cried mysel' ter sleep many er night fo love ob you an' yo mama, but dere weren't nuthin' I cud do ter fin' where he'd sol' you to. Nobody knowed, or effen dey did, dey wudn't tell me. But ol' Beulah up t' da big house, she tol' me dat she'd oberheard Mister an' Mistress Clarkson talkin' 'bout me one day an' 'bout *Carolina*. She didn't know dey'd jes' sen' me dere for a spell, an' she thought dey'd sol' me an' dat I wuz a slave on some plantashun in Carolina an' she tol' me she'd tol' yo mama dat I wuz in Carolina. An' dat tore at my heart all da more, knowin' dat she didn't know dat I wuz back right dere an' dat you might er been jes' a few miles away but dat I cudn't fin' you."

He stopped and wiped at his eyes and face, tears pouring down his rough black cheeks to live the memory all over again.

"Den came anudder day when everythin' changed agin," he struggled to go on. "Mr. Clarkson, he had him a partickerly ornery horse dat no one cud break. He wuz a cruel man an' he took delight in watchin' dat animal hurt whoever tried ter ride it. One day came when he an' anudder plantashun

owner had been drinkin' more den dey shud, an' Mr. Clarkson started talkin' big ter da men gathered roun' an' den he
shouted out ter his slaves, more showin' off ter his friend den
anythin'. He said, 'Whoever kin break dis horse, I'll gib you
yo freedom.' He figgered we wuz all so scared ob dat horse,
none ob us wud try, or, effen we did, we'd git trampled ter
death an' he wudn't have cared. But I'd been watchin' dat
horse's habits an' by den I knowed everythin' I needed to
'bout dat wild beast, an' I wuzn't scared ob what it might do.

"So I steps up an' I looked Mr. Clarkson right in his eyes
an' I says, 'You gib me yo word on dat?' He wuz half drunk,
but Mr. Clarkson laughed an' looked ober at his frien' an' den
said he did. I don't figger he dreamed dat anythin' wud come
ob it 'cept maybe dat I'd git trampled.

"'How much you figger a trained horse like dis be worth?'
I axed. 'As much as a man-slave?' 'I always say a good horse
is worth twice as much as a slave!' said Clarkson, lookin' at
his frien' an' laughing.

"'So I got yo word dat if I deliver dis horse ter you
trained, it be worth my freedom?' I said.

"'Sure, whatever you say, Patterson!' He laughed agin.

"So I walked inter dat corral an' I start talkin' real soft like
I duz wiff horses. An' I reckon dey wuz a mite amazed when
dat wild thing wuz lettin' Mr. Clarkson himsel' ride him
before dat day wuz done. Mr. Clarkson wuz furious wiff rage,
thinkin' dat I'd duped him wiff some trick. But because he'd
gib his word in front ob his neighbor, he had no choice but
ter gib me my freedom. I begged him ter tell me where you
an' yo mama wuz. But by den he hated me all da more, an'
he jes' laughed in my face an' tol' me ter git off his property
wiff my paper er freedom.

"After dat, I traveled roun', gittin' what work I cud, but
when da war started dat wuz hard enuff. All I wanted wuz ter
put enuff food in my stomach ter keep me alive so dat I could
fin' you an' yo mama. I searched everywhere. I must hab axed

MEETING

28

J AKE STUMBLED OUT, A HURRICANE OF CONFUSING thoughts exploding within him.

Could he really have been . . . so *wrong* all these years? Had his father truly *loved* him, and yet he had harbored such anger and bitterness toward him?

Could his years of anger all been based on misperceptions, on things that his childish eyes had seen twisted and contorted from what had really happened? Had the anger originated *within him* more than from anything his father had actually *done*?

The questions were too huge. He could not face them. They probed too deep into his youthful pride. He had lived so long by feeding off his anger toward his father. Suddenly he hardly knew who he was. Was he willing to find out what kind of person he might be . . . if somehow the anger in his heart was *gone*?

He halfway came to himself standing on the street. Suddenly he remembered Mr. Watson. He broke into a run back to the mill where he was supposed to be working.

He found Mr. Watson growing a little perturbed at his lengthy disappearance.

"I's sorry, Mr. Watson," he said. "I didn't eben stop ter

think after you said dat name."

"I am afraid I don't understand what it's all about," said Mr. Watson.

"Dat man up at da livery, Hank Patterson—he's my pa," said Jake. "I been lookin' fo him. I had no idea where he wuz till I axed you."

"If that don't beat all!" said Mr. Watson with a smile. "I've heard him mention you!"

"He talked 'bout me?"

"Not too often. But I knew he'd been keeping an eye out for his son for years. Every time he'd start to say something, a look of pain came over his face and I figured I oughtn't to ask any questions."

He shook his head again. "I just had no idea!"

"Neither did I, Mr. Watson."

"Then I think this calls for a celebration. You take the rest of the day off, Jake. Go be with your pa. Come back to work tomorrow."

"Dat's right kind ob you, Mr. Watson. Kin I still sleep in yo barn out yonder?"

"Of course, Jake."

Jake left the mill and walked slowly back in the direction of the livery, full of many thoughts. Suddenly his life had been turned upside down, though he wasn't quite sure how. His father was standing at the entrance waiting for him.

Neither spoke, but as he approached, Jake extended his hand and looked into his father's face. They shook hands.

It was a beginning. All relationships take time. Sometimes the ones closest take the most time of all.

"I been workin' at Mr. Watson's fo a spell," said Jake. "I ran down ter tell him why I lef' him so sudden."

"You need ter git back ter work?" asked the older man.

"He said I cud come back tomorrow," answered Jake. "I tol' him what happened—'bout you an' me."

As they spoke, they began walking along the street, no

destination in mind. They were just walking as they talked.

"Mr. Watson's a fine man. How you'd happen ter be workin' fo him?"

"He saw me at anudder town a few miles away. He axed ef I needed work an' I tol' him I did. So he tol' me ter come see him, an' I did."

Down the street a wagon was coming toward them. Two girls were seated on it. As Jake glanced toward it, he thought they looked a little young to be wielding a big wagon and team of horses by themselves.

"By the way," said Jake's father, "duz you min' ef I call you by yo real name dat me an' yo mama gib you?"

Momentarily Jake bristled at the negative memories the name had held for so many years. But the reminder of his mother softened his reply.

"I reckon not," he shrugged. "Ain't nobody called me dat in years."

"It'd mean a lot ter me, son. It'd remin' me ob yo mama."

The wagon coming down the street drew closer. Henry looked toward it, then paused and tipped his hat to the two girls. Jake could now see that one of the girls was white and the other was colored. He thought it strange that both were sitting on the seat together. Usually black folks bounced along in the back of a wagon.

"Mo'nin' to you, Miz Kathleen," Henry called out.

"Hello, Henry," said the white girl, pulling back on the reins.

Henry walked toward the wagon and spoke to the white girl for a few minutes. That in itself seemed unusual to Jake—if not dangerous. His father seemed mighty familiar with her, more so than with the colored girl sitting beside her.

"How's yo mama, Miz Kathleen?" his father asked.

"Uh . . . everything's just fine, Henry."

Jake noticed that the girl didn't answer the question directly. And from the funny expression on his father's face, he had noticed it too. Jake felt the eyes of the colored girl on him. He glanced up at her, but she quickly glanced away. Jake guessed she was about his own age, or maybe a year or two younger.

The white girl turned to look at her as well.

"This is Mayme," she said. "She's going to . . . to be working for us."

Jake heard the hesitation in her voice and wondered what that meant.

"Dat right nice," said Henry. "How'do, Miz Mayme. Ah's pleased ter make yo 'quaintance."

Henry glanced toward Jake and then back to the two girls. "I don' bleeve you two ladies has eber made 'quaintance wiff my son Jeremiah.—Jeremiah, say hello ter Miz Kathleen an' Miz Mayme."

Jake took off his hat and looked down at the ground, feeling suddenly embarrassed. Despite himself, he liked the way his full name sounded when his father said it.

"How do," he said, trying to smile up at the girls. "Glad t' know you both."

"I never knew you had a son, Henry," said Kathleen.

"I neber talked about him much," replied Henry. "It hurt too much ter 'member him. 'Twas all I could do ter keep from cryin' downright like er baby when I thought 'bout it. Him an' his mama, dey wuz sol' away from me when he was jes' a young'un. An' after I got my freedom, I search high an' low ter fin' 'em, but I neber foun' so much as a tiny noshun where dey might hab git to. But Jeremiah come alookin' fer me. It took him a heap er years, but his mama'd tol' him enuff where fer him ter come all dis way here ter Greens Crossing, an' he dun foun' me jes' a little while ago."

Once or twice while his father was talking, Jake stole another glance at the girl named Mayme from the corner of his eye. Her hair was covered in a kerchief, but he thought her face was real pretty. Her skin was lighter than his own, and her hands, held stiff in her lap, were rough from hard work. She glanced up and saw him looking at her, then quickly looked away again. Her eyes were nice too, he decided. But from then on, she kept those nice eyes of hers on her lap.

"Is your wife here too?" asked Kathleen.

"I'm sorry t' say she ain't, Miz Kathleen. She din't make it through da war."

"Oh . . . I'm sorry."

"Dat's right kind er you t' say, Miz Kathleen.—Say, hit seems ter me dat bridle er yers is frayin' an' 'bout ter break. You don' want ter hab no horse runnin' loose wiffout a good bit in his mouf. Why don' you two come ter da livery an' let me an' Jeremiah put on a new piece er leather? Won' take but er jiffy."

"Uh, we don't have time just now. We've got to get back. Well . . . good-bye, Henry," said Kathleen, giving the horses a swat with the reins.

The two girls went on their way. Father and son watched them go, each intrigued for his own reasons.

⤳ ✳ ⤲

One of those girls was me. My name's Mayme. Mayme Jukes. And that was the first time I had ever laid eyes on Jeremiah Patterson.

I had seen Henry a time or two before that day but had never been introduced to him. My friend and I— well, she was more than just a *friend*, but that part of the story I'll have to tell you later—we had come into town and had just left the general store when Henry greeted us from across the street. She had known Henry for years. My friend's name was Kathleen Clairborne, or Katie for short. She was white. I was colored.

As Katie spoke with the man named Henry, I couldn't

help looking at the black boy a year or so older than me who was standing beside him. And once or twice while Henry was talking, I could tell that Jeremiah was looking at me out of the corner of his eye too. I felt my neck and face getting hot all over, but I tried to keep staring down at my lap and pretend I didn't notice.

As we rode away down the street, I was dying to glance back, and almost did too. But I didn't, because I could feel their eyes watching us ride away.

"Did you notice that look on that fellow Henry's face?" I asked. "He didn't seem too altogether pleased with your answer after he asked about your mama."

"He's always been nice to me," Katie said, "nicer than just about anyone. But I didn't really notice Henry too much with his son standing there. I can't believe it. And to think that they haven't seen each other in all those years."

I didn't reply. I didn't know what to say about Henry's son.

As Katie and I rode away, both of us were quiet, lost in our own thoughts. Katie likely thinking of how she had fooled that nosy ol' Mrs. Hammond at the general store and me thinking about the all-too inquisitive look in Henry's eyes—and about his son. I have to admit, I couldn't help thinking about the boy called Jeremiah for the rest of the day. In the eyes of a fifteen-year-old colored girl, he was just about the best-looking boy I'd ever seen.

So that's how Jeremiah and I met. Now that you know how Jeremiah—or Jake, as he used to go by— came to be in Greens Crossing that day and about his search for his papa, I reckon I'd better tell you a little about Katie and me and what *we* were doing there.

REMEMBERING
29

*K*atie and I had met by accident a couple of months
before that, right about the time the War Between the
States had ended. In those days right after the war,
things were a mite different than they became later. But
in another way of looking at it, I don't reckon things
really are ever all that different. People are still people
and they still have to live together and get along. People
of different skin still have trouble sharing this old world
together. Kinda funny, it's always seemed to me. You'd
figure folks would enjoy their differences and wouldn't
all want to be the same. But strange to say, that's not
how it is. All through history, I suppose, people haven't
liked those who were different from them. You might
say that's just about been at the root of all the world's
problems. I don't understand it myself, but then that's
the way it seems to be.

When it comes to the differences between people of
white skin and people of what you'd call colored skin,
that's where the differences and disputes and conflicts
seem to be worst of all.

After the war, slaves like Jake and me had been
freed from slavery, but we hadn't been freed from the

white man's feelings against black people. In a way I reckon you might say those feelings had even gotten worse since freedom had come to us. Before that, colored folks were more or less just taken for granted in lots of ways. As a race, I don't think whites figured colored folks were worth hating. We were just stupid in their eyes, so why bother hating us?

But after the War Between the States and the Emancipation Proclamation, hatred started to grow between whites and coloreds. And while nothing is as bad as slavery, we weren't *really* "free," because hatred and prejudice creates an invisible bondage of its own, just as sure as had the chains of the white masters.

I know what both kinds of bondage are like, 'cause like Jeremiah I used to be a slave too—I'm only half colored, but in the eyes of whites that makes you what people now call "black," though my skin isn't anywhere close to that. My skin's brown. That's about the best way to put it.

Now in one way I don't reckon Katie and me were so unusual. We were just two girls that circumstances happened to throw together. But the fact that we became such good friends—one of us white, the other black—was one of the reasons we always considered our friendship so precious—*because* we were different, not because we were the same. In fact I think our differences made us closer than we would have been otherwise.

Katie and me were different in more ways than just the color of our skin and her blond hair and my black hair. We were different people *inside*, with different personalities and different ways of looking at things. Those differences were what made our friendship stronger.

Katie and I grew up to be women together during

those years when white people were looking at colored people in different ways. Some white folks were looking at them and realizing that they were people too, just like them in many ways, and learning to care about them and even love them. Other white folks were looking at colored people and beginning to hate them.

During our years as young girls, Katie and I never knew each other. In fact, we'd never so much as laid eyes on one another, even though the plantations where we grew up were only a few miles apart.

The war between the North and the South came in 1861, but it didn't change things in my life as it did Katie's. Slaves kept right on working like before. For a colored girl like me, who was only eleven when the war broke out, I hardly even knew what the fighting was all about. None of us knew at first when Northern president Mr. Lincoln freed all the slaves, 'cause most Southern slave owners ignored his proclamation anyway. The South had declared itself a separate country, so why did they need to pay any attention to what Mr. Lincoln said? For us slaves, life just went on day after day as it always had. But as I turned twelve and then thirteen and then fourteen, I began to wonder what would happen to *me*. It's God's mercy I was skinny as a rail and nothing much to look at, and that kept anything *too* bad from happening to me—except for an occasional whipping by Master McSimmons or one of his sons.

But for Katie, it was different. The war changed everything about her life. Until then, her life had been pretty calm and pleasant. She had been able to grow up in the kind of luxury that daughters of plantation owners enjoyed all over the South. Then suddenly the war came and her daddy and brothers left to fight, and Katie's mama had to run the plantation all by herself.

As Katie got older, her mama depended on Katie for help and the hard work was new for her.

Then came a terrible day just after the war ended when Katie's and my lives would change forever. A band of bad men called Bilsby's marauders rampaged through the region and killed all the rest of Katie's family, and everyone at the slave village on the plantation where I lived except for me. We were both left all alone in the world—at least we thought so at the time—on the same day. I set out from home mainly just to get away from anyone who might want to hurt me. I didn't have any idea where I was going. Eventually I wound up at Katie's house.

Those were awful days, getting used to being alone, remembering the killing, burying Katie's family. We were a fifteen-year-old black girl and a fourteen-year-old white girl who didn't know each other. But we survived and became friends.

A little while later another slave from the Mc-Simmons plantation wound up living at Rosewood too. Her name was Emma and she was a tall, scatter-brained colored girl. She was real good-looking—so good-looking, in fact, that she'd got herself pregnant by Mr. McSimmons, who was now looking for her and trying to kill her and her little baby called William.

So besides keeping ourselves alive after our families were killed, Katie and me were trying to protect Emma and William from anything bad happening to them.

During our time together, Katie showed me books and helped me learn to read better. And I taught her how to do things like milk cows and chop wood and sing slave songs. She read me stories from books and I told her stories I'd heard and made up. And it didn't take long before Katie was doing all kinds of things for herself. Even though I was older, and Katie was always telling me that she wouldn't have Rosewood anymore if it weren't for me, if anybody could have been said to be in charge around the place, it was Katie.

Just before Jeremiah arrived in Greens Crossing, Katie had come up with an idea that would keep people from finding out we were alone at Rosewood. We didn't want people to know we were alone together because of how young we were and what might happen if anyone found out. I called it "Katie's scheme." What it meant was that we were trying to pretend that everything was normal at Rosewood, and that it was still functioning like a regular plantation ought to. To do that meant pretending that Katie's mama was still alive. Rosewood was far enough away from Greens Crossing that nobody in town knew about the massacre that had killed Katie's family.

What we figured was that if no one knew we were alone, they wouldn't come and take us away or hurt us, and that none of Katie's relatives—she had three uncles we were worried about—would come and take the plantation for themselves and put Katie in a home for people without parents and do something even more awful with me.

So that was our scheme—to keep secret that we were alone.

We had just begun Katie's plan about a week before. In fact, that day when I first met Jeremiah was our first trip to town after Katie'd thought of it. So we were a mite nervous, especially because of a certain nosey shopkeeper named Mrs. Hammond, who also kept the mail and who we were afraid might figure out what we were doing.

We were nervous about Henry too, because we didn't know what he might do if he found out either. I thought he'd looked at Katie a little suspicious a time or two. So we were anxious to get out of there after he'd introduced us to Jeremiah. We didn't want Henry asking too many questions. But as we bounded off on the wagon on our way back to Rosewood, I was thinking about the boy I'd just seen for the first time!

But now I reckon I should tell you a little more about what Jeremiah was thinking and feeling at the same time, right after he met me and Katie.

⌒ ❋ ⌒

CHANGES
30

H ENRY AND JEREMIAH WATCHED THE WAGON AS IT
bounced down the road, the two girls sitting close
together on the seat, heads close, talking.

"Sumfin mighty strange goin' on," Henry muttered.

Jake wasn't sure what he meant, but something strange
was going on inside him when he looked at that girl called
Mayme. As the wagon disappeared from sight, Jake stared
after it. But gradually his thoughts returned to the present.

He had located his father. But it wasn't at all what he had
expected.

Now he found himself having to do some serious soul-
searching. He had thought one thing was true for so long that
it was part of him. Could he really believe what his father had
told him? Could everything he had always believed about him
not have been right at all? After everything his pa told him,
Jake was more confused than he'd ever been in his life.

His father's voice interrupted his thoughts.

"Now dat I tol' you sum ob what happened ter me,"
Henry said, "I'd be right pleased ter hear 'bout you, Jeremiah, an' what happened . . . an' 'bout yo mama."

The words brought Jake back to the present and reminded
him of the conflict he was feeling inside. He was not quite

ready to tell his father everything. But as they resumed walking along the street, he told Henry a sketchy version of events.

When Henry heard what his former owner Clarkson had done and what his overseer had said, he was both furious and heartbroken. A righteous indignation rose inside him at the cruelty of such men. How could they toy with a child's feelings, and then tear his family apart?

"I's so sorry, son," he said in a soft and tender voice. "I wud neber hab said sumfin like dat."

For the first time, Henry understood what had happened to him and his wife and his son. Suddenly it all made sense. Clarkson's motives had only been to get back at him.

"I loved you and yo mama so much!" Henry blurted out after a minute.

His own words turned his thoughts again to the woman he had loved. A new stab of pain went through Henry's heart at the reminder that she was dead.

"You wuz da apple ob dis father's eye," he added. "I's so sorry you had ter hear a dreadful thing like dat man said. I can't even imagine da pain ob how dat must hab hurt!"

Henry's heart was twisted in knots. And for the son he never expected to see again to lash out in angry accusation as he had a few minutes earlier was almost more than Henry's tender heart could bear.

"I tried ter fin' you after I come back," Henry went on, his eyes wet with tears. "But dey wudn't tell me nuthin'. Dat Clarkson, he jes' laughed at me an' my tears. I tried everything ter fin' what had happened ter you an' yo mama. Den after I got my freedom an' Beulah tol' me what she tol' yo mama, I spent a few years roun' dere axin' everywhere an' travelin' about, an' den figgered to come here."

The father's words softened the heart of the son. But inside remained many swirling and conflicting emotions. It was not so easy to suddenly erase a lifetime of memories just because his father now told him they weren't true. The hurts of those memories for Jeremiah were real enough. The pain had been real, even if the facts causing them hadn't been. Even hearing the truth didn't remove the pain from Jeremiah's heart.

The first days after that between Henry and Jeremiah were awkward. Gradually they got used to being around each other and were able to talk more freely. The awkwardness was mainly on Jeremiah's side. For Henry's father-heart, the years were gone in an instant. He could have taken Jeremiah in his arms and poured out his love as he had so freely done in the years that were now mostly lost to Jeremiah's memory. But for Jeremiah the years did not so easily fall away.

Whether Jeremiah's resentments had been based on a falsehood or on reality hardly mattered. They had been real because the pain of supposed rejection had been real. Jeremiah's anger was so deeply ingrained by now that its chains were not easy to break. He needed to be freed from them. But the key to that freedom was forgiveness. The fact that those perceptions had been born in his own mind only made it harder for forgiveness to reach into him.

Slowly Jeremiah and Henry established a new footing for their relationship. But most of the change came because of Henry's deep love, and the free forgiveness in his heart. But Jeremiah didn't yet recognize how wrong his own anger toward Henry had been.

For now that remained something he could not face.

For the next few weeks, Jeremiah went through a lot of changes, getting used to having a papa and living in one place for the first time in years. He and Henry were having more talks, though it was hard learning to be a father and son again. Jeremiah found himself remembering his many conversations with Micah Duff and wondered where the young soldier was now.

Eventually Jeremiah moved in with Henry, sharing his

father's two rooms behind the livery stable, but he kept working at Mr. Watson's mill.

One morning, Henry asked Jeremiah, "What you doin'
today, son?"

"Nothin' much. Mr. Watson don't need me today."

"How 'bout doin' me a favor?"

Jeremiah shrugged. He had been looking forward to lying
on his pallet most of the morning. His father didn't seem to
notice his apathetic gesture. He stood staring out of the small
room's single window.

"I been thinkin' 'bout dem two girls," Henry began.
"Wonderin' . . ."

Suddenly Jeremiah didn't feel quite so lazy. "You talkin'
about those two girls we met a while back? That white girl
and colored girl together?" He propped himself up on his
elbow.

"Dat's right. Miz Kathleen and Miz . . . Now what wuz
dat udder girl's name . . . ?"

"Mayme," Jeremiah answered.

"Dat's right. Miz Mayme. Reckon you might walk on out
to the Clairborne place and check on dem? I kin tell you jes'
how to find it."

Jeremiah couldn't help thinking of his reception at the
Dawson place. "I'm jes' gonna show up at some white man's
place and ax 'how'do'?"

"Word is Mr. Clairborne an' his sons ain't made it back
from de war," Henry said, "an' Mistress Clairborne has
knowed me fer years."

"But not me."

"Dat's all right. You see Mistress Clairborne, you tell her
who you is. *Effen* you see her."

"Why you want me ter go?"

"You 'member dat bridle er ders? Seems ter me it wuz
frayin' an' 'bout ter break. Don' want no horse runnin' loose
wiffout a good bit in his mouf. It wud ease my min' effen you

cud check on dat for me. Mebbe eben fix it. Reckon you know how?''

"I learned some when I rode wiff the army. An' I seen you do it 'nough times dese last few weeks."

"I shore wud feel better effen I knew Mistress Clairborne wuz all right. Ain't seen her since I don't know w'en."

"Miz Kathleen's mama, you mean?"

"Dat's right. You ax after her, you hear? An' ef you git no answer 'bout where she is an' don't see her wiff yer own eyes, you make sure dose young ladies is all right."

Jeremiah wasn't sure what his father meant about Mistress Clairborne. Truth be known, he didn't care all that much. What he did care about was an excuse to see Mayme again.

Jeremiah washed up and put on his best shirt and struck out, following the route his father had described. He walked and walked, wondering at the welcome he might receive at this place called Rosewood. Jeremiah was beginning to think he'd lost his way when the roof of a large house finally came into view. The house was white and two stories tall, with a porch that ran around two sides of it. There were several other smaller buildings and sheds nearby, a smokehouse and a little shed that sat on top of the ice cellar. There was a big barn with stables connected to it and a fenced-in pigpen. Fields stretched out around the house on three sides, woods on the other with a stream running through it. It was a big place. Nicer than the Clarkson place had been. But still, something didn't seem right. The place looked run-down and it was too quiet. He saw no one about. As Jeremiah reached the house, he began to understand his father's concern.

SURPRISE CALLER
31

*D*uring the time since I'd first seen Jeremiah, I'd gone back to visit my old home at the McSimmons plantation and had seen one of the house slaves there who hadn't been killed in the massacre, a big loving lady named Josepha. I was relieved to know Josepha was all right, but I was a mite sad to see the old place again and relive memories of my years there. I still missed my family and grieved for them, but I was glad to be living at Rosewood now.

One day, Katie and me, along with the pretty colored girl named Emma, were all in the kitchen together. When we heard the knock on the door, we all stopped what we'd been doing. Katie and I glanced at each other. We'd been so involved in making cheese at the time that we hadn't heard anyone coming toward the house.

Katie looked at me again, then slowly got up and walked to the door. I didn't know whether we should all run and hide or stay and pretend that nothing was wrong. We'd hardly had any visitors to Rosewood since deciding to pretend Katie's mama was still alive. We didn't know how to act or what to do not to give our secret away. It was too late to hide anyway—there we all were messy and with our sleeves rolled up, and there was the figure of whoever it was standing at the kitchen door.

Slowly Katie opened the door. Standing in front of her was the last person either of us expected to see— the boy we'd met only once before.

"Afternoon t' you, Miz Clairborne," said Jeremiah. "My pa thought dat you might be needin' dat bridle ob yers fixed so it don' break on you."

Taken by surprise, Katie just stood for a second or two. From where I was on the other side of the room I saw that Jeremiah was holding some leather and tools.

"Is . . . uh, Miz Mayme here?" he asked.

I heard the question in his deep voice. I don't know if Jeremiah saw me or not, but my heart started beating faster the minute he said my name.

"Mayme," Katie said, turning her head. "Henry's son . . . uh, Jeremiah came to mend that broken bridle—would you show him where it is . . . in the barn?"

I could tell from her voice that she was nervous. I knew she didn't want anyone, least of all someone who was curious, looking too closely at what was going on inside the kitchen—though Jeremiah was standing right there at the open door. In Katie's mind I was the logical one to get him away from the house.

I walked toward the door and stepped past Jeremiah onto the porch. The instant I was outside, Katie shut the door behind me.

I didn't look at Jeremiah, but walked down the steps and toward the barn. He followed. I glanced back and saw Katie's face in the window.

"Where's your horse?" I asked.

"Don' have one, Miz Mayme," said Jeremiah. "I walked."

"All the way from town?"

"Yes'm."

"That's a long way."

"My pa thought Miz Clairborne mite be needin' dat bridle. He's been worried it would break."

I thought to myself that I wished Henry showed a little less concern about us!

"An' I been wantin' a chance t' try ter see Miz Clairborne an' yersel' agin," he added, speaking slowly. Heat rose up the back of my neck. I didn't say anything and didn't dare glance over at him.

"Ain't too many young folks my age 'bout town," he said. "Leastways, no coloreds. Now dat we're free, dey all lef', I reckon.—Is you free too, Miz Mayme?"

"What do you mean?" I said. "Of course—don't you know about whatever it's called, that proclamation?"

"I know, but why you still here, den?"

"Where else would I be?"

"Why ain't you lef'?"

"I've got no place to go. This is my home."

"Your ma an' pa here too?"

"No."

"Where are dey?"

"I don't know."

"Don' you want ter fin' dem, now dat ye're free?" asked Jeremiah.

"I can't find them," I said. I was getting uncomfortable with so many questions, especially about my kin. "I told you—this is my home. I don't have anyplace else to go. I don't want to go someplace else."

"Mister an' Mistress Clairborne pay you?" Jeremiah asked.

The question took me off guard. I didn't know what to say.

"I've got all I need," I said. "I've got food and a bed, and . . ."

I paused briefly.

". . . and folks who care about me," I said.

"Yep . . . I reckon dat's mighty important."

"And Katie . . . I mean, Miss Clairborne needs me," I added.

I don't know why I was talking so much, but it was easy to talk to Jeremiah. I'd been around plenty of boys of my own color before. But this was different than any situation I'd been in . . . just *talking* to a black boy my own age. It was different than it would have been back at the colored town when I'd been a slave. If there'd been a black boy like Jeremiah and me standing together, we wouldn't have been talking. We'd have been standing there keeping our mouths shut while some white man looked us over wondering what kind of babies we'd make together.

But now we were just two people . . . two *free* people. Nobody was watching us. Nobody was thinking anything. We could just talk. It felt good.

"You make it soun' like you an' Miz Clairborne's frien's," said Jeremiah.

"We are," I said with a little laugh. "What's so strange about that?"

"I jest neber thought ob it afore, I reckon."

"Miss Katie couldn't get by without me . . . or me without her either," I said. "I don't know what would become of us if we hadn't—"

I stopped myself. Feeling comfortable talking to Jeremiah was one thing, but I didn't want to be the one to give away Katie's scheme!

"I mean . . . *they* . . ." I said, fumbling to correct

myself, "—*they* took me in and helped me, and—well, that's all."

Again I stopped. Jeremiah was looking at me funny.

"What do you mean . . . took you in?" he said. "Weren't you one ob dere slaves?"

"Uh . . . yes—that's what I meant to say. I mean, they let me stay."

"Where's Mister and Mistress Clairborne?" he asked. "My pa wanted me t' ask dem somethin' fo him."

"Katie's pa ain't back from the war."

"What about Mistress Clairborne—she in da house? I din't see nobody but jest two other girls, an one ob dem was colored."

"She's . . . she's somewhere and it ain't . . . well, it ain't none of your business where she is," I said.

I turned and led the way into the barn.

"Here's that bridle," I said. "Just fix it and mind your own business."

Jeremiah set about his work with the straps of leather and few tools he had. I saw him looking around the barn. I knew he was noticing things.

I walked outside, more mad at myself than him. I hoped I hadn't got us into a worse fix. I went back to the kitchen. Katie and the others were waiting for me.

"I don't think he'll be too long," I said. "We can finish the cheese when he's gone."

Then I went back outside and waited on the porch.

Five or ten minutes later Jeremiah came out of the barn.

"Got it mended," he said. "Reckon I'll jes' tell Miz Clairborne."

He climbed the steps and knocked on the door again. Katie had been watching and immediately opened it.

"Bridle's fixed, Miz Clairborne," said Jeremiah.

"Thank you," said Katie.

"Anything else you'd like dun aroun' da place?"

"Uh, no . . . but thank you," said Katie. Then without waiting for anything further, she closed the door.

Slowly he came back down the three or four steps to where I was standing.

"Well . . . reckon I'll be headin' back t' town," he said slowly. "You, uh . . . you min' if I come out agin?"

"I don't think Miss Katie, I mean Miss Clairborne—" I started to say.

"No, Miz Mayme . . . I mean, does *you* min' if I comes fer a visit?"

"What would you want to visit for?"

"I thought maybe I'd come t' visit you, dat's all. An' my pa, he said dat if I asked 'bout Mistress Clairborne an' got no answer 'bout where she was an' din't see her wiff my own eyes—dat he wanted me ter make sure you young ladies wuz all right."

"What did he mean by that?" I said.

"Nuthin', miss . . . just what I said. Dat's why he wanted me ter come out an' men' dat bridle, 'cuz he wanted ter know if you an' Miz Clairborne wuz all right."

"Well, you can tell him we're fine," I said. "And that he ought to mind his own business too."

I shouldn't have said it. Jeremiah looked at me funny. Then he shrugged and turned and started walking along the road back toward town. I watched him a minute, then suddenly ran after him.

"Jeremiah!" I called out.

He stopped and turned back toward me.

"Please . . . don't tell," I said.

"Tell what?" he asked.

"What you saw here—who you saw in the

kitchen . . . what you said before about only seeing us girls."

He looked at me seriously, and it was the first time we'd both looked in each other's eyes.

"What you really want me not ter say," he said after a few seconds, "is what I *ain't* seen, an' dat's Mistress Clairborne—ain't dat right, Miz Mayme?"

"Please," I said without really answering him, "you *can't* tell. Please promise you won't tell anyone."

"Dat's a hard one, Miz Mayme," said Jeremiah finally. "Reckon I'll have ter think on dat some on my way home."

That was the first day Jeremiah and I talked alone together. That part of his coming out had been nice. But suddenly, without us planning it, someone knew that something fishy was going on at Rosewood—and that someone was Jeremiah Patterson! I knew if he thought long enough about what he'd seen, he'd start figuring out Katie's scheme.

❧ ✻ ❧

TO THE RESCUE
32

JEREMIAH DIDN'T SEE MAYME OR KATIE AGAIN FOR A while. He was busy working in town, and Rosewood was a long way from Greens Crossing.

But then one day, when Jeremiah was helping his father in the livery, he heard a galloping horse approaching. He didn't think much of it until he heard Katie's voice out front.

"Where's Jeremiah?" she called, clearly in a panic.

"Back dere cleanin' out da livery," began Henry. "But what's you—"

Before he finished his sentence, Katie ran past him through the doorway.

"Jeremiah . . . Jeremiah!" she called in the dim light. "Jeremiah—it's Katie Clairborne . . . please, I need your help. Mayme's in trouble."

Jeremiah dropped the pitchfork in his hand and stepped forward.

"Some men have got Mayme," said Katie frantically. "White men . . . and I'm afraid. Can you help us?"

"Jest lead da way, Miz Clairborne."

Katie turned and ran back outside as Jeremiah hurried to catch up.

"I ain' got no horse er my own," he said.

"You can ride with me!" said Katie. She ran to her horse and jumped onto its back. "Climb up and sit behind the saddle."

Less than a minute later, Katie was flapping the reins and galloping through town, leaving Henry watching them go, along with townspeople no doubt shocked to see a white girl and colored boy on the same horse.

Jeremiah caught a glimpse of the storekeeper, Mrs. Hammond, as they flew past her store, a disapproving scowl on her face. He didn't doubt news of this ride would reach the ears of the white boys in town. But he couldn't worry about that now.

"I'm going to say the same thing to you," said Katie, glancing behind her as they slowed a few minutes later and turned the horse off the road, "that Mayme told me she said to you before. Please . . . don't tell what you see or who you see or anything. I can't make you promise because there's no time to worry about it. But I hope you'll keep quiet."

Before Jeremiah could reply, Katie had stopped the horse and was dismounting.

A pretty black girl was crouching near the side of the road. "Who dat!" she called out as they approached, clearly frantic.

"Never mind who it is," said Katie. "He's the boy who came out to the house. He's going to help us.—Jeremiah," she said, turning back to him, "would you ride behind Emma on the other horse?"

In another minute they were on their way again, traveling more slowly as they approached the McSimmons place. As they went, the horses side by side, Katie briefly tried to explain the situation.

"These are mean people, Jeremiah," she said. "If they see too many black faces, there is no telling what they might do.

For reasons I can't tell you about, if they catch so much as a glimpse of Emma, they're likely to kill her. So we've got to stay out of sight.''

"What dey want wiff Miz Mayme?" Jeremiah asked.

"Mayme used to be a slave here. I'm guessing they think she knows where Emma is and are trying to get her to tell them.''

"An' if I know what she's doin' right now,'' Emma began tearfully, "it's dat she's not tellin 'em where I's at. She's in danger on account er me.'' She began wailing.

"Shush, Emma,'' said Katie sternly. "Now, Jeremiah, I don't want you to be in danger either. If anything bad happens, you get away and take her with you. Get as far away as you can and take her back to my house until I get back.''

"What about you, Miz Katie?'' asked Jeremiah.

"If anything happens, I just want the two of you to get away as fast as you can. They won't hurt me—I'm white.''

"What you plannin' ter do?'' asked Jeremiah. "If dey's got Mayme, how you gwine fin' her?''

"I don't know. We need to sneak up to the house somehow,'' she said. "There's a black servant lady named Josepha that we've got to find without anyone seeing us.''

"I can git in da house, Miz Katie,'' said Emma. "I know where dere's a way in wiffout bein' seen. I snuck in an' out lots er times. I'm sorry, Miz Katie, but I was a crackbrained coon an' I dun things I shouldn't hab dun.''

"We won't worry about that now,'' said Katie.

Ten minutes later Katie and Emma had managed to sneak into the McSimmons house through the cellar and were asking Josepha if she'd heard anything about Mayme.

"I'm feared, Miz Kathleen,'' said Josepha, tears filling her eyes, "I'm mighty feared dey was fixin' ter take her out to da big oak.''

Emma gasped. "Da big oak!'' Her eyes filled with terror.

"What is it?'' said Katie.

"Come wiff me, Miz Katie," said Emma without answering the question. "We gotter git outer here!"

"If Mayme's in trouble, then we're going to help her. Do you know where the oak is, Emma?"

"Yes'm, but—"

"Emma!" said Katie. "Remember—we came to help Mayme."

"If they've taken her to da big oak, chil'," said Josepha, breaking into sobs, "dere ain't nuthin you can do fer poor Mayme now."

Katie and Emma left the cellar of the house as they had come, and ran back to where Jeremiah was crouching behind a tree, holding one of the rifles Katie had brought along.

"What are you doing with that!" exclaimed Katie.

"Listenin' ter you talk about how dangerous dese people is, I figured I'd best be ready ter shoot if dey was comin' after da two er you."

"Nobody saw us . . . come on!"

Two minutes later they were back in their saddles and Emma was leading the way as best she could remember.

It took them ten or twelve minutes to reach the place.

"Dere it is—dat's da big oak!" whispered Emma. "An' see—dere's men on horses all dere together! Oh, Miz Katie, I'm mighty feared 'bout what dey's doin', an' I'm feared we be too late!"

They dismounted and tied up their horses and crept to the edge of the trees.

"No—look, there's Mayme in the middle of them," said Katie. "We're not too late. She's on one of the horses and—"

Suddenly Katie gasped in horror.

"She's blindfolded . . . and they've got a rope around her neck!" she exclaimed. "It's tied over that limb up above!"

"Dat's what I feared, Miz Katie! Dat's what I been tellin you."

"Dey's fixin' ter string her up, all right," whispered Jeremiah. "I heard 'bout dis eber since da war. I almost got in some trouble like it mysel' wiff some white men dat'd been drinkin'."

"Oh, Miz Katie—Mayme's so good," Emma was babbling. "She be gwine git herself strung up fer me."

"Shush, Emma! We're *not* going to let them kill Mayme."

"No, we ain't," added Jeremiah, anger rising in his voice. "I'm goin' t' git one ob dose guns!"

"Just a minute, Jeremiah!" said Katie. "We've got to think first.—I wonder why some of them are wearing white hoods over their heads."

"I heard ob it," said Jeremiah. "Some kind er white man's religious thing."

"What should we do, Jeremiah?" asked Katie.

"I don't reckon I kin shoot 'em all," he said. "Dere's too many. To tell you da truf, I neber shot a gun like dis in my life, an' I don' know if I could kill a man—"

When his memory caught up with his words, a chill went through him even as he added, "—eben effen he's white."

"We don't have to kill anybody," said Katie. "We can just try to make them think we are. It's a trick Mayme showed me.—Let's get the guns."

They ran to the horses and pulled out the rifles.

Quickly Katie explained as she and Jeremiah each took a handful of shells. Then they split up.

A minute later, from where she was hiding in the trees, Katie fired a shot over the heads of the men.

She'd forgotten what a kick the gun had. It knocked her backward and she nearly lost her balance. Emma cried out from the sound as Katie steadied herself and fired again. Then came the sound of Jeremiah's first shot.

As the echo died away, Katie fired again, then a few seconds later heard three or four more shots in rapid succession come from Jeremiah's gun.

Surprised and confused, the men yelled and swore as they looked about.

Katie fired again. A loud curse sounded. She'd accidentally hit William McSimmons in the leg!

"Let's get out of here!" he cried. "She's practically dead now anyway—we'll let the tree finish the job!"

He gave the horse Mayme was sitting on a great swat with his whip. The horse lurched forward and ran straight out from under Mayme as McSimmons galloped away after the others.

Katie's first thought was elation. Then she saw Mayme dangling from the tree with the rope tight around her neck!

"Mayme!" she screamed. She dropped the rifle on the ground and ran toward the tree.

Jeremiah came out of the woods and ran after her.

"Jeremiah!" cried Katie. "Go back and bring the horses! Hurry, Jeremiah!"

"Mayme . . . Mayme!" called Katie, tears filling her eyes. "Mayme, we're here now—we're going to help you."

But when she reached the tree, she realized there was nothing she could do. Mayme's hands were tied behind her back and the rope was pressing so hard against her windpipe that she couldn't make a sound.

"Mayme . . . Mayme . . . oh, Mayme—God, help me!" Katie cried frantically, grabbing her friend's feet where they dangled up in the air almost as high as her shoulders. She tried to lift Mayme's legs to take the pressure off her neck. But Mayme was so close to unconsciousness that she was just hanging limp.

By then Jeremiah was racing toward them on one of the horses, followed by Emma pulling the second by the reins.

Jeremiah reined in and walked the horse forward to get it under Mayme. At the same time he was fumbling with his hands trying to grab hold of her.

"Mayme . . . Mayme, sit up on the horse!" cried Katie from the ground.

While Jeremiah tried to steady the horse, Katie tried to push Mayme's legs over its back. But in the confusion the horse kept moving about and Jeremiah couldn't get it to stay still. All the while Mayme was hanging there like dead weight with her neck stretching further and further.

"Emma," cried Katie, "the knife! Get the knife. It's in the saddlebag. Climb up the tree and cut the rope!"

A minute later Emma was scurrying up the trunk with the help of a few low limbs while Katie kept lifting Mayme's legs and Jeremiah was trying to hold her up around the waist to take the weight off her neck.

"Be careful, Emma," cried Katie. "Don't fall—but hurry!"

Ten or fifteen seconds later the rope gave way from Emma's knife. Mayme dropped into Jeremiah's arms. But the sudden weight of her body made him lose his balance and they both fell into a heap on the ground. Frantically Katie struggled to loosen the noose around her neck.

"Mayme . . . oh, Mayme!" said Katie, smothering her friend's face with kisses. "Please God . . . oh, Mayme, don't be dead!"

Slowly Mayme's eyelids fluttered open and Katie went wild with joy.

"Oh, Mayme!" she cried.

Mayme opened her eyes a little wider and tried to force a feeble smile to her lips. Emma and Katie began crying, but Mayme didn't seem to have the strength to cry. She just lay there. She glanced over to where Jeremiah knelt behind the girls. He smiled at her and she tried to smile back.

"Dose men be boun' ter come back before long," said Jeremiah. "If dey fin' dat we spoiled dere lynchin', dey's like ter string up all three ob us."

"You're right," said Katie, "we've got to get out of here."

They got Mayme to her feet. Jeremiah lifted her onto one of the horses. She winced as he did so, biting her lip to keep from crying out. He tried his best to be gentle. He knew she was hurting from the cuts and bruises. He wondered if she had broken bones too.

"Jeremiah," said Katie. "You're stronger than me. You ride with Mayme and keep her in the saddle."

He climbed up behind Mayme, putting his arms around her to grab on to the saddle horn. But it was all he could do to keep Mayme in the saddle, limp and exhausted as she was.

Katie mounted the other horse, pulled Emma up behind her, and the horses galloped away. After riding about twenty minutes, Mayme began to slump and collapse in Jeremiah's arms. Realizing she needed a rest, he slowed and he and Katie began looking for a place they could stop for water.

When Katie and Jeremiah helped Mayme down off the horse she nearly collapsed at the river's edge.

"Water . . ." she tried to say, ". . . thirsty."

Katie ran to the river, took off her bonnet, scooped it full of water, and hurried back to Mayme. She helped her sit up and held the water to her lips before most of it soaked through the cloth to the ground. But Mayme managed two or three swallows.

Katie went back and after a few minutes had managed to get some water into Mayme's stomach and to wash her face.

Mayme smiled faintly. "Thank you," she whispered.

"Oh, Mayme," Katie said, "it breaks my heart to see you so weak!"

She embraced her. Mayme stretched her arms around Katie and they held each other for the longest time. Mayme reached toward Emma and the girl came forward and embraced Mayme too. Jeremiah saw Mayme cringe as Emma threw her arms around her back. Then Mayme smiled at Jeremiah again, likely too worn out to wonder what he was doing there with the others.

"I feel better now," Mayme said. "I've hardly had anything to eat or drink in two days. I was just feeling faint."

"Then let's get you home," said Katie.

When at last the white buildings of Rosewood appeared in the distance, Jeremiah heard Mayme sigh with happiness. He followed her gaze as Mayme looked over at Katie. Katie's eyes were wet with tears.

"Welcome home, Mayme," she said.

Jeremiah got down and carried Mayme toward the house. Katie led the way inside and up the stairs. A minute or two later Mayme was lying on the bed while everyone scurried about fetching water for the tub and talking about getting some food and liquid inside her.

Jeremiah stood in the kitchen, watching all the commotion. It was plain that Katie's mother wasn't anywhere around, and that there wasn't sign of any other grown-up either. Katie was clearly mistress of the place.

Katie walked over to Jeremiah and led him outside.

"I don't know how to thank you, Jeremiah," said Katie. "I couldn't have done it without you."

"I'm jest glad Miz Mayme's safe," he said, "an' dat I could help."

"Please . . ." began Katie after a few seconds, "you won't tell . . . will you? Someday . . . maybe we can explain what is going on here. But for now, nobody can know."

He stood looking at the serious expression on Katie's face.

"I reckon I can do dat, Miz Clairborne," said Jeremiah slowly. "'Tis mighty strange, I gotter say, seein' colored an' whites livin' in a big house like dat t'gether. But I reckon I can keep my mouf shut fer a spell. But ya'll tell me someday, I hope, 'cause you got me mighty curious.''

"I will try to," said Katie with a relieved smile. "Thank you, Jeremiah.—Do you mind walking back to town? I'd let you take one of the horses, or ride you in myself, but . . ."

"Don' mention it, Miz Clairborne," said Jeremiah. "Dat'll give my pa an' dose other folks in town dat was watchin' us a chance ter settle down an' ferget what dey seen. I'll jest sneak in a roun'bout way so no one sees me."

"Maybe you're right," said Katie. "Thank you again!"

New Boy in Town
33

W
ORD OF COURSE GOT AROUND TOWN ABOUT
"Henry's boy," especially after his gallop through
town on the back of Katie's horse. But all it did was bring
Jeremiah more to the attention of the kind of young whites
that were up to no good. That Jeremiah was alone made him
an easy target for their rowdy pranks and insults. And that he
was free and was working at a man's job, and receiving good
pay from a white man for a job some of them might have
wanted but would have been too lazy to keep, irritated them
all the more.

A seventeen-year-old boy called Deke Steeves was the
worst of the troublemakers. By himself Jake could have
whipped him with one hand behind his back. But Deke was
the kind of boy who took pleasure in making other people,
especially if they were black, suffer. And he made sure that
he was never alone. Being big for his age, and a bully, young
Steeves always attracted a crowd of younger admirers whenever he was on the prowl.

On one particular day, Steeves and his small following had
been roaming about town with little to do. Deke himself was
in a surly mood. His father had yelled at him earlier in the
day and now Deke was on the hunt for someone weaker than

himself to take out his anger on. A few minutes earlier, he and his cohorts had seen an elderly Negro woman coming out of Mrs. Hammond's store and swooped down upon her. That's when Jeremiah caught sight of them.

He broke into a run toward the scene. As he drew closer he saw that they were tossing pebbles and small stones at her. She was pleading with them to stop, but her cries only encouraged them the more and brought jeers and cruel taunts along with them.

Jake stooped down, grabbed up a half dozen good-sized rocks from the street, then ran forward until he was close enough to make sure he would hit them and not her. He began to hurl the stones at the biggest of the white boys. Two or three found their marks, one small rock directly on the back of Deke Steeves' head. He cried out in pain, swore a few times, then backed away. The younger cowards followed his lead and ran across the street. Jeremiah scooped up another handful and kept up a volley of stones until they were out of sight.

As soon as she was safe, Jake hurried to the old woman's side.

"Did dey hurt you, Miz Barton?" he asked.

"No, I's be fine now, young man," she said. "But dey's a troublesum lot, dose nickums."

She paused and looked at her defender a little more carefully.

"Ain't you ol' Henry's boy I heard 'bout?"

"Dat's me, Miz Barton."

"Henry's a good man. He's been er big help ter me."

Jeremiah nodded. "I's jes' walk you back partway ter yo place," he said. "I got me a feelin' dose bullies still might be roun'bout sumplace."

"Dat right nice er you. What dey call you?"

"My papa calls me Jeremiah. My mama used ter call me Jake after I got big enuff dat I weren't jes' a little tyke. I didn't like the Jeremiah fo a while, but I's gettin' used ter it agin."

"I can't hardly imagine you a little tyke," chuckled the old woman. "You's a big'un now, dat's fo sho!"

Thirty minutes later Jeremiah walked back into the mill, where he encountered Mr. Watson.

"I's sorry ter be gone so long," he said. "I saw sum whites botherin' ol' widow Barton an' throwin' rocks at her. So I helped her home."

Watson nodded. "I see," he said. "Who were they, do you know, Jake?"

"One ob dem was dat blamed Steeves kid, an' a bunch er younger ones."

Again Watson nodded, this time more seriously.

"You watch yourself, Jake," he said. "You stay away from Deke Steeves. His father's a bad one, and so is the boy. I've heard some things I hope aren't true, but if they are . . . well, you just keep clear of him, that's all."

"I cudn't let dem hurt an ol' lady."

"I suppose not. But just watch yourself, Jake. That's all I'm saying. These are dangerous times. Just watch yourself."

COTTON
34

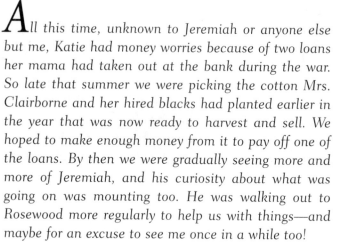

*A*ll this time, unknown to Jeremiah or anyone else but me, Katie had money worries because of two loans her mama had taken out at the bank during the war. So late that summer we were picking the cotton Mrs. Clairborne and her hired blacks had planted earlier in the year that was now ready to harvest and sell. We hoped to make enough money from it to pay off one of the loans. By then we were gradually seeing more and more of Jeremiah, and his curiosity about what was going on was mounting too. He was walking out to Rosewood more regularly to help us with things—and maybe for an excuse to see me once in a while too!

One morning we were out in the fields picking when I glanced up and saw Jeremiah walking toward us.

I paused and stood and stretched my back. About the same time Katie noticed him too and walked over to meet him near where I was standing.

"You ladies is workin' mighty hard," said Jeremiah. "I been watchin' the goin's-on at Mr. Watson's mill," he went on. "It seems t' me dat you could use a couple more han's."

Katie smiled a weary smile. "I'm not going to

pretend that we don't need help, Jeremiah," she said. "But what about your father? Does Henry—?"

"He don' know where I went. I ain't sayin' he ain't been askin' lots er questions. But I ain't tol' him nuthin' 'bout what I seen here."

"Thank you, Jeremiah. We are all very appreciative of your help."

Katie went back to the row she was working on. I started in picking again too and Jeremiah started working beside me. We noticed a difference right away in how fast the wagon filled. As we went Jeremiah and I talked a little, mostly about how life used to be when we were slaves. I suppose picking cotton couldn't help remind us.

We were dumping our pickings into two wagons on each side of the field. By the end of that day, with Jeremiah's help, we had one of them nearly full. Jeremiah came back the next day, and the day after that. We found another bag in the barn and now started moving even faster. The second day we worked till about noon, then finally stopped to get ready to take both wagons into town.

We ate some lunch, then hitched a team of two horses to each wagon. To get all the cotton to town I'd have to drive one of the wagons myself. It couldn't be helped. Jeremiah jumped up beside me. I shouldn't have been surprised, but I was. Pleased too. I felt his eyes on me and kept my own eyes straight ahead. I called to my two horses and followed Katie onto the road.

"You min' me ridin' wiff you?" he asked.

I shook my head. "No, I don't reckon I mind."

"Dat's good."

"I was right sorry to hear about your mama," I added after a bit.

I felt him stiffen beside me, and I quickly regretted my words. We rode in silence for some time before he finally said anything more.

"She wuz a fine woman."

"I'm sure she was," I said. "Your papa too."

He shrugged, and I was confused by the expression on his face. "Effen you say so," he said.

"I lost my mama too," I said. I blinked away sudden tears and focused on following the wagon ahead of me. Jeremiah didn't reply. I figured that was probably just as well. Talking about my family could lead to more questions I wasn't ready to answer.

About a mile from town, Jeremiah said suddenly, "Slow down an' I'll jump off here."

I realized that was a good idea, so nobody in town would see us ride in together. I slowed the horses to a walk and just before he jumped off, he surprised me again by reaching for my hand and giving it a quick squeeze.

"I's sorry 'bout yer mama too," he said, not quite meeting my eyes. Then he hopped off the wagon and disappeared across a field.

We rode into Greens Crossing a short time later on the two wagons, bouncing along the street toward Watson's Mill, Katie leading, me following. Out of the corner of my eye, I saw Henry as we passed the livery stable. I could tell he was watching us with an expression of growing curiosity.

⌒ ❀ ⌒

A Stranger Who Wasn't
a Stranger
35

JEREMIAH DIDN'T HEAD OUT TO ROSEWOOD THE
next day, since the girls were planning to take the day to
catch up with their regular chores about the place and get a
little rest. Jeremiah had his own catching up to do, both at
Mr. Watson's and at the livery. It seemed his father thought
he had some explaining to do too.

"Where you been dese las' few days, Jeremiah?" Henry
asked.

Jeremiah shrugged, determined to keep the girls' secret,
but not wanting to lie to his father if he could avoid it. "Here
and dere," he answered.

"What you keepin' from me, boy?"

A bit of Jeremiah's old anger flared up. "Don' be callin'
me boy," he said. "No need to be fussin' over me neither. I
been doin' fine on my own fer years."

"Hab you? Hab you truly?"

Jeremiah looked away from Henry's searching eyes. No,
he hadn't done fine, not always. But no use his father knowing
that.

Henry sighed. "I ain't fussin', son," he said. "I's worried
'bout you is all. Mr. Watson come here lookin' fer you. Says

you din't show up at the mill all day."

"Well, I'm jes' fine. I be working at the mill all day today."

The day after that, he was out again in the fields around Rosewood, picking cotton with Mayme, Katie, and Emma.

They worked all morning, though not quite so fast and frantic as before, laughing and talking and almost enjoying it—if a black person in the South could ever be said to enjoy picking cotton. Suddenly Jeremiah looked up and saw a rider approaching. The rider caught them all by surprise. Beside him, Jeremiah noticed the others stop working too and stand still, watching the man on horseback come from the direction of the house.

Jeremiah glanced at Mayme, but she was looking at Katie. He glanced next at Emma, who had a look of terror on her face. Suddenly Emma dropped her satchel, ran to grab William from the buckboard where he was sleeping, then bolted for the house. Jeremiah was giving mighty serious consideration to bolting in the opposite direction himself. But he stood there and waited with the others.

As the rider came closer, Jeremiah saw the look on Katie's face change from fear to relief. She gasped and it was clear she recognized the white man on the horse. She set down her satchel and began walking toward him as he reined in.

"Well now," the stranger said, and even from where Jeremiah stood he could see his teeth glisten white as he flashed a mischievous grin, "are my eyes deceiving me! Is this my sister Rosalind out in the fields, or would this be . . ."

He hesitated, still with the grin on his lips, but also with a sudden look of doubt, as if he wasn't sure anymore who this tanned, strong, hardworking girl actually was.

"It's me," said Katie, walking up to where he sat on his horse, "—it's me . . . Katie."

"Well . . . Kathleen!" said the rider. "You have turned into a woman since I saw you!"

He began to dismount. "And you look so much like your mama," he went on. "You've got her hair, her eyes, and—"

Before he could say anything more, suddenly the man found himself smothered in the girl's embrace. Taken by surprise, he stood a moment with Katie's arms around him as if he didn't know what to think. Then slowly he put his arms around her and hugged her back.

Tired and worn though the man seemed, he looked like a dandy in Jeremiah's eyes. His white shirt had ruffles and bright buttons down the front. Showing from beneath the end of his fancy jacket were cuff links sparkling from the ends of his shirtsleeves. If he wasn't rich, he sure dressed like a man who was. Jeremiah saw the man look over Katie's head at Mayme for a few seconds with a puzzled expression.

Jeremiah took a step closer to Mayme. "Who dat?" he asked softly.

Mayme turned to face him. "Katie's uncle, I think," she whispered.

"You know him?"

"I've never seen him before."

"Does he know . . .'bout . . . ?"

"No. But it seems likely he will before long."

"What you think he'll do?"

"I don't know."

Mayme turned again to Jeremiah. "Maybe you oughta go," she said. "One less person for Katie to have to explain will make it easier for her." She smiled, though it wasn't quite convincing. No doubt she was worried about what this man's coming would mean to their future. "Thank you so much for your help."

"Don' mention it, Mayme," he said. "I jes' hope no trouble comes fer you."

"We'll try to get word to you. I don't know what me and Emma will do if he makes us leave, but I'll come see you somehow, whatever happens."

KINFOLK
36

I watched Jeremiah walk away across the field with his long strides and the broad stretch of his shoulders. Yes, sir, he was a strong and mighty fine-looking boy.

I turned back to where Katie still stood in her uncle's arms, just holding him tight. The man was obviously uncomfortable. He relaxed his own arms and tried to ease away.

"Where's your mama, Kathleen?" he said. "I need to have a talk with her."

"Oh, Uncle Templeton!" cried Katie. "—she's dead! They're all dead!"

She burst into the most mournful wail and began to sob, like a dam that had been held back all these months was bursting inside her. At the word *dead,* her uncle's face went ashen. Katie's wailing and sobbing left no doubt that she was telling the truth.

He stood there stunned, his eyes wide, his face white. After a few minutes, Katie put her hand in his and led him in the direction of where she and I had buried her family. I followed them, but from a distance.

Katie took him to the spot, then stopped. They just stood there looking down at the graves, not saying a word. Slowly her uncle stretched one of his arms around Katie's shoulders and pulled her to his side. She leaned her head against his chest and shoulders and again began to cry. I figured they needed to be alone and didn't need prying eyes staring at their backs. As I turned and walked away, I took one last look back. Seeing Katie leaning into her uncle's arms, I knew my life was about to change forever.

Katie's kinfolk knew. Everything was bound to change because of that. Without even consciously trying, my brain was working hard to brace itself for whatever this was going to mean, even if it meant that in a few days I'd be gone from Rosewood and might not ever see Katie again.

After a while, I saw Katie and her uncle walk slowly back from the graves and into the house together. He still had his arm around her, and she was leaning against his side as she walked, as if it was the most natural thing in the world. As nervous as I was about what all this might mean, it warmed my heart to see them together like that.

When I entered the kitchen a short time later, Katie and her uncle were both seated at the table quietly talking. Katie's eyes were red. She glanced up at me and tried to smile.

"Hi, Mayme," she said. Her voice was still husky from crying.

"Hi," I said.

"I told him everything, Mayme . . . I couldn't help it. I hope you're not mad at me."

"Of course not, Katie," I said, glancing toward her uncle. "You had to . . . he's your kin."

As her uncle watched, he seemed moved by our obvious love for each other. But I could see he was looking strangely at me, just as he had in the field. I was used to that. White folks always look different at blacks than they do their own kind. But something about the way Katie's uncle did it was strange. It made me feel funny in a different kind of way than any feeling I'd ever had.

"This is Mayme, Uncle Templeton . . . Mayme Jukes," said Katie. "She's the best friend I've ever had."

My eyes started blinking fast to hear Katie's words. I knew it wouldn't do much good for me to start crying too. But it was all I could do to keep from it.

"I am happy to know you, Mayme Jukes," said Katie's uncle. "My name is Templeton Daniels, and from what Katie has told me, I suppose I owe you my thanks—for helping look after her, for helping look after the place . . . and for helping bury my sister and her family."

I nodded and forced a smile. I didn't know what to say.

At last Katie broke the silence by jumping straight into the middle of it.

"Does Rosewood belong to you now, Uncle Templeton?" she asked.

Katie's words seemed to sober her uncle all the more. I reckoned the poor man was having a lot thrown at him at once. He'd just found out that his sister was dead and that his niece had been running the plantation with an assortment of colored kids. And now suddenly his own future had changed as much as ours.

Mr. Daniels looked at the two of us staring at him, then chuckled a little nervously.

"I don't see how that could be, Kathleen," he said. "I'm no kin to your pa."

"Does it belong to Uncle Burchard, then?" Katie asked. "You won't tell him, will you, Uncle Templeton?"

"I've never met your father's brother. I only heard

Rosalind mention him a time or two."

"I don't want to go live with him."

"We're not going to do anything until we have a chance to think this thing over a bit."

Katie looked up at me. "I told him about the gold, Mayme. And about the men who came here looking for it. He says the gold was Uncle Ward's—that's Mama's other brother."

"And do you know if he's coming back for it, sir?" I asked, finally sitting down with them.

"Naw . . . Ward's dead, as far as I know," he replied. "At least that's what I heard. I haven't seen him in years, and the last time I did there were men after him. I tried to pick up his trail several times, but it always went cold. Take the gold and use it, I say. He's never coming back."

"We already did," said Katie. "But it was only about fifty dollars. That wasn't enough to pay off Mama's loan."

"Hmm . . . I thought there was more. Those men sure think there is more," he added.

"Why, do you know them, Uncle Templeton?"

"I've run into them a time or two—that is, if it's the same bunch. They're convinced I was in on it with Ward."

"If there'd been more, we wouldn't have had to pick the cotton," said Katie. "But we earned over three hundred dollars, didn't we, Mayme?"

Mr. Daniels whistled in astonishment. "That is a lot of money! It must have been hard work."

"It was. We paid off the first loan, but there's still one more loan to pay off. That's why we're still picking cotton."

We talked a bit more, but I soon excused myself and went upstairs to my room, feeling downcast and wondering what was to become of Emma and me.

Suddenly a sound disturbed my thoughts. I turned around and there was Mr. Daniels standing in the doorway looking at me.

"I was just—" I started to say. But the sudden look that came over his face silenced me. His face went white and he gasped. It was such an odd expression that I couldn't take my eyes off him either. The two of us just stood there for a minute, staring at each other. Suddenly, he turned and stumbled away and down the stairs. But just before he turned away, I thought I saw tears in his eyes.

Some time later, I was outside hanging some wash on the line when I heard footsteps behind me.

I turned and there stood Mr. Daniels only a few feet away. Again he was staring at me strangely.

"Hello, Mary Ann," he said. "I'm sorry . . . didn't mean to startle you."

"How did you know my name?" I asked, trying to hide that he had startled me and that I'd nearly jumped out of my skin to see him standing there so close.

"I asked Emma," he said with a smile. "She told me."

"Nobody calls me that," I said, going on with the laundry. "Nobody except Katie when she's funning me."

"It's a nice name," he said. "A pretty name."

"Thank you," I said.

"I meant it," he said.

"It ain't like a white man to think kindly about coloreds," I said. I regretted the words as soon as they left my mouth. It was probably a stupid thing to say to a white man I hardly knew, though it was true enough.

Mr. Daniels chuckled lightly. "You're right about that," he said. "But I've always been a little different than other white men in that regard."

"Why's that?" I asked, starting to relax a little.

"I reckon because that's how my mama taught me—that's Kathleen's grandmother, her mama's mother. Eliza Jane Daniels, that was her name. She taught Rosalind and Ward and Nelda and me that everyone was equal in God's sight, and that if God had seen fit to make people with different-colored skin, then the least we could do was treat everyone equal."

"Lots of white men go to church but are as mean as can be to coloreds."

"I reckon that's so," he said. "But our mama taught us different." He paused, then looked at me closely. "Mary Ann," he said, "would you mind . . . mind telling me . . . what was your mama's name?"

His words were so unexpected that I just stood there staring back at him. What could he possibly care about that?

"I don't know why—" I began.

"Please, I know you may not understand," he said, and his voice sounded almost urgent, "but it is important to me."

"All right, then. I don't reckon there'd be any harm in it," I said. "Her name was Lemuela . . . Lemuela Jukes."

The instant I said the word, his face showed a momentary look of shock, as if I'd slapped him across the mouth. He took a step back, still staring at me with an expression stranger than all the rest. His mouth seemed to go dry and his face was pale.

"And . . . and she was killed along with everyone else?" he asked, his voice low and husky-like.

"Yes, sir," I said, suddenly feeling very strange.

Mr. Daniels said nothing more. He just turned and walked slowly away.

The next morning when we got up, Templeton Daniels was gone.

"Do you think he'll be back?" I asked Katie when I found her in the kitchen.

"I don't know," Katie replied. "With Uncle Templeton . . . you never know." She sighed and squared her shoulders. "Well, uncle or no uncle, we have more cotton to pick."

⌐ ❀ ⌐

Cotton-Pickin' Henry
37

*O*nce we had milked the cows and tended the other animals, we went back out in the field to work again. It was tedious, especially without Jeremiah's company, and we worked slower and went along in rows next to each other. We had been working two or three hours and the weariness had begun to set in.

Katie sighed and said, "I think these rows are getting longer every time we turn around."

"That's the way cotton is," I laughed. "It seems like it's never going to end!"

When Katie suggested it was time for a water break, no one argued with her.

We walked toward the wagon where William was sleeping and where we had jugs of water and milk. As we walked, Emma asked why we had to keep picking cotton, since we had already given the man at the bank his money. Katie began explaining how her mama owed the bank a lot of money and they still had another loan to pay, when all of a sudden she stopped talking right in the middle of a sentence.

I looked over at her. She was standing still as a statue. I turned around in the direction she was looking. There was a tall black man walking slowly toward us from between the long rows of cotton.

It was Henry!

Suddenly we forgot all about water! We just stood there stock-still as he walked toward us. I was sure that Jeremiah hadn't told him. But there was no way around his papa finding out now more than we'd wanted to tell him. It seemed like our secret was suddenly spilling out all over the place.

Henry sauntered up and stopped and just looked us over one at a time. I figured we were in big trouble now and that the worst of it'd come on me. But Henry just stood there a few seconds. Then he finally spoke, and it wasn't what I had expected.

"Y'all got anudder satchel a feller cud use?" he said, as if there wasn't anything unusual going on at all.

I took mine off and handed it to him. I wasn't quite sure what he wanted it for, but I figured I could use the big pockets in my dress for a while.

He slung it over his shoulder, then stooped down and started picking away on the next row beside mine. Katie looked over at me, and we all looked at each other, and then started slowly in again, none of us saying a word.

It was dead silent. All you could hear was our feet shuffling along the dry ground as we went back to where we'd left off and then slowly began inching our way from one plant to the next.

"Yep," Henry finally said, "eben wiff dose clouds up dere, a body cud git mighty tard in dese ole fields er cotton."

Again it was quiet, with just our feet moving slowly along the ground.

"Yep," he said again, "dis ole cotton'll make yo han's ruff an' red an' full er prickles. Ain't da kind er work

mos' white folks eber done. Ain't dat right, Miz Kathleen? Right unushul work fer mos' white folks!"

"Yes, sir," mumbled Katie, keeping her head down.

Again we shuffled along in silence.

"Who's dis yere frien' er yers, Miz Kathleen?" he
said, looking toward Emma. "Who you be?"

Emma glanced toward Katie with big eyes of question. Katie nodded for her to speak up.

"Dat's right," said Henry. "You kin tell me. I'm jes' a
colored like you what ain't gwine hurt you nohow."

"Emma," said Emma. "My name's Emma."

"Emma . . . I see. So dere's Miz Kathleen, Miz
Mayme, an' Miz Emma all workin' out chere togeder,
sometimes wiff a boy called Jeremiah helpin' 'em, ain't
dat right? Mighty strange situashun it 'peers ter me."

There was a long silence. None of us knew what to
say. Every now and then I'd try to sneak a look over at
him.

He paused and looked up, shielding his hand from
the sun peeking through the clouds. "Gettin' kinder
'long tards da time mos' folks take er break from dere
work," he said. "You ladies knows how ter fix a man
somefin t' eat?"

"Uh . . . yes, sir," said Katie.

"Den I say we go t' yer house an' git somefin t' eat
an' drink."

Without asking us any more questions, Henry
straightened his back and stood up and started walking
out of the field toward the wagon. Katie and I looked
at each other, both of us silently saying, What do we do
now!

Slowly we followed him. He dumped the cotton out
of his satchel into the wagon, then walked off toward
the house. Emma retrieved William from the buckboard and hung back behind the rest of us. Still not

saying anything, we followed him and gradually he slowed down so we could catch up.

"An' a young'un too," he said as he saw Emma. "My, oh my . . . yes, sir, dis indeed be some kine er mighty unushul situashun."

I saw Henry glance over at the four graves as we approached the house. He hesitated for a second, but followed the rest of us inside. There he stood standing until Katie told him he could sit down. Finally he sat down at the table.

"Now, Miz Kathleen," he said, then looked over at me, "an' Miz Mayme, ah seen dem stones markin' what looks ter me like graves out dere, an' ah got me an idea. But ah'd rather hear you tell me 'bout it yo'selfs."

Slowly Katie started to cry.

Henry waited a minute.

"Yo mama and daddy's lyin' under dem stones, ain't dey, Miz Kathleen?" he said quietly.

"Yes!" she whispered softly.

Henry got up from the chair and ambled toward us. He took Katie in his arms now and held her as I stepped back. Seeing how much he loved her made me realize he hadn't been trying to be mean with all his questions.

"It's gwine be all right, Miz Kathleen," said Henry. "Da Lord's watchin' ober you, an' He ain't 'bout ter forget none er His chilluns—white, black, or any udder color."

Then Henry looked over at me.

"What 'bout you, girl?" he said. "Yo mama an' daddy dead too?"

I nodded.

"Was dey Rosewood slaves?"

"No, sir . . . I lived at the McSimmons place."

"Ah see," he nodded. "An' you?" he asked Emma.

"I don' know 'bout my mama and daddy," she said. "Dey wuz sold an' I wuz sold an' I don' eben hardly remember dem. I ain't got no notion where dey is."

"Wha'chu doin' here?"

"I got myself in a heap er trouble an' I ran away an' Miz Katie an' Mayme, dey helped me."

"I see . . . well den, come here all er you," he said, opening one of his hands toward me and Emma. "I reckon dese ole black arms is big enuff ter hol' all er you at once."

I went forward and he drew me toward him. I felt Katie's arm go around me too, and the three of us stood there for a few seconds in Henry's wide embrace. Emma followed and started blubbering like a baby.

It was such a relief having Henry hug us. He wasn't mad at all, like I'd expected him to be. I don't know why, but he was as compassionate as could be.

Finally we stepped away and Henry went back to the chair where he'd been sitting.

"What happened, Miz Kathleen?" he said.

"Some terrible men came, men on horses . . . they were shooting and killing."

"Where wuz you?"

"In the cellar."

Henry nodded. "I heard 'bout dem marauders, dey was called. How 'bout you, Miz Mayme?"

"The same men killed most all the slaves at the McSimmons place," I answered.

"When all dis happen?"

"Last April," said Katie.

Henry nodded again, then looked at Emma.

"Emma ran away from where she was," said Katie, answering his silent question. "There were people trying to kill her because of her baby."

Henry nodded again and then it got real quiet for a minute or so.

"Are you going to tell on us, Henry?" said Katie. "Are you going to get us in trouble?"

"Well, I don' rightly know," he said. "Tell what? What is it dat you's so feared er folks findin' out dat y'all gotta sneak roun' town pretendin' an' carryin' on like y'all been doin'?"

"We're . . . we're trying to make people think my mama's still alive," said Katie.

"Why's dat?"

"So they won't put me in an orphanage and take Mayme away."

"What 'bout yo kin?" he asked. "As I recollect, yo papa's got a brudder somewheres?"

"Yes, sir," said Katie. "But I'm not sure exactly where he is, and I don't like him."

Henry glanced back and forth between us all again, seemed satisfied for the time being, and sat for a minute or two thinking.

I finally got up and got us all some milk and cheese and bread and butter to eat. Nobody said too much. We were still anxious to know what Henry was thinking, and Henry just kept thinking and hardly saying a word.

After we had finished eating, he rose back up to his feet.

"Well, I got me some work I gotter tend to back at da livery," he said.

"What are you going to do, Henry?" Katie asked again as we walked. "Are you going to tell on us?"

"I don' rightly know yet, Miz Kathleen," he said. "Who wud I tell, an' what wud I tell 'em? Afore I do anyfing, ah needs ter spen' some time ruminatin' an' prayin' an' axin' da Lord what He thinks 'bout dis whole thing. It's da Lord who tells me what I'm ter do. So I got ter fix mysel' on what His mind is on it—den I'll know what I'm ter do."

We watched him go, but didn't talk much amongst ourselves after he was gone either. Like she was with her uncle, I think in a way Katie was relieved that Henry finally knew.

☙ ❋ ❧

RAIN
38

T HE NEXT MORNING, JEREMIAH GOT UP EARLY AND set out for Rosewood at dawn. When he arrived, Mayme was just leading the cows out after the morning milking. He waved to her and she waved back.

"You're here early," she said, giving him a big smile as she walked over to meet him.

"My daddy tol' me what's goin' on wiff you and Miz Katie," he said. "An' he said you's needin' mo help wiff de cotton."

Half an hour later they were all out again in the field. Everyone seemed glad not to have to pretend anymore. Jeremiah noticed right away that Mayme smiled and laughed more, now that she didn't have to watch her words to protect their secret. Katie and Emma were in especially good spirits too. Even Jeremiah himself was more talkative than usual.

But it was chilly and windy. Dust was flying about getting in their hair and eyes. Every now and then Jeremiah would look up into the sky and shake his head.

That evening Henry came out again. With Jeremiah and his papa working, the cotton mounted twice as fast. The next day they both came out a little before lunchtime, and they finished the field the girls had begun a month ago and got started on another even bigger one a little farther from the house.

All the while as they worked that day it got chillier and chillier and windier. Henry kept picking faster and faster and was mumbling to himself as he glanced up at the clouds swirling above them.

Gradually they began to feel the moisture in the air. They kept working frantically, nobody saying a word.

Suddenly the wind stopped. The air became calm and still.

Henry looked around in every direction, sniffing in the air and still muttering.

"Hit's comin'," he finally said aloud. "Hit's comin' fo sho.—Jeremiah!" he called. "We gotter git dis yere wagon hitched up!"

Jeremiah looked at Mayme and without another word both started running for the barn to fetch a horse.

Suddenly a terrific blast of thunder exploded above them.

"Hurry, Jeremiah—we ain't got no time ter lose.—Miz Kathleen," Henry called to Katie, "come wiff me . . . we gots ter git dat wagon under cover!"

Within seconds a few huge drops of rain began to fall. Jeremiah and Mayme reached the barn ahead of Henry and Katie, who were hurrying as quickly as they could. Mayme led Jeremiah to the corral. Three minutes later they were racing back to the field with horse and harness. Henry and Katie were hitching up another horse to pull the full wagon of cotton into the barn and out of the rain.

As Jeremiah and Mayme fussed with the harness, already their faces were wet. Mayme jumped up onto the seat and grabbed the reins. Jeremiah leapt up beside her. She yelled at the horse, and off they clattered toward the house. The rain poured down in torrents. By the time they flew into the wide open doors of the barn, they were soaked to the skin. Mayme's dress was clinging to her, and water was dripping from her hair and ears and chin and nose. The two horses were in a frenzy of excitement from the rain and thunder and sudden exertion and the close quarters of the barn. Henry hurried to them and began talking to them and stroking their noses one at a time while Jeremiah and Mayme unfastened the harnesses and got them free from the wagons.

Ten minutes later the horses were in their stalls munching on oats. Katie ran back from the house with a handful of towels, and they all dried their hands and faces. She was still not aware of the danger. But Henry was running his hand through the cotton, pulling out handful after handful to feel how wet it was. Gradually Katie must have realized that his expression was serious.

"It's all right, isn't it, Henry?" she asked.

"I reckon we got it in time," he said thoughtfully. "I reckon Mr. Watson'll take it."

He sighed and walked to the big open doors and took a couple steps outside where he stood and stared out. The rain was pouring down in sheets.

"Unforturnt'ly, Miz Kathleen," he said as he stood staring out into the storm, "hit ain't dis yere cotton I'm a worryin' 'bout. Hit's da cotton still out dere in dem fields dat we gotter be worried 'bout."

"Why . . . can't we just pick the rest of it when the rain stops?" asked Katie.

"Effen da rain stop soon, I reckon we might at dat," said Henry. "But it's gotter stop real soon, Miz Kathleen—*real* soon. Effen it rain like dis fer anudder hour er two an' dat cotton goes down, den da whole crop be los'."

"Lost!" gasped Katie. "But . . . but what about all the other plantations around?"

"Dey mostly had dere cotton in an' under cover or sol' ter Mr. Watson weeks ago. Dat's why I been wonderin' what's goin' on at Rosewood when I seein' you bring in dem scrawny little bales so slow an' I'm wonderin' ter mysef, *What dat*

Mistress Clairborne wastin' so much time fer—don' she know dat she's gotter beat da rain? Dat's why I come out. But hit 'peers I was jes' a mite late 'cuz here's da rain an' dat cotton's still on da stalk.''

The four of them stood there silently staring out as the water poured down. Beside him, Jeremiah felt Mayme's fingers brush his own, and he slowly reached out and closed his big hand around hers. He glanced down at her, then at Katie, and saw tears falling from their eyes. They knew it too. The rain wasn't going to stop.

MOONLIGHT STROLL
39

A FTER THE COTTON HARVEST AND THE FLOOD THAT
followed, Jeremiah was glad that he and his papa were
in on "Miz Katie's scheme," as Mayme called it. Jeremiah
thought of his own secrets, but he wasn't ready to share those
yet. Maybe not ever. But he liked being able to help Mayme
and the other girls, to protect them some too. He couldn't
help but compare Miz Katie with that other white girl,
Samantha Dawson. But Kathleen Clairborne was so completely different.

Jeremiah began planning his next visits to Rosewood, getting to the mill early and saving up his time off. He even
braved Mrs. Hammond at the general store to buy some soap
to clean up with.

One evening, a couple weeks before Christmas, Jeremiah
came to call. It had been a warm day and sunny and everything smelled wet and warm and nice. Jeremiah had gotten all
cleaned up with the new soap and thought he didn't smell too
bad either. He couldn't keep a smile from his face when
Mayme came to the door.

"How'do, Miz Mayme," he said. "I thought . . . uh,
maybe you an' me could go fer a walk."

Mayme nodded and stepped outside.

They walked away from the house. Dusk was settling in. A full moon was coming up over the trees. It was as nice an evening as he could imagine. Neither of them seemed to have anything to say. As they walked he took Mayme's hand and they kept walking and walking till they were in the woods and the house was out of sight.

"What you gonna do now dat ye're free?" Jeremiah asked. "You gonna keep working fer Miz Katie?"

"I don't know. I hadn't thought about it," Mayme said. "But I could never leave Katie."

Jeremiah wasn't sure he liked the sound of that. "Why not?" he asked.

"She's my friend."

"But she's white."

"She's like a sister to me. It doesn't matter what color she is."

"Seems ter me it matters. Whites an' blacks is different, ain't they?"

"Not down inside," Mayme said. "Don't you figure if you could open us up, our hearts'd be the same color?"

"I reckon I never thought 'bout dat."

"What about you?" Mayme said. "What are you going to do?"

"I'd like ter save a little money," said Jeremiah, "an' maybe git me a livery er my own someday."

"That's sounds like a fine idea, Jeremiah."

"My daddy's happy enuff ter work fer Mr. Guiness," he went on. "He's pleased enuff ter hab a job an' ter be a free black man. But now dat young folks like you an' me is free, maybe we can do eben more—jes' think, a black man *owning* something. Don't it jes' soun' right fine!" He heard the excitement in his own voice and felt a little foolish.

"You can do it, Jeremiah," Mayme said. "But I'm not ambitious like that. Besides, I'm just a girl. Girls can't do things like that."

"Why not? Maybe dey can . . . someday."

"Not colored girls."

"Why not? You's free, ain't you?"

"I reckon."

"Ain't nobody can tell you what you can an' can't do. So don't dat mean you can do whatever you want?"

"I never thought about things like that before. Although Katie gave me twenty dollars an' that almost makes me feel like I could do anything."

"Twenty dollars!" exclaimed Jeremiah. "Ob yer very own . . . real money!"

"Yep. It's in the bank in town with my own name on it."

"Why, ye're rich, Mayme!"

She laughed.

"I had twenty dollars once too," said Jeremiah.

"You did! Then you were rich too. Why did you say you *had* twenty dollars?"

"Because it's gone now. I used it mostly all up before I got here."

"How did you get it?" I asked.

Jeremiah told Mayme about being with the army company and about the Dawsons. It was the first he'd told her about the story of his past. They walked on and finally turned around. It was pretty dark by now. It was such a nice contented feeling walking along hand in hand, knowing they were really *free* people. Was this how it had always been for white boys when they got to this age, meeting a girl and then taking her hand and treating her like she was special?

He found himself thinking about his papa and wondering if he'd felt this way when he'd first met his mama. Suddenly, without thinking through what he would say, Jeremiah asked, "You eber think . . .'bout gettin' married?"

Mayme looked startled at his words. Jeremiah felt embarrassment creep up his neck and heat his face. He was glad it was dark!

"I reckon," Mayme answered softly. "Doesn't every-body?"

"But it's different now, you know," Jeremiah went on. "Wiff no masters tellin' us what ter do. Now we can make up our own minds who ter marry an' what we wants ter do."

They came out of the woods into the clearing of fields and open space. The moon made everything glow a pale silver. He was wondering what Mayme would say to that, but she never had a chance.

Suddenly they heard voices yelling.

"There he is!" shouted a voice. Jeremiah could tell it was a white boy's voice.

"Look—he's got a nigger girl with him!" yelled another one. "Let's get them!"

Jeremiah tensed. Mayme trembled beside him.

"Who is it!" she asked.

"Jes' some no-goods dat must hab follered me from town.—You run, Mayme. You git back to da house an' you an' Miz Kathleen, you lock dem doors!"

"But, Jeremiah, what about—"

"You go, Mayme.—Go now!"

She gave him a frightened look, then turned and ran for the house.

"There she goes—after her!" shouted one of the white boys.

One of them tore off from the others toward Mayme. Jeremiah bolted after them both. Mayme kept running, but the boy was a lot faster and in just a few seconds had nearly caught her. Mayme looked over her shoulder and screamed.

Jeremiah rushed at the white boy and knocked him over, and they both thudded to the ground and wrestled against each other to get to their feet.

"Why you cussed nigger!" the white boy yelled in a fury, "I'll kill you for that if I—"

Jeremiah silenced him with a whack of his fist.

The others quickly caught up and knocked Jeremiah off their friend and started pounding and beating him something fierce. The pain was terrible, but from the corner of his eye Jeremiah saw Mayme disappear into the house. At least she had gotten away. He fought them off the best he could. But there were three of them, and within a minute he was nearly unconscious from the pain of several broken ribs.

When Jeremiah heard the explosion, he thought maybe it was the final death blow. It took a few seconds for him to recognize the sound for what it was, the blast of a shotgun. The sudden shot brought the fight to a halt. Above him, the white boys stopped kicking and pounding on him. Lying on the ground, Jeremiah opened his eyes a crack. A woman with a man's hat pulled low over her face, shotgun at the ready, was marching straight toward them.

"All right, you've had your fun!" she yelled and Jeremiah recognized the voice. It was the voice Katie used when she was pretending to be her mama. "Now get out of here before I use this again. If I have to get my husband out of bed to see to you thugs, he won't be none too happy."

"He's just a nigger, lady," said one of them, slowly climbing off Jeremiah's chest. "We was just having some fun."

"Well, have your fun someplace else. Now get out of here!"

Muttering and swearing, the three started wandering away.

"You can move faster than that!" yelled Katie.

They started running slowly in the direction of town. When they were about fifty yards away, she fired another shot. This time she was aiming closer and they started yelling like they were mad and scared all at once and tore off out of sight.

Relieved to be alive, Jeremiah tried to lie quietly, but a groan escaped his mouth. "Jeremiah . . . Jeremiah." Suddenly there was Mayme, kneeling down close beside him. "How bad is it?"

"I's be all right," he moaned. "I think some ob my ribs is broken, but dat ain't too bad. I had dat once before."

"Can you stand up?" Katie asked.

"I don't know . . . I reckon."

They helped him to his feet. Holding on to both of them, with his arms around their shoulders and with Katie still lugging the shotgun, the two helped him to the house. Once they were inside, where the light from the lantern showed on his face, Mayme looked away. He must look real bad, he thought to himself. He could tell his face was bloody and swollen and one of his eyes was already starting to swell up. But Katie wasn't queasy and was already tending to him with a wet cloth. Emma immediately went into a babbling fit. They washed him up as best they could and then got him to the couch in the parlor.

"You're spending the night here, Jeremiah," said Katie. "I'm worried about those white boys. I'll ride into town and get your daddy in the morning."

Jeremiah didn't argue. Mayme tried to get him to eat and drink something, but he was in too much pain to eat and fell asleep soon after that.

They locked the doors, and Katie kept the gun loaded all night.

The next morning, Jeremiah was hurting something terrible. He tried to be brave but he was in a lot of pain. One eye was swollen shut and he could hardly move or turn over from the broken ribs. He was just glad they were on the other side of his chest and weren't the same ones that had been broken before, when he was at the Dawson place during the war.

Katie rode to town and was back with Henry by midmorning. There wasn't much he could do for Jeremiah either. Since he hadn't come home the night before, Henry was clearly relieved that Jeremiah was all right, but was pained to see him in such a state. Together they decided Jeremiah should stay at Rosewood another day or two, until enough of the soreness had gone down so that he could get on a horse.

No Ain't No Answer
40

*T*hrough the opening months of the new year 1866, Katie and I were anxious to get to planting the new year's crop of cotton. But Henry kept saying it wasn't time yet and that we had to be patient. I missed Jeremiah something awful while he was laid up in town, but after he recovered, he walked out to Rosewood whenever he could to help us with our work.

By late February the weather slowly started to turn warmer, and Henry came out and ploughed one field. He told us what to ask for when we went to Mr. Watson's to buy cotton seed, which we soon did.

Together we got one field planted, and Henry and Jeremiah got to work on ploughing another. Now all we could do was wait till the cotton grew up and then we'd pick it again. Unfortunately events weren't so patient and didn't wait for the cotton.

A few days later we were out planting a field when the men came. The second I saw them, terror seized me. Even though there were only three of them, the reckless way they were riding reminded me of the marauders that had killed my family. They came galloping straight across the vegetable garden, kicking up the fresh dirt and destroying the seedbeds and young shoots that had started to grow, then tore toward us across the nice furrows Jeremiah had worked so hard at with his ploughing. It seemed they were trying to do as much damage as they could. Even their horses looked angry.

"It's just a bunch of kids and darkies!" said one as they reined in close to us, as if they were trying to scare us.

"Where's Clairborne!" yelled the one who seemed to be the leader.

Nobody spoke.

"You all deaf!" he shouted with a menacing tone.

"I'm Kathleen Clairborne," said Katie, stepping forward.

"Yeah, well I asked for Clairborne, not some kid. Who are you?"

"I'm his daughter. He's not here."

"Where is he?"

"He's away. He's up north."

"Say, young lady, you look uncommonly like your ma," said one of the other men, riding his horse over next to Katie and brushing alongside her. Even as he said it, he eyed Katie with a look I didn't like.

"That's what people say," said Katie, staring straight ahead and trying to ignore him, which wasn't easy to do.

"Except that you're a lot prettier.—Can't you look at me when I'm talking to you, girl! I said you was pretty. Don't you like that?"

Still Katie kept staring forward.

Now the man reached down from his horse and felt Katie's hair, then started running his hand slowly across her cheek.

Beside me, I felt Jeremiah take a step toward him.

"Jeremiah," I whispered, "don't. She'll be all right."

"Cut it out, Hal," said the one called Jeb. "Time for that later when we got what we come for." Then he turned back to Katie. "Now, little girl, you listen to me," he said angrily. "It's your ma we want if your pa ain't here—or what she's got. And that is her brother's gold."

"I'm sorry . . . my mama isn't here either," said Katie.

"Well, maybe that's so, but I reckon you know about that gold too."

"I've only heard about it, sir."

"And you have nothing to tell us about Ward Daniels?"

"No, sir," said Katie. "I've never seen my uncle Ward."

The man let out an exasperated sigh. It was obvious he was losing his patience.

"Now, look," he said, "we're tired of fooling around. Fact is, Ward Daniels stole some gold from us and we aim to get it back. Your ma told Sneed there was no more, but you see, we ain't convinced."

"What if . . . there isn't any more?" asked Katie in a shaky voice.

"If your ma was playing it straight and don't know where it is, then we'll have to find it ourselves, 'cause it's here, whether you or she know it or not. And we aim to find the rest of it. It's ours. It don't belong to Ward, and it don't belong to your ma or pa or you neither. We ain't gonna take no for an answer. No ain't no answer at all."

Katie just stared back at him.

"So I'm asking you straight out—has your ma got the gold?"

"I'm . . . I don't know, sir. There's no more gold."

"All right . . . if that's the way you want it, you tell

your ma she's got twenty-four hours to stop whatever game she's trying to play, or else to find it. Then we'll be back—noon tomorrow. You tell your ma that if she don't give us the gold, we'll take her place apart board by board if we have to. We'll have our guns, and we'll burn you out if we have to."

He spun his horse around and rode off and the second man followed. The third waited, then went up close to Katie again and reached down from his horse to touch her hair and neck. "And just maybe I'll help myself to a little of this too, after we find your gold!" he said.

Then he laughed a horrible laugh and galloped away after the other two. Right then I think I could have killed him.

As soon as they were gone, I went to Katie and took her in my arms. Every inch of her body was trembling.

"I don't know what we're going to do, Mayme," she said, tears filling her eyes. "We fooled them before, but they're not going to let anything stop them tomorrow."

That put an end to our cotton planting for that day. After all, what was the use of planting cotton if the men were going to come back and knock the house apart, or even burn it down?

The first thing we knew we had to do was tell Henry. Jeremiah left for town immediately to do that. Both men came out later and had supper with us and offered to stay the night. But having Jeremiah there wasn't like I wished it could be because we were all so scared.

Katie and I didn't know what to do. There *was* more gold. We had found some stashed in an old lantern in the cellar. We had taken some of it to the bank and used the money to buy seed. If Katie gave the men what was left of the gold, the bank would take Rosewood, and the men might still not believe it was all of it and might do those other terrible things regardless. But if she didn't give it to them, they might destroy Rosewood before the bank could do anything anyway.

It seemed there was nothing we could do that wasn't bound to have a bad ending.

Knowing Henry and Jeremiah were spending the night close by in the barn, we somehow drifted off to sleep. But when morning came it brought no answers to our dilemma.

And now noon was only a few hours away.

≈ ❀ ≈

By midmorning the tension was so great that Jeremiah could hardly stand it.

Katie went down to the cellar and came back a while later with a canvas bag. Jeremiah could tell by the way she carried it that it was heavy. She clunked it down on the sideboard in the parlor.

"Well, there it is," she said.

"You gwine gib it t' dem, Miz Katie?" asked Emma.

"I don't know, Emma," said Katie with a sigh. "I just don't know. But I've got to be ready to give it to them if it seems like it'll help."

From the tone of her voice, it appeared Katie had about given up all hope of saving Rosewood. The bag of gold sitting on the sideboard was the only hope left—and now she was ready to give it away. Jeremiah exchanged looks with his father across the table, but Henry only shook his head thoughtfully before bringing his coffee cup back to his lips.

Slowly the morning passed.

About eleven, Jeremiah couldn't sit still a moment longer. He jumped up from the kitchen table.

"I don' know 'bout da res' of you," he said, "but I'm

gettin' me a gun.—Miz Katie, show me da gun cabinet, an' wiff yer permishun—''

Henry rose to his feet.

"Now jes' wait er minute, Jeremiah," he began. "We don' wants ter go git all riled. Ain't no good comes from killin', nohow. We ain't gwine do no shootin', not unless hit becomes a matter on life er death, which ain't likely ef gold's sittin' at da root ob it—''

"Look, Papa," interrupted Jeremiah. "Dose men ain't gwine ter be feelin' too kindly tards Miz Katie when dey come, an' wiff respec' t' yer feelins' in da matter, I ain't gwine let dem hurt her, or any ob da res' ob dese girls. I ain't neber shot nobody in my life. But I's takin' one ob Miz Katie's guns an' I'm hidin' myself in dat barn, an' effen dey lay a han' on her or Mayme or Emma, or you either, den I'll shoot 'em. I'm sorry, Papa, but I ain't gonna stan' by an' watch dem do what white men sometimes does. Dey's carryin' rope too, an' dat fears me right fearsome. You can whip me later ef you wants to, if you an' me's still alive, an' I won't gib a squeak er protest. But right now . . . —Miz Katie, show me yer guns!''

Henry kept silent. Jeremiah wasn't sure if his papa was upset or if he agreed with Jeremiah. He hoped it was a little of both.

Five minutes later Jeremiah was on his way out to the barn carrying a loaded rifle and a shotgun in his two hands.

Mayme called after him, "Jeremiah, please . . . be careful.''

He turned back to her. "I'll be as careful as I can be," he said. "I'll jes' bide my time till I see's what's gwine happen. I won't start nuthin'. An' Lord knows I's scared a da thought ob it all. So I's keep quiet, res' assured a dat, till I sees what dey's gwine do. But I ain't gonna let 'em rape Miz Katie, or hurt Emma or . . .''

He paused a second and looked down into Mayme's eyes.

In that moment he knew he'd die himself before he'd let anything happen to her.

"An' I sure ain't gonna let dem hurt you," he said. "An' if dey lay a finger on my daddy, den I'll kill 'em."

Suddenly he stepped forward, leaned toward Mayme and kissed her. Then he turned and hurried off toward the barn.

A Welcome Surprise
41

I watched Jeremiah walk away toward the barn holding the two guns, leaving me standing there with my heart pounding about twice as fast as it should have been. It wasn't how I'd imagined the first time being kissed by a boy—with us worrying whether we'd live through the day.

I returned to the kitchen to wait with the others. At quarter till noon we were all the more on edge and scared. Even Henry was sober and silent and just sat in a chair calmly waiting. He still had no gun. As was clear enough from what he'd said to Jeremiah, he wasn't a fighting man. He just sat there praying, though I could never have guessed the direction his prayers were taking. I reckon he would say that was his kind of fighting. We hadn't heard any more from Jeremiah since he'd gone out to hide in the barn.

Suddenly we heard a horse outside. The moment we'd been waiting for had come!

I didn't know if Katie'd decided what to do or not. At a time like this, as much as we'd shared of our life together, what we were facing on this day involved decisions she had to make herself.

A tense minute went by. We heard the horse walk up and stop. A few seconds later a knock came on the door. It seemed so loud it nearly made us all jump right out of our chairs.

We looked around at each other. I could tell that Katie didn't know what to do. But she was the mistress of Rosewood now.

She hesitated a moment, then got up from the table and went slowly toward the door. Slowly she opened it.

"Uncle Templeton!" she exclaimed. The next instant her visitor found himself smothered in a tight hug of joy.

The words flowed like a wave of deliverance into the room. The rest of us let out big sighs of relief accompanied by smiles, and of course Emma started carrying on immediately.

"Hello, Kathleen," said Mr. Daniels. Even as he embraced her at the door, I saw his eyes searching past the entryway into the kitchen until they found me. He smiled above the blond hair of Katie's head buried against his shoulder, and I knew the smile was meant just for me.

"You came back!" said Katie, still holding him.

"That I did, Kathleen," he said. "I can't keep running forever. So here I am."

He stepped back from Katie, and the two of them walked into the kitchen, Katie beaming with pride. Like he had before, he was looking straight at me and gazing deep into my eyes. Now I knew why. And at last I wasn't afraid to return the look of love in his eyes.

"You and me are going to have to have a long talk, Mary Ann," he whispered, ". . . a long talk about your mama, and about you, and me."

I just nodded my head, and for a moment the whole kitchen was silent.

"We're so glad to see you!" said Katie, excitedly interrupting the quiet moment between us. "We're in trouble, Uncle Templeton. Those men I told you about . . . they're back. They're coming today, real soon . . . they said they were coming with guns! Jeremiah's outside right now with a gun. I'm afraid he's going to shoot them. We don't know what to do!"

A serious expression came over Mr. Daniels' face. That's when he noticed Henry standing on the other side of the room.

He walked toward him and stretched out his hand.

"I take it," he said, "that you must be Henry."

"Yes, suh," said Henry, shaking his hand.

"Templeton Daniels," said Katie's uncle.

"Henry Patterson," said Henry with a nod.

"Well, I'm glad to know you, Henry," said Mr. Daniels. "From what these girls of mine tell me, you've been a mighty big help to them. I should have been doing more myself. I want to thank you. I am most appreciative that you've taken it upon yourself to watch over things here. I hope we will be good friends from now on."

A little taken aback to have a white man treat him with such courtesy and respect, Henry hesitated a moment before saying, "Miz Kathleen's right 'bout one thing, Mr. Daniels," he said. "Dem men's comin' back. Dat's what I'm doin' here. Dey's after Miz Kathleen's gold, an' like she say, my son's out dere right now—"

But Mr. Daniels didn't hear the rest of what Henry was about to say.

"What!" he exclaimed, spinning around. "You found it!"

"Oh yes! I almost forgot," said Katie excitedly. "We found it, Uncle Templeton. There really was more gold after all."

"Where?"

"In a lantern down in the cellar."

"A lantern! Well, I'll be."

"I tried to tell them there wasn't any more, but they didn't believe me. They said they were coming back today and that if we didn't give it to them, they were going to ransack the place. They even said they would burn us out if they had to."

"Looks like I got here just in time," said Mr. Daniels, taking in everything Katie had said.

He sat down with a serious and thoughtful expression on his face, then let out a long sigh.

"What's this about your son, Henry?" he said after a minute, glancing toward Henry.

"He took two guns, an' is hidin' out dere right now."

"We got any more weapons?"

"Don' know, suh," said Henry, shaking his head. "Whateber else Miz Kathleen's got, I reckon. But I ain't no man ter use er gun. Dat ain't my way."

Mr. Daniels thought a minute, then looked up at Katie.

"Where is the gold, Kathleen?" he asked.

Katie went and got the bag and set it down on the kitchen table. "So what should we do, Uncle Templeton?" she asked.

He stared at the bag. "Why don't we just . . . give it to them?"

"What about the loan at the bank?"

"It's not worth anyone's getting killed over. We can

take care of it. We're a family now. I'll talk to the banker. I'll tell him what's happened and about Rosalind and the rest of your family. Surely he'll understand. I'm certain he'll extend the terms a few months. I'll work. We'll harvest crops.—That's possible, isn't it, Henry?" he said, glancing toward Henry.

"Dat it is, Mr. Daniels," replied Henry. "Dese ladies here, dey picked dere own cotton las' year an' wiff all da lan' out dere, ain't no tellin what can be done."

"There, Kathleen, you see. It's just like Henry says. We don't need gold, we've got land, and that's better than gold. And we've got each other now too. We don't need that little bag of gold to be a family and to make Rosewood prosperous again. All we need is each other."

Suddenly the sound of horses from outside interrupted him.

Our brief enthusiasm vanished. Suddenly tension filled the room again. Unconsciously every eye in the room went straight to Mr. Daniels. Whether he liked responsibility or not, he was in charge now. He walked toward the open window and looked out.

"It's them, all right," he said. "There's four of them."

He thought a minute.

"All right ... Henry, you take these ladies upstairs."

"What about you, Uncle Templeton?" said Katie.

"Right now I'm more worried about the rest of you," he said. "I'll talk to them and give them the gold. But I want the rest of you out of sight in case they're on a short fuse."

"Should we hide in the cellar?"

"I don't think there's any need for that. I'm going to

try to handle this thing peaceably."

Reluctantly we all left the kitchen and Katie led the way upstairs.

In spite of what he had said, the moment we were gone, Mr. Daniels went to the gun cabinet, took out a rifle, loaded it, and walked with it back to the window, carrying a box of shells.

By then there were already shouts coming from outside.

⤛ ❄ ⤜

SHOOT-OUT
42

J EREMIAH HAD BEEN SURPRISED AND RELIEVED TO SEE
Katie's uncle ride into the yard. He watched him disappear into the house. Things were quiet for a few minutes.
So quiet that Jeremiah was just starting to think about heading back into the house himself when the pounding of horse
hooves filled his ears. He peered through a crack in the barn
door and watched tensely as four riders galloped up to the
house, sending dust flying in all directions.

"Hey in there . . . you Clairbornes!" yelled the lead rider.
"Time's up. We're back like we said we'd be. We're here for
what belongs to us."

"All right," a voice shouted back through the window.
"We've got the gold and we're not going to put up a fight."

It was Katie's uncle's voice. A voice the men clearly
hadn't expected. The rider seemed momentarily puzzled as
two of his partners rode up alongside him.

"That you, Daniels?" he finally called out.

"Yeah, it's me, Jeb."

"What are you doing here?"

"I'm here. That's all that matters."

"I figured you'd be back for the gold one day. Now I can

settle my score with you for that money you cheated me out of."

"I never cheated you, Jeb. You're just a bad poker player, that's all. You should never have called, holding just a pair of sevens."

"We'll see about that, Daniels," the man shouted back. "The way I figure it, I got the winning hand now."

"You're right, Jeb—no argument there. You got me dead to rights. That's why, like I told you, I'm just going to fold and let you walk away with the gold."

"Yeah, well, maybe it ain't that simple, Daniels. You ever think of that? Maybe it's gone too far. Maybe it ain't only the gold we want."

"What else could you want, Jeb? We've got nothing else."

"Yeah, well, maybe we're just gonna take the gold and that pretty little girl in there for Hal here. And maybe I'll just kill you to boot."

"No need for all that, Jeb. I told you, you can have the gold. You don't want to get yourself into even more trouble than you're already in."

"Why should we trust you, Daniels? Ward lied to us. The woman lied to us. The kid lied to us. And you're all kin. We're going to take it . . . all of it."

Another man rode up alongside the fellow called Jeb—the fourth rider who hadn't been with them when they'd come before.

"They're all cut out of the same lying cloth," he now said. "If the rest of you want to keep talking, that's fine. But I say we get this done and get it done the quickest way to make sure nobody lives to talk about it."

His voice was harsh and cold and cruel.

⤺ ✳ ⤻

Upstairs, inside the house, Katie couldn't stand it anymore, whatever her uncle had said about staying out of sight. She was so worried about him that she couldn't stay put. All at once she got up from where she sat on the floor beside me and dashed for the stairs. Henry tried to stop her, but by then Katie was out of sight.

"Emma, you stay here with Henry," I said. "He'll make sure nothing happens to you."

I jumped up and hurried after Katie. The two of us crept downstairs where Mr. Daniels stood just to the side of one of the open windows.

"What in blazes!" he said. "What are you two doing here?"

"I was afraid for you, Uncle Templeton," said Katie. "I wanted to be with you."

"Just keep your heads down."

We crouched beside him. But soon my curiosity got the best of me. I raised myself up and snuck a peek out the bottom of the window.

"Something about that voice seems mighty familiar . . ." said Mr. Daniels, more to himself than to us. Then he glanced over at me. "Keep your head down, Mary Ann!" he said. "What are you trying to do, get yourself shot?"

But I had seen enough.

It wasn't only the man's voice that made me start shaking.

Through the window I had seen a face I knew I'd never forget, with reddish hair and a thick mustache, and those horrible huge eyes of white. It was the man who had killed my family and trampled my grandpapa under his horse's hooves. A chill seized me and I began to tremble in terror.

Almost the same instant, I heard Mr. Daniels say

his name. The sound of it filled me with dread.

"It's Bilsby!" said Mr. Daniels. "What is he doing here!"

"Who is he?" asked Katie.

"He's the meanest cuss I ever knew," he replied. "I didn't know he was hooked up with the rest of them, but I should have figured it. He'll kill us all even if we do give him the gold. I may not be able to talk my way out of this."

Suddenly a shot exploded and sent the glass from the shattered window above our heads tinkling all over the floor.

"You girls get outta here!" said Mr. Daniels. "Bilsby's a guy who plays for keeps!"

He knelt below the windowsill, stuck the barrel of the rifle out of the broken window, and fired back two or three shots. A rapid volley of gunfire came back and broke several more windows. Mr. Daniels fired back again and the room filled with the echo of loud shots coming from everywhere.

Katie was yelling and crying in panic—horrified to see the house she loved being shot up, yelling at everyone and terrified that someone was going to get hurt.

"Stop . . . stop!" she yelled. "Stop it!" But her voice was drowned out by the blast of gunfire and shattering glass and splintering wood and ricocheting bullets all around us.

Suddenly she jumped up from the floor, ran to the table, and grabbed the bag of gold. Then she darted for the door.

"Katie!" I cried.

"Kathleen, get back—" shouted Mr. Daniels.

But it was too late. Katie flew straight out toward the yard and into the middle of the gunfire.

"Stop . . . stop!" she cried in desperation, running

toward the men. "Here's the gold, you can have it! There's no more . . . this is all there is! Just take it and stop shooting and leave us alone!"

Beside me, the rifle Mr. Daniels had been using crashed to the floor. Katie's uncle jumped to his feet and tore through the door after her.

I stood and looked outside. One man was already down. Then I looked at Bilsby and watched in terror as an evil grin came to his lips and he raised his pistol.

I screamed in terror and dashed after them.

Running as fast as he could, Mr. Daniels threw himself in front of Katie and knocked her to the ground. The same instant a puff of white smoke burst from Bilsby's gun and a deafening roar filled the air.

Bilsby turned and saw me running from the house. I glanced toward him and saw the same wild look in his eyes that had paralyzed me with fear more than a year before. He lifted his gun and pointed it straight at me. But then a second shot exploded from behind me. The same instant a huge splotch of red burst from the middle of Bilsby's chest. I saw the light of life instantly go out of his face, and he crumbled from his horse onto the dirt.

"Katie, Katie!" I cried, running to where she lay partially covered by her uncle's body. I was in such a panic at the sight of blood splattered all over Katie's dress that I thought nothing of where the second shot could have come from.

~ ❄ ~

Jeremiah knew where the shot had come from. He now walked deliberately out of the barn, shotgun in his hands. He was not looking at Mayme but toward a second-floor window of the house, stunned at the sight that met his eyes. There stood his father with the rifle in his hands, still smoking, that had ended Bilsby's life.

"Let's get out of here," cried Jeb. "If they find us with him, we'll swing from a tree. I don't want to hang for the rest of Bilsby's murders!"

The bag had flown from Katie's hand as she fell. Gold and dirt and dust were strewn everywhere. With one last fleeting glance at the half-empty bag on the ground, the man called Jeb thought better of it, then spun his horse around and galloped away with his one remaining comrade, just as Jeremiah sent a barrel of buckshot after them.

Mayme knelt sobbing beside Katie. Blood covered her back and neck as she lay motionless. "Katie . . . Katie, please . . . please don't be dead!"

Jeremiah felt helpless. He hurried over and knelt beside Mayme. Suddenly Katie tried to roll over. "I'm . . . I'm all right, Mayme," she groaned. "I think I just fell."

Mayme smothered her friend with kisses, hardly realizing that she was getting blood all over her hands and sleeves. For a second or two, Jeremiah was so relieved that Mayme and Katie weren't hurt, it didn't occur to him to wonder why there was so much blood.

Slowly the truth dawned on him. Then on Mayme. She leaned back onto her knees and took in the horrible sight. The blood splattered on Katie's dress wasn't hers at all.

As Katie struggled to get out from under her uncle and to her feet, Templeton Daniels lay unmoving on the ground, with the bullet from Bilsby's gun now lodged about an inch from his heart.

Jeremiah still knelt beside Mayme. He heard footsteps, then turned to see his papa emerge from the house. He stood and studied his father's face. Never had he seen a face so full of love and grief and grim determination at the same time. The two men stood gazing into each other's eyes a second or two. Then Jeremiah extended his hand. Henry grasped it silently.

"Thank you, Papa," Jeremiah whispered for his father's ears only. "I wuz mighty feared I'd lose her. . . ."

"I knows it, son. I know. . . ."

Jeremiah squeezed his father's hand, blinking back tears. He knew what getting that rifle had cost his father in his heart, and knew the sacrifice and pain it had taken for him to pull the trigger.

"I'm proud of you, Papa," he said.

Henry let out a deep sigh, released Jeremiah's grasp, and put a hand on each of his son's shoulders. Then with a nod he stepped back and walked to where Bilsby lay. He stooped down to see for sure whether he was dead.

Henry bowed his head and closed his eyes. Jeremiah knew he was praying. When he rose a minute later, tears flowed out of Henry's eyes.

After a moment, Henry stooped down and rolled Katie's uncle partially onto his side. The man's eyes were closed. A trickle of blood oozed out of the side of his mouth.

"Hit don' look good," mumbled Henry. "He's hurt bad."

He glanced up at Katie and Mayme. "You girls, you don' need ter be lookin' at no dead man's face," said Henry, "effen dat's what dis is.—Jeremiah," he said, glancing up at him, "you git t' town an' bring da doc. Effen he hesitates, you tell him hit's a white man. You git him here soon, boy. Don' take no fer an answer."

Jeremiah ran for the barn.

"—you ladies," said Henry again, "git back. Y'all can't do him no good now. He an' dose other two layin' dere—dey's in da Lord's han's now."

Aftermath of Death
43

J EREMIAH RETURNED AS SOON AS HE COULD WITH THE doctor. He and Henry pulled the two dead bodies off to the side of the yard, then carried Mr. Daniels into the kitchen.

"Where can we lay him?" asked the doctor, glancing around as they struggled to hold the limp body.

"There's a big couch in the parlor," Mayme said. "Or there's beds upstairs."

"No, we don't want to carry him upstairs in his condition."

"You mean he's alive!" Mayme exclaimed.

"Just barely," said the doctor, "and hanging on by less than a thread. Show me the parlor."

Jeremiah couldn't help wondering what the doctor thought of seeing so many coloreds in the house without sight of any familiar Clairborne face.

"And who is this fellow again?" the doctor asked as they eased Katie's uncle down onto the couch.

"Mistress Clairborne's brother, suh," said Henry.

"Is he the only one who's hurt? What about the rest of them?"

"Yes'uh—dey's all fine. Where's Miz Clairborne, Miz Mayme?"

"Upstairs," Mayme answered.

"What about Richard?" asked the doctor.

"Mr. Clairborne's away, sir—he's up north," Mayme said quickly. "But Mistress Clairborne's fine . . . she's asleep upstairs."

The doctor nodded and seemed satisfied.

"Well, as soon as we're done here," he said, speaking again to Henry, "I'll ride over to Oakwood and send the sheriff out for those two bodies. You got any idea who they are, Henry?"

"No, suh."

"I do," Mayme said. "The man with the reddish brown beard is called Bilsby."

"That's Bilsby!" exclaimed the doctor. "How do you know?"

"Mr. Daniels said he recognized him. I heard him say so just before the shooting started."

The doctor let out a low whistle.

"Bilsby! This is going to cause quite a stir!" he said. "They've been looking high and low for him. Sheriff Jenkins is going to be mighty interested to hear this! There might even be a reward, for all I know. This Daniels fellow shoot him?"

His question was directed to no one in particular. The doctor still didn't seem to know what to make of the fact that he was standing and talking to a room full of blacks, none of whom answered him.

"'Bout dem two bodies, Doc," said Henry without answering the question. "Don't trouble yerse'f—Jeremiah an' me, we'll load 'em into one ob Mistress Clairborne's wagons an' take 'em ter town ourse'ves. We don' want dese yere ladies havin' dem layin' dere no longer'n need be."

"Suit yourself," said the doctor. "Just the same, the sheriff's going to want to talk to you about what happened."

"Yes'uh."

"Bilsby," he repeated, shaking his head. "I can't believe it.—All right, I'll go get my bag. And you," said the doctor, looking at Mayme, "I'm going to need some boiling water. I'm going to see if I can get that slug out of his chest."

When the doctor returned to the kitchen about a half hour later, his face was grim. He was holding his surgical knife and wiping it with a white cloth. Both were stained with blood.

He cleaned up at the sink, then went back to get his bag and coat. Ignoring the others, he nodded to Henry as he walked to the door. Henry followed him. Mayme stepped next to the window where broken bits of glass still lay strewn all over the floor and strained to listen. Jeremiah stood next to her.

". . . got the slug out . . ." the doctor was saying. "Doesn't look good . . . hasn't lost that much blood, but . . . too close to the heart . . ."

Henry nodded and said something they couldn't hear.

". . . did what I could . . ." The doctor went on to say, "but I wouldn't hold out much hope. . . ."

At that, Mayme turned toward Jeremiah and began weeping in his arms.

Somehow the day passed. Henry and Jeremiah drove the bodies to the sheriff's office in Oakwood and returned. For the next several hours Jeremiah did what he could around the place, helping with a few chores—milking the cows and tending the other animals. The girls kept busy in the house, cleaning up the mess of broken glass and other things in the kitchen.

Emma fixed some supper and they all ate in silence, too aware of the man lying near death in the next room to do much talking.

"Y'all want me an' Jeremiah ter stay da night in da barn, Miz Kathleen?" Henry finally asked.

"If you don't mind, Henry," replied Katie. "At least one

of you. I just . . . we wouldn't want to be alone if . . . you know, if—"

"We's bof stay," said Henry. "Mr. Guiness an' Mr. Watson, dere biz'ness'll keep, ain't dat right, son?"

Jeremiah nodded. "We be here jes' as long as you wants, Miz Katie," he said.

What he didn't say was that Jeremiah was a mite puzzled by how Mayme was carrying on. Of course it was hard to see a man get shot, especially Katie's uncle. But was there more to it than that? The way Mayme kept sitting by the man's bed as the afternoon wore on—tending him, crying over him— was beginning to make Jeremiah wonder just what were Mayme's feelings for the man. Wasn't he just an ordinary white man, almost a stranger? Why was she so upset?

The next day brought no change. The doctor came back out, changed Mr. Daniels' dressing, and left again, his face grim. He offered no words of hope, saying only "time will tell" and told the girls to try to get him to swallow a bit of water every few hours.

On the morning of the third day, Jeremiah came into the kitchen, stiff from another night in the barn. He'd slept in many barns before and even out on the open ground, but he reckoned these months on the soft pallet in his father's room had softened him some. He poured himself a cup of coffee as Katie came into the kitchen from the parlor.

"Coffee, Miz Katie?" he asked.

"No thanks, Jeremiah," replied Katie. "Just some milk, I think."

"How be your uncle dis mornin'?"

"The same, I'm afraid." She poured herself a cup of milk to take with her into the parlor. "I'm going back to sit with him."

"You seen Miz Mayme dis mornin'?" Jeremiah asked.

"She sat up with him most of the night."

"She sleepin', then?"

"No. She went for a walk."

As Katie left the kitchen Jeremiah went to the window and scanned the yard. He saw Mayme walking around the length of the field toward the river. He finished his coffee and waited.

Half an hour or so later, Jeremiah left the house. He found Mayme sitting on the bank and watching the river silently move past. Tears were flowing down her cheeks. She glanced up as he came across the field, then stood and smiled.

"How'd you know where to find me?" she asked, standing up as he walked up the bank toward her.

"I watched you go when you lef'."

Without any more words he took her in his arms. They stood for a minute or two, holding each other quietly.

Jeremiah took Mayme's hand and they sat down together. They sat for some time, just staring into the river, neither saying a word. Jeremiah wanted to ask her what she was feeling, about Mr. Daniels, about *him*, about everything, but he couldn't make the words come.

Finally Mayme broke the silence. "I been sittin' here," she said. "Prayin' for him. For me too, I reckon. I'm not ready to say good-bye. There are so many things I want to tell him. . . ."

"It's right kind of you, Mayme," said Jeremiah, "caring for Miz Katie's uncle so."

He felt her studying him, but kept his eyes on the river.

"That's right . . ." Mayme said slowly. "You were in the barn when he came back, so you didn't hear. Then with all the shootin' and everything . . ."

"Didn't hear what?" asked Jeremiah, glancing over at her.

"Something I've wanted to tell you. But now . . . I'm afraid to all of a sudden. I hope it won't change how you . . . how you think about me."

"What is it?"

"Jeremiah," said Mayme slowly, "Mr. Daniels is more than just Katie's uncle. Though of course she loves him. But I . . . I love him too."

"You. . . . *love* him?" he said in a husky croak.

"Well, I didn't right at first, when I found out. At first I was angry. But now I'm afraid I'll lose him."

"Found out what?"

"You understand, don't you, Jeremiah? I mean, you thought you lost your father, but you wanted to be with him again, so you didn't give up until you found him. . . ."

"Miz Mayme, I ain't sure I . . ."

"My father. Can you believe it, Jeremiah? Templeton Daniels . . . is my father."

"Your father?" Jeremiah repeated in surprise.

"Yes. I know it's hard to believe, but it's true."

"You got my head spinnin' round so fast, I don' know what to think," said Jeremiah. "You bes' start from the beginning."

"I know what you mean," said Mayme. "I was plumb dumbfounded myself. Seems my mama and Katie's mama grew up together, friends like, though I suppose my mama worked for the family, though she wasn't exactly like a slave. When Katie's folks came here to Rosewood, my mama came along. And this is where my papa—Mr. Daniels—met her and they fell in love. He wanted to marry her, but Mr. Clairborne, Katie's father, he didn't like the sound of that at all. He got angry and sold my mama to the McSimmons. My papa tried to find her, but never did. He never knew she was expecting me neither, not until he saw me here."

"I wondered why he looked at you funny!"

"Me too!"

"Well, dat explains it. You must look a powerful lot like your mama."

"My papa says so."

"Your mama must have been one fine-looking woman."

Mayme smiled and looked down, embarrassed.

"You don't mind, then?" she said timidly.

"Mind?"

"About me being half white?"

"You cud be half green an' I wouldn't care."

Mayme laughed and squeezed his hand. They sat for a few minutes. Then they both grew more serious.

"I don' know. I never thought much about such things. I suppose it can't help but change things some."

"What do you mean?" asked Mayme.

"Don't you think dis might change things fo you? You got a rich white papa an' I'm jes' a poor slave boy. . . ."

"You ain't a slave no more."

"I's still poor, though."

"My papa's poor too," said Mayme. "Though you wouldn't know it to look at him. I thought he was a dandy when he first came."

"Me too," Jeremiah chuckled, then asked more seriously, "You don't think he'll mind effen I court his daughter?"

"You'll have to ask him."

Jeremiah looked over at Mayme and saw tears begin to fill her eyes again. He knew she was fearing her papa wouldn't live long enough for anyone to talk to again. He released her hand and put his arm around her shoulder.

How long they sat together, Jeremiah didn't know. For a long spell, the only sound between them was the sound of the river. Gradually another sound intruded into his ears. Slowly Jeremiah turned his head and glanced back over the fields.

Someone was running toward them.

"Mayme . . . Mayme!" a voice called.

Now Mayme heard it too. She turned and looked back toward the house in the distance. Katie was running toward them.

"Mayme!" Katie cried again.

Beside him, Jeremiah felt Mayme stiffen, fearing the

worst. He helped her to her feet. Together they hurried down the embankment.

"Mayme!" Katie cried again as she got nearer. "Come . . . hurry. He's awake!"

Mayme flashed Jeremiah a quick look of joy, then turned and dashed toward the house, leaving Katie out of breath and Jeremiah hurrying to catch up.

When Jeremiah climbed the porch steps and made his way into the house a minute or two later, pausing to catch his breath, happy sounds of talking and laughing met his ears. He stopped at the parlor door and peeked around the doorframe.

Mr. Daniels still lay on the couch, but now his eyes were open. Even though he still looked pale—he was a white man, after all—Jeremiah thought he looked a little less white than he had before.

"Where've you been, little girl?" Mr. Daniels asked as Mayme knelt down beside him. "I've been asking everyone where you were."

His voice was weak, but Jeremiah saw the hint of a smile on his face.

"Oh, Papa!" Mayme burst out. "I was just so afraid. I thought—"

"That I was going to die? Naw . . . I told you that you and I were going to have a long talk. And from now on, I intend to be a man who keeps his promises. I told you, I'm not about to lose you now."

Mayme laughed through her tears.

"But I am about as thirsty as I've ever been in my life," Mr. Daniels said. "How does a man get a drink around here?"

Mayme jumped up and ran toward the kitchen. Seeing Jeremiah standing there, she gave him a great smile and threw her arms around him, then hurried to the pump for a glass of water. Seconds later she ran back into the parlor.

"Help me sit up," Mr. Daniels groaned. "I'm sick of lying here."

Jeremiah was about to step forward to help, but Mayme was already there, putting an arm behind the man's shoulders and trying to ease him up as he struggled forward. Mr. Daniels winced in pain.

"Aagh . . . ow—it hurts! What happened to me anyway?"

"You got shot, Papa," Mayme said. "You got shot saving Katie's life."

"Did I, now? Well, that sounds mighty heroic! Seems I do remember something about chasing her out of the house when suddenly everything went black."

"If you can sit up a little more, I'll give you a drink of water."

With Mayme's arm around him, he managed to lean forward enough to reach the glass.

"Ah, Mary Ann . . . that feels good," he said as he sipped at it. Mayme tipped the glass higher until he managed to drink down the whole thing. "I need more. I'm parched!"

Mary Ann, Jeremiah thought. *Mayme's name is Mary Ann?* Well, he supposed, he used to go by Jake and now went by Jeremiah, so why shouldn't Mayme have two names too!

Within minutes all the girls were clustered around, all talking at once and trying to help Mr. Daniels get comfortable. Mayme sent Jeremiah upstairs for pillows and blankets while she ran into the kitchen for more water. Emma began bustling about, asking what he wanted to eat.

"My, oh my," Mr. Daniels said as Jeremiah came back down the stairs, "I don't know if all this attention is good for me!"

"It be good fer us, Mr. Daniels!" said Emma. "We all thought you wuz gwine ter die, an' it's been so quiet roun' here I jes' about cudn't stan' dat silence no mo'!"

At Emma's words, the whole room rang with laughter. How quickly life had returned to Rosewood!

SO MANY UNCLES!
44

*U*ncle Templeton—my papa—recovered quickly and made good on his promise to stay and take care of things with the bank. We were able to retrieve enough of the gold Katie had thrown on the ground to pay off the second loan. Papa lived at Rosewood for the better part of the next year helping to get the plantation on a firm footing again. He learned all about crops and weather and ploughing and animals and cotton and wheat. He helped with our second harvest of cotton, getting blisters on his fingers, and his face and arms growing tan. He even learned how to milk cows!

After the harvest, we all enjoyed a quiet winter. I loved having my new family all together. Emma and William, my papa, and my cousin—*cousin!*—Katie. Add to that plenty of visits from a certain handsome young man, and I couldn't remember a time I'd been so happy. Fact was, I was beginning to think things were going along a mite too smooth to last.

I was right.

Our new troubles began in the spring of 1867, when my papa announced that he had to leave again. The new cotton crop was in and starting to come up, and *he figured it was a good time to be gone. He assured us it was only for a little while, a few weeks at most. He said he had some things to take care of from the past. He'd taken part in some less than upright business dealings and it was time to make amends. Once he took care of that, he said, he would be back. Back to stay.*

And that's why we were alone—two years after Katie's scheme began—when the thing we'd been most afraid of finally happened.

≈ ✳ ≈

Jeremiah was standing in for his papa in the livery when Mayme came riding up the street on horseback, a second horse on a lead behind her. He was so pleased to see her that he didn't think to wonder much why she had the other horse. Maybe it had thrown a shoe. It didn't matter. He was always glad to see Mayme. He had been out to Rosewood a few days back for a visit, so he hadn't expected to see her again so soon. They had spent a fair amount of time together over the winter and he was just beginning to think the time might soon be coming for him to ask her a certain question. Not just yet, though. He was saving all the money he could from his job with Mr. Watson—and from helping out at the livery. Maybe by the end of the summer.

With this happy thought, he lifted a hand toward Mayme as she rode close, a smile of welcome on his face. But his smile soon faded when he saw the expression on Mayme's face.

"Mayme, what is it?" asked Jeremiah as he grabbed her horse's reins and helped her down.

"Oh, Jeremiah! It finally happened!" she said.

"What?"

"He came! Katie's uncle Burchard from Charlotte! Her pa's brother. He's the one Katie's been worried about all this time! He wants to see Katie's ma."

"What are you going to do?" Jeremiah asked.

"We put him off once already and he's madder than a hornet. He's not like the others. He's not going to give up."

"What do you think he wants?"

"Rosewood, I'm guessing!" Mayme said. "And he can't stand coloreds, that's for sure! You should have seen how he looked at me, like I was a dog or something! Oh! I wish my papa was here!"

"No word?"

"No. And it's been nearly two weeks!"

"Well, my pa's not here right now either," Jeremiah said. "But I 'spect him back anytime."

"What are we going to do, Jeremiah?" asked Mayme. "There don't seem any way around the fact that our scheme is about over now. That man is going to find out and send us away!

"I'll have to go look for a paying job," Mayme continued. "Though I don't suppose a sixteen-year-old white girl and a seventeen-year-old black girl could make enough to live on their own without a house like we've had these last few years. And what'll become of Emma and William!"

"Nothing bad's gwine happen," Jeremiah said, doing his best to encourage her. "My pa will be back soon and he'll help us figure somethin' out."

But Henry didn't have any answers either. He did ride out to Rosewood that same evening on the horse Mayme had left for him and talked to the girls and prayed for them. But at the time, it didn't seem to them that all his praying did much good. When Katie told her uncle Burchard about her mama and daddy being dead, he showed her not one bit of kindness. Instead he got the lawyer Mr. Sneed to draw up a new deed to the place—in his own name—since, according to him, Rosewood should have belonged to him all along anyway. Worse yet, he said they all had to leave, just as Mayme had feared. Katie could stay if she wanted to, since she was kin, but he didn't want any coloreds around the place.

None of them knew how much time they had, but Katie and Mayme started watching the road more and more closely, hoping more than ever that Templeton would come back and help them figure out what to do.

FINAL NOTICE
45

Someone did arrive at Rosewood the next day, but it wasn't my papa. It was Josepha, the former house slave from the McSimmons place where Emma and me used to live. The big woman was crying and worn out from the long walk, but relieved to find us. Katie and I didn't want to spoil Josepha's happiness at being away from Mrs. McSimmons, but we had to tell her how things stood with Katie's uncle, and that none of us would likely have a home there for long.

When Katie's uncle Burchard came back a few weeks later, he gave Katie notice that we all had to be off the place by the end of the week. So me and Emma and little William, as well as Josepha, packed up our few belongings and got ready to head north. We didn't know exactly where we would go, just that we had to leave the next morning. I had no idea what would become of me, or whether I'd ever see Katie or Jeremiah again.

Henry and Jeremiah came out that evening to say their good-byes too. Ever since all this had been happening, Henry had been sorely grieved about the talk of us leaving. But he didn't have any solution to suggest. He and Jeremiah didn't have room to take us in. Henry just rented two small rooms behind the livery from Mr. Guiness, the man he worked for. Even if there was room for three women and a baby, Mr. Guiness would never have stood for it, not to mention the townspeople. If the whites around had seen anything like that, they'd have had a fit. Henry didn't think Katie ought to leave, though, especially since she needed to be around when her uncle Templeton came back. So we all promised to keep in touch. It was still plain that Henry and Jeremiah didn't like the idea of us leaving. But what else could we do?

Jeremiah and I went for a long walk. But it wasn't anything like the ones we'd had earlier, because we knew we were saying good-bye and might not see each other for a long time. I thought Jeremiah wanted to ask me to marry him, and might have been fixing to. But he didn't, and I was glad. There wasn't any way I could leave Emma, not now, not the way things were. And Josepha'd never be able to take care of her alone. I thought down inside Jeremiah knew it too, and didn't ask 'cause he knew I'd have to say no. It wasn't that we didn't love each other. At least I knew I loved Jeremiah and was pretty sure he loved me too. But sometimes life gets in the way of love. And sometimes being black gets in the way of how you wish life could be.

It was a quiet walk. There wasn't much to say. My heart hurt, I was so full of love. The next day I was going to have to say good-bye to Katie, and tonight I was saying good-bye to Jeremiah, and the thought of that made me feel so full and so sad at the same time.

We walked a long way hand in hand in silence.

"I wish dere wuz sum way fer you not ter go," said Jeremiah after a while.

"I'd give anything not to have to," I sighed. "But Katie's done everything she can. And . . . Emma and

Josepha need me to go with them."

"Why can't y'all stay in Greens Crossing sumplace?"

"Where, Jeremiah? Where could we stay? And Emma can't stay here. She's in danger. She's got to go somewhere else."

"I reckon."

Again it was quiet for a long while.

"I don't like da thought ob not seein' you agin," said Jeremiah. "I'm a little feared dat you won't come back, dat you'll forgit all 'bout me an'—"

"Jeremiah," I interrupted. "I will never forget you. I'll come back, just as soon as I can."

"But what if you can't? What if sumfin happens ter you an' I ain't dere ter help you?"

"We'll be all right."

"Dat soun's good, but sumtimes bad things happen an' folks can't do what dey want ter do."

He let out a nervous and frustrated sigh.

"It's jes' dat I thought dat sumday . . . you an' me, you know . . . might . . ."

I squeezed his hand. I *did* know! I had hoped so too. My heart was aching. I didn't want to leave him. But Katie's uncle would own Rosewood the next morning, and one thing he didn't want around the place was Negroes. We still didn't know where my papa, Templeton Daniels, was and hadn't heard from him.

"I will come back, Jeremiah," I said again. "I promise. You just promise me you'll be here and won't go leaving looking for me or something and then neither of us ever find each other again."

"I reckon I dun enuff travelin' lookin' fo my pa," he said. "I figger I'll stay put roun' here fo a spell. Don't know where I'd go anyway."

We arrived back at the house and Jeremiah gently took me in his arms and kissed me softly. "I best stop now. Knowin' my luck, effen I keep on kissin' you, dat's right when yer pa *would* come back."

I smiled but tears filled my eyes. "Then kiss me again," I whispered, one teardrop spilling over and down my face.

He leaned close and kissed my damp cheek. "Dat ain't a kiss good-bye, hear?"

"What is it, then?"

"A promise to be here when you come back."

After all our tearful good-byes, the next day we were in for a huge surprise. One of Katie's other uncles that she'd thought was dead suddenly turned up with the deed to the property. For someone who thought she had been left all alone in the world such a short time before, Katie sure had lots of kin that always seemed to be showing up! This Uncle Ward, Templeton Daniels' brother, had been the rightful owner of Rosewood all along, not Katie's uncle Burchard.

Burchard Clairborne was madder than he could be. But with Ward Daniels standing there holding the deed to the plantation and its land, there wasn't much for him to do but storm off.

Katie had never seen Ward Daniels before. For all she knew he would want us to leave too. But he turned out to be nothing like her uncle Burchard. He said we could all stay and that Katie could keep running Rose-wood just like she had been. He didn't even seem to care that half of us were colored!

The only problem was that Emma, William, Josepha, and I had already left! So Katie and her uncle Ward came after us on horseback, leaving Henry and Jeremiah waiting back at Rosewood.

About an hour later, Mr. Daniels galloped back into the yard on Miz Katie's horse—alone. Jeremiah, already sweating, ran a worried hand over his face.

"Easy, son," Henry said and stepped forward to help the man dismount.

"You Henry?" Mr. Daniels asked.

"I is," Henry replied.

"Kathleen sent me back, said you wouldn't mind helping me. Hope that's right."

"Dat's right, all right."

"Good." The man smiled. "My niece wants me to bring back a wagon."

"You found dem!" exclaimed Jeremiah.

"Yep. All three, no, four," said Mr. Daniels. "Katie said Henry would know which wagon and which horse would be best."

"Dat I do. Come, Jeremiah, gib me a han'."

Father and son made short work of hitching up the wagon, and soon Mr. Daniels was climbing up on the seat board.

"Much obliged," he said, then glanced at Jeremiah. "You want to come along, son?" he asked.

"Dat I would, suh!"

"I thought as much," smiled Mr. Daniels.

⤙ ❊ ⤚

I sat beside Katie on the grass, near the spot where she and her uncle Ward had found us, listening as she told us about all the excitement we had missed back at Rosewood when her uncle Ward had put such a sudden end to her uncle Burchard's plans. How quickly everything had changed!

We talked excitedly and Katie told us all about how her uncle had ridden up right at the last minute and about how mad her uncle Burchard had been. We all laughed and asked so many questions that the time went by quickly. Before we knew it, we heard the sound of the wagon coming along the road. And there was Jeremiah sitting beside Katie's uncle on the seat board! Now I was even happier than ever!

I smiled and waved, and before Mr. Daniels had even reined in the horse to a full stop, Jeremiah leaped down from the wagon and caught me in his arms and swung me around. Then he seemed to notice all the others standing around and he stepped back a bit sheepishly.

He cleared his throat. "Uh . . . good to see you agin, Miz Mayme."

Everyone burst out laughing, and William ran forward and jumped into his arms, saying he wanted to be swung around too.

Katie told her uncle who we all were. Then Mr. Daniels turned the wagon around, and we all loaded up and began the ride back home. Jeremiah sat with me and the others in the back while Katie sat up front with her uncle. Jeremiah didn't say anything, but he couldn't seem to stop looking at me and smiling. Content, I sat back and listened as Katie and her uncle talked.

"How did you hear about what was going on, Uncle Ward?" asked Katie.

"I read about the two of you in a paper up north. That's how I found out Richard and Rosalind were dead, and I figured I ought to come down and see if there was any way I could help out, you being kin and all."

"Did you know about Uncle Burchard's saying Rosewood was his and having a new deed drawn up and everything?"

"There was just a mention of a brother of Richard's in the paper. But I didn't know any more than that till

I got to Greens Crossing. I saw a notice up on a sign-board and I asked somebody about it. That's when I figured I'd better hightail it out there so I could have a say in the matter."

"I'm sure glad you did!" said Katie.

"And just in the nick of time, by all appearances," he said.

"I'm sorry about us using up all your gold, Uncle Ward."

"I didn't come back for the gold, Kathleen. But tell me again what happened with it?"

"We used it for Rosewood," answered Katie. "My mama had taken out two loans when my daddy was away at the war, and after they were killed, the loans came due. Mayme and I found the gold and paid off the loans."

"Well, no matter. I'm glad it got put to good use. I came back to see if you were okay and to tell you how sorry I am about your ma. If my hard work in California helped save the place from some banker, well then, I figure maybe that's worth it."

Suddenly, Katie's uncle Ward turned to look at me. "And what about you, Mayme?" he asked. "I read in the story in the paper that you lost your family too, just like Kathleen. You want to stay on at Rosewood too?"

"Yes, sir, Mr. Daniels," I answered. "Rosewood's my home. This is the just about the only family I've got left."

I smiled at the man, then turned to Jeremiah and whispered, "I only just thought of it—he's *my* uncle too!"

≈ ❉ ≈

TOGETHER AGAIN
46

*L*ife around Rosewood changed a lot after that, when Katie's two uncles, Mr. Templeton Daniels and Mr. Ward Daniels, finally came to live at Rosewood for good. Of course, first we had had to find my papa, who was still missing. Turns out he had run into some problems up north, when one of the men he wanted to repay had him thrown in jail instead. But after Mr. Ward and Katie made a trip up north, and with the help of a young deputy there, I finally had my papa back home with me again.

Mr. Ward said we could all stay—me, Emma, William, and Josepha—and that Katie could keep running Rosewood just like she had been. He didn't even seem to care that most of us were colored!

One of the biggest changes of all was Katie and me trying to get used to the fact that we were cousins. But other things were going to take longer to sort out. Knowing that Templeton Daniels was my father made me feel like I had to figure out all over again who I really was.

I reckoned the changes in me were similar to the kinds of changes that had come in Jeremiah's life, finding his pa, realizing his past was different than he thought, and now suddenly having a place to call home. That was new for him too.

Even our names were new. Jake was calling himself *Jeremiah* now, to please Henry. And even though I had grown up as Mary Ann Jukes, now that I knew about my real father and how he and my mother had been in love, I began calling myself Mary Ann *Daniels*.

Once the two Daniels brothers were sort of in charge of Rosewood, though they let Katie and me mostly do what we thought best, there was no longer any need for Katie's scheme. Besides, everyone around Greens Crossing knew what had happened after Burchard Clairborne shared the secret with Mrs. Hammond. And, of course, the newspaper articles and all. Mrs. Hammond at the store tried to make like she'd known it all along!

After that our lives became a little more normal, if living on a plantation with three whites and four coloreds all together under the same roof could ever be called normal!

We were all growing up—Katie and me and Emma and Jeremiah. Katie and I had met when we were fourteen and fifteen. Jeremiah had come to Greens Crossing when he was seventeen.

But by the time the year 1867 gave way to 1868 and we began planting new crops for yet another year's harvest, Katie was seventeen and would soon turn eighteen, and I was eighteen and would be nineteen about the time of the harvest in August. Jeremiah was practically a grown man now at twenty. Even little William wasn't so little anymore.

We'd all changed a lot since 1865. To me, it seemed that Katie had changed most of all. She was tall and shapely, with that long, curly blond hair of hers, and just about as pretty as anyone could imagine. She often wore her mother's dresses now. They fit her real good. Her mother sure knew how to pick pretty clothes. She must have been a real lady.

The South wasn't the same as it had been before the war. But if it had been, I could almost imagine Katie as a Southern belle at her daddy's plantation with all the young men clustered around her asking her for a dance at a party or ball, and trying to win her heart and ask for her hand. Of course, that South of plantations and balls and parties and slaves was gone forever now.

Katie's mama and daddy's plantation had changed more than most, I reckon. There were more blacks living under Katie's roof than whites. We were quite a mixed-up family—blacks and whites and half of each, uncles and cousins and brothers and friends—all coming and going and working together around the place. That made a lot of the local people, like Mrs. Hammond, pretty upset. But Katie was determined in her love and loyalty. She made all of us feel that we really belonged to the "family" at Rosewood. And four of us—Katie and me and Ward and Templeton Daniels—really were blood kin to Katie's mama. Emma and her son, William, and Josepha, were still living with us too. And with Henry and Jeremiah living at the livery in town but coming out to see us all the time—no, the townsfolk didn't like the goings-on at Rosewood one bit. They thought it was scandalous all the mixing up of black and white as if skin color didn't matter at all.

But I didn't think it was scandalous. I thought it was right nice. It reminded me of the tunes Katie played on the piano in the parlor. All kinds of notes mixing together to make beautiful music.

Like the day I walked into the kitchen and heard

the strangest thing. Josepha was talking in what sounded like a foreign language! It was followed by the sound of Henry chuckling.

They glanced toward me as I entered.

"What was that, Josepha?" I asked.

"What wuz what?"

"Whatever you were saying. It sounded like some other language or something."

"It wuzn't nuthin'. I wuz jes' tellin' Henry 'bout sumfin dat happened a long time ago, dat's all."

I had heard and told plenty of slave stories in old "black grandpapa" language—but even I didn't understand what they were saying!

Josepha glanced toward Henry and they smiled at one another, like there was a secret they alone shared.

The next moment Uncle Ward came in from outside and Katie came downstairs. Katie went to the pantry, and Josepha asked Mr. Ward if he wanted a cup of coffee. My papa came in and asked Henry's advice on fixing the plough, and out on the porch, Emma was singing an old field song to little William.

That's the way Rosewood was—whites, blacks, half-whites, men, women, old, young . . . and we were all a family together!

The whole South was changing as fast as things around Rosewood. With the war over and slaves free, nothing was like it was before. The old way of life was gone. Northerners called "carpetbaggers" were coming down to the South. There were lots of resentments against free blacks. Greens Crossing was starting to grow with new people coming and going.

The Rosewood plantation slowly began running halfway normally. We were growing crops and tending animals and making enough money and growing enough vegetables to feed us all and even to have a little money to spare—something Katie's mama never had during the war.

My papa and Uncle Ward were so different than they had been before! It was like they'd been running a plantation all their lives. Everyone at Rosewood thought the world of them and felt so safe now that they were in charge of things.

But the rest of the community wasn't so pleased, and didn't think quite as much of the Daniels brothers as we did. In fact, there was a growing tension between Rosewood and the rest of the townspeople. The two "Northerners," as people thought of them, were "nigger-lovers" and people hated them for it. People thought of Templeton as a Yankee dandy and carpetbagger himself, just because of the way he used to dress and the polished way he spoke. Some people in town resented him and Uncle Ward all the more too because they seemed to be making a successful go of Rosewood again. When a lot of the plantations in North Carolina were struggling without slaves, here was a crazy little family of whites and blacks and kids and a former house slave . . . and we were making money.

People didn't like it.

❧ ❀ ❧

A DADDY FOR WILLIAM
47

ONE DAY JEREMIAH CAME AROUND THE SIDE OF THE house and saw Emma sitting on the steps of the big wide front porch. She was shelling peas and watching William running around on the grass playing with one of the dogs. Jeremiah walked over and sat down beside her.

"Hey, girl, wha'chu up to?" he asked good-naturedly.

"Jes' shucking sum peas."

"I kin see dat," said Jeremiah, reaching into the bowl and taking a small handful, then popping a few in his mouth.

"Hey, you stay outta dere!" laughed Emma as she slapped at his hand. "Dose is fo our supper!"

"Well, den, I's jes' havin' myself sum supper right now!"

"Dat right, dat right . . . you's jes like all da rest!"

"What dat supposed ter mean!"

"Jes' what Josepha sez—dat men's always thinkin' 'bout dere stomachs."

"I reckon dere ain't no way ter keep from dat aroun' here, with such good vittles as dere always is. It looks like dat boy ob yers been makin' good use ob it too. He's turnin' into a right chubby little feller, all right."

Emma smiled and they sat for a few seconds watching William.

"Yep, dat William be growin' up like er weed," said Jeremiah as they quieted.

"Dat he is. An' I owes it all ter dis place," said Emma. "I can't hardly imagine what I'd dun effen Miz Katie an' Miz Mayme hadn't taken care ob me like dey dun."

William came toward the porch, stared at Jeremiah, then walked up the steps and put his arms around him.

"Hey, what dis, little man!"

"Will you be my daddy, Jer'miah?" said William, staring up into Jeremiah's face with wide, innocent eyes.

"Shush yo mouf, William!" said Emma, embarrassed.

"He only been mostly aroun' white men," she added to Jeremiah. "He ain't neber had no black man up close afore you and Henry come. He's always looked at you dif'rent."

Emma reached out to pull William toward her. But Jeremiah stopped her.

"Dat's all right," he said. Then he looked into William's face and pulled him up into his lap.

"I can't be yo daddy, William," he said. "But I kin be yo frien', jes' like I's yo mama's frien'."

"Why can't you be my daddy?"

"'Cuz I jes' can't. But sumday I reckon dere'll come a time when yo mama'll fin' sumbody dat'll be a daddy ter you."

Emma glanced over with a strange expression.

"You mean dat, Jeremiah?" she said. "Duz you really think so?"

"Why not, Emma? Look at all da changes dat's comin' ter black folks like us. Jes' think—we ain't slaves no mo. We got people an' frien's and even a little money ob our own. Dis is a good time ter be colored. I figger we's 'bout da luckiest colored folks dere eber wuz. An' it's gwine git better too, so I figger you'll meet sum black man one day who'll take care ob you an' William jes' like Miz Katie an' Mayme hab dun up till now."

It got real quiet for a while. William sat contentedly in Jeremiah's lap. From the corner of his eye, he saw Emma brush a tear or two away from her eyes.

Jeremiah looked up and saw Mayme bringing in the cows for the afternoon milking. She waved when she saw them sitting there. Jeremiah waved back.

After a minute or two, William got up and scampered off again. Finally Emma spoke up.

"You's real sweet on Mayme, ain't you?" she said in a thoughtful tone.

"Yeah, I reckon so," nodded Jeremiah. "She's about the prettiest thing I ever saw."

"I see da way you look at her, like you can't take yo eyes off her."

"You's real pretty too, Emma," said Jeremiah. "Dat's why I said what I did. Sumday a man'll come along dat'll look at you dat way too."

"But it's diff'rent wiff you an' Mayme. Da way you looks at her's not like dat. It ain't da way men look at me. I know dat look men gives girls like me. I used ter think I liked it, but now it scares me right down ter my toes. But what I see in yo face is different. You ain't jes' looking at how pretty Mayme is. You's lookin' at sumfin inside her."

Jeremiah did not reply immediately. He watched Mayme lead the cows toward the barn and thought about Emma's words. He wanted to get up and go help Mayme, but he reckoned there was more Emma wanted to say.

"I shore hope sumday sumbody looks at me wiff dat kind er look," Emma went on, "like dey's lookin' at who I is inside. Dere wuz a time when dere might not er been much down dere ter see. I don't reckon I wuz too smart. But bein' aroun' Miz Katie an' Miz Mayme . . . I reckon I'm changin' an' growin' sum jes' like William. Maybe we's both growin'—but I hope I's growin' *inside*."

Jeremiah looked at her and smiled.

"I reckon you are," he said.

"You think dat person you said would come along sumday fo me—you reckon he'll see sumfin in me ter love like you see in Mayme?"

"I do, Emma. Yes, I do," said Jeremiah. "He's gwine see a mighty fine young black lady an' a real good mama ter her son. Dat's what he's gwine see."

Emma sniffed and glanced away. Her eyes were wet again.

꙳ ＊ ꙳

Strange feelings went through me at the sight of Jeremiah and Emma sitting there on the porch together, Jeremiah holding William on his lap. On one hand, it made me feel warm inside to see Jeremiah with William like that. I reckon every girl likes to see a young man she's fond of being nice to children. But at the same time, it made me feel funny as I watched them, like there was a bond between them that I couldn't share. I wasn't jealous of Emma exactly. But for the first time, I did wish Emma wasn't quite so good-looking.

When Jeremiah walked into the barn a few minutes later where I was milking the cows, I still felt unaccountably strange.

Slowly he began milking one of the cows too. For a few minutes the only sounds were the *zing-zing* of milk hitting the pails.

"Dat William," Jeremiah began, chuckling. "He shore is a cute one."

"Mm-hm . . ." I muttered. I was still feeling unsettled from seeing Jeremiah and Emma laughing and talking together.

"You know what he axed me jes' now?" Jeremiah asked. "He axed me if I could be his daddy."

My hand stilled on the teat I was holding. I could

feel my heart starting to beat faster.

"Da way dat little boy was a lookin' at me, eyes all shinin' and hopin'," Jeremiah went on, "made me think of my own daddy. How things was between us, afore. . . . well, dat's anudder story."

I wondered what he meant but was too busy holding my breath to ask about it now.

"Know what I said?" Jeremiah continued. "I said I couldn't be his daddy. Know why?"

"Uh, no . . . why?" I said.

Jeremiah's face appeared over the stall wall. He must have heard something in my voice. "Mayme. You ain't jealous of Emma, is you?" he asked.

"No," I answered.

"You got no call to be. Emma is pretty, all right. Real pretty. But I tol' her I was shore some nice black man wud come along someday, ter take care of her an' William."

I heard the sound of boots crunching through straw. Suddenly there was Jeremiah standing beside me. He leaned down, hands on his trouser legs, and looked straight into my eyes.

"Mayme. You knows I like 'bout everything 'bout dis place," he said. "I like how dem Daniels brothers treat us all de same, and you knows I think Miz Katie's 'bout the finest white woman dat ever lived. I like Josepha's cookin,' an' I like lil' William lookin' up ter me, makin' me wish I was as fine a man as he thinks I is. And, yes, his mama is mighty fine lookin'—mighty silly to boot. But none ob dem is why I keep makin' dat long walk out ter dis place. You knows why I came here dat first time and why I keep comin' back, don't you, Mayme?"

I reckon I did know, but I didn't reply. Already I was feeling a little foolish for worrying about Emma.

"I come ter Rosewood ter see one Miz Mary Ann

Daniels," said Jeremiah, "ter be with her, ter talk with her and see her smilin' at me. Mayme, ye're da reason I come here."

I smiled up at him and he smiled back. He leaned down, like he meant to kiss me. But the cow, impatient with waiting, turned her head and butted Jeremiah's back, nearly pushing him over.

"All right. All right." Jeremiah chuckled, straightening up. "I get your meanin'." He smiled at me once more. Then we both went back to work.

≈ ❊ ≈

MR. THURSTON'S BOX
48

M R. WATSON WAS WAITING FOR ONE OF HIS WAG-
ons to get back before Jeremiah could load it for a
delivery. While they were waiting, he sent Jeremiah to Mrs.
Hammond's store to pick up his mail.

By now Mrs. Hammond knew who Jeremiah was and how
he was involved with the goings-on at Rosewood. But even
though she pretended to have been in on the scheme all along,
that didn't make her treat Jeremiah any nicer. It didn't make
her treat *any* of them nicer. Jeremiah reckoned she enjoyed
being ornery and contrary. Some folks are like that.

Mrs. Hammond glanced up when Jeremiah entered her
shop, her nose tilting slightly into the air.

"Mo'nin' ter you, Mrs. Hammon'," said Jeremiah. "Mr.
Watson sent me ter fetch his mail."

"I'm not about to give . . . *you* someone else's mail," she
said.

"Why not?"

"Because I'm just not, that's why."

"All right, den," said Jeremiah, turning to go. "I's jes' tell
him I axed for it an' dat you refused to give him his mail."

He took several quick steps toward the door.

"Wait . . . young man," said Mrs. Hammond behind him.

Mr. Watson was one of the town's leading citizens and she didn't want to anger him. "I . . . uh, don't suppose there is any harm in it . . . that is, *if* he told you to pick it up for him."

"Dat he did, ma'am."

Mrs. Hammond handed him Mr. Watson's mail.

"Thank you, ma'am," said Jeremiah with a mischievous grin.

He left the store and walked along the boardwalk.

A wagon was rumbling along in front of the store. The man guiding his team of two plough horses gave a wave to Jeremiah as he passed. A few seconds later a small bump in the street caused a box on the back of the wagon to jostle and fall to the ground. Jeremiah saw and ran after it.

"Mr. Thurston," he called. "Mr. Thurston, you's los' one ob yo parcels!"

Mr. Thurston, one of the few local men who had developed a friendship with the Daniels brothers as their closest neighbor, reined in and looked around at the voice calling at him. He saw Jeremiah running into the street to pick up the box and bring it to him. He also saw Deke Steeves, Jesse Earl, and Weed Jenkins from Oakmont on the other side of the street where they had been watching Jeremiah since before he had gone into Mrs. Hammond's, trying to decide how to cause him trouble without too much danger. They were afraid of Jeremiah's fists, so they had to plan their mischief carefully. Steeves was holding a length of wood about three feet long he had picked up somewhere.

"Hey . . . nigger boy, what you think you're doing!" called out Steeves' voice from where he stood leaning against a post.

Jeremiah stood up with the box he had just picked up. He glanced toward them, then walked toward the wagon where Mr. Thurston had just bounced to a stop.

"Hey, we're talking to you," said young Jenkins in a high-pitched boy's voice, trying to sound tough. His nickname had been given him because he was tall and scrawny as a weed, and he had a voice to match. Though Steeves was the obvious ringleader, the other two were anxious to show Deke they could be as mean as he.

"That's a white man's box, boy," added Jesse Earl. "He didn't want your filthy nigger hands all over it."

Jeremiah continued to ignore them and walked toward the wagon.

Steeves now strode into the street in front of Jeremiah with a cocky swagger, running his left hand up and down the club he held in his right. Jeremiah stopped. Steeves walked toward him.

"You don't seem to hear too good, boy," he said. "We're talking to you. Now you set that box down. I'll see that it gets back up on the wagon."

Jeremiah stared into his eyes, but did not flinch.

Behind him, he heard Mr. Thurston jump down from his wagon onto the dirt.

"Steeves, you are a good-for-nothing blowhard," he said, walking toward them. "Now get away from this young man and stop trying to bully him into a fight. He would pulverize you anyway. If he didn't, I'd horsewhip you myself."

Stunned to hear the white man taking Jeremiah's part, Steeves took a step or two back with a look of disbelief and rage on his face.

"You young fools," Mr. Thurston went on, glancing back and forth between Steeves and the other two, "if you had half the sense of this boy here, you'd try to make something of yourselves instead of going about causing trouble."

Jeremiah handed him the box. Mr. Thurston thanked him, and turned back toward his wagon.

"Hey, Deke, look what I found," cried Weed Jenkins behind them. "He dropped some letters."

Jeremiah glanced about and suddenly realized he'd set down the mail in his hands when he went after the box.

"I didn't know niggers could read or write!" said Earl. "What do they say, Weed?"

"I don't know . . . I'll open them and find out!"

"Hey, dat's Mr. Watson's mail, you gimme dat back," said Jeremiah, walking toward them.

But seeing Jeremiah make a move toward them, still holding the envelopes he had picked up, lanky Weed Jenkins took off running in the opposite direction. Three seconds later he was tackled from behind and sent sprawling to the ground.

Jeremiah climbed off him and began to stand up when a shadow fell on the street beside him. He glanced up to see Deke Steeves standing over him, the piece of wood now in both hands and raised in the air. The look on his face said clearly enough what he intended to do with it.

Again Mr. Thurston's voice put a stop to his plans. "Don't even think about it, son!" yelled Thurston. "You so much as make a move to hurt that boy, you'll regret it."

He walked to the scene, grabbed the club from Steeves' hand, and tossed it away as Jeremiah climbed to his feet.

"Now you, young Jenkins—pick up the man's mail."

Weed glanced toward Deke Steeves, then back at Mr. Thurston.

"Go on . . . pick it up," repeated Thurston.

Muttering something to himself, the boy did so, then stood.

"Now hand it back to Patterson here."

Again Jenkins glanced at his ringleader. But even at three to two, Deke Steeves was not anxious to tangle with Mr. Thurston, who was a big man and who knew how to handle himself.

Steeves stood silent. Slowly Weed walked forward and handed Jeremiah Mr. Watson's mail. Jeremiah nodded, then turned and walked away. When he was gone, Mr. Thurston also turned and went back to his wagon.

"You'll pay for this, Thurston!" Steeves called after him, incensed to appear so powerless in front of his friends. "You'll pay, I tell you. I won't forget this!"

A Thoughtful Day
49

*I*t seemed like washday sure came around often. I reckon there were more of us now, and we were washing all the men's clothes, and there were four of them and they all worked hard and their clothes got dirty. It was a lot of work running a plantation!

Papa and Uncle Ward had dragged out the big pots and got the fire ready the night before. Then as soon as it warmed up the next morning, Katie and Emma and I got started on the wash. Josepha let us do most of it ourselves. She was a hard worker in the kitchen, but she wasn't too keen on washing, though she'd help us hang the clean clothes on the line sometimes.

It was a hot day and we started to get silly like we had that other day right after Emma had come. Pretty soon we were splashing water on each other and laughing and running around as if we were little girls again. By the time we were almost finished, we were soaked. I was just filling a bucket half full of water to throw at Katie when suddenly I realized we weren't alone.

I looked up. There was Jeremiah watching us and grinning real big.

It took me so by surprise, and I guess I was a little

embarrassed to have him see me like that, and I forgot about the others. Emma took advantage of the distraction and suddenly I felt a bucketful of water dump on *my* head! Emma was nearly beside herself with delight at having gotten me so good. She ran off toward the pump to refill her bucket and go after Katie.

Jeremiah walked toward me while the others went on, still laughing and throwing water at each other. He was staring at me with the oddest expression.

"What . . . what are you looking at!" I laughed, water dripping from my head.

"You's jes' real pretty, dat's all."

"I'm a mess!"

"Dat's not what I's talkin' about. It's who you are dat's pretty. You's even pretty when you's all wet."

"My mama used to say men could be exasperating—but I didn't expect it out of you!"

"What you talkin' about!" laughed Jeremiah.

"Just you talking about me being pretty on a day like this."

"Why shouldn't I? You are."

"The other day I was all dressed up in my new brown dress and you didn't even notice. But now that I'm soaking wet, you go saying those kinds of things about being pretty. I know I'm not pretty anyway."

"I did notice you dat day," said Jeremiah. "I saw you standin' dere on da porch as I wuz walkin' up."

"I never saw *you*," I said.

"I wuz comin' up behind you. But den I saw you kind ob lookin' out, wiff a thoughtful expression on yo face, and I stopped. It didn't seem right dat I should disturb you right den. But if I had, it would er been ter tell you dat you wuz da prettiest girl I'd eber seen, an' dat you looked so old an' growed-up, jes' like a real lady. An' dere I wuz in my work clothes an' my dirty hat . . .

you looked too good fo me. Dat's why I stopped an' didn't come no further."

I looked away and felt the heat rising up the back of my neck. I remembered the day vividly. I had been thinking about Jeremiah at the very moment when he'd been watching me and I hadn't known it. I'd been wondering what would become of us, what our future would be. I was wondering if I was good enough for Jeremiah, just like he had been about me!

"So what did you do," I said, "on that day, I mean, when you saw me standing on the porch?"

"I jes' looked at you fo anudder little bit, and den lef' an' went back ter what I'd been doing," said Jeremiah. "But seein' you like dis—all happy an' laughin' and workin' hard an' havin' fun . . . it's different. Den it's jes' shinin' out from inside ob you. Like I said— you's jes' real pretty, dat's all."

"That's about the nicest thing anybody's ever said to me, Jeremiah," I said, looking toward him with a smile. "Thank you."

Suddenly a shriek put an end to our conversation.

"Mayme!" shouted Emma. "Kin you run after dat wet little scamp!"

I looked where she was pointing and saw William running after one of the barn cats. He was heading behind the barn.

Jeremiah and I ran after him. I was more than a little relieved. I wasn't used to talk about how pretty I was!

❧ ❀ ❧

A DAY TO REMEMBER
50

*T*hen came a special day I'll never forget.

It was a day when a young man came calling to Rosewood. How's a girl ever going to forget a day like that!

It was a warm day late in May of 1868. Katie had just turned eighteen. I was eighteen too and would be nineteen in three months. I'd done considerable growing up and changing just like she had. Whether I was shapely or not or any prettier than I used to be when white folks called me ugly, I don't reckon I could say. But my father always said I was about the prettiest girl he'd ever seen except for my mama, and if he and Jeremiah thought I was pretty, that was enough for me.

Late spring has always been one of my favorite times of the year in North Carolina. The days were getting longer and warmer, but it wasn't yet too hot like it gets in July and August. On that particular day, most of the crops were already in the ground, things like cotton and wheat and some oats and potatoes, along with our big vegetable garden. Everything was growing and smelled so nice. It was a time of the year when the earth seemed fresh and alive and full of hope, and when you just couldn't help thinking that no matter what happened, somehow everything was going to turn out all right. It was a time when you wanted to go on long walks through the fields and woods, and along the streams and rivers, just to be part of the life that was bursting out everywhere.

That's how I felt on that special day. I was happy and grateful for my life and my little family and that I had a place to call home.

It was really *Katie's* house and her uncles'. But in a way it was *my* home now too.

I don't know if there's a way to make you understand what a big change it is for a colored person like me to say a thing like that. It was such a short time ago when slaves hardly had anything to call their own. I remember what a turning point it was in my life when I first held some money in my hand that was actually *mine*. It was only eleven cents, but it made me feel like a whole new kind of person. And now I had a bank account with my own name on it with over fifty dollars in it, and here I was talking about my "home." And Katie and my papa were paying real wages to Josepha, and giving Emma a little money too every once in a while. Things had really changed for black folks in just a few short years.

Two days before what I'm going to tell you about next, Jeremiah had come to see my papa, Mr. Templeton Daniels. Though I didn't know it yet, it was *me* they had talked about.

Then came that special day.

Emma ran yelling through the house to find me. "Mayme . . . Mayme!" she called, tramping up the stairs like a buffalo caught in too small a space and frantic to get out. "Mayme . . . Jeremiah's at da front door, an' he's axin' fo you . . . an' he dun brung flo'ers!"

When I came downstairs, I saw Emma had left the door ajar. I hurried to open it all the way. There stood Jeremiah, holding a little bouquet. He had a sheepish look on his face, which wasn't like him, and he smelled of lilac water, which was even less like him!

Immediately I felt the back of my neck getting hot!

"Here," he said, handing me the flowers. "I brought dese fer you."

I took them and smiled.

"I thought maybe we cud go fer a walk or sumthin'," he said.

I started to go out the door with him. Then I stopped.

"Do you mind waiting just a minute?" I said, then turned and dashed back inside and up the stairs. When I came back down a few minutes later, I was wearing the fancy brown dress Papa had bought me in Charlotte, the same one Jeremiah had seen me in that day we'd talked about when I was standing on the porch. He smiled when he saw me. I glanced away. I still couldn't get used to the idea that he actually thought me pretty!

As we left the house together, I knew something was different about this visit, and I more than halfway suspected what it might be. I had a feeling too that Katie and the others were probably watching from the windows of the house!

Jeremiah was so nervous. I might have felt a little sorry for him if I hadn't been nervous myself. If Jeremiah was going to say what I expected him to say, I'd been thinking some already about what I would say too.

"I talked ter yo papa da other day," said Jeremiah after we had walked a ways. "I been aroun' here close on three years an' you an' I's gettin' older. An' I figger it's time we wuz thinkin' 'bout sum things. So I . . . uh, axed yo papa if he thought I wuz da kind er young man he'd approve ob ter be wiff you. And he said I wuz an' dat he'd be right proud ter call me son. An' den he shook my hand an' tol' me ter talk ter you, an' so here I am an' I reckon I'm axin' if you'd like ter be my wife."

My, oh my! He just blurted it out all at once!

I had been expecting it, but it was so sudden that it took me by surprise. Jeremiah let out a big sigh of relief at having said all of what he had to say in one mouthful. I was hot and nervous and happy, and felt like I was just about the luckiest girl in the whole world.

I didn't know what to say!

Sometimes you have too many words and they come out so fast you stumble over them. Sometimes you don't have enough words and you can't think of anything to say. But this was a time when I had a mountain of words I *wanted* to say, but couldn't manage to get a single one out!

I had to say something! But it was several minutes before I did.

"Of course I want to be your wife, Jeremiah," I said softly. "I can't imagine being married to anybody but you. I'm so happy when I'm with you. I love you and . . . I reckon my answer's yes."

I could tell Jeremiah was relieved. It must be hard to ask a girl to marry you, not knowing what she might say.

He took my hand and we continued to walk. I'd been thinking about this so much, but now that the moment had come, the words and thoughts were all confused in my brain. Suddenly I was in an emotional whirlwind.

"Jeremiah . . ." I tried to begin again, though my tongue felt like it was stuck to the back of my mouth, "I do want to be your wife . . . more than anything in the world. But . . . I don't think I'm ready yet to leave Rosewood."

He glanced over at me. It wasn't what he'd expected.

"I'm still getting used to being free and to having a family again," I said. "It's all still so new. I've just discovered my papa and you just found your papa too not long ago, and . . . I reckon what I'm trying to say is that I don't feel I'm ready to get married yet. Can you understand?"

"I reckon so," he said. I could tell there was disappointment in his voice, but he was trying to hide it. "You're sayin' dat you got you a family now an' a life here at Rosewood dat you's not anxious ter leave ter start a new life an' new family jes' yet."

"Yes, that's it! Oh, thank you, Jeremiah! You're not *too* disappointed, are you?"

"I don't know 'bout dat exactly. I reckon I'm a mite disappointed, but I kin understan' what you's sayin'. Or . . . *maybe* I kin. I ain't exactly got me a home like you. Da back ob da livery where me an' Papa live, it ain't exactly like sleepin' in a white man's house, wiff da smell ob horses an' what dey do all 'bout everywhere. I ain't complainin' 'cause I's glad ter be wiff my pa an' ter be free an' ter hab a job. I's a lucky young man, all right. I's jes' sayin' dat it's a mite different fo me, dat's all. So I's thinkin' dat being married might be a pretty nice thing."

"Oh, it would be nice, Jeremiah. It *will* be nice! And I will be happy with you even if we live in a barn or a livery stable or anywhere. It isn't Rosewood I'm not ready to leave, it's Katie and my papa and the others. I just want to be part of my family a little longer. Maybe it's got something to do with finding out who I am. I'm still learning who *Mary Ann Daniels* is. It's like the slave girl called Mayme Jukes is trying ter grow up to become Mary Ann Daniels, a free black woman. Sometimes I'm not sure who that person's supposed to be. Family is part of that, just like you are part of that too."

"I reckon I kin understan'," said Jeremiah. "I reckon I've had ter do sum changin' inside too after findin' out dat my papa wuzn't like I always thought he wuz. Dat's made me hab ter figger out who I am too, like you's sayin'. I reckon dat's a good thing fo us both. Maybe I still gots more ob myself ter figure out too."

"We're both still young, Jeremiah. I know slaves used to get married a lot younger than we are. But that was because the masters wanted them to make babies to have more slaves. But we're free now. We can take time to learn about who we are and what we want. We can think about things we never could before. I don't want us to get married . . . until we're both *ready,* and until we know who we really are and who we're supposed to be."

Jeremiah nodded. I slipped my hand through his arm and leaned against him and we kept walking in silence. I was so content and happy. I hoped Jeremiah understood as much as he said he did.

It was so different to be two *free* black young people, free to think, free to love, free to decide things for ourselves, free to become what we wanted, free to be the people we wanted to make ourselves, not what somebody else wanted us to be.

It was different than anything we could have expected when we'd been slaves . . . but exciting. We had our whole lives ahead of us. We could make them anything we wanted them to be!

Things were never the same with Jeremiah and me after that day. We'd been good friends for a long while, but now he and I sort of "belonged" to each other.

Jeremiah'd spoken for me and everybody at Rosewood knew it. We would be married someday!

Sometimes at the supper table, or when we were out working, we'd catch each other's eyes and smile. It was like we knew what the other was thinking. It was a good and peaceful time in our lives.

I knew Jeremiah was a mite disappointed that we didn't get married right away. My papa had told him that he and Mr. Daniels would help him build a little house for us just past the barn. Jeremiah said he'd be just as happy to fix up one of the old slave cabins. But my papa wouldn't hear of his daughter ever living in a slave cabin again. He said he would never forgive himself for leaving my mama to get sold off as a field hand and then killed. He wanted me to have a good life and to live a free life as the daughter of a white man, and now all black people, should be able to do. He said when the time came that I was ready, then we would all work together to build a nice little house right nearby where he could be near his little girl—even though she would be Jeremiah's wife. He wanted to be part of my life even after I was married, and it made me feel so warm and good inside to know that.

I felt like just about the luckiest black girl alive. But deep down I knew it wasn't luck at all. I'd been reading in my ma's Bible for a pretty long time by now, and I knew more than ever how God had been watching over me. As much as I missed my ma, and as bad as I hurt for Papa, I could see how the bad of her dying had turned into the good of me being here at Rosewood with a cousin and a father and a family . . . and now a future husband!

❧ ❖ ❧

Voices in the Night
51

W HETHER IT HAD ANYTHING TO DO WITH ASKING A
certain young lady to marry him or not, Jeremiah
began to be plagued with reminders of the past. With them
came increasing pangs of guilt. More and more often Micah
Duff's words returned to plague him. It was like his conscience was speaking through Micah Duff's voice. He
couldn't escape the probing words whenever he was alone.
They came to him especially at night when he lay awake. As
the weeks passed they became more and more insistent.

One night Jeremiah couldn't sleep at all. He tossed and
turned nearly the whole night. Over and over the words
Micah Duff had said to him hounded him like a dog chasing
him.

"There's freedom inside and outside," he heard him in his
mind. *"There's lots of men who are free on the outside, but
aren't free inside. They aren't free from themselves."*

It had been several years, but it was like he had heard
them yesterday. How vividly he recalled the day Micah had
been chopping wood and had stopped to examine several
pieces of it.

"Look at this piece of wood," he had said. *"Its grain is all
gnarled. When I look at this chunk of wood, I see a person who's*

twisted up, who's confused and doesn't know which direction he wants to grow, and doesn't know what kind of person he wants to be. He's all mixed up inside."

And Jeremiah remembered the day he had come upon Micah sitting in the darkness waiting for the sunrise. Micah had always loved the early morning hours. How often, Jeremiah thought, had he spoken about light.

"God chases darkness away . . . defeats the darkness in us so that we can be more full of light. God is trying to get His light inside us to chase away the shadows and clear out the dark corners of our heart. When we fall in with how God means us to be, that's when our grain grows straight and true. Life can't be a good and happy thing if we don't go along with that purpose."

It seemed that on this one night Jeremiah was reliving his entire three years with Micah Duff! Most poignant of all were the challenging words Micah had spoken straight to him about his attitudes.

"When are you going to let the light all the way inside your heart, Jake? When are you going to let it shine into those dark spots that are keeping you from being clean and whole?"

The words had angered him at first. As he lay alone in the night they now bit deeper and deeper. If he let them, they would anger him again and make him upset at Micah all over again. But *why* did the words anger him? Could he be honest with himself? Could he admit that the very fact that he had gotten angry with Micah confirmed all the more the truth of what he had said?

"You're an angry young man," Micah had said pointedly more than once. *"I can see it in your eyes. That anger is like a darkness inside that you haven't let the sun reach yet. You're trying to run from it, trying to hide from the light. But you can't escape it, Jake. That anger is making you grow crooked inside."*

Jeremiah continued to toss and turn, becoming all the more agitated and uncomfortable. Micah's words probed deep into places he did not want to look. But alone on his pad in the night, he could not stop Micah's voice. That voice had now become like a beam of light itself, shooting straight into him.

"The real fearsome kinds of things are inside us. Most men go through life trying to prove how brave and tough they are. But a real man is one with courage to face what's inside where no one else sees. Growing into a man with that kind of courage is a hard thing. But it's the only way to be a whole man.

"Who knows where anger comes from? But lots of men are filled with hidden anger and don't even know it. It takes courage to look inside ourselves. It takes humility to forgive. But no one can be a whole man without being able to do both."

Jeremiah dozed and gradually fell into a fitful sleep. Uneasy dreams floated into his brain. Slowly the images took more shape and form.

He was running . . . running . . . running . . . trying to escape . . . he was galloping like a horse.

He glanced to his side. There *was* a horse . . . he was hitched to a team of horses . . . he was one of them, running with them! He was running on two feet, they on four . . . but he was galloping like them.

He glanced to his side again. The horse beside him leered at him. It was a familiar yet grotesque face . . . a horse but not quite a horse. Why was the horse's face so strange yet so familiar? Why was it leering at him, as if it knew some dark and horrible accusation it would speak against him if it could? The horse was silent and could not speak, but its eyes looked like they wanted to speak.

Suddenly the great *crack* of a whip sounded. The same moment the pain of its merciless thong split the skin of his back.

He screamed in agony.

But his dream-scream was silent. Again came the whip down upon him. Again and again. The horse beside him seemed to feel nothing. Jeremiah cried out over and over but no one heard. And still the whip cracked relentlessly against his back. The pain was the torment of hell itself!

On they ran . . . and ran . . . and ran. The whip drove them ever faster.

He struggled to free himself from the cords that bound him to the team of horses. He had to get free . . . free from their leering, grotesque faces . . . free from their silent accusations . . . free from the secret the horse's head held against him, free from the secret only the horse knew. But he was bound to them. How could he escape! He had to get free from the terrible sting of the whip!

Suddenly he broke free. The cords of bondage were loosed! He ran and ran and ran like the wind. He had to get away . . . get away . . . get away!

The horse was gone . . . but still he ran. Still the whip chased him, cracking its cruel lash on his back . . . whipping . . . beating . . . snapping at his flesh . . . for the whip knew his secret and must torment him for what he had done. Why could he not escape it!

He came to a small incline. It led up to the tracks!

There he would be safe! He could get away. If he could jump onto a passing train, he could escape and be free from the persecuting and tormenting whip of justice!

He ran up the hill, legs tiring. He could feel himself slowing. His persecutor was gaining on him! In desperation he ran on. But his legs were now heavy as lead. He stumbled and nearly fell.

An evil laugh sounded behind him. The next instant the whip cracked again, this time lashing around his ankles and yanking them from beneath him. He sprawled across the tracks. A great groan of despair rose from within him.

He struggled to rise. But fatigue now overpowered him. His pursuer caught him, and now stood above him and brought the cruel whip violently down upon him . . . whack . . . whack . . . whack until he was nearly unconscious from the pain. Still his screams of agony were the tormenting silent cries of helplessness.

In the distance a train whistle sounded. He shrieked in terror and called for help. But his cries were drowned out by the evil laugh of his tormenter. Who could do such evil!

Hands were fumbling with his feet and wrists . . . he could do nothing to stop them . . . they were tying him with the same whip to the railroad tracks! They were tying him in front of the train!

Again the cruel laugh rang in his ears.

"Stop . . . no!" he tried to yell. But his voice was frail and weak, the voice of a child pleading with a monster. "Please, don't—"

He looked up at the man binding him to the tracks. It was a black face, the man who had chased and whipped him and was now doing his best to kill him . . . a face he knew . . . it was the face of his father!

"No!" he screamed. "Why are you doing this? Why are you tormenting me?"

But his cries fell on a face stern and hard. Its expression was without compassion. It held no look of father love.

"No . . . please . . . stop!"

Still hands fumbled at him, pushing and poking and shaking him now.

"Get away!" he yelled. "Get your hands off me . . . don't touch me . . . stop hurting me!"

"Son, son," said a voice, jarring strangely into the world of his dream. "Son . . . Jeremiah . . . wake up."

"No, stop . . . the whip . . . please . . ." Jeremiah's eyes opened wide with terror. The face of his tormentor was standing over him!

"No . . . Daddy, please don't . . . stop . . . don't whip me, Daddy!" he cried. "Don't tie me down!"

"Son, it's me . . . it's yo papa," said Henry, gently shaking him. "You's safe wiff me. You's dreamin'. It's not real. I'd neber whip you, son. Dere's no whip no more.''

Gradually Jeremiah's eyes came into focus. He was drenched in sweat and breathing heavily. In panic his wide eyes stared confused into Henry's.

"You's had a nightmare, son," said Henry softly. "You's had a dream 'bout some massa whippin' you. But I's here now. You's safe wiff me. You's safe wiff yo daddy."

Panting for breath, Jeremiah glanced around, at last coming fully awake. Slowly he relaxed, closed his eyes, and lay back and began to breathe more easily. After a moment, Henry left him.

But sleep did not return that night. Jeremiah lay wide awake and alone with his thoughts. But though the dream was gone, the torment continued. Which was his real father—the tender Henry of his waking, or the persecutor of his dream? *Could* he believe that Henry was really a kind and loving father, and had been all along?

Then again came Micah Duff's words:

"When you're facing something inside yourself—that's what takes real courage. That's when you have to find out if you're really a man. Isn't it about time you took a look inside yourself at that anger eating away down there?

"Nobody's got a perfect daddy, Jake. No daddy can be perfect. They make mistakes. They're just men like the rest of us. But they gave us life. If it weren't for them, we wouldn't be here at all. No matter what they may have done, and no matter what we may think they have done, they deserve our love and honor for that alone. The anger you've got toward your pa will kill you if you don't summon the courage to face it. All of us have got to learn to forgive."

But Jeremiah could tell no one what he was thinking. He was not quite ready to let the light shine all the way inside. For now the secrets and confusion in the heart of Jeremiah Patterson remained locked inside him.

NIGHT RAID
52

ONE NIGHT, ALL OF ROSEWOOD AWOKE IN THE middle of the night to the sounds of shouts and gunshots and galloping horses. Katie sat up in bed and screamed out in terror, reminded of the night her family had been killed.

All through the house, voices called and people leapt from their beds. Strange lights flickered against the windowpanes like fire.

Katie ran into Mayme's room and the two girls hurried to the window. Outside a dozen riders wearing white robes with hoods over their heads, some carrying lit torches, were tearing about on their horses, yelling, shouting, shooting.

"Nigger-lovers!" were the only words they heard clearly.

Something was burning on the ground. The girls couldn't tell if the riders were setting the barn on fire or what. Then came the sound of breaking glass from rocks thrown through several windows.

A few seconds later the girls heard tramping feet behind them. They turned to see Ward and Templeton running for the stairs with rifles in their hands. Neither girl had ever seen Ward Daniels holding a gun. He always said he hated guns.

The girls hurried after them, trembling and afraid. By the

time they ran outside, the hooded horsemen had done what they wanted to do and were disappearing in the distance. They all stood on the porch looking at a strange sight.

The shape of a cross was burning in the grass.

"What was that all about?" asked Templeton.

"I don't know, but nothing good, that's for sure," said Ward. Suddenly he seemed to notice the rifle in his hands. He looked at it a minute, almost in disgust, then threw it to the ground. Templeton stared at him with a funny expression, then went down the steps and began to stomp out the fire. Slowly the others walked into the house and back to their beds, though no one slept much after that. Long after everyone else went to bed, Templeton Daniels sat on the porch with his rifle across his legs.

He was still sitting there in the morning, dozing in the chair, when Mr. Thurston rode up. Startled awake, he tensed and grabbed at the gun. When he saw who it was, he relaxed.

"I see you had the same kind of trouble here last night that I did," said Mr. Thurston, nodding toward the blackened cross on the ground in front of the porch.

"Why . . . you get paid a visit by those white riders too?" asked Templeton.

Thurston nodded. "Probably right after you did. Same thing—they burned a cross in front of my house, fired a few shots, yelled and broke a few windows, then took off."

"Got any idea who it was?"

"Nope. Nearly frightened my wife to death."

Four hours later, three men with serious expressions rode side by side down the main street of Oakwood. As they went a few townspeople stopped to stare. A few of them mumbled comments that it was best weren't heard. Some of the women, sensing trouble, hurried away.

The three men stopped in front of the sheriff's office, dismounted, tied their horses to the hitching rail, and walked inside.

Sheriff Jenkins glanced up from his desk. He did not seem entirely surprised to see them.

"Morning, Daniels . . . Thurston," he said to Templeton Daniels and Mr. Thurston. "You must be the other Daniels brother I've heard about," he added, glancing toward Ward.

"Ward Daniels," he said, extending his hand. Sheriff Jenkins shook it, though without much enthusiasm.

"I take it this isn't a social call," he said.

"We had a problem at both our places last night that we want to report," said Templeton.

The sheriff eyed him with a cool expression.

"Our homes were paid a visit by a band of riders," said Mr. Thurston. He went on to explain what had happened. "There was some damage done. We'd like it looked into."

"Who were these riders?" asked Jenkins.

"They were cloaked and hooded," replied Templeton. "We couldn't tell."

"How do you expect me to do anything if you don't know who they are?"

"You've got to do something, Sam," said Thurston. "You can't allow this kind of thing to go on."

"You're not really surprised, are you, boys?" said the sheriff, glancing back and forth between all three. "I must say, Thurston," he added, "I'm surprised at you getting involved with these two and their colored friends. My son tells me you took a nigger's side in a ruckus over in Greens Crossing. No wonder you got paid a night visit—you riled some folks."

"You know as well as I do, Sam, that Deke Steeves and his father are troublemakers."

"At least Dwight Steeves is white."

"I'm aware of that, Sam. But he's a troublemaker. All I did was keep his boy from killing Henry Patterson's kid."

Sheriff Jenkins shrugged. "Well, boys," he said after a pause, turning again toward the Daniels brothers, "I suggest you think about getting them coloreds out from under your roof. That'd go a long way to settle this community down and keep anything like this from happening again."

"That could almost be construed . . . as a veiled threat, Sheriff," said Templeton. "Are you saying that as long as we *don't* do what you say, and as long as we have blacks living with us, you're not going to help?"

"Now you heard every word I said, Daniels, and I said nothing like that. All I'm saying is that you came in here asking for my help, and I'm just telling you that folks don't take kindly to treating coloreds like whites. The war may be over, but this is still the South. We got our own way of doing things. That's something you boys might oughta try to understand. Maybe you Northerners don't know better, but Thurston . . . you know how things are here."

After the incident, and after realizing that the sheriff was going to be no help, Templeton Daniels started carrying a small pistol inside his coat pocket.

Out of the Depths
53

*E*verything was quiet and somber for several days. Every time we went outside, the burned cross in the grass reminded us that a change had come. Our danger really sunk in after that. It was good that we blacks were free. But it was becoming more and more dangerous to be colored in the South. I could tell that my papa and Uncle Ward were worried. Mr. Ward especially got real quiet and was acting strange. Ever since the moment I had seen him with that gun, somehow he had seemed different.

We were all jittery. Katie . . . Josepha . . . Emma . . . each one of us had our own personal fears. The riders in white had frightened us all. Suddenly we were very conscious of our skin color . . . and knew that people hated us because of it. It is an awful feeling to be hated for who you are, not because of anything you have done.

Even though they hadn't been there, the incident changed Jeremiah and Henry too. They knew that they were at the center of the storm, even more than we three women.

Jeremiah got real quiet for two or three weeks.

Whenever I saw him he hardly said a word. I could tell something was on his mind. I figured it was about what had happened. But it wasn't. The incident had triggered deeper things inside him than that, things about his past, things I could never have guessed.

It's a hard thing when men get quiet. You can never tell what they're thinking. It's easy to figure they're angry. Their expressions don't give away as much as a woman's. When they're gloomy and silent, it can almost be frightening.

That's how Jeremiah got. I thought he was mad at me, though I didn't know why.

Then a horrible thought occurred to me. What if he was upset with me for only halfway saying yes, but then saying we had to wait? Or what if he had changed his mind about wanting to marry me! What if he was afraid to tell me?

Before long I was sure that's what it was. I couldn't imagine anything else.

Finally I couldn't stand the silence. I knew that I had to talk to him. We were walking in from one of the fields alone and I just blurted it out.

"Jeremiah," I said, "what's the matter? You're so quiet. Are you mad at me?"

He looked at me almost as if I'd slapped him in the face.

"Why wud you think dat?"

"I don't know . . . you've been so quiet and glum."

"Yeah, I reckon," he said with a sigh. "But it ain't you."

"What is it, then?" I persisted.

He glanced away.

I waited. Suddenly I realized that he was trembling. I reached out and put my hand on his shoulder. Slowly he turned to face me. His eyes were wet.

"Oh, Jeremiah . . . what is it!" I said. I'd never seen him like this!

"I . . . I haven't been honest wiff you," he said in a broken voice.

"What . . . how do you mean?" I asked.

"I haven't tol' you everythin'."

"About what?"

"I don't reckon I been honest wiff my papa either," he said. "But . . . but if we's eber gwine git married, you an' me, I mean . . . den we's gotter be so honest wiff each other dat we's got no secrets. An' dat's what's been tearin' me up sumfin dreadful inside—"

His voice broke and he looked away.

"Jeremiah, what *is* it!"

"I . . . I got a terrible secret," he struggled to continue, "an' it's killin' me. It's killin' me worse dat I axed you ter marry me wiffout tellin' you. 'Cause you got ter know what kind ob person I am, an' dat maybe I ain't what you think. It's like I lied ter you an' I hate myself fo it. But I can't lie no more."

"But you can tell me now," I said. "It's all right that you didn't tell me before."

He sniffed and wiped at his eyes. He drew in two or three breaths to try to steady himself. But even when he started again, his voice was shaky and soft and broken. Whatever it was, he was right—it was tearing at him inside. I could see that he was in torment.

"I tol' you about my mama . . ." he began.

"Yes," I nodded.

"But I didn't tell you da whole truf, dat her dying— oh, God!—it . . . wuz my own fault!"

The words filled poor Jeremiah with anguish. They stung him with a pain I can hardly imagine. I could see it in his face. He was trembling to keep from bursting into sobs.

He closed his eyes and swallowed hard. He could hardly get anything out.

But now that he had made the admission that had haunted his nightmares and even his waking hours, he couldn't stop. He had let the healing knife go down into the deepest place where the tormenting secret had hidden so long.

"I wuz such a cantankerous an' selfish boy," he said. "I wuz full ob anger. My mama wuz as good a lady as dere is. But I wuz so full ob myself I cudn't see past my own nose. She did everythin' fo me. She wuz so strong when dey sol' us an' sent us away so dat Papa cud neber find us. She wuz about as strong an' courageous a woman as dere cud be. But I wuz jes' selfish an' angry. An' when dat day came when Massa Winegaard tol' me ter go ter dat white drifter wiff sum tools, my anger got da better ob me. I got angry at Mama too, an' I gots ter live wiff dat terrible thought. I got selfish an' lazy, an' so Mama went instead. An' dat white no-good drifter, he tried ter rape her an' he hit her an' she fell and got hurt real bad. An' a week later, she wuz dead an' it wuz all on account er me. If I'd jes' dun what I wuz tol' . . . she'd still be alive! It wuz my own fault!"

The last words came out in a forlorn wail of remorse. I could hardly stand the awful sound of it—to see someone I loved in such torment!

Jeremiah stopped and almost shuddered in horror. He was blinking hard but couldn't stop the flow of tears from his eyes. I was in an agony to see him suffer so! I couldn't imagine how terrible the guilt must be.

"I went crazy wiff rage," he said. "I shud hab seen den what an evil thing da anger inside me wuz. I shud hab seen it. But I wuz too young an' selfish ter see my heart fo what it wuz. I can't hardly recollect what happened next. When I saw dat white man an' my mama lying dere an' him wiff his clothes half off, I lost my head. An' I ran at him an' attacked him wiff a fury I didn't eben know wuz in me. An' I hit at him an' den grabbed a rock an' just kept hittin' an' hittin' him. An' when I came ter myself, dere wuz blood everywhere. I knew he was dead an' dat I'd killed him. I knew I'd be hanged if dey foun' out. I looked aroun' an' saw da stream dere, an' I drug him to it an' washed away all da blood an' tried ter git it off my hands, but it wudn't wash off. Den I drug him down past where I thought dey'd fin' him, where dere wuz a little falls where da stream dropped in ter da river. I pushed him over an' watched dat body float away. An' den I went back an' got my mama an' ran fo help. I cud hardly sleep for weeks after dat, knowin' what I'd done. An' a week later, Mama was dead."

Jeremiah stopped and at last broke down sobbing with the most bitter grief I've ever heard.

"Oh, Jeremiah!" I said, trying to comfort him. I was holding his hand. He was sweating and trembling.

"Mayme," he said, "I killed a man. I got da blood ob a man on my hands an' it won't come off. I's a murderer, Mayme, an' I can't live wiff myself for da torment ob it. You won't neber want ter marry me now, an' I got ter bear da guilt ob my own mama's dyin' wiff it. I got two people dat's dead on account ob me, an' da guilt ob it's more terrible den I kin live wiff. I'd die myself ter take away da voices haunting me at night!"

He was sobbing uncontrollably. All I could do was gently stroke his hand and sit with him. There were no words to comfort him. Only forgiveness could do that. It would be a hard forgiveness for him to find.

It was a long time before he began to breathe more easily. When he next spoke his voice was barely more than a whisper.

"Ain't no good comes ob anger, Mayme," he said. "It's a bad thing. But even den, after all dat, I cudn't see dat it wuz all *my* anger dat was da cause ob it. So I got angrier an' angrier at my pa, trying ter blame him when it wuz *me* I shud hab been lookin' at. Da guilt wuz so terrible dat I cudn't look at myself. So I blamed him. Anger's a terrible thing, Mayme. It kin jes' destroy a man inside. What kind ob person am I ter hab lived such a lie all dis time!"

Again Jeremiah quietly wept. Several minutes went by. Gradually the storm passed.

We continued to talk. Eventually Jeremiah told me most of what happened since that time. He must have talked for more than an hour, telling me things he never had before, about his childhood as a slave, about his father's leaving, about Micah Duff and his years with the army company, then about the Dawson family he'd met. Once he started talking about his past, it was like a dam across a river had burst and he wanted to tell me every single thing that had ever happened to him. I think that's when I first began to think that his story needed to be told too, just like Katie's and mine. That's when I realized that mine and Katie's story wasn't *only* our own story but that it was a story about a whole lot of people and an important time in the country when a lot of people's lives were changing. Jeremiah was one of those. His story was my story, just like, in a different way, Henry's was too, and Katie's and Josepha's and Emma's, and maybe even Micah Duff's, for all I knew. Anyway, that's how it seemed to me at the time.

"When I met dem Dawsons," Jeremiah said, "wiff everythin' Micah Duff wuz sayin' ter me, dat's when a first bit ob light began ter dawn on me dat anger wuz sumthin' dat destroyed people inside. Dat place wuz plumb full er hate, Mayme. But dat didn't stop me from lashin' out an' still blamin' my papa when I saw him. But den when I met you an' Miz Katie, if anyone had da right ter feel anger, I reckon, it's you an' Miss Katie. Yet dis place here is as filled wiff love as dat Dawson place wuz ob hate. Dat's when I started thinkin' 'bout some ob what Micah Duff tol' me. He wuz a good man too, maybe jes' like my papa. He did nuthin' but good ter me. He saved my life twice. But finally I got angry at him too, an' jes' lef' him wiffout a word. Da same thing I got angry at my daddy fo doin', but dat he never did, I *really* did ter Micah Duff. All my blamin' other people . . . I shud hab been lookin' at myself! I jes' lef' Micah. How cud I do dat ter such a kind man? What kind er person wud do such a thing! Dat's when I began ter think dat no matter what happens, nobody *has* ter let anger get a root inside ter grow an' fester like I saw it had done in me. Dat Dawson girl wuz so full er hate. But nuthin' so bad had happened ter her as ter you an' Miz Katie. She *let* herself git full er hate. It wuz her own fault, jes' like my anger wuz my fault. I didn't *hab* ter get angry, but I did. I cud hardly stand ter look at myself an' see dat I wuz jes' like dat Dawson girl. I wuz full ob anger too. Mine wuz jes' more hidden so folks didn't see it. But it was dere. I convinced myself dat if Papa hadn't lef' us, Mama'd still be alive. But dat wuz jes' 'cause I cudn't look at myself. I wuz jes' tryin' ter hide from my own guilt. Da anger and da blame—it's been dere all along, cuz I *let* it be dere. Ain't nobody's doin' but my own."

He stopped and looked up into my eyes, almost like a little child.

"What shud I do, Mayme?" he asked. "What kin I do ter git rid ob da terrible guilt?"

"Have you talked to your papa?" I said.

"Some, but not 'bout dis."

"Don't you think you ought to tell him?"

"I reckon so. Dat'll be hard."

"There's no other way for it to be clean between you," I said.

"I reckon you's right. If it's what I got ter do, den it's what I got ter do. I reckon it's time I started doin' what's right. Micah Duff wud say dat's what it takes ter be a man."

⁓ ✳ ⁓

FATHER AND SON
54

J EREMIAH WAS SPENT. THE TALK AND HIS CONFESSION
and the tears had all drained him.

But Mayme was right. He knew he needed to talk to his
father. The forgiveness he needed could only come between
father and son. With the flood of emotions already flowing so
freely, it seemed this was the day for it. He needed to allow
himself at last to accept his father's love completely.

Mayme left Jeremiah sitting where he was, and went looking for Henry. She found him in the barn.

"I think you need to talk to Jeremiah," she said.

Henry looked straight into her eyes with question.

"Is he ready?" he asked hopefully.

"You knew?" she asked.

"How cud I not see dat he wuz mighty troubled inside,"
nodded Henry. "I seen da gnawin' away in his soul all dis
time. I knew he wuz strugglin' wiff blaming me fo sum kin'
er trouble inside him. But my seein' it wudn't do him no
good. He had ter see it fo hisself."

"I think he does now," Mayme said. "I think he's ready
to tell you about it."

Henry nodded again and left the barn.

He saw Jeremiah seated out away from the house. Softly he approached.

"Mayme tells me you an' her's been talkin' 'bout sum hard things," he said.

Jeremiah glanced up and half smiled. It was a sad and weary smile, but almost a peaceful one, as if the hardest battle of the war had already been fought. There was no trace of hostility in his expression as there might once have been at Henry's words.

"Did she tell you everythin'?" he asked.

"She said dere wuz sum things I needed ter hear from yo own mouf."

Jeremiah nodded. "Dat soun's like Mayme, all right," he said.

Henry sat down. "You want ter tell me 'bout it?"

Jeremiah nodded again. "I reckon I finally do."

They sat for five or ten minutes. For Jeremiah to tell Mayme what he had done was one thing. But to confess his guilt to his own father took all the more courage. He didn't find it easy to begin.

Once he did, the story and his confession flowed out in a torrent of relief. At last he was unburdened from his dreadful secret. Henry's tears were even more plentiful than Jeremiah's. There is no pain so deep as that of a loving father's suffering on behalf of his son. If Jeremiah had been worried that his father would condemn him after his admission, nothing could have been further from the truth. Henry's weeping sorrow was all for Jeremiah. His tender words of compassion wrapped the son in a cloak of forgiveness. And at last Jeremiah was ready to let that cloak embrace him.

"I's so sorry, Papa," said Jeremiah. "I let myself think wrong things 'bout you. I shud er known dey wuzn't true. I know I wuz wrong. You wuz a good man an' Mama always said you wuz a good father ter me . . . I's so sorry! When I said before, right when I came, dat I didn't want you ter call me yo son, dat wuz da cruelest thing a son cud say ter his own father. Dat wuz so wrong er me. I's so sorry, Papa! I'm proud fo you ter call me yo son now. An' I's proud ter *be* yo son."

Henry's heart filled with quiet gratitude. His prayers, not for himself but for his son, had been answered!

"We's all dun things we's ashamed ob," he said, blinking back the tears in his eyes. "I blamed myself fo talkin' too much an' angerin' Mr. Clarkson. We kin both say it wuz our fault. An' dat ain't ter say dere ain't sum truf in dat. But now we gots ter look ahead. We dun what we dun. So we ax da Lord's forgiveness, den we look ahead. Den we forgive ourselves an' each other too, an' keep lookin' ahead."

Jeremiah nodded. It would take a long time for the full reality of what had just happened to sink all the way inside him and do its complete work. But the change had begun. Forgiveness had begun to live in him.

Then he remembered.

He reached into his pocket and pulled out a tiny object, held it a moment, then handed it to Henry.

The sight of the carved wooden horse, worn smooth and shiny from years in his son's pocket, brought a new flood of tears to Henry's eyes. The sight was full of the memory of the wife of his youth.

"She tol' me ter fin' you an' gib you dis," said Jeremiah. "I don' know why I didn't gib you dis afore . . . jes' didn't seem like da right time, I reckon. But here it is now. An' she had sumfin she wanted me ter say. As angry as I got at you in my mind, I cudn't ever forget her words."

Henry waited. His heart was too full of too many things to speak.

"She said ter tell you dat you wuz da bes' man she'd ever known, and dat she loved you and never stopped lovin' you, dat she never loved anudder man in her life an' dat you wuz the best man da Lord cud hab given her."

Henry broke down and wept freely at his dear wife's words.

He stood. Jeremiah also rose to his feet and faced him. Father and son embraced.

The sunlight of the father's forgiveness had sent away the darkness of the son's enmity. The grain of Jeremiah Patterson's character was at last ready to grow straight and true. A great weight had been lifted from his shoulders.

His anger gone, he was at last free to *live*.

A Woman's Honor
55

*T*he sense of danger didn't go away.

Everyone for miles knew about the two cross burnings. And everyone knew why they had happened.

Whenever any of us went to town now, there were some people who were nice and others who refused even to look at us. Some people who might have wanted to be friendly seemed afraid to act too nice toward my papa and Mr. Ward, as if someone might see them and then *they* would be in danger themselves. Mr. Thurston had stepped in to help Jeremiah against Deke Steeves. That had angered certain men and now he was in danger too. People didn't want that same thing happening to them.

By now Deke Steeves was older than when Jeremiah had first come, and so was Weed Jenkins. His voice had finally changed and he had put a little meat on his bones. Both boys were mean as sin. Everyone in town was afraid of them. If they took it into their heads that they didn't like someone, broken windows and all kinds of mischief might result. Deke Steeves was not the kind of person you wanted as your enemy.

And everyone knew that Sheriff Jenkins wouldn't do

anything about it because Weed was his own son.

Finally the undercurrent of hostility and anger on both sides boiled over.

It was probably a mistake, but one day Katie and I both went into town with my papa. We hadn't been in so long, because of what people were saying about us. But on this day we wanted to go with him. Papa had business with Mr. Taylor at the bank. Katie and I both had a couple errands we wanted to take care of.

"Everything will be fine," said Papa. "We'll just go into town, take care of our business, say hello to Henry and Jeremiah, and be gone before anyone even knows we're there."

So we got dressed up and headed for Greens Crossing.

It was September. I had just turned nineteen a couple weeks before. It had been a cold summer and the weather had delayed the cotton harvest. We were planning to start in a few days without any idea that calamity was about to break in on our lives.

Papa parked the wagon on the street near the general store. He walked off in the direction of the bank. Katie headed into the store, and I went up to the livery hoping to see Jeremiah for a few minutes. But he wasn't there. Henry said he'd been at Mr. Watson's all day.

I left and walked back along the boardwalk toward the store to rejoin Katie. I had gone about halfway when from across the street I saw a group of white boys who hadn't been there a few minutes earlier. I didn't know where they'd come from, but they were there now. And they were watching me.

I quickened my step. But the worst thing you can do in a situation like that is show you're afraid. The minute you try to run from a dog, it takes off running straight at you. The boys had seen me glance in their direction and start walking faster. It was all the bait they needed. Immediately they came out into the street toward me, walking diagonally to cut me off before I could get back to Mrs. Hammond's. I didn't know who they were, but they were some of the same boys who had bothered Jeremiah before.

"Hey, pretty girl," one of them called out. "What's your hurry? Come over here."

My heart was pounding and I began walking faster yet.

"What do you want to talk to a nigger girl for, Deke?" said one of the younger boys, running to catch up with the boy who was talking to me.

"Haven't you heard, Jesse—that lady there's half white. Ain't that right?" he said, now breaking into a run and jumping up onto the boardwalk in front of me. I had no choice but to slow down. I tried to keep moving and get by him. But he wouldn't let me.

"I asked you a question, girl," he said, pushing at me. "We hear you're half white. That must be why you're so pretty."

By now the others caught up and gathered round me and surrounded me. "You like white men, little black lady?" said the boy who had stopped me. "How'd you like it if you and me get to know each other a little better?"

Some of his friends laughed and made bad comments. They inched closer and closer and started touching me and saying horrible things. I was terrified. There was no way I could escape.

"Get away!" I screamed. "Leave me alone . . . please, stop touching me!"

Jeremiah had come out of Watson's Mill in time to see me walk away from the livery. He was just about to go back inside and ask Mr. Watson if he could take five minutes to go see me when he saw the group of boys heading across the street. Immediately he started toward me. The moment I screamed, he bolted toward us.

My screams brought a rude slap across my face from one of the white boys. But the next instant Jeremiah burst into the center of the group, sending a couple of them to the ground. They got up and began pelting Jeremiah with their fists. But he knocked them away and turned toward Deke Steeves.

"Leab her alone, Deke," said Jeremiah. "She ain't done nuthin' ter you."

The only answer he received was a charge like a bull straight toward him.

The two exchanged several blows, blood poured from Steeves' nose, and I yelled for help. The rest of the boys jumped back into the middle of the scuffle, trying to grab Jeremiah and hold him so that Steeves could hit and kick him. Dust was flying and there were yells and curses and a few cries of pain whenever someone landed a blow.

Suddenly another figure rushed right into the middle of the fight.

"Stop . . . stop it!" she cried, whacking at Deke Steeves' head and trying to push several of the smaller boys aside.

It was Katie! She seemed to be afraid of nothing!

Their surprise, and their natural reluctance to hurt a white girl, temporarily put a stop to the fight. Everyone looked around, breathing heavily and sweating. Jeremiah stood and regained his balance. Slowly he began to back out of the center of the fray.

"Come, Miz Katie," he said, "you git out ob here. You don't want ter be gettin' hurt."

But now Deke advanced on Katie. Slowly a menacing grin came over his lips. "Well now, who's this?" he said. "You be Miss Clairborne I heard about? Why don't you come with me. You'll find that I'm not such a bad fellow."

A few lewd cracks and whistles sounded from Steeves' friends. Never dreaming that Jeremiah would go to such lengths to defend a white girl, Steeves reached out his hand and began to feel Katie's hair. She shuddered and backed away. The move angered Steeves. He took another step forward and reached toward her again.

"Don't you go be getting unsociable when Deke Steeves is talking to you, you nigger-loving white girl!" said Steeves. Rudely he grabbed hold of her arm.

"Ow!" cried Katie. "Ow . . . stop—you're hurting me!" She had been carrying a letter ever since leaving Mrs. Hammond's. Now it fell to the ground.

The next instant Jeremiah's fist crashed against Steeves' jaw and sent him staggering backward. He tripped over the edge of the boardwalk and fell in the street, swearing in a violent rage.

Jeremiah took hold of Katie and eased her behind him. The two slowly began backing away as Jeremiah kept his eyes on the rest of the group.

Incensed almost more to see Jeremiah touch a white girl than for what he had done to him, Deke Steeves jumped to his feet.

"You cowards!" he cried to his friends. "Don't you see that? Get him!"

The whole group rushed forward. Katie and I ran backward to get out of the way, yelling and calling for help. There were quite a few people gathered around from the surrounding stores by this time, but no one stepped forward to help. Nobody seemed to mind if they killed Jeremiah!

In less than a minute Jeremiah was on the ground surrounded by Deke Steeves and five others pounding and kicking at him.

"Help!" I cried at the people watching. "Why won't any of you help him!"

Suddenly a gunshot rang out.

The beating stopped and the heads of the ruffians all turned toward it.

There stood Papa with his pistol in his hand! Katie and I ran to him.

"Get away . . . back away from him, all of you!" he yelled at the white boys.

Slowly they got off Jeremiah, hatred in their eyes.

"Get out of here, you no-goods!" said Papa.

A few eyes turned toward Steeves. He stepped back, wiping at the blood on his face with his shirt. They looked like a pack of wild dogs deprived of their prey. He looked straight at Jeremiah.

"You're dead, nigger!" he spat, then shot a glance of hatred at Papa. Finally he slunk off, followed by his friends.

Papa walked over and helped Jeremiah to his feet.

"You okay?" he said.

"Yep, I'll be fine," said Jeremiah. "I gib Steeves da worst ob it."

Jeremiah and I clasped hands briefly, then Jeremiah went back to work. Katie went over and picked up the letter she'd dropped that she'd gotten from Mrs. Hammond. It was all crumpled and wrinkled from the fight. Then Papa helped her and me back to the carriage, twenty or thirty silent onlookers watching us. Then we headed home.

"Who's the mail from?" Papa asked, no doubt trying to distract us from the ordeal.

"I haven't read it yet," said Katie. "I don't want to

open it until I've calmed down. I think it's from Rob Paxton in Baltimore."

Wonder what he's got to say, I thought to myself, remembering the young deputy who'd helped bring my papa home. I figured Katie would tell me about the letter when she was ready, but in the aftermath of what came next, the letter was soon forgotten.

ABDUCTION
56

*W*hoever planned these kinds of things didn't wait long to carry out the threats Deke Steeves had yelled during the fight with Jeremiah. It was almost as if the white men who had been listening, or those who heard about it, had gotten together that day to take revenge on Jeremiah for hitting a white boy and touching a white girl.

A few evenings later Henry and Jeremiah were at Rosewood after helping us with the cotton harvest that we'd just begun. We were eating a late supper after a day in the fields. It was already dusk and probably nine or nine-thirty.

"If you'd like our help in da mo'nin'," said Henry, "Jeremiah an' I cud sleep in da barn an' gib you anudder half day afore gittin' back ter town."

"We would appreciate that very much," said Uncle Ward. "You two pile up the cotton faster than all the rest of us combined, don't they, Templeton!" he added with a laugh.

"You're right there, Brother Ward!" said my papa. "There's no way we can express our gratitude, Henry. And to you too, Jeremiah," he added. "We've got the two *of you to thank that Rosewood's on its feet again."*

"What 'bout us?" said Emma. "An' Miz Mayme an' Miz Katie, dey dun did everythin' afore anyone else come roun'."

"Of course, of course, Emma!" laughed my papa. "We all know that and love them for it, don't we?"

"An' me too!" said Emma's William, who was now just over three and never let an opportunity pass to add whatever was on his mind.

"You're all right!" laughed Mr. Ward. "It's a family adventure all the way around!"

"It may be a family advenshur," now said Josepha, "but you ain't gwine git *me* out in dose fields er cotton!"

"But you have the most important job of all," said my father with his familiar smile and a brief wink in my direction.

"An' jes' what dat be, Mr. Templeton?"

"You keep us fed!"

When we were through with supper, we were all tired after the long day. Henry and Jeremiah went out to the barn, the rest of us went upstairs to our beds.

The last thing I remembered about that night before falling asleep was how dark it was outside. There was no moon. It was just black and quiet. Little did I know what would soon approach Rosewood through the night.

Several hours later, somewhere in my dreams I heard a few barks from the dogs. But I rolled over and continued to sleep. But when the sound of galloping horses intruded into my dreams, at last my brain began to come awake. The dogs were howling now.

A minute later a dozen riders galloped into Rosewood. The dogs ran about in a yowling frenzy. Chickens were cackling and the cows mooing. I heard my father and Uncle Ward stirring in their room, then running for the stairs. Torches of flame from the riders' hands cast eerie shadows on the house and open space in front of it. But the torches would burn no crosses on the ground tonight. The hooded riders had other plans.

"Hey you inside!" called a voice. "You got a nigger in there—we're here for him!"

I snuck to the window and glanced outside. The band of men sat waiting. I felt Katie creep up beside me and look out. She was trembling. Hearing the word *nigger* filled me with dread. Were they after *me*?

After a long minute, we heard the door open downstairs. My papa stepped out onto the porch holding a lantern.

"We're here for the nigger . . . you know why!" said the rider.

"You know who we've got here," replied my father. "We've got an older Negro woman and a girl that's half white, half colored. They're none of your concern."

"That young buck made himself our concern the other day," the man spat back. "This is what comes of being too friendly with that little white girl of yours. Now he's going to pay! Hand him over or these torches'll be through your windows and your house be cinders come morning."

"You know as well as I do that he doesn't live here."

"Word has it he's been out—"

"Hey, Dwight—" interrupted another voice.

"Shut up, you fool," spat the spokesman, turning in his saddle. "—I told you . . . no names."

"But I got him . . . he was in the barn!"

All eyes turned toward the voice of a tall slender youth whose white cape barely went down past his waist. He was dragging Jeremiah, struggling and kicking, out the barn door into the torchlit night.

"That's him!" cried another of them.

Half the saddles emptied and the small crowd began kicking and beating Jeremiah viciously into the dirt. In the upstairs window, I couldn't watch. I looked away and buried my face sobbing in Katie's arms. She comforted me for a few seconds, then stood, hurriedly dressed, and left the room.

"That's enough—plenty of time for that later," yelled the leader. "Get the rope around him and put him up on that horse."

"All right, you boys have had your fun," said my father. "He's done nothing to any of you."

"He forgot what color his skin is—that's enough!"

"Ain't no good can come to a nigger-lover around here, mister. You and your kind ain't welcome in these parts."

The door of the house opened again. I wiped at my tears and looked out. There was Katie walking outside toward the fidgeting horses!

"He meant nothing by what he did," she said to the lead rider. "It was my fault, not his. I shouldn't have interfered."

"Then he should have known better, miss—and you should have yourself. Now that it's done, he's got to pay."

The others were shoving Jeremiah onto the back of a horse. They had already tied his hands behind his back. One of the other men forced a noose over his head and down onto his neck.

"Get it tight!" yelled a voice, which I now recognized as the voice of Deke Steeves.

"You can't do this!" cried Katie in a pleading voice. "He's done nothing wrong! He was just trying to keep me from getting hurt!"

But rude hands yanked her away. My papa took several steps forward, struggling to hold back his anger.

There was nothing he could do against so many. Katie ran to his side.

I couldn't stand it anymore! I jumped up, threw on a robe, and flew down the stairs.

"Let's go, Dwight," yelled one of the men, "—we got him!"

The riders swung their horses around.

I ran through the door and straight for Jeremiah. Before they could stop me, hardly realizing what I was doing, I threw myself against the horse, clinging to one of his legs.

Jeremiah looked down and tried to reassure me with a smile. But the look of it broke my heart! I started crying again, terrified that I would never see him again.

Our eyes met but for a moment. Though the noose had already begun to choke his neck, Jeremiah tried to speak.

"I love . . . we'll—" he began.

A rude slap across the mouth from the nearest of the horseman silenced him. The same instant, a booted foot from another shoved me away.

"Get away from him, nigger girl!" he yelled as I stumbled and fell. "Otherwise we'll string you up beside him! We got plenty of rope for the two of you."

A few shouts and slashes from whips and reins and they galloped away. On the ground, I picked myself up and ran after them.

"No!" I wailed. But my protests were lost in sobs. I hardly felt the arms of my papa and Katie as they led me whimpering back into the house, while the dozen riders disappeared into the darkness.

❧ ❃ ❧

LYNCHING
57

A S JEREMIAH BOUNCED AWAY FROM ROSEWOOD INTO
the night, he thought back on his whole life and everything that had brought him to that moment—about his
younger years and Henry's sudden disappearance, how his
anger had begun and how he and his mama had been sold,
about what had happened to her and how he'd set off on his
search to find Carolina and had finally arrived in Greens
Crossing, and about the changes and healing that had come
to him, and finally about him and Mayme and asking her to
marry him.

But the last few minutes were a blur. Jeremiah had awak-
ened to the swinging light of a lantern and the sounds of a
blow and his papa falling to the straw of the barn floor. The
hooded man grabbed Jeremiah before he could get to his feet.
Hand on his head, Henry had tried to rise. Fearing the man
would strike his papa again, Jeremiah urged him to stay where
he was. Then the hooded man had dragged him from the
barn. When Jeremiah saw the riders, dread filled his heart.
Were they here for him alone? For one terrifying moment, he
thought they would take Mayme too. He could still close his
eyes and see that tearful desperation on her face.

Now, bound and riding farther and farther away from

Rosewood—and from any hope of rescue—Jeremiah realized
this was surely the end. Maybe it was better that he die alone.
Still he wished he had lived long enough to marry Mayme.
What might have happened had he never come to Carolina?
What if he had stayed with the army and Micah Duff? But
then he wouldn't have found his papa, wouldn't have known
forgiveness, wouldn't have known Mayme. No, he wouldn't
go back, wouldn't change it, even if he could. If only he had
left those white boys in town alone. He only hoped they
would leave the others alone.

He knew it was time to pray. Strangely enough, for once
he felt no anger, not toward his captors, nor even toward God
himself. Instead Jeremiah Patterson asked God for mercy, and
to take care of the others—especially Mayme and his papa—
when he was gone.

Templeton helped Katie and Mayme, who were still crying, inside. Henry followed from where he had been watching
from behind the barn door. He looked as shaken as they had
ever seen him. The moment they were inside, Templeton
glanced at the other two men.

Without a word spoken, Ward turned and left the room.
When he came back thirty seconds later he was holding
Katie's father's prized Spencer rifle and loading it with shells.

Templeton looked at his brother. Their eyes met and they
just stared at each other for a second or two.

"But . . . I thought—" began Templeton.

"I do," said Ward. "I hate everything about them. I hate
the feel of it in my hands. When I left California I swore I
would never touch a gun again in my life."

As he spoke, the expression on his face and the sound of
his voice sent chills through Katie and Mayme. They didn't
know what he meant exactly, or why he had made such a vow,
but they could tell that whatever was behind the words, it
went deep into him. That look on his face was one none of

them would ever forget. It was almost . . . a look of death.

"Put that thing away, Ward. Henry and I'll go—" began Templeton.

"Look, Templeton," said Ward as he shoved seven bullets into the chamber of the rifle one after the other. "No offense, but you ain't so good a shot. Not from the distance we're going to be at. We're only going to have one chance. I figure I'm the only one who can save the boy before a rope breaks his neck."

He strode toward the door and hurried to the barn to saddle a horse. Templeton glanced at Henry, then went to the gun cabinet himself and came back with two more rifles. Then they both ran out after Ward.

The girls watched the three men gallop away two minutes later, following the faintly flickering torches still just barely visible as a glow in the distance. When they were younger, Katie and Mayme had done some daring and stupid things. But neither of them even thought about chasing after them now. They knew they could be no help. All they could do was wait, and cry, and pray. The men would come back sooner or later, and they would either be carrying Jeremiah's dead body over the back of a horse, or he would be riding along with them. They would just have to wait to find out which.

Templeton and Ward and Henry lashed at their three horses with whips and tore dangerously fast through the black night. If one of the horses slipped and fell, it could mean broken legs and death. But it was a risk they had to take. Jeremiah's life was at stake.

They kept to the road toward town. About halfway to the Oakwood road, a horse trail wandered off to the right and up a fairly steep incline toward a thickly wooded slope that led to a place called Shenandoah Summit. They slowed as they reached the path. Could the riders have turned off?

The torches were no longer visible. They stopped to

listen. But with the breathing and movement of the horses, it was impossible to hear anything.

Henry dismounted and ran a short distance from the others, cocked his head, then hurried back and jumped onto his horse again.

"Dat's dem," he said. "Dey's headin' fo da summit!"

They swung their horses off the road and followed the faint sound. They had to pick their way more carefully now, for the footing was uneven. But they pushed through the night as fast as they dared. About halfway to the summit, gradually the lights of burning torches again began to glow in front of them as they caught up with the mob. Two or three minutes later they halted. They could see better now. The riders had stopped. Several of them had taken their hoods off and were looping a rope above a high branch of a huge oak. Jeremiah was sitting helplessly on a horse's back beneath it.

There was some low talking, but most of the men were just waiting and watching. None had participated in a hanging before this night and possibly the long ride had jostled a few of their consciences out of their slumber. If so, they had not come awake enough to make themselves heard. No one spoke a word of objection.

"What you want to do, Ward?" whispered Templeton.

"All I need is to get close enough to have a few good shots," replied Mr. Ward. "I think I like that direction over there," he added, pointing to his right. "I'd rather be on the uphill side."

"What you want us ter do, Mr. Ward?" asked Henry.

"I want you to stay out of sight, Henry," replied Mr. Ward. "If they see you, you'll be in the same fix as Jeremiah. You stay here and be ready to get Jeremiah's horse if it goes wild."

"I kin do dat."

"I know you can. But keep your gun ready too. They may try to shoot Jeremiah if they see their hanging spoiled. You'll have to shoot anyone who turns a gun on him first.''

Henry did not reply. He had already shot a man to save Mayme's life. There wasn't much doubt he would do so again if he had to, to save his own son.

In the meantime, Ward was thinking hard to come up with the best plan.

''Templeton,'' he said, ''it's a big gamble, but how'd you like to risk your life by walking out there and distracting their attention?''

''I don't think this is one I'll be able to talk my way out of with my silver tongue, Ward, if that's what you're thinking.''

''All I want is for you to buy me a minute or two. If I can sneak closer from up there while they're watching you, I just might be able to do it. The light's bad, but it's the only chance we got.''

''Just tell me what you want me to do.''

A few seconds later they parted, Ward toward the uphill side of where the riders were gathered, Templeton in the opposite direction, and Henry remaining where he was trying to keep the horses quiet and watch. By now the rope was tied up over the branch and they were tightening the noose around Jeremiah's neck. There wasn't much time!

When Templeton thought he had waited long enough, suddenly he walked out from among the trees straight into the lights from the burning torches.

''Hey, look who's here!'' called out the man who first saw him, ''—it's the nigger-lover!''

All the heads turned to see Templeton Daniels walking out of the woods toward them.

''And look,'' added another, ''he's got him a gun! Maybe he's after some trouble himself!''

''Now look, boys,'' said Templeton, ''I followed you out here to appeal one last time to your good judgment. You don't need to do this. Do you really want murder on the conscience of this town? I'll talk to the boy. I'll tell him that he's got to be more careful and watch—"

"Look, Daniels," interrupted a voice. "It's too late for all that. He had his chance."

"Let's string him up with him!" shouted a voice.

"Shut up, Deke, you fool. We don't want a white man's blood on our hands."

"Watch what you call my boy, Sam," now said the man who had led the charge into Rosewood.

"Take it easy, Dwight, all I meant—"

The brief argument went no further. Suddenly a shot rang out from the darkness behind them.

Several of the horses whinnied and reared as everyone spun around. None had yet noticed the half-frayed strand of rope two feet above their captive's head.

A second shot followed.

"What the—" yelled someone. But he was drowned out by more shouts of anger and confusion. No one yet realized that at the first shot, Templeton Daniels had sprinted back for the cover of the trees. He now lay on the ground with his own rifle cocked and ready.

A third shot split the rope at the same moment the horse bearing Jeremiah bolted, leaving him dangling momentarily from the tree.

Suddenly frightened and angered as well as confused, some of the men tried to fight back. But they could see nothing of their enemy. They peered into the night as they drew their pistols. But no sooner had they lifted their guns from their holsters than—

Bang! one, then . . .

Bang! two . . .

. . . and guns were flying from their hands!

"I'm hit!" cried one of the gunmen. His torch fell to the ground as he grabbed the wound. "My hand's broken! I'm not waiting around to get killed!"

Five shots had now been fired from the woods. Two more sent another pistol and one rifle to the ground. More yells mingled with the echoing explosions. Then came a volley of shots from Templeton's rifle on the opposite side. The riders realized they were caught in the crossfire of a gunfight they could not hope to win.

"Let's get out of here!" cried three at once. They bolted after the first rider, who was already disappearing down the trail past Henry without even seeing him.

As their lights bounded away, the torch that had fallen still flickered enough to give a little light. Ward, Henry, and Templeton hurried out from different sides of the woods.

"That was some shooting, Ward!" said Templeton.

Mr. Ward nodded. "Don't remind me," he said. "I just hope I never have to use one of these again."

But Henry ran past them and stooped to the ground to see if they were in time.

Decision of Love
58

*H*ow long we waited back in the kitchen at Rosewood, I couldn't say. It seemed like ten hours!

Finally it was Josepha who cried, "I hear sumfin—dey's comin'!"

We all ran out the door and looked out. As the riders gradually came into view I realized with sickening horror that I only saw three horses.

No! I cried, and ran out into the night. My heart was in an agony of grief. Had I found love only to lose it like this? I was sobbing as I ran. Gradually the forms of the three riders came into clearer focus. It was my papa, Mr. Ward, and Henry. There was no sign of—

But then Henry stopped and began to dismount.

Another rider sat on his horse! He had been sitting behind him!

"Jeremiah!" I shrieked.

Henry had barely managed to help him to the ground when I pushed past him and threw my arms around Jeremiah's shoulders.

I was so deliriously happy at that moment that if the question of marriage had come up right then I would have married Jeremiah in an instant! I was so relieved and happy and excited and full of love, nothing else mattered.

And actually, the subject did come up again. You'll probably be surprised when I tell you that it was *me* who brought it up. I don't suppose it was too ladylike for me to be so forward. But who cared about being ladylike at a time like this! I was just so happy Jeremiah was safe.

The first chance I got, after a couple days when he had recovered and felt better and we could talk alone, I told Jeremiah what I was thinking.

"Jeremiah," I said, "I've changed my mind."

"About what?"

"About not marrying you yet. If you still want me to, I've decided that I am ready to marry you whenever you want."

Now it was Jeremiah who didn't say anything, but looked away. He had a funny expression on his face. Suddenly a terrible thought struck me—maybe he didn't want to marry me now! Had I just made a big fool of myself for saying what I had!

All I could do was wait to find out what he was thinking.

"I . . . uh," Jeremiah began. "I, uh . . . don't know exactly how ter say dis . . . but I been thinkin' about it eber since da other night . . . an' now it's me whose changed my mind—"

Jeremiah saw the look of shock and dismay on my face.

"It ain't like dat!" he said. "I hope you's not mistakin' my meanin'. I ain't changed my mind about *you*. I *want* ter marry you more den eber. It's jes' too perilous, Mayme. So now it's me who ain't ready yet. I'm thinking dat it jes' ain't safe yet wiff all dis."

Finally I understood. I should have realized how

shaken he had been by what had happened.

"Dis danger ain't gwine go away," he went on. "Ter git married now wud mean puttin' you in da middle ob dat danger too. I can't do dat. I love you too much."

By now I was crying. For someone who didn't used to think I was emotional, I sure cried a lot!

Slowly Jeremiah took me in his arms and held me. How can I possibly describe all the feelings that were going through me at that moment! In a strange way I almost felt a quieter joy than when he had asked me to marry him. I felt so content and safe in his arms. He was looking out for me. He wanted to protect me. He was thinking of me even more than of himself.

I felt *loved*!

Jeremiah loved me enough *not* to marry me. He loved me so much that he would rather not marry me to protect me than to marry me and have it be danger-ous for me. What a lucky girl I was to be loved that much.

"I love you, Mayme," he said softly in my ear.

"I love you too, Jeremiah."

"Our time'll come, an' it'll be da right time."

I stepped back, wiped my eyes, and smiled. "You're a good man, Jeremiah Patterson," I said. "I'm sure glad you found Carolina, so I could find you!"

❧ ❀ ❧

ENDINGS AND BEGINNINGS
59

*J*eremiah talked to my papa again the next day and told him what he'd decided and what he'd said to me and that we'd decided to wait.

"I've been thinking about it all too," said my papa. "You're right about the danger not going away. And I'm not altogether comfortable with you and Henry so far away from us and in town by yourselves."

"But what kin we do, Mr. Templeton?"

"Ward and I have been thinking that maybe it's time you went to work for us."

"I ain't sure I knows wha'chu mean, Mr. Templeton."

"What I'm saying is that you're working for Rosewood from now on. And if you're going to work here, you ought to live at Rosewood too."

"You mean it, Mr. Templeton!"

"Ward and I've already got it figured out. We'll fix up the best of the old slave cabins. You and your pa can use it like it's your own. You can stay here, or at Henry's place in town, however you like. You're also going to each have a horse of your own, so that if you need to get here fast, you'll be able to."

"But won't all dat put you in more danger too?"

"We'll handle it together," said my papa. "If you're going to marry my daughter someday, I need to keep an eye on you!"

When I heard about it, of course I was happier than I could be.

And that's how two more boarders came to stay at Rosewood, though Henry kept his quarters and job at the livery in town too.

Even though Jeremiah and I weren't married, I got to see him and work with him and talk with him every day. That couldn't help but make us all the more ready to be married someday.

I hadn't thought my little family at Rosewood could get any better.

But it had! Jeremiah was now part of it too!

❦

Epilogue

M RS. ELFRIDA HAMMOND, OWNER OF THE GENERAL
store in Greens Crossing, North Carolina, and keeper
of the town's post office, took her responsibility seriously.

If the United States government, now that there was only
one government again, entrusted her with so sacred an obli-
gation as to distribute its mail, then it was her solemn duty to
know everyone in the community so that the mail went where
it was supposed to.

Along with that duty, she also tried to know everything
about everyone.

Whether or not the government would have felt it important, that was the greatest benefit of her job. It was certainly
more rewarding than the small fee she received each month
for her services. Her deepest satisfaction came from the
knowledge that her gossip-loving mind managed to pick up
from day to day. It gave her the delicious power in the community she imagined she held.

She gained her information any way she could. It might be
from snatches of overheard conversation or the memory of a
return address—and she read every one the moment the mail
was delivered and had a brain that never forgot such details.
Or it might be from a letter held up to the light to see what
she could see through the envelope. Or she might learn something from all the informal questions—seemingly innocent

but each calculated to add to her storehouse of information on every resident for miles—she made part of her transactions with every man, woman, or child who walked through her door. However she did it, Mrs. Hammond's devious mind was in a constant state of activity concerning everyone *else's* affairs.

But it was not merely possessing information that fed her obsession. She must do something with it. Thus she doled it out in whatever circumstances would add to her own supposed stature in the minds of those she chose to share her secrets with. She liked to be seen as the one "in the know." To hold such influence placed her at the center of the life of the community.

That her preoccupation with town gossip was but a disguise for her own loneliness was a sad fact Mrs. Hammond would not have guessed in a hundred years. Whether there was anyone she would have regarded as a friend, it was certain that no one in the town considered her *their* friend. She had not been invited to dinner after church except once, and that was years ago, by Reverend Hall and his wife. Whether she felt the aloneness of her existence during the long winter nights in her small sitting room above the store, no one could have said. But when every new day came, she was there to greet the morning's first customer when he or she walked through her door with the optimism of her twin callings—to sell and to learn.

But even Mrs. Hammond had her scruples.

She was a Southerner through and through. She didn't like all this business with colored people coming and going as if they were like everyone else.

She couldn't decide whether it was the war and President Lincoln who had changed everything in Greens Crossings, or those two girls out at the Rosewood plantation who went around like they were friends, pretending that skin color didn't matter.

There was no doubt—things had changed because of them. And those two Daniels brothers! They were the worst of the lot. They should know better.

It seemed that there was always somebody new coming to town, and that it always had to do with those two girls! First it had been the dandy from the North, Rosalind Clairborne's brother, God rest her soul. Then Mr. Clairborne's brother from Charlotte, God rest Rosalind's husband's poor soul too. Then Rosalind's other brother from California. Then that son of Henry's.

Would it never end!

For all she was concerned, everyone at Rosewood could just stay away from Greens Crossing forever!

Yes, Mrs. Hammond had her scruples. And most of them had to do with black people and poor people. She had no use for either.

So when the bell rang and Mrs. Hammond glanced up to see who was walking through her door early in the year 1869, her first response was to tilt her nose slightly in the air. No smile would greet *this* customer on *this* day.

Whatever information he might either need or possess, she wasn't interested. For he was a black man. She had never seen him before, and good riddance.

"Morning to you, ma'am," he said. "Might you point me in the direction of the livery?"

"It smells like you just came from there," she retorted. She sniffed once or twice with an unpleasant expression.

"Sorry, ma'am. I've been traveling awhile."

"It's down that way," said Mrs. Hammond, pointing along the street, wrinkling her nose again.

The man thanked her, turned, and left. From force of habit, she wandered to the window and watched him slowly make his way in the direction she had pointed. She muttered a few comments to herself, then returned to her counter.

Hoping she had seen the last of him, Mrs. Hammond

could not know that this stranger would cause a greater stir in Greens Crossing than all the rest.

He did not yet know it himself. But his presence would bring mysteries to light that Mrs. Hammond herself could never have dreamed—secrets that would turn this community, and even the whole state, on its ear.

Author Biography

CALIFORNIAN MICHAEL PHILLIPS BEGAN HIS DISTIN-
guished writing career in the 1970s. He came to widespread
public attention in the early 1980s for his efforts to reacquaint
the public with Victorian novelist George MacDonald. Phillips is recognized as the man most responsible for the current
worldwide renaissance of interest in the once-forgotten Scots-
man and is one of the world's foremost experts on MacDonald. After partnering with Bethany House Publishers in
redacting and republishing the works of MacDonald, Phillips
embarked on his own career in fiction, and it is primarily as a
novelist that he is now known. His critically acclaimed books
have been translated into eight foreign languages, have
appeared on numerous bestseller lists, and have sold more
than six million copies. Phillips is today considered by many
as the heir apparent to the very MacDonald legacy he has
worked so hard to promote in our time. Phillips is the author
of the most widely read biography of George MacDonald,
entitled *George MacDonald, Scotland's Beloved Storyteller*.
Phillips is also the publisher of the magazine *Leben*, a peri-
odical dedicated to bold-thinking Christianity and the legacy
of George MacDonald. *A Perilous Proposal* is Phillips' 48th
original novel and 102nd published work. Phillips and his
wife, Judy, alternate their time between their home in Eureka,
California, and Scotland, where they hope to increase awareness of MacDonald's work.

FOR ADDITIONAL RESOURCES FROM MICHAEL PHILLIPS

SEE:
www.MacDonaldPhillips.com
www.PrayingDangerously.com

If you enjoyed *A Perilous Proposal*, you will be sure to enjoy the companion series to CAROLINA COUSINS—SHENANDOAH SISTERS, the four books about Katie and Mayme and their scheme at Rosewood. The first book in the series is entitled *Angels Watching Over Me*. And don't miss Michael Phillips' other newest titles *Is Jesus Coming Back As Soon As We Think?* and *Dream of Freedom*.

For contact information and a complete listing of titles by Michael Phillips and George MacDonald, write c/o:

P.O. Box 7003
Eureka, CA 95502
U.S.A.

Information on the magazine *Leben*—dedicated to the spiritual vision of Michael Phillips and the legacy of George MacDonald—may also be obtained through the above address.

MORE HISTORICAL FICTION
from Michael Phillips

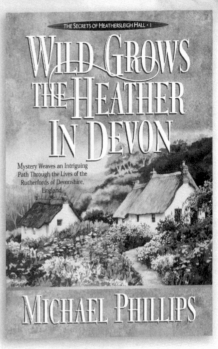

**...S UNITED THEM,
...PE SEES THEM THROUGH**

...ght together when their families were
...in the Civil War, two Southern girls
...rely on each other to survive. One the
...hter of a plantation owner, one the
...hter of a slave, they fight against
...ything they'd been taught about the
...r in order to trust, survive, and see the
...r day ahead. An inspirational histori-
...eries from a bestselling author.

*Angels Watching Over Me
A Day to Pick Your Own Cotton
The Color of Your Skin Ain't the Color of Your Heart
Together is All We Need
By Michael Phillips*

A JOURNEY FOR TRUTH

Among the gently rolling Devonshire
downs of southwest England, the
Rutherford family lead a peaceful and priv-
ileged life at Heathersleigh Hall, their
country estate. But there are secrets
beneath this prosperous and contented life.
The Rutherfords are about to set out on a
journey of truth that will change each of
them in ways they never imagined. A saga of
adventure, long-held secrets, and romance.

*Wild Grows the Heather in Devon
Wayward Winds
Heathersleigh Homecoming
A New Dawn Over Devon
By Michael Phillips*

BETHANYHOUSE